RAN'S DAUGHTERS

AN ALTHINGI SAGA

KAITLIN FELIX

Rán's Daughters

Published by Outland Entertainment LLC
3119 Gillham Road
Kansas City, MO 64109

Publisher: Jeremy D. Mohler
Creative Director: Cullen Bunn
Editor-in-Chief: Alana Joli Abbott
Senior Editor: Scott Colby
Games Director: Anton Kromoff

ISBN: 978-1-964735-01-6 trade paperback, 978-1-964735-02-3 ebook
Worldwide Rights
Created in the United States of America

Editor: Joshua Gillingham
Copy Editor: Ariel Kromoff
Cover Illustration & Design: Shannon Potratz
Interior Layout: Jeremy D. Mohler

Printed and bound in the United States.

Visit outlandentertainment.com to see more, or follow us on our Facebook Page facebook.com/outlandentertainment/

This one is for my parents, who taught me to love stories and to believe in the magic of words. This voyage began with you. Thank you for everything.

PART ONE:
AL-ANDALUS

PROLOGUE

It is well known that when a child on the shore waves to their parent as they stand in the beast-prow of a ship of oak, journeying from the home-fjord to a far land and plunder beyond reckoning, that child goes away from the sight wishing to one day sail the swan-road after them. Often, they do. Still more often, they die in the doing.

Thus, it should also be known that such aspiring sea-striders must learn.

Cracked hands and sunbaked skin teach the lesson of how salt and heat can dry you like jerky, and kill if left too long without fresh water. Broken backs and snapped oars teach how the god Njörd wrestles with rowers, hoping to drown them. Thus, muscles must strengthen until arms and necks are as corded as the ropes that lash the sail and until the hull of the vessel cuts through waves like a thief's knife through purse strings.

The most important lesson a child must learn before anything else is that an ocean storm can be worse than battle. Worse than standing in a broken shield-wall with your closest kin bleeding and dying on either side. Worse even than the splitting, gushing death of mothers when a babe comes too early or too swiftly. Worse still than drowning in a river after falling out of a fishing boat, for though that is a straw-death, the drowned can still claim the simple glory of the desire to feed their families.

But drowning in a storm is not glorious. It is the way to be forgotten. For who will remember the drowned? There are so many it would take a skald endless nights to recite them all.

There are no sagas of drowned sailors. But what child thinks of that?

Sometimes, a few hardened voyagers return to the home-fjord with tales of adventure, of the letting of blood and of bright, shining silver. And those are the tales that are most dangerous, for children will dream despite the danger, and dreams of that kind do not fade with time.

It had proved thus for Gyda *Fiskwif* years before, when she had been that child waving to a parent who never came home. So it would prove again for years onward, until the burning of the world at Ragnarök.

CHAPTER ONE

If ocean storms were sea-beasts, then this was the most dire of monsters.

Blood-dark water burned our eyes. Salt spray flung from waves as tall as the ship's mast ran down to sting and crust around our lips. The gale-wind hammered us and howled as if *Sea-Wolf*'s own prow-mounted beast had come alive to swallow the sea and everything in it.

Yet we, Rán's Daughters, fought.

A voice reached out to me through the gloom, coming from the cargo hold in the center of the ship.

"Sail's secure, Lady," Eir called. "Take this and fasten yourself to it!"

She stood among the crates and barrels stacked near the mast-step. Already, a measure of water sloshed around her knees. The wind scattered her words like gaming pieces from a *tafl* board, but I, crouched under the prow-beast in the bow, heard her well enough.

The rope she threw flashed out of the mist and thunked against my arm. I took hold of it and threaded the end through the belt around my waist.

"Another swell! Brace yourselves," yelled Rúna, my steers-woman. She hauled on the tiller, cursing as the water surged and threatened to break our rudder.

My hands shook. The knot would not fasten. When the wave hit, I slipped, falling against the sheer strake. Pain erupted in my left shoulder and I lost my grip on the rope. It slithered away into the flooded bilges.

Cursing, spitting salt, I dug my fingernails into the weathered oak strake and pulled myself up. Hand over hand, I made my way toward the hold.

"One more wave like that and *Sea-Wolf* could be lost to the water," I said, raising my voice to be heard over the tumult. Eir held her bailing bucket in one hand and the length of her lifeline in the other. She grimaced at me through sodden mats of hair.

"That bastard Thor has a temper as foul as yours, Lady," she said.

"Maybe Rán spit in his stew and he's returning the favor," I answered.

Dropping the bucket on a crate, she stepped up onto the deck. Threading her rope through my belt, she made a knot, then yanked it to check the tightness.

"It is meant to be summer," she said, half-smiling. "Yet even the sun is afraid of Thor's fury. What sort of war are the Æsir waging?"

I rubbed my shoulder. It was bruised, or worse. "*Sea-Wolf* isn't safe yet. Get yourself a new lifeline. I won't have my second-in-command falling over the side."

She nodded. "Astrid and Liadan can bail. I'll row with Guðrun."

A fresh spate of rain pelted us, thrumming against the deck and rigging. Her gray-eyed gaze dropped to my shoulder and she frowned. "Are you taking Rúna's place at the tiller?"

"I will row, just as before."

There were more oar-ports in the bow, with spaces for the journey chests that served as our benches, but we were a crew of only six. We had not the number to fill all the benches and bail at the same time.

"Are you certain you can manage?" Eir's tone was careful, but I scowled up at her.

"Just get to it!"

She whipped away, calling out my orders to the other women on the stern benches.

Under my feet, *Sea-Wolf* groaned with the tossing sea. I gripped the strake to keep balanced. My line—Eir's line—was anchored to the mast alongside the others, all fastened as the storm rushed in. There had been no time to fasten mine before we were swamped and blinded with the rain. My line always came last. It was my strictest rule on this ship, and so it should be. *Sea-Wolf* was not safe until its crew were safe.

An unfurled corner of canvas snapped overhead as the tempest kicked up.

"Would it not be better to get a covering over the hold, Lady?" said Astrid, joining me. "Bailing is a waste of energy in a gale like this, isn't it?"

Astrid was our youngest, only sailing with us for a handful of seasons. Her skin was still unblemished from the relentless sun and scouring winds.

If I were a patient woman, I could answer her question. But I was not patient, nor forgiving of ignorance. And if indeed this was not ignorance, then it was a question of authority, and I could not ignore that either.

"Eir gave you my order. Get your bucket and *bail,* girl, before I flay you from arse to oxter and use your skin as our sail!"

Paling, Astrid backed away and stumbled into the hold. She cried out as the cold water soaked through her leg wraps and trousers.

Liadan, bearing herself with far more grace, followed Astrid into the hold. She was Irish, and could not speak, but she needed no words to be understood among us.

Astrid emitted distressed noises like a lamb with a leg stuck in a trap as she bailed, and Liadan turned to give me a long-suffering eyeroll. Among all of us, she was the most patient, but Astrid's naivety grated even on her.

Thunder rolled and the wind kicked up. No time left.

"We must outrun this storm or be swallowed by it," I yelled. "You know your work. Show Rán what good Daughters you are!"

"Yes, Lady," they called back.

Rúna remained at the tiller. Eir and Guðrun took opposite benches. I chose a starboard bench, my numbed fingers latching around the spruce wood of the oar.

"Pull," I screamed.

Muscles bulged, jaws flexed, the oar-blades sliced into the churning water, and *Sea-Wolf* strained forward.

I pulled on my oar, cursing the fire-ache in my shoulder. It was nothing, I told myself. A pathetic hurt, and I would be damned before letting the sea claim my Daughters or my ship for it.

"Come on!" Eir urged. She sat in front of me. Our rowing was uneven, but Guðrun made up for it with sheer effort, groaning as she pulled.

Rain lashed the deck. We were wet to the bone, shivering, breaking our backs to fight this storm.

Rúna's steering made the best use of the wind. "Njörd!" she called. "Remember us!"

"Remember us!" echoed Guðrun.

The prow-beast's gaping maw dipped and rose with the waves, snarling its defiance.

Astrid and Liadan followed the new rhythm. Row. Bail. Row. Brace for a wave. Row again. The world narrowed, becoming nothing but the blinding rain, our oars and buckets, and ourselves.

"Drowning is for *niðingar* and fools!" Eir crowed. "We are neither. We are Rán's Daughters! Favored of the goddess and of kings and merchants the world over! This storm is nothing to us."

We roared together, voices lifting over the wind.

"A *dvergr*-hoard awaits us in al-Andalus," I yelled. "Row for your swords. Row for silver. Row for your silks and your spices!"

"We'll be as wealthy as old Olavi in Dyflin," Rúna said. "And just as well-fed!"

Our strength surged. Oars bit the white-capped waves. *Sea-Wolf* plunged on, twisting and writhing, a sleek beast of singing timber and tackle.

"Thor's fury is passing," Astrid said, pausing her bailing to look up at the sky. A glob of run-off from the sail chose that moment to fall. It smacked her forehead and she jerked back, squawking and flailing as if stung by a bee.

Liadan's face split into a silent laugh. Lifting her bucket, she heaved it back and doused the girl with seawater.

"I'm already miserable, you horrible cow!" Astrid cried. "Did you really need to do that?"

Liadan spread her arms, inviting Astrid to return the favor.

"Back to bailing," I ordered through my laughter.

Though the rain still fell in sheets, the clouds did not seem so malevolent, nor so smothering. Even the waves buffeted our hull more gently.

"You catch sight of coast yet?" Guðrun said to Rúna. Her grin was as wide as her shoulders, which rippled and moved under her woolen tunic as she drew hard on her oar. "I want to be in a warm bed before half-dead Hel wakes in her hall wondering where we are!"

"I have not strayed from our course, my love," Rúna answered confidently. "And take care to remember I will be in that bed with you!"

"A wonderful way to stay warm," I said to both of them. "But not dry!"

Between the grunting efforts of the work, more teasing and filthy comments flew across the deck from all sides. But then an urgent, rapid pounding cut off our talking. Our eyes went to Liadan, who dropped her bucket and pointed out to sea.

My heart stuttered. The wind had changed, building a swell that rose higher than any we had yet endured. It would hit *Sea-Wolf* square on, which could capsize the ship and drown us all.

I twisted, leaping from my bench. Rúna stared at the water open-mouthed. I took the tiller from her limp grasp. The sail snapped and *Sea-Wolf* groaned as the arm moved.

"Help me, Rúna," I yelled. "Everyone brace!"

Together, we pressed our combined weight against the tiller, and the ship turned.

Not fast enough. The surge slammed at the stern. Our screams rent the air, all of them cut off as the ocean rolled over us.

My fingers were wrenched from the tiller. The weight of Rúna's body fell away, lost in the dark chaotic torrent. I groped for my lifeline. With my other hand, I grasped anything solid I could hold.

Crushing, unrelenting, the wave tipped *Sea-Wolf* far onto its side.

Salt water filled my throat, my nose, my eyes. I couldn't see, couldn't hear. Had the lines broken? Would we be swept away, sinking to Rán's underwater hall, never to breathe air again?

My dead husband's face appeared in my mind. Would I meet him among the seaweed and shipwrecks? He had drowned so long ago, would I even recognize his fish-eaten corpse?

Rage rose in my chest. I dug my fingernails hard into the wood. *Not like this,* I thought.

The surge fell, and the ship fell with it. I hung on, gasping and choking on the salt and the fear. It was over.

Across the deck, scattered ropes and spilled journey chests littered the surface. The lashings around the cargo had come undone and the crates lay splintered, their contents smashed in sodden clusters inside the hold or spread over the planking. Half of the crates were missing, having gone over the side into the sea.

I raked my eyes over the ship, counting heads. There was Eir, eyes squeezed tight, arms locked around her oar and gunwale. And there were Liadan and Astrid, pressed against the mast together with faces white as new wool.

"Rúna!"

I whirled. The broken cry came from Guðrun, who had been slammed against the starboard strake. She was halfway over the side, reaching into the sea, tears and snot flowing.

"Rúna," she screamed, leaning further.

I flew across the deck and yanked her back by the neck of her tunic. "Don't be a fool!"

The woman's knees buckled and she sagged in my arms. "Her line snapped," Guðrun howled. "She's gone! She's gone!"

Eir and Liadan rushed to us. "Rúna?" Eir said, her eyes wide, stricken by grief.

Quick as thought, I pushed Guðrun into Liadan and leaned over. There was debris, and water, and the empty expanse of the merciless ocean. No Rúna.

"There! She's there!" Guðrun pointed. "Oh, gods."

Among the broken wood and floating cargo, Rúna's white face bobbed, one arm slung around a smashed crate and the other waving. She was weakened, carried too far from the ship for a line to reach.

"Someone get an oar, now," I barked.

I would have to be quick. Even a summer sea could petrify a body's muscles from cold or cramp, and the storm had not yet blown itself out.

Clambering onto the strake, I dove into the sea without hesitation.

Salt and iron filled my mouth as the water closed over my head.

My arms moved rhythmically, powerful from years of rowing and hauling ropes and weaving my own tunics, sails, and shrouds.

I broke the surface, kicking hard. Ahead, Rúna draped over the broken crate. She was no longer moving.

Already, fatigue pulled at my limbs. Only a few spear-lengths more. And then she and I would drown, or else we wouldn't. Only the goddess Rán knew.

Left behind on *Sea-Wolf*, the Daughters yelled for me, calling me back. Grieving before they'd even lost me.

The line tied to my belt tugged. I swam on, hoping that I had only caught on something, and not that I had run out of slack. But then it tugged again, harder. Salt water went up my nose, stinging and tasting of fish.

Twisting, I yanked on my line and waved. "No," I yelled. "I'm almost there!" Rúna was close. So close. She floated still, pale and pelted by rain.

Liadan stood at the strake with an oar, ready for me to return and use it to haul myself out of the water. Astrid was at her shoulder, arms around Guðrun.

"Fucking *hear* me," I snarled.

Seeing my waving, Astrid turned to yell. Eir must be in the hold, reeling in my line. I tugged it again.

"Not yet, Eir, damn you. Please!"

The rope jerked once more, then slackened. Eir appeared at the strake, a longer coil of rope in her hands. She waved and tossed the extra length into the water.

I surged forward, my limbs eating the remaining distance. Soon I had Rúna in my grasp. The broken crate supported both our weights.

"Wake up." I struck Rúna's cheek, barely feeling the sensation in my palm. I kicked my legs to keep the blood flowing, and struck her again. "Rúna!"

Her eyes fluttered. "Lady," she murmured. "This is a lovely swim, isn't it?"

"The fish may think so," I said, giving her a smile. "I've never taken to it myself."

"It's exhausting," she said, her sigh as heavy as her eyelids.

I shook her. "Kick, Rúna. Stay awake, or I'll slap you again until your pretty white cheeks bleed and Guðrun swears to cut off my hand."

But Rúna did not respond.

"Freyja's tits," I muttered. Releasing the crate, I wrapped my arm around Rúna's chest and shut my mouth tight as her weight pulled us both under. She was spare in body, but as dead weight she might as well have been made of iron.

My shoulder twinged as I maneuvered Rúna into a floating position on her back. Her dark hair sloshed into my face like a clump of seaweed. Once she was secure, I tugged my line twice. There was an answering pull, and then the water parted around us. I flailed, legs uncoordinated and numb. Fists balled in Rúna's tunic, I ceased kicking and allowed our bodies to float.

When we finally bumped against *Sea-Wolf's* oak hull, the sea had calmed to a smooth roll, as if the gale had been nothing but a summer squall. Even the rain had lessened to a pitiful dribble. Thor was mocking us, the great wet shit.

Guðrun leaned over the side, reaching for Rúna's prone form. Snot dripped from her chin. "She isn't—?" Her voice broke.

"Stop weeping and get us out!"

Liadan lowered the oar, and with Astrid behind her for leverage, they pulled Rúna and I out of the water and dumped us like a sack of eels onto the slippery deck.

Guðrun tore Rúna from me and gathered her in her wide lap. She pressed a kiss to her limp hand. "She's cold! One of you idiots get a fire going!"

"But it's too wet for a fire," said Astrid. She trembled as she stared at Rúna's white face.

"Fetch the brazier, girl," Eir barked.

Kneeling beside me, Liadan draped a blanket over my shoulders, then pressed a pair of mittens into my hands. They were wool, made by nalbinding, and were warm even when wet.

It was kind of Thor to blow himself out, eh? she signed, smiling.

My teeth clacked together hard, my answering smile more of a grimace.

"You're in better shape than Rúna," Eir told me. "But that could change quickly. What are your orders?"

"Get back to the benches," I rasped. "We need to reach the channel before night falls."

Guðrun twisted to yell over her shoulder. "Move your scrawny arse, girl. Get that brazier here now!"

"It's too heavy for me," Astrid called from the hold.

Casting her eyes to the clouds, Liadan rose and went to help her.

"She isn't dead, you know," I told Guðrun. Drawing on the mittens, I flexed my stiff fingers.

"She will be dead if she doesn't wake up soon," Guðrun responded. "She needs to get dry." She rubbed Rúna's forearms, then removed her waxed sea-cloak to spread over her torso. I passed my blanket over to add to it.

"Get her out of the wet things first. Find her thickest tunic and trews. If you have extra socks or leg wraps, put two pairs on. A hat, too. It will keep the warmth inside."

With Liadan's help, Astrid got the heavy brazier into position between two benches. As it was a fire hazard, we used it only for the coldest days of sailing. If the need was great enough, we boiled fresh water and roasted fish. Long-ships full of warriors, like the sleek *drakkar* or *snekkja,* could pull onto shore and make camp for such things. But on a bulky *knarr* like *Sea-Wolf,* speed was everything. When traveling for days or weeks with a belly full of cargo, every moment under sail meant more profit. Spoiled wine or rotting foodstuffs would never catch the best price in the markets.

"Give me your fire striker," Eir told Astrid, and the girl handed it over.

Eir had already cleared the deck of debris, dumping clothing, furs, and sacks of clanking weapons back into our journey-chests. Even with the brazier loaded with dry wood taken from the stores in the hold, it took several tries with the fire striker before the wood finally hissed and caught. The fire was small and smoked heavily, but soon enough heat emanated from the grate to thaw my muscles.

Once I could move, I pushed myself to stand, groaning as I did.

At forty-three winters, I was no longer young, and my body was prone to stiffness in even the best circumstances. I went to the tiller bench and knelt. From under the bench I pulled out my sea-chest. A puddle of red spread like blood across the planks and the heady scent of wine hit my nose.

"*Skitr*," I cursed. "That was a gift from Sigtryggr. The flask must have broken with the wave."

Behind me, someone tapped the strake. I turned.

"You are a fool, Gyda *Fiskwif*," Eir pronounced. Her cheeks were blotchy with anger.

There was no place on a ship where true privacy could be found, and so we never cared for discretion, either in modesty or in conversation. Eir had not attempted to make this confrontation a quiet one, and so I hardly felt surprise at it.

Behind her, gathered around the brazier, the others tensed as they waited for my response.

This was not my first conflict with Eir. We were old friends, almost sisters, for how often we argued. But a direct challenge?

I lifted my chin and met her gaze with a smile. "A fool? Come now, what is your lecture this time?"

"You leapt into the sea with no thought and no warning to the rest of us." She said this like an accusation.

"None of you were able," I said, flipping a hand. "Rúna lived, so it needed doing."

"And if you'd drowned in the doing?" Eir demanded. "We're already short of hands, by the gods! Who would keep us safe if you'd failed? How could we row back to Jórvík with no leader?"

Guðrun emitted an angry sound, and Eir nodded at her deferentially.

"Of course, I am happy Rúna is safe," she said. "But Gyda, you must think of the rest of us before you give yourself to the mercy of the sharks."

"Stop clucking! I'm as strong a swimmer as any of you, and I had my line."

Eir made an exasperated noise, which I ignored. Turning back to my sea-chest, I threw the lid off, tasting wine on my tongue. It was good quality, used only for the king's table, but even the best wine eventually soured into vinegar. I would need a new chest.

I dug through my things until I found a roll of waxed canvas. It dripped but was not sodden. I opened it over the deck and sorted through folded garments. I had both men's and women's items, some richer in fabric than others. From these I chose a linen tunic, a pair of simple trousers, and an embroidered over-tunic.

I stood and began stripping off my damp things, shuddering as the cold wind bit the skin of my bare legs.

Eir was still behind me.

"Are you dense as well as water-logged?" she said. "Think of Ragnar. What would he say if you are not with us to meet him? You made this deal, Gyda. If we're sailing into danger, we're all fucked without you."

"Eir is right," said Astrid in a small voice. She shrank back from my glare, but Liadan thumped her chest in support of the girl.

"What are you really trying to say, Eir?" I said, shoving my head through the neck of the under-tunic. "This isn't about Ragnar. Someone else would happily haul his carcass to Iceland, and for far less dear a price."

Being sized for a larger body, the under-tunic was easy to put on, but my arm caught in the tighter sleeve of the over-tunic. I hissed, pulling on the scratchy linen to force it.

Eir clicked her tongue and stepped close to help, guiding my arm through the sleeve. "We shouldn't be here, Gyda," she whispered. "We should go back to Dyflin and forget about Ragnar. Olavi will forgive us."

Before I could answer her, a groan rose from the mountain of blankets and furs next to the brazier.

Guðrun leaned over Rúna, clasping her pale hand. "My love?"

Rúna sat up and coughed, her hair like dark kelp stuck to her head. She pointed to starboard. "Land," she rasped. "I see the channel! We made it."

CHAPTER TWO

Fog and gathering night shrouded the ship as we whispered up the channel.

I had the tiller, its pine handle smooth in my palm as *Sea-Wolf* followed the drift of the current. At the stern benches, my Daughters' oars sliced the water with hardly a ripple. With the storm gone, there was no wind to drive us. Our yard and sail rested in their brackets. Our prow-beast had also come down, hidden in the belly of the ship to avoid offending the land-spirits.

We made for a small fishing harbor at the end of this channel. Down the coast, there was a rocky bay and a port meant for trade-ships. But we needed a quieter berth, something discrete to venture into town unnoticed. We were a poorly lot, sore and tired to the bone. We needed shelter and rest before dawn arrived with all its danger.

Our meeting with Ragnar had been planned since the end of last summer. He was a steady ally, if not a friend to us. We had met him, or rather *stumbled over him*, in the belly of *Sea-Wolf*. Fleeing accusations of murder, he had stowed away among the furs and crates before Rán's Daughters set out from Dyflin. He had nothing to his name then: no property, no lord, and no wealth beyond the large gold collar he wore—a gift from his dead Córdoban lover. Ragnar Goldmane, he'd styled himself. A grand name for a man of grand dreams and little luck. So little luck that he got himself into a *holmgang* with Helgi, the youngest son of Jarl Olavi of Dyflin.

Helgi was master of trade in Jórvík, and therefore in direct competition with Rán's Daughters. More than that, his father Olavi was my benefactor and patron, the sole reason *Sea-Wolf* had the protection and freedom to sail into any lucrative port with confidence.

Worse than all this was that Helgi was also a dishonorable, shit-stained coward.

When Ragnar challenged him to a duel, and then won the duel,

Helgi pulled an axe when his back was turned. Against my own interests and better judgment, I stepped between the two and ripped a hole in Helgi's guts with my seax. Rán's undersea hall received the tribute of Helgi's bloody corpse as we sailed away.

After these events, Ragnar and I struck our agreement. He would continue his voyage to al-Andalus, earning the favor of the Emir of Córdoba as a sell-sword. Then, if a year passed and he still lived, Ragnar would board *Sea-Wolf* once again and go to Iceland, intending to establish himself as a wealthy landowner.

I set my price at nothing less than Ragnar's own weight in silver and tradable goods. He'd accepted without argument. After all, he owed me his life. What was there to argue?

"Do you think Ragnar is waiting for us?" asked Rúna. She huddled on the bench in front of me. Though wrapped in two thick cloaks, she sniffled and shivered hard enough for her bones to rattle. "A berth and a bed would do me well, I think."

She punctuated this with a violent sneeze, and Astrid, rowing in front of her, cringed as the product hit the back of her neck.

"A bath would be better," she groused.

"Not long now," I told them. "Keep up your rhythm. We'll be stuck until morning tide if we get caught on a sandbar."

"That would be just our luck," Guðrun said, grunting as she pulled back on her oar. "Where did Ragnar get the Loki-cunning to set all this up anyway? Whatever favor the gods give out, I never thought a man as stupid as he is would get such a troll's share."

Eir laughed. "None of us thought he'd live this long," she agreed. "But luck seems to follow him as much as tragedy."

"He's a bodyguard. That's enough luck for me," Rúna said. "He'll make certain we'll be as safe as bairns in our beds."

"He's a household guard in the Emir's palace," I corrected. "And a beloved member of his harem. I doubt he cares about luck at all."

"His *harem*?" Astrid said, and Guðrun answered with a lusty whistle.

We snickered as the girl hunched bashfully over her oar. She'd never been with a man, or a woman, and so knew little of these things.

Liadan let go of her oar and signed, her motions barely visible in the moonlight. *Fortunately for Rán's Daughters, such an occupation brings a great deal of wealth, and we don't even have to work for it!*

"If *Sea-Wolf* isn't the place for you, perhaps a soft bed in a lord's grand hall is more to your liking," Rúna added cheerfully.

Astrid covered her face with her cloak, and there was no quieting ourselves after that.

The closer we got to land, the higher our spirits rose. This town was the perfect meeting place. It was of little import, a fishing hub with no defensive stronghold. There was a force of men, allotted by the Emir to guard the town and hold the peace, but they numbered less than fifty. This posed little credible threat to a tiny group of traders, even if we were women. To anyone seeking a place to arrive and depart unheralded and untroubled, Ragnar could not have chosen better.

We had used an amber merchant to pass messages between Córdoba and Jórvík, our current berth. Ragnar met with the man late in the spring, but it took until late summer, when the merchant sailed home, for us to learn of it.

We had left in haste to make it to Ragnar in time. Every day, the route to Iceland grew more treacherous with the weather. Even if we were to meet him and sail on the very next tide, we would be fortunate to avoid the floating ice fields in the north.

And that was to say nothing of raiders looking for a fat-bellied *knarr* full of silver as their next target.

After some moments of silence, Guðrun spoke. "This wall spooks me."

"And me," Eir replied.

The moon had vanished behind a wall of cloud and now there was no light save for the distant glow of a torch, hung at the entrance to the harbor to guide vessels through the channel.

"It's just a wall," said Astrid. "What is there to be afraid of?"

"Plenty, girl," Guðrun growled. "I'd rather not get a skull full of arrows loosed from some goat-turd I can't see. We're being watched from that wall, and I don't like it."

Her fear had basis. The wall was a hulking shape on our left, as ancient as a jötun. Once it may have been a formidable shoreline defense. Now it appeared weather-beaten and crumbling, as good as abandoned. Yet even a weak wall could hide a great deal.

"Of course we're being watched," Rúna murmured, her voice thick and nasal. "They'd be fools not to."

On our other side, there was a wide spit of flat rock, and beyond that the open sea. *Sea-Wolf* was not a vessel that skated the waves like a quick, bright fish fleeing open-throated birds, nor was its bulk easily maneuverable. If it came to it, there was no turning back. We could only plough on, and hope Njörd and Rán looked on us with favor.

As we slipped past the decrepit wall, the sounds of the night withdrew. Little waves lapped at our hull like a lullaby. A veil of quiet fell over us.

"You mentioned that bed, Rúna," I said softly. My shoulder ached with the twist of the current. I switched hands to relieve it, then stifled a yawn. "I'm yearning for a bowl of something hot and meaty."

"Gods, yes," groaned Guðrun. "And a fur-lined blanket. Fucking luxury, that would be."

That set the rest off, and they whispered to each other in the dark as they rowed. Liadan, of course, remained silent, but she looked back and nodded along.

I felt Eir's eyes on me. We had not spoken of our disagreement, but her previous words, whispered so the others would not hear, lodged in my ribs like a knife.

Once we settled for the night, there would be ample opportunity to speak.

"It is strange, is it not?" Eir said, turning her gaze away. "There are no torches on the wall. Just ancient earth and stone to mark our passage. Like we are entering a cave."

Liadan half-turned to her, a question in the tilt of her head.

"What kind of coastal village neglects their own security?" Eir said, catching Liadan's intention. The Irish woman thumped her oar to confirm.

"They've likely been raided before," rumbled Guðrun. "Even if they are watching us, we are only six. Their lives are worth less than that piss-soaked wall if *true* Sea-Norse came calling in their longships. Better for the town to submit to fate and the weave of the Norns."

Being a survivor of such raids, Liadan threw Guðrun a rude gesture, which the woman shrugged off.

"I wish you wouldn't say such things, Guðrún," chided Astrid. "We aren't raiders. But they might think we are and drive us out if they hear you."

"In that case, you'll have to bring out that axe you hide in your sea-chest. What a shame, girl. Those fine hands of yours will get bloody." Guðrun cackled, throwing her head back. The sound echoed off the wall.

Letting go of her oar, Liadan signed furiously at both of them.

When the ship veered, I snarled. "Shut your mouths! And your hands. We're here."

The channel opened, funneling us into an oblong natural harbor. It was not so dark here; torches hung over the water, casting circles of red-gold reflections. Fishing skiffs bobbed around the edges of the harbor, tied to jetties and posts sunk into the silt.

Guðrun swiveled on her bench to look around. "It's as quiet as a fucking grave-mound," she said. "It's worse than that wall."

Rúna also leaned forward. "I don't see Ragnar," she said. "And there's no one else here. Not even a harbormaster has come to greet us."

"This feels like some Loki-trick," Eir said. "I don't like it, Gyda."

"We've only just arrived," I told her. "And we don't have to like it. We're here to retrieve our cargo and our passenger, and then leave. Who cares if there's no harbormaster?"

"You don't think he lied, do you?" Astrid said in a small voice, which made it worse because it was what everyone was thinking.

"If he's not here, he either lied or he's dead," Eir said.

Liadan signed something, but Guðrun spoke over her.

"I knew we couldn't trust him, that troll-born cheat!"

"What choice do we have but to trust him?" Rúna protested. "Ragnar is the only reason we can return to Dyflin without shame!"

Silence fell over the others, and Rúna winced. Turning to me awkwardly, she lowered her gaze. "I didn't mean that, Lady," she said.

"Enough," I said. "All of you, get your wits back in order. Raise oars. I see a berth."

The oars rattled in their holes as the Daughters took them from the water.

A dock jutted out into the center of the harbor, large enough for two ships to tether on either side, though we were the only vessel making use of it. A single torch guttered in a bracket at the end. I maneuvered the tiller, making *Sea-Wolf* rock and creak as we approached.

When our hull butted against the dock, Liadan stood to cast a loop of rope. When the loop caught, she hauled, tightening it. It held fast and she grinned.

"Make ready, Daughters," I ordered. "And be quick about it!"

Al-Andalus was a land of many religions and many cultures. So many that deep-minded Oðinn himself would labor to fathom them all. It was as practical as it was wise to provide for every occasion, and so we kept a variety of kit and clothing. The others rifled through their chests now, pulling cloaks and shawls to wear over their hair, as was the custom in these lands.

I preferred to wear loose trousers of wool with my iron-ringed *brynja* under a linen tunic. Tonight, I would forgo the mail and arm myself with my seax, which I carried everywhere, no matter the occasion.

With their contents either chosen or left behind, sea-chests went into the hold next to the cargo. Planks were placed over the top to conceal it. Knots were tightened, ropes coiled, and the sail tethered down. We were ready.

The Daughters stood before me, waiting for my orders. I met each of their gazes.

"I know we are all exhausted," I began. "Tired to the bone. Eye-bruised and slope-shouldered with faces like mound-dwellers. But we are alive."

Guðrun put an arm around Rúna and smiled down at her. Without returning the smile, Rúna leaned against the solid bulwark of her shoulder and closed her eyes. The chill of Rán's deep-water grasp would not easily be forgotten by either of them.

I went on. "By next evening, Rán's Daughters will leave these shores with more wealth than we have ever had possession of. No more skulking behind the goodwill of a man. *Any* man."

Eir looked away, but the others leaned in, hungry for my words. An old, familiar fire rose in my chest.

"With the spinning of the Norns and the weave of our fate, we make our own fortune. Tonight, we will drink and sleep like the sea-striders we are. Rán's Daughters! Strong and fierce and brave!"

Like thunder rolling across a storm-split sky, my women stamped the deck and crowed. I relished the hum of it under my skin.

I will feed these women destiny, I thought. *I will make them thrive with silver and my own guiding hand. Our fate changes tonight.*

It was as I tied my scabbard to my belt that Eir chose to speak.

"These people do not like us arriving in the dark of night," she began.

As she stood, leaning against the stern strake, her gray eyes reflected the torchlight. She had a shawl of dyed silk to cover her, and it complemented her pale hair.

"Can't do anything about it now," I said. "If they didn't like it, they should have said so before we tethered to their dock."

She didn't respond. Her expression said enough for her, and none of it good.

The silence stretched. The others were up on the dock behind *Sea-Wolf,* tucking their own weapons beneath clothing and against skin. Eir herself had an eating knife in the small loop of her belt. She put a hand on it to check the fastening.

"Stop staring and say what you want to say."

Her jaw flexed and her gaze went past me, looking at the women. "What of Olavi, Gyda?"

I huffed. "What of him?"

She shook her head. "Don't make this an argument. We can't go back to Jórvík after this. It has been a year. None of us can stand any more."

I turned away, as much to hide my face as to gather myself.

"After Iceland, we need to go back to Dyflin," she pressed. "We need to go *home.*"

"Dyflin isn't home."

"Neither is Jórvík."

I pressed my lips together, thinking.

"Ragnar's payment ensures we will be women of means," I said carefully. "After all our journeys, all our trading, we'll finally have something to show for it. Our months away were not wasted, Eir. We have a connection to Jórvík's markets now, and to the smaller coastal merchants. We can be independent traders. With new resources, and maybe an agreement of supply with Sigtryggr, we can look to Chester or even Orkney as our next haven of demand. We don't need Dyflin."

"All those things are good," she said. "But this is not about Ragnar, and it's not about Dyflin."

I snorted. "Olavi never held my oath, Eir. There is no obligation. I owe him nothing. *You* owe him nothing."

She straightened, earnest, her eyes bright. "And what of his obligation to us? Our husbands were oath-men. By his own honor, he is bound to care for us as widows."

"That brings its own troubles," I countered. "Do you want to spend your years beholden to a Jarl who resents you?"

Her mouth twisted and she looked away, out over the harbor. "That is not what I meant."

Realization dawned as I studied her. "Ah," I said. "You meant Hákon *Stáli*."

A flush spread over her cheeks, or perhaps it was torchlight.

"You know better than to waste your hopes on him," I said, not bothering with kindness. "Hákon will be Jarl one day. And he likely hates us as much as his father does."

"You mean he hates you," she said softly.

"Eir," I started.

"What happens if one of us dies?" she said, pushing off the strake. "You know it is a fair question. I never wanted this life to last forever. The others are still young. *I* am still young. I could marry again. I could bear —"

"Think of the freedom we have now," I sputtered.

"It's hardly freedom if we have to hide," she pressed. "This cannot last, not like this. If Olavi is kind enough to take us under his protection, we cannot refuse it."

"The blood of his youngest son is on my hands, Eir! What am I meant to do, offer him my belly like a kicked hound?"

She raised her hands. "Helgi was a shit," she said evenly. "His own treachery would have gotten him killed eventually. I'm confident, if you humble yourself, Olavi must forgive you. If not for his honor, then for his reputation."

I stared at her.

"You speak of his honor," I said. "His reputation. What of mine?"

Undoing the straps hanging from my belt, I unfastened the scabbard. Gripping the seax's handle, I pulled it from the finely-tooled leather and thumbed the edge, letting the length catch the torchlight.

"This has tasted the blood of many enemies," I said, holding her gaze. "It is my best weapon. Part of me."

"It is a good blade," Eir said, frowning.

"Olavi's *son* died by this blade. None of the rest of it matters. I have known the Jarl since we were both children. He will demand an answer for the loss, and I must provide that answer. One day. But not yet. I will not bow to Olavi. My reliance on him is finished."

"Gyda, please."

"Fear keeps us alert," I said. "Our weapons keep us safe. But it is our *unity* that keeps us alive." Breaking off my stare, I sheathed the seax and fastened it to my belt once more. "Are you with me, Eir? Are *they* with me?" I jerked my head towards the women on the dock, now sitting on barrels and talking as they waited for us to finish our business.

"I am," Eir said, and there was no hesitation. "By the gods, I am. We all know your love for us."

"Even if my course does not lead back to Dyflin?"

"We all would follow you to the gates of Helheim," she said. It pained her to say it, but it was the truth.

"Then will you trust me?" I pitched my voice low.

She softened, her hands loosening by her sides. She stepped closer and touched my shoulder. Her warmth seeped into the muscle. "I trust you with everything, dear friend," she said. "But I am tired of hiding. I need to change. Please understand."

I leaned in, touching my forehead to hers. "I do," I said, though I was not certain if I spoke the truth.

There was time enough to think about what she'd told me, what it meant for our lives as Rán's Daughters, but not now.

"I swear on my life," I went on. "If you still wish to sail to Dyflin once we leave Ragnar behind, I will take you there."

"Thank you," she breathed, and for a moment, neither of us moved. But then I shifted, stepping back to straighten my tunic and tighten my belt.

"First, we will have what he owes us," I said firmly. "We will not live in shame any longer."

"You are dauntless," she said, eyes misting.

"What I am is bone-aching and hollow-bellied," I said, stepping away to climb onto the strake and gangplank. "Let's see if this silent town has any beds for our weary carcasses."

Huffing a laugh, she followed me onto the dock to join our friends.

I whistled a low note and their attention went to me, their fists tightening around their knives.

"We are foreigners," I said. "Few in number and bringing nothing of worth to trade in the markets. And we are women. Observe the customs, Daughters. Make no friends here. Sharing a meal and a bed may seem like good fortune until the smiles turn to sneers. A knife can slip into your ribcage as easily as a thief's finger slips into your coin-fold."

Astrid gasped and dropped her knife. It clattered on the planking. This earned a snide laugh from Guðrun.

I exchanged a look with Eir, then turned to the girl. I held her gaze longer than either of us were comfortable. Finally she dropped her eyes. Still I stared until she dipped her head.

"Apologies, Lady," she said.

"One more thing," I said. "Remember that though this land seems peaceful, people are the same. Dangerous. Full of their own violence and hunger. Go canny, and keep your knives close."

I unbuckled my weapon belt and held it out to Astrid.

"You have earned yourself the most important job," I told her. "Go into the town with Eir and find us a place to stay. We will follow behind. Take my seax. You will protect her with your life. And if I don't receive that blade back, I'll use it to teach you some sense."

"Y-yes, Lady," Astrid said, but didn't move.

With a roll of her eyes, Guðrun kicked the back of the girl's legs. She tripped forward, then rushed to retrieve my seax with a red face.

Eir stepped forward and gripped Astrid above the elbow.

"Let's get moving," she said brightly, and marched up the dock towards the large timber gateway that led to the town.

"That girl is going to get herself killed," Rúna murmured, shaking her head as Astrid and Eir vanished.

"Killed or married," Guðrun rumbled, and Liadan's heaving, silent laughter infected all of us.

CHAPTER THREE

The town's main artery was paved with large stone, worn by years of traffic. Pits of rainwater across their surfaces reflected the burnished torchlight. We walked carefully, leather shoes scuffing and echoing in the stillness.

I walked at the back of the group, and Liadan walked with me, her gait easy. She scanned the alleyways like an owl, sharp and eager for the hunt. All around, doors were shut tight, oil lamps snuffed out, and if any figure peered out of cracked windows to watch us pass, they took care to hide themselves well.

Guðrun led our group with Rúna two paces behind. They laughed and whispered to each other. Such cheer put them at odds with the oppressive quiet.

I reached for Liadan's arm, then stopped. She did not tolerate surprise. To a former thrall, any uninvited touch could feel like a threat. I cleared my throat instead and she turned to me, eyebrows raised. I dipped my head at the two ahead of us, and we slowed to watch them.

Rúna said something lewd, and Guðrun choked on her laughter. When she turned to reply, her leading foot slipped, squelching into the runnels of mud and shit alongside the road. Yelping, she leapt back, curses echoing off the walls and rooftops. The howls of several dogs followed, and Rúna pressed her hands to her mouth to smother a laugh.

Guðrun tugged her shawl down to hide her burning cheeks. "My apologies, Lady," she said.

Where one thing glitters, another festers, Liadan signed, grinning. *Better get rid of that or you'll bring the dogs on us.*

Guðrun wiped the befoulment against the stones. "A ripe welcome, this is," she said darkly.

We walked on. Far larger than first perceived, the heart of the town fanned out with a maze of streets and courtyards. Near the harbor, the houses were packed close, built with timber or wattle and daub, like the houses of Dyflin and Jórvík. But as we approached the center of town, the buildings increased in size and grandeur. Long avenues branched off the main road, leading to market squares or boat-yards and smithies. Dyed tapestries swayed on lines hung between roofs, ghostly shadows in the dark. And still, not a single person showed themselves to us.

Eventually, the road opened onto the largest area we'd yet seen.

"An open market," Rúna whispered, eyes turned up to the star-speckled sky. Her nose dripped and she wiped it on her sleeve. "It's so quiet here."

"Quiet and empty," I said, peering across the square. Torches lit the area, but most had burnt out. It gave the space a bleak, secretive atmosphere.

Guðrun drew her antler-handled knife, gesturing with it.

"This place is strange," she said. "All these arches and carvings. And quiet, like a Christ-temple. You can't fart without some priest shushing you."

"It is all lovely," Rúna countered. "This place is strange only because you've never been ashore in these lands."

"And you have? You know as much as I do, woman."

Rúna shrugged, wrapping herself tightly in her shawl. "That may be true, but think of what our fathers would say. They'd die of jealousy to see all of this."

A disordered row of timber frames stood nearby. Fishing nets and scraps of ripped sail hung from the wooden spokes. With the tip of her knife, Guðrun lifted a corner of one net, disgust twisting her mouth.

"I'd think our fathers would piss themselves over what poor state these people keep their tackle." She dropped the net and sheathed the knife with a huff.

"Córdoba is indeed a beautiful place," I said. "And the people are as well. Look at that."

Across the square, there was a tall building. Perhaps a mercantile or a religious structure, a courtyard and fountain fronted it. Shadows played across painted arches, star-shaped windows, and carved needle-like roof spindles. Other decorated buildings surrounded us, each as vibrant as the others.

"Think of the skill it takes to shape stone and brick in such ways," I said. "I have heard tales of the great temples in Serkland. Towers so tall they scrape Ýmir's brains. Think of the mind one must possess to achieve such feats. Think of the wealth and the collected knowledge."

Liadan and Rúna drank in the buildings with greedy, shining eyes, seeing all the beauty that I had conjured.

Guðrun harrumphed. "Strange buildings, stranger town," she said. "This quiet makes my teeth itch. Eir and Astrid better find us beds soon."

Liadan turned her head to the left and sniffed. Then, wrinkling her nose, she raised two fists to each side of her mouth. Her sign for horses.

I inhaled. Manure from stables and other livestock wafted on the breeze, overlaid by the pungency of fish and brine.

"So there is life here," Rúna said, brightening. "Is there a festival on? Or is it their gods that forbid the people to come greet us?"

"Doesn't matter. It's a land of *niðingar,"* Guðrun said. "We are so fearsome even the old drunkards dare not walk abroad."

"Brazen words, braggart," I said. "I doubt even you could stand against their drunkards in a fight."

Rúna laughed and Guðrun's face fell. "You hear this, my love?" she grumbled. "The Lady mocks me, her own best warrior."

Something moved at the edge of my vision. Liadan saw it too, and she scowled.

"Stay here and keep quiet," I said to the others. "Liadan, with me."

The two of us slunk down an intersecting street, hidden by the semi-darkness. Like the rest of the town, these houses were shut tight, with fabric covering the windows and any lamps inside doused.

Liadan signed something, and I caught only the end of it.

...Eir and Astrid?

"No," I whispered. "Someone else."

A scuffing, gravelly sound, two spear-lengths away, made us pause. Liadan hissed.

"I see it," I said.

A house stood back from the road, darkened and fronted by a

walled garden. A canopy hung from two posts off to the side. Concealed beneath it, crouching against the wall, there was a person wrapped in a cloak. They blended with the night so well, I had to squint to make out their shape.

As we approached, the sensation of being watched prickled my skin. I rested my hand on my weapon belt. I had an eating knife. If this person posed a danger, I would be ready.

When we reached a safe distance, I ventured to speak. "What has your people so snug in their houses, friend?" My skill in the language of this land was out of practice, so I pronounced the words carefully, then waited to see if my meaning came across.

The shape moved. A skinny fist, veined and gnarled with bone-swells, protruded from the cloak.

"Silver," they creaked.

I squatted, peering into the folds of fabric, though I could discern no features. "Silver, is it? You have none of your own if you make your bed in the dirt. Answer my questions and you may find new friends and better fortunes tonight."

The figure made an indiscernible noise and withdrew their hand. Muttering obscure curses, they rummaged around in the depths of the cloak. With a grunt of triumph, the figure produced a coin, dull and bent and hardly the size of a fingernail.

"Silver," they said again, then made a fist and gestured up and down the street. "For silence. Quiet streets tonight. No strangers. We do not speak. We do not see. We do not hear."

Dread unfurled in my belly. "Is that so? Who gave such an order?"

They shrugged, more of a sensation than an actual movement.

"Is there danger in the town? What is the reason for all this?" I touched my hand to my eating knife again. "Tell me, pestilence."

They wheezed, showing the coin again. "I am quiet," they said. "I earn my silver."

Liadan stepped to my side and thumped her chest. She signed, her gestures broad and expressive so I could see them.

I released the knife handle and straightened, taking my coin fold from my belt. "Would more silver loosen your tongue?" I brought out three pieces of hack-silver, no bigger than the coin. I let them clink against each other in my palm. "My crew-mates and I are looking for a place to rest our heads. A shame you have no friends to take you in. With this, perhaps your problem and ours could be solved. Tell me what I ask, and you can have it all."

With a creak, they leaned forward eagerly, stopping just short of reaching for the silver.

I waited, unmoving, confident their need would overcome their fear.

"Lady," called Rúna from the end of the street. "Eir and Astrid have found us."

The figure shrank away, pressing themself against the wall. "Away from me," they hissed. "No more speaking."

"Such a shame," I said, returning the hack-silver to my coin fold. "Sleep well in your dirt, old one."

It was when Liadan and I were halfway down the street that they called after us.

"No friends here," they said. "Only death. Silver and death."

Our companions stood in a semi-circle at the far edge of the square.

"What was that about," Eir said as we reached them. "Did you find Ragnar?"

Not Ragnar. Someone else. There is trouble here, Liadan signed, her expression sober in the torchlight. *These people were paid to keep their doors shut against strangers.*

"All of them?" said Rúna. She leaned against Guðrun's chest, shivering and half-sleeping.

"It appears so," I said. "But we couldn't find the reason for it."

"You don't think it has anything to do with our arrival?" Eir's frown deepened.

"This is something that takes time to prepare, and a large purse. No one other than Ragnar expected us. This is something else."

We stood in heavy silence, trying to fathom what this meant.

"What now?" ventured Guðrun. "Do we go back to *Sea-Wolf* and leave?"

"We can't!" Astrid stepped forward, eager. "I've found us a place."

When I looked to Eir, she inclined her head solemnly. "The girl did well," she said.

Astrid raised her chin. "I did better than well. We'll have hot food, and there are rooms for all of us. Here is your seax, Lady." She shoved the scabbard forward.

Slowly, I reached for the blade and refastened it to my belt. "You did well," I told her, thinking my pained grimace would dampen her pride.

Her jaw remained firmly set. "I know," she answered.

Shifting her weight between her feet, Guðrun spoke up. "Wait, now. There's trouble, and you all still want to sleep under a stranger's roof? Thor's balls, but that's the most foolhardy thing I've ever heard."

"There are no other taverns," Astrid said defensively. "This one is perfect for us. And it's only a single night."

Rúna, sensing how the thunder gathered, moved away from Guðrun.

As the argument grew in volume, Liadan shook her head. *Once they start, there's no stopping. We'll be here all night now. The girl should know better.*

"It's Guðrun's fault, really," Eir said. "She's always looking for a reason. Once she's latched onto something, nothing penetrates that skull. I'm tired enough now to consider using a knife."

Liadan's shoulders shook. *A knife would bounce off,* she signed. *Better to use a hammer!*

Rúna clicked her tongue, and tried to speak. Three delicate sneezes arrested her words.

"My apologies," she murmured, dabbing her nose. Her eyes were red-rimmed and swollen. "I took a chill from the water. This is likely why Guðrun is…," she paused, then shrugged. "Guðrun is Guðrun. It doesn't matter why."

Unfastening the iron fibula at her shoulder, Liadan removed her cloak and offered it. With her other hand, she made her sign for an apology.

"A place to lay my head would serve me better," Rúna said with a polite smile. "Should I get between them, Lady?"

I stifled a yawn. "Oh, let the girl hold her own against Guðrun a moment longer," I said. "It'll do her good."

"I'm not sleeping in a hovel smelling of fish-guts and ball-sweat," Guðrun shouted. Her broad chest heaved like a forge-bellows. "If this is the only place with an open door, that should tell you something. If you had anything in your skull besides cracked eggs you'd know it means nothing good!"

Astrid, hands on slender hips, stared back, looking every bit the petulant teenager waiting for a lecture to blow itself out.

"The more you carry on like a wounded ox, the more people know we're here. Which means we need shelter, and I have found it. If anyone is foolhardy, it's you."

"A night of lice and suffering the snores of my neighbor isn't a good exchange. I'd rather sleep in *Sea-Wolf*'s sodden bilges!"

"Thick-headed arse," I muttered.

"She has a point," Eir said. "This tavern was the only one to open its doors when all others refused. Something boils under the surface here, and I want very badly to know what it is."

I rolled my neck, considering.

If this tavern flouted the bribe, all the better for us, Liadan offered.

"I just need a bed," Rúna said pensively. "I don't care about the rest of it right now."

I nodded. "Let the morning bring the answers. We can rise early and return to *Sea-Wolf* before anyone knows we're here. Lead us on, Eir. Those two idiots will follow."

Fish-guts and ball-sweat, Guðrun had said, and could not have been more wrong. I turned in a circle, mouth agape.

"Beautiful, like *Folkvangr*, isn't it?" Astrid said.

"Like *Folkvangr* and Lady Freyja herself." Rúna smiled at the girl.

Hanging braziers and torchlight revealed the truth of Astrid's discovery. This was no simple tavern. A cluster of buildings surrounded an ancient stone courtyard. The primary structure was at the northern edge, with annexes branching from all corners to enclose the square.

Long wings of rooms and promenades surrounded us, all sculpted and decorated in similar styles. Each wing stood three stories tall and boasted tiled roofs. The central structure, which I surmised to be for brief stays, had just a single floor above the main level. Oil lamps flickered in arched, open-air windows.

It was evident this complex catered to respectable guests, those with ample coin to spend. Once richly painted, the structures boasted a faded grandeur, their best days behind them, and now they enjoyed a dotage of regal memory. We stood at the door of the main structure. Astrid had banged heavily on it, and now we waited to see if our luck would hold.

"I believe this is called a funduq," Eir told me. "Travelers and merchants often stay. And there are storage rooms for cargo and other goods. This one looks rather aged."

"I have heard of these places," I said, still breathless. "They are friends to those like us. You did *very* well, Astrid."

Astrid ducked her head.

"Careful, Lady," Rúna said, smiling through her sniffling. "You'll spoil the girl and she'll forget she's the worst sailor of all of us."

That dampened Astrid's spirits, but brought weary laughs from the rest, except Guðrun, though her eyes creased at the corner.

A shaft of golden light hit us as the door swung open on rusted hinges. A dark-haired woman poked her head out and spoke urgently, beckoning us in.

Once we'd gathered in the small entryway, the woman shut the door and faced us, eyes wide and intent.

Astrid stepped forward and nodded respectfully. "This is the alewife," she explained to us. "She told Eir that she has rooms for us."

The woman was the same age as Astrid, not more than twenty summers, and beautiful, with black hair and smooth brown skin. Her garments were not new, but they had been fine once, dyed silks and linens. Now they were clean but shabby.

She spoke, her voice deep and her words rapid.

I held up a hand. "I speak a little of your language," I said. "But not this dialect."

"She said we must follow her," Eir translated.

A crease appeared between the girl's brows, but then she turned, waving us through another door.

"I will take you to my mother," she said, switching dialects. This one I understood.

As we filed through the entry, Eir bent close to my ear.

"She is not happy to see us," she murmured. "When it was only Astrid and I, she was much more welcoming."

"She is certainly not at ease," I whispered. "Stay alert."

"What's that burning stink?" Guðrun said as we entered the inner room. She waved a hand and coughed. Tendrils of smoke hung in the air, clinging to our clothes and making halos around the candles.

"It's called incense," replied Rúna. "It smells better than you do, my love."

Astrid snorted, then coughed as the smoke hit the back of her throat.

Though the outside had been faded, the inside of the funduq was anything but old. The room we'd been led to was white-washed, lit by expensive candles, and hung with intricate tapestries of every color and shape and pattern. Large cushions and carpets spanned the floor, inviting in their plush comfort. The center of the floor was stone and inlaid with hundreds of green and blue tiles arranged in brilliant patterns of fish and waves.

Astrid and Liadan gaped at a wall hanging with the figure of a man. He was dark-skinned and sported a great black beard. Medallions of gold and precious gems hung from his neck, and at his hip hung a wickedly curved sword. A small, serene smile touched his lips and roses bloomed in his full cheeks.

"You like this man?" asked the young woman, smiling at Liadan.

Liadan looked to me for an interpretation.

"Do you like him," she repeated, and put a hand out to tap Liadan's shoulder.

Liadan stiffened and took a quick step back.

"I speak to you, Lady." The young woman's warmth left her voice.

Liadan straightened, clasping her hands in front of her and focused on the wall above the alewife's head.

"Does she refuse to speak to me," she demanded, turning on her heel to glare at me as if I were at fault. "Is she rude, or just without sense?"

"Liadan does not speak," I said, after receiving a nod from the Irish woman. "And she does not suffer disrespect. We are here for your hospitality, girl, not for your questions."

"Why doesn't she speak? Did a man hurt her? Is this why you travel without one?"

Anger simmered through us, a bubbling murmur as shoulders tensed and fingers curled. But it was Liadan herself who held up a hand.

She lifted her braided blonde hair from her neck, tilting her head so that the flesh caught the candlelight.

The young woman's dark eyes widened. Her fingers went to her own throat. "Ah, I understand," she breathed.

Liadan lowered her hair again, covering the scar. She signed, which I relayed.

My owner did this. Liadan's face twisted with bitterness as she remembered. *He believed there is no true freedom for thralls. I have been marked by the sisters of death, but they have not claimed me. My voice was their price, but I received my freedom.*

"Forgive me, I am a fool," the young woman said, lowering her gaze.

You are not a fool, Liadan told her. *But you are young. Take care the next time you have guests.*

When I finished translating, I cleared my throat and straightened.

"Where do you lead us," I demanded. "We came here for food and beds. Where is your father and mother? You are far too young, and far too lacking in sense to own such a house. I would speak with them."

The young woman tensed at my tone, then plastered on an affected and fawning smile. "Yes, we have food," she said. "We have beds. I will call for my mother. Wait, please." She scurried off, through another door at the other side of the room.

Eir leaned close to me. "We should follow."

"She hides something," I replied. "But I suspect we know it already."

"We do?"

"Her mother is not aware we are here," I said. "She hopes that, by telling her now, when we are already past their entry, her mother's anger falls on us instead of her."

Eir laughed a little. "How do you know that?"

"I know because it is exactly what I would have done in her place."

From the passage beyond the door, a raised voice echoed, followed by a younger, pleading one.

"As ever, your wisdom astonishes," Eir said wryly. "I should call you *seiðkona*."

The mother and daughter were still arguing as they came into the chamber. No one could mistake their relation; both had dark features, though the mother's hair was bound in elaborate long braids and streaked with threads of shining silver. Their garments were similar: loose pants, a tunic with silk ties at the clavicle, and a shawl to cover their shoulders and hair when needed.

Their hands flew like startled birds as they argued. I took my knife and rapped the butt three times against the doorframe. Both women's necks swiveled.

"I am Gyda of Dyflin," I told them, switching to Norse. "We need sleep and food. Do you understand my words?" I paused, then switched to *Gaeilge*, the Irish language, and asked again.

The mother, not much older than me, scowled fiercely. "I understand," she answered in Norse. "Not well, but it is enough. We have had many of your people stay here. But you are not welcome here, Gyda of Dyflin."

Her daughter shrank behind, bowing her head.

"These are my women," I said, turning to allow each of the Daughters' faces to be seen. "Eir, Liadan, Guðrun, Rúna, and Astrid, our youngest. She is near the same age as your daughter."

I bared a smile, but the Daughters did not. Rúna was the only one to even attempt. She gave a watery half-grin, which fell from her face as she smothered a small sneeze. Guðrun put a protective arm around her shoulders.

"We come for warm beds and food," I said. "We need only one night, and we can pay you well."

Curiosity pulled at the mother. I saw it in the way she leaned closer, with her brows lifting and mouth pursing. But as she studied me and the seax hanging from my belt, wariness overcame her interest. She gathered her shawl around her and turned her head. "I do not know what my daughter has told you, but we have no room. No place for you here."

"Is that so? Ah, well. When one's loyalty is bought so cheaply, then it is no great burden to buy it back."

Taking my coin fold from my belt, I opened it outward. The woman and her daughter widened their eyes at the hack-silver and coins inside.

"Whatever you were given to say this to us, I can multiply it ten times," I said.

The mother considered a moment, twisting a golden ring around her right forefinger. But then she inhaled and took a firm step back.

"No," she said. "I can give you food, as my faith asks of me, but you must sleep elsewhere tonight."

I concealed the coins once more. "Tell me," I said, keeping my voice even. "What kind of proprietor would turn down good silver and paying patrons? Your home falls apart around your ears. And the damage to your reputation as a house of hospitality…," I clicked my tongue and shook my head. "I am disappointed. Surely you risk shame in the eyes of your devout neighbors."

"Your words are goading, and they stink of pig shit," the mother spat. "What do you know of shame?"

Though I doubted she understood much Norse, the daughter stepped forward to whisper in her mother's ear.

Eir took the same opportunity, moving to my left. "This is not worth the trouble, by Freyja," she said. "Let us go back to *Sea-Wolf*. We will be safe there, and perhaps finally get some sleep."

"We stay here. Wait."

Eir made an impatient noise. "I don't have it in me to argue all night long! Rúna needs rest, and the rest of us are holding ourselves up by our belts."

"Wait," I said through gritted teeth.

Eir's face darkened. "Of course, *Lady*," she bit out. "We are at your command." She stepped back.

"My name is Hadiyya," the daughter murmured then, her voice reluctant but clear. "My mother is called Nashwa. I will take you to your rooms and bring the food. Please be quiet."

Weary exhalations of relief emitted from Astrid and Rúna.

As Hadiyya led us out, Nashwa kept her head turned, mouth creased flat.

Before I ducked through the inner door to follow the others, I paused. "We will speak in the morning, Nashwa," I said. "You will have your payment. I promise, you will not suffer reprisal for housing us this night."

Nashwa shut her eyes tight and jerked her head. "Just go. You will leave early and you will not return. My daughter was foolish, but she has a good heart. I do not. Our door will not open to you again."

"That is fair," I said, and left the woman alone.

CHAPTER FOUR

I lay awake, one arm behind my head and the other trapped beneath the slumbering weight of Liadan. It was long since I'd lost feeling in it, though I did not move. A little numbness in the arm was better than the ache of my pulled muscles.

Liadan breathed softly, curled up and facing away. The bed was enormous; our limbs splayed out like children on their parents' sleeping platform. Though averse to touch in waking hours, Liadan enjoyed company while sleeping. The warmth and security reminded her of her sisters, now long lost. It seemed a gift she feared no touch in her sleep; I knew too many women who did. Her form in profile was a lump of dreams and dried sweat, but she was peaceful. Her plait rested over her shoulder like a rope of moonlit gold.

I dug my fingernails into my scalp. My hair itched with dried salt and smelled of fish. I should have bargained for a bath along with the food and beds.

Dawn was yet far off. I kicked a leg, throwing off the linen and silk covering. It was too hot for blankets. Too hot to sleep. Too hot for anything. Except, of course, fear; that was always present with me.

I listened to the darkness outside. Crickets droned somewhere below the window and there was the faint breathing sigh of the ocean. Nothing else. The town slept, as quiet as it was when we'd arrived.

We had three rooms between us at the end of a passage. Guðrun and Rúna had claimed the largest room, and Eir bunked with Astrid across the hall. There had been a cold spell on us for the rest of the evening. Eir said not a word to anyone, choosing to sit and eat alone. We all felt the strain, though none more than me.

I scratched my scalp, the debris crusting under my nails.

What kind of leader was I, bringing my Daughters here? We'd lost Ragnar within the bowels of a snake-pit town, and there was no guarantee we could find him. Whatever writhing, twisting scheme this bribe was, I now wished I had kept us out of it.

Liadan twitched, gusting a sleep-heavy sigh as she curled tighter. The movement broke my dark thinking.

I loved these women; they were everything to me.

Eir and I had been together for years, sisters more than friends. Widowhood bound us together, and Rán's Daughters were born from that bond. We were ill-fit women, too odd for our families, like Guðrun and Rúna, or unfairly deemed too 'difficult', like Liadan. The girl Astrid had left her home to escape violence, and we had become her new parents. We were a family, the six of us.

Yet Eir wished to leave?

Outside, beyond the grated window covering, a bird called. The crickets crouched in the shrubbery, singing their night song and fearing nothing. I listened, wondering if the creatures had ever felt anything beyond the need for survival. The need to mate and eat and hide.

Once, I had felt as weak as an insect, dependent on men with more power than me, men who ordered my steps and dictated where I lived. I came to Dyflin with my husband, a dull man who had once raided alongside Jarl Olavi. In his later years, Jörund cared little about things like *legacy* or *reputation.* He could not understand how deeply those things mattered to me.

Most female reputations and fortunes hinged upon their husbands or fathers or sons. With no children and a husband who turned to fishing as a pastime, my byname became *Fiskwif*—fishwife.

I couldn't go to the market or trudge through the muddy roads without being greeted by this name. When my husband drowned in the dark water of the river, it became my widow's mantle.

Gyda *Fiskwif*. It was a term of endearment from the Daughters, but an insult from my competitors. The memory of what it first meant was a thorn that still pricked me.

I pulled my arm out from under Liadan and rose, hissing as blood rushed to my fingertips. Padding to the window, I stared through the star-shaped holes into the lower courtyard.

Some people became warriors and raiders. Some turned a trade or crafted goods and trinkets. I was a woman of the sea, a daughter of silver and salt. I would live on the waves or die in the depths. *Gyda the Grim*. Ragnar had named me thus after I'd killed Helgi. That name suited me best.

From a fish-stinking wife in a cold, drizzly settlement on the arse-end of the world, to a fish-stinking merchant commanding a ship I owned, I had forged my reputation across multiple lands. My Daughters were chosen for their strength and their determination. Tomorrow, we might well be the richest of women, simply because I had taken pity on a grieving man and killed the youngest son of a Jarl.

"See what the *Nornir* spin, eh, crickets?" I whispered. "What will the fate-weavers make for me now?"

The cricket's song held no answer.

I stood a moment longer, rubbing my shoulder. Then I turned away from the window and went back to bed. My thoughts spun and spun, like driftwood in a current, until even the crickets ceased their singing.

Dawn broke with a throat-ripping scream. I was in the hallway with my seax in my hand before the last echo died away.

"Open!" I flung myself at the door, striking it with my fist. "Open now! Astrid, Eir!"

On the other side, there was a grunt of effort, followed by the sounds of splintering wood, a clattering, a short, deeper cry of pain, and then nothing.

Liadan appeared beside me, thunder on her brow from being woken. Rúna also stepped into the hall, her face as pale as bone. She wore nothing but a short linen *serk*. "What is happening?"

Guðrun followed behind, blinking away sleep. She wore even less than Rúna. "Thor's hairy balls, what was that noise?"

"Get this door open!" I stepped back and Guðrun and Liadan moved in. Before they could batter it down, Eir opened it.

"No need for that," she said. "We are all right."

She wore her tunic and trousers, with the bed-covering slung over her shoulders. Her unbound hair floated like pale clouds.

I shoved past her and aimed for the left side of the bed, where Astrid rested with her hand cradled in her lap.

"Who did this?" I demanded.

A large, broken window frame gaped to our left. Though most of the fragile grate had splintered outward, slender pieces of wood scattered across the floor. I stuck my head through the window and looked down. A chunk of grate had shattered in the alleyway below. Beyond that, I saw nothing else.

Shouts echoed at the head of the alley. I pulled my head back in and looked to Astrid.

"The town guard is coming. Who was it, girl? What festering troll-son dared this?"

Astrid quailed, stammering.

"Open your mouth!"

"We think it could have been Ragnar," Eir put in.

"Ragnar?" Guðrun slapped her knee. "What would Ragnar be doing climbing up a wall like a stink bug?"

"More likely it was some ball-aching *bak-rauf* who thought that peeking on sleeping women was a worthy use of his cock," I said.

Liadan broke into silent laughter and Eir's face flushed scarlet.

Guðrun's broad chest was bare. Unconcerned, she put the whole of her upper body outside the window to look out. "Whoever it was, they're sniffing around out there for him now. Might want to hurry. They'll be up here next."

"How many?" I said.

"At least ten."

"Fuck."

Eir went to the bed and draped the blanket over Astrid's shoulders. "Let me see that," she told her gently.

Astrid flexed her knuckles, hissing with the soreness. She placed her hand in Eir's and looked away. Eir tilted it to catch the dim morning light.

"It is bruised, not broken. We'll have to pick a few splinters from your knuckles, but that is easily done."

"I can do that," Rúna said, coming around to the bed. "We'll soak it in honey-mead and bandage it."

"Tell me exactly what happened," I said again, striving to keep my voice even. "Before they send the guard up here."

"There was a sound," Astrid said. "It woke me and I went to the window, thinking it was a bird, but there was a man. His face was covered. He said something about a house and a wall, but I was too startled to understand. I screamed and punched the window grate to break his nose." She paused, flushing red. "I think he broke his ankle. He lost his hold and fell straight down. I didn't see where he went afterwards. And then you were shouting and banging on the door."

"Who knew the girl had fight!" Guðrun grinned, but there was an edge of mockery in it. "But your soft hands, what a pity."

Astrid raised her fists. "Who found you a bed last night? These soft hands can still break *your* nose."

Eir's mouth creased with worry. "The owner and her daughter don't need this trouble," she said. "Until we learn what this town is hiding, lingering anywhere is unwise."

Her warning came too late; raised, angry voices resounded from the ground floor.

Five pairs of hands flew to hips for weapons and came up empty. Only I had my seax, and my fist tightened around it.

Mingling with Nashwa's protests, the voices, all male, stalled at the foot of the stairway near the end of the passage.

"We're fucked if they come up here," Guðrun said, but she joined the line of the other women as they fanned out behind me.

So it was that Nashwa found us, clothed or otherwise, and ready for violence.

"Ai!" The woman threw up her hands and turned away, hiding her face in her shawl. "Cover yourselves!"

I lunged forward and grabbed her arm. "Who is downstairs?" I demanded in her language. "Did you send for them?"

"This is not my doing!" Nashwa let her shawl drop and yanked her arm from my grasp. "There are men, town guard and…others. Like you. They want to know what happened. Hadiyya is with them."

She came into the room, removing her shawl. "At least cover your shoulders." She swung the fabric around Guðrun. It fit her poorly, like a doll's blanket strung up for a sail.

Guðrun looked down. "You can still see my tits," she said in Norse. She pulled on it, but the shawl failed to cover her.

"It's either one or the other," Rúna said with a barely stifled smirk. Guðrun rolled her eyes and let the shawl hang however it wanted to, which was not at all. It fell in an undignified heap.

Nashwa, face aflame, ignored this and turned back to me. "They're not likely to wait long. There is a way out, through the alley. I can take you."

"Why would you help us?" I exclaimed. "You turn us away, then you seek to hide us. How can I trust you?"

She eyed me like a noisome insect. "I have hosted you, and did not poison your food or put a knife to your throats while you slept. You destroy my property before the sun rises, and you have the boldness to question if you can trust *me?"*

I said nothing, matching her stare.

"By the Prophet, peace be upon him, you will bring calamity on me." Nashwa pulled on her knuckles, looking to the hallway as she considered her next words. "You promised you could protect us. Did you speak the truth?"

I nodded.

"Then I will tell you what I know, and I will show you the way out. Everyone must dress, and be quick. I will go down and delay as long as I can."

"You said they were like us," Eir interjected, her accent strong. "What did you mean?"

"I mean they speak like you. Walk tall like you. And they know your names."

Eir looked at me, gray eyes full. "You don't think…?"

"He's here." Astrid's whisper sent a shiver through all of us.

Olavi.

"We need to go," I said. "Make yourselves ready, Daughters."

Nashwa came for us as we left our rooms.

"I told them a lie," she said. She stood at the top of the stairs, leaning against the wall as her chest rose and fell. "They will be drunk soon. I keep a stock of beer for foreigners. I left my daughter to serve it with fresh flat bread. Though I doubt this will keep their attention long. Their anger boils."

"We are ready," I said.

"Then follow me. Keep silent."

One by one, we descended, taking care not to tread on any loose boards. I walked ahead with Nashwa, while Eir brought up the rear.

We moved quickly, hands on our weapons and muscles bunched tight. There had been no time to speak as we dressed, no time to think. Olavi had come to al-Andalus, and he had come with oathmen. Warriors.

At the foot of the stairs, Nashwa halted. "I will take you to the end of this," she said quietly.

The passage had a dozen doorways, each leading to more rooms and halls, spreading out like boughs of a tree. Smoking oil lamps hung from hooks above every door.

"Are there other guests staying here? We should avoid them," whispered Eir.

"None," Nashwa answered. "Hush now, not a sound."

The fourth door on the left was open; a sliver of warm light shone through the crack. There was laughter inside, mingled with the clinking of ceramic beer cups. Hadiyya's voice threaded over several men's deeper timbres. Hers was light and brave and young. I did not recognize the men's voices. The ones who spoke were not Norse.

We crept past the room, hearts in our throats.

"Where are the others, the ones like us?" I mouthed to Nashwa.

She shook her head. "I left them in that room," she whispered. "If they departed, I did not notice."

The passage stretched, made longer by our caution. When Hadiyya's laughter rose to a nervous pitch, Nashwa's face twisted.

"She will not be harmed," I murmured, touching Nashwa's shoulder. "When we are gone, tell them we threatened you. Their wrath should not fall on your heads."

Nashwa jerked away from me. "You don't know what you speak of," she hissed.

"You owe me answers, Nashwa," I said. "And you are afraid. I need to know if we are to protect you and your daughter."

"I owe you nothing." Her voice was low and sharp. "But I will hold that promise to you like fire to your feet."

We reached the end of the passage. To the left and right, there were walled walkways with high windows to let in the morning air. There were no people in sight.

"There is someone I know," Nashwa whispered to us. "A dung-eating coward. His name is Afzal. He leads the guardsmen. And he wants my property. It has been two years and I still refuse him. You see the decay of this place. Because of him, I no longer entertain many travelers." Her mouth creased in bitterness. "They stay at another inn. It is little better than a bathhouse, but Afzal owns it."

"What does he have to do with anything?" Guðrun said, but I held up my hand to listen.

"We used to house so many," Nashwa said, her gaze unfocused and soft. "My rooms would be full of stock and trade goods. There would be food served all day, and stories told all evening in the common areas. We would run out of floor cushions, there would be so many guests. Now we are little better than an empty barn." She drew her shawl around her and leaned against the wall.

"You will turn left here," she said wearily. "And then right again. We are at the outermost edge of the building. The second to last door in that passage will let you into the garden. From there, follow the path to an iron gate and into the alley. Leave this place, go to your ship, and do not return."

"Is Afzal —"

"No," she said, jerking her chin up. "Afzal is not why I turned you away last night."

"Then why, Nashwa? Tell me now."

"By the prophet, be quiet," she hissed. "There is another man, like all of you, but he came from the city of Córdoba on business for the Emir. He arrived two weeks ago and stayed with us. The next day he met with Afzal. Something went wrong. There was a fight in the street. I don't know what happened, but he did not return. After, we were told to close our doors. Anyone harboring a foreigner would be turned out of their homes. We have kept our doors locked for days, not knowing why. When you came here with your blades and your silver, I knew you must be involved."

"Gyda," Eir hissed. "There is no time for this."

"Is the man from Córdoba alive?" I demanded. "What is his name?"

Nashwa shrank against the wall, her black and silver hair falling forward. "My brother serves in the guard. Your man is wealthy, and he has influence. He may be alive, but we are afraid. All of us are afraid. It is not the first time people of your kind have come here to thieve and to torment, and it will not be the last."

"It has to be Ragnar," Astrid said excitedly. "He's here for us. He must have been the man at my window."

"No doubt of it," I said. "What did he say to you?"

She cringed under the force of my glare. "I can't remember."

"*Think,* girl!"

"Ah-a red house," she said, squeezing her eyes shut. "And the wall. East of town. That's all!"

"It must be a meeting place," Rúna said.

Looking past us, Nashwa's dark eyes widened. "You need to leave. Now!"

Angry male voices rang out. I whirled, hand on my seax. Down the passage, two men had seen us. They called to their friends, and two more spilled from the room.

"Hadiyya!" Nashwa lurched. I grabbed her by the shawl.

"Don't! You cannot fight them."

Nashwa stared open mouthed at me, then at the men. "I can't fight them," she said. "But I can delay one or two. Go!"

Nashwa left the shawl hanging from my hands. She screeched, tearing at her clothes and her hair, weeping as she ran towards the angry men. "My brother, my brother," she cried. "I cannot find him!"

The others were gone already, racing down the left passage with Eir and I chasing after them.

"Wait, Eir," I called, slowing as I looked back at Nashwa. But Eir grabbed my hand and dragged me. My shoulder flared with the movement and I cried out. There were more loud voices coming up the passage. Nashwa's screeching stopped. Eir slowed. The voices were Norse.

"Run!" I snarled at her. "Get the others out. I am behind you."

She dashed ahead, her stride longer and limbs more athletic than mine.

I pressed my arm against my side and jogged, out of breath from the pain and the fear and the frustration. What if the stranger described by Nashwa was Ragnar? What had happened to him? Did that mean our agreement was void? Had he brought Olavi down on my head to cheat me?

I bared my teeth. No. Ragnar was a fool, but he was honorable. Whomever intimidated this poor fishing town had no honor. He was lower than a turd, no better than a *niðingr*.

I turned the corner to the final passage.

"Fuck!"

More doors, but no Daughters. Which led to the garden? The second one?

A shout rattled my ears. My hand found my seax, already striking with it before I'd fully turned around.

The man screamed as his fingers parted from the hilt of his knife. Blood pulsed from the stump of his thumb. His Jarl-given arm ring, silver and twin-ended with boar's heads, gleamed in the sunlight.

"Who sent you here," I demanded. "Who threatens this town? Give me his name."

"A curse on your head!" His florid face was stretched in a wide grimace. He pressed his mangled hand against his belly.

His knife had fallen to the right. He lunged for it at the same time as I moved to kick it away. My foot connected with nothing but air.

I stumbled away from his reach. He laughed. More were coming. I could hear their shrieks and curses. Which door was it?

The man lunged for me again, wildly, clumsily, with the knife in his weaker hand. I wheeled, striking across his shoulders as he brushed past. He arched and screamed. Red soaked his white tunic.

I grabbed the knife from him. "Who sent you here? Are you Olavi's man? Tell me!"

"Fuck you, dog-faced bitch!"

The man went for me unarmed, and this time, I stepped into his embrace.

My seax slid into his gut like silk. He was of a height with me, and so when his mouth opened to exhale a rank-smelling '*guh!*', a glob of spittle wet my cheek.

I ripped my seax out and shoved him off.

The second-to-last door opened with a kick and I fell onto the sandstone path of the garden.

I ran, flicking my seax clean of the man's blood.

The garden was long and a containing wall ran the extent of it. Large shade trees and shrubberies decorated most of the inner area, and more paths of sandstone gravel twisted and turned throughout.

I took a path that ran west, perpendicular to the wall, which stood higher than my shoulder.

"Iron gate," I huffed, searching the foliage.

Cries of rage reached me. "Here! She is here!"

Vaulting over a stone bench, I landed hard in a row of brambles. My fine trousers and leg wraps snagged on thorns. I crashed through and cut across the patches of herbs and around fruit trees, aiming my trajectory for the wall. I continued along the perimeter, pushing away vines hanging from overhead trellises. The pounding of feet dogged me.

Another path appeared several spear-lengths ahead. Its sand was kicked up, strewn about by the passage of recent feet. I flew towards it, then turned and passed through the iron gate. It had been left open to the alley, and I did not slow to shut it.

My lungs burned. My mouth was parched. My shoulder ached. But I did not stop.

There was a square ahead, full of people. They milled around the tented stalls and browsed the market stands. Colored silks and linens hung like garish flags in the sun. The smell of spiced meat and sweet rolls were heady in the air.

I bolted through the stands, shoving and hurdling and screaming, "Make way!"

Women pulled their children aside and yanked shawls over their eyes. Men reached out to grab me and drew back just as swiftly, seeing the blood on my tunic and the blade in my belt. There would be no hiding now.

Voices behind me: angry, deep shouts and curses.

With pulse pounding fast like the drums at a *blót,* I turned a corner, and then another. A narrow, empty street opened before me and I took it. I did not stop running until the number of houses lessened and the alleys led me to an abandoned dwelling built of red stone blocks which was tucked against the eastern corner of the town's surrounding wall.

Ragnar's meeting place.

"Took you long enough to find us," said Guðrun when I fell through the door. She perched on a stool with the others around a smoking cook-pit.

"Fuck you," I said. "Get me a drink."

CHAPTER FIVE

"Ah, fuck!"

"Hold still." Eir pulled the knot of linen one more time, then tucked it behind my shoulder. "You're finished," she said. "Keep that sling on until the soreness fades."

I clenched my jaw, knowing that if I spoke now, it would be nothing but curses.

Dragging her wooden stool to the other side of the cook-fire, Eir sat and rested her elbows on her knees. She fixed me with a sober stare. "So, you killed one of Olavi's men and then ran through the market covered in his blood. Well done."

Guðrun grinned hungrily. "Which one was it? Was it Logi? I've had a *seiðr*-curse on him for years."

"I told you before," Rúna said. "That woman in the market was as false as the bits of polished tin you gave her. Your *seiðr*-curse was nothing but dried grass in a pouch, my love."

"It's the thought that makes the curse," Guðrun said stubbornly.

Rúna shook her head and took another drink from the steaming horn cup in her hands. Astrid offered her ladle, refilling the cup with the fragrant tea boiling in the cauldron. She filled another cup taken from her belt and offered it to me. It wasn't ale, but it would do. I accepted the cup and sipped, appreciating the bite of thyme and sage.

"Did you expect me to yell," I said to Eir, who still watched me. "Defend myself?"

"Do you think you need to defend yourself, Gyda?"

"Do you want me to, Eir?"

She drew a hand down her face and straightened. "You may think you're at your best when belligerent, but I don't have the patience today. This isn't an interrogation."

"Then why are you staring like I'm a rabbit in a snare?"

She jerked her head at the others, all of whom kept their faces carefully blank.

"We're missing someone," Eir said. "Ragnar isn't here."

She raised her hands, counting off fingers as she spoke. "We come to a town that's as silent as a barrow-hill. All doors are locked. When we do find beds, we suffer an intrusion, followed by a visit from the town guard and Jarl Olavi's fighters. You kill one, and now we squat in an abandoned house at the edge of the town, waiting for an injured outcast to show up towing his own weight in coin."

"So there's been a few squalls! We've weathered worse."

Astrid snickered and Liadan glared at her until she fell silent.

"Ragnar is not here, Gyda," Eir said flatly. "What are we meant to do?"

"You say that like you already have an answer."

She took a breath. "I think we should go to Olavi," she said. "We should do it before his men find us and drag us to him by our necks."

None of the others expected that. Guðrun's cursing made even Rúna wince. Astrid and Liadan stared at Eir with eyes as big as goose eggs.

I stood and drained my cup. "If you've got nothing else to say, I think we're finished here."

"Don't do that," Eir said, coming around the smoking hearth. "You can't wall yourself off because you don't like what is said to you. Ragnar is not coming, Gyda. Perhaps he never intended to. Even if he did, he's gone now, or dead. We are in serious danger now."

"Then I say we should be gone as well," put in Guðrun. "Let's get back to *Sea-Wolf* before it is taken, or we are. Olavi can eat goat-turds for all I care."

I didn't shrug off Eir's hand on my arm, nor put a fist in her face, though every instinct in me wanted to. I didn't because fear came off her like smoke. It came off all of them, showing in their faces and in the slump of their shoulders.

"I cannot go to Olavi," I said. "I can't stop you if that is your wish, Eir. But hear me: whatever hope you hold for his mercy, forget it. He came in all his force. The warrior I killed was not bargaining. There is no mercy for us. Olavi wants blood."

She dropped her hand. "Gods, I am tired," she said. "I don't want to bring corpses back to Dyflin. The longer we avoid Olavi, the farther we flee, the bloodier this life becomes."

I turned to the others. "Do you all feel the same? Don't be afraid to speak."

Astrid leaned against the back wall, near a stack of dusty crates. She cleared her throat to be heard. "I don't want to go against the Jarl. But when it's safe, I'd like to go back to Dyflin. I miss my mother."

Guðrun made a derisive noise. "If Ragnar isn't here, we are wasting our time."

Wiping her fingers on her tunic, she looked over at Rúna, who had stuffed her nose with bits of linen to keep it from streaming.

"She'll catch a fever if we stay. This place is hot like a fire giant's ball sack. I say we go back to Jórvík and beg that wolf-headed King Sigtryggr for a new trade route. Orkney or something more northerly. We can keep to the sea for a while. Olavi will forget about us if he can't find us."

"But how did he find us at all?" Rúna said. "And how could he have known when we'd be here?"

I shook my head. "That amber merchant could have passed on his knowledge to any other merchant on their way to Dyflin. Ragnar was a prominent man of Olavi's before he was a bodyguard for the Emir."

Eir nodded at Liadan. "And you? What are you thinking?"

She stood from her crouch and glowered at all of us. She signed: *I want to stay. Ragnar will come. I haven't lost my ambition or my courage, even if you frightened hens have.* Her hands flicked the last sign, her disdain evident.

Guðrun's brow darkened, though she did not get the chance to argue, because there was a cracking sound in the corner, followed by a squeal.

"A snake, a snake," Astrid yelled. "It's biting me! Oh Freyja, help me!" Her eyes squeezed and her face turned white as new spun wool.

She had shifted her weight, causing one foot to plunge through what appeared to be reed matting protecting a void in the dirt floor.

Being the closest, Guðrun reached out. "Hang on to me," she said, laughing. "Don't move or your *friend* might turn into a pair of shoes."

Astrid looked down. A deep flush replaced her paleness. "It's just a piece of leather," she said meekly.

"Come on, then." Guðrun hauled Astrid out of the hole, and as her foot and the leather came out, there was a distinct and musical *clink*.

For the span of a heartbeat, all of us gaped at each other. And then we dove for the hole, ripping up and tossing away handfuls of dirt and reed matting.

Eir sat back on her haunches. "May Thor strike me," she breathed, eyes wide.

Inside this shallow earthen cellar, we had found something truly wondrous.

Guðrun whistled low. "Fáfnir's hoard, this is. I've never seen such shine!"

None of us had. Hidden beneath the dirt floor and woven reeds was silver. Unfathomable amounts of it. There were stacks of ingots the size of my fingers, pouches of hack-silver and whole coins. Small vessels full of spices. We ripped the lids off of them to inhale the aromas. There were strings of amber beads and precious stones, ivory and pelts from beasts we had never seen, sacks of fine silks and fabrics spilling out. It was a dragon's hoard, and more.

I shoved my fist in a pouch of coins, squeezing so hard the edges dug into my flesh. This was beyond anything I'd expected. Beyond what Ragnar had promised. This hoard was wealth and power and status and everything I'd wanted for countless years. Everything I deserved. Everything Rán's Daughters deserved.

And that fact complicated everything.

I glanced at Eir. From the lines appearing between her brows and the fingernail she chewed, she knew it too.

"Why do you look like you've swallowed a pair of live eels?" Guðrun buried herself in a sack and brought out handfuls of dark amber beads. "Look at these! Proof enough that Ragnar was good for all his promises."

"Maybe," Eir said. "But where is the man himself?"

"Pah! He's broken his leg," Guðrun grunted. "Holed himself up somewhere like a badger or moldering in a jail. Better for us. We can take this and leave for Jórvík as soon as we pack it into *Sea-Wolf*'s belly."

Astrid lifted a length of goldenrod silk to her cheek and held it there. "This will make a wonderful new *serk* for my mother. Her linen ones are so old and stained. Surely we can go back to Dyflin now!"

Gathering myself, I stood and went to the door. I found a crack in the weathered wood and looked out.

It was quiet. No animals occupied the pen in the yard. No one walked the street. We were alone here.

I moved back, studying the crumbling plaster on the walls and the packed earth floor with its small cook-fire and secret hoard. Ragnar had been here, and recently. But would he come back?

There was a sound next to me. I turned.

You are afraid, signed Liadan.

I scowled, hating my answer before I even gave it. "The others are right," I said. "We should leave."

Eir joined us. "I heard that. So you have seen my side of things?"

"Hardly," I scoffed. "But I won't deny all this sits poorly in my gut. This place isn't safe for us to linger."

What of Ragnar? Liadan's hands were hesitant. *We have our payment, but no passenger. He cannot speak for himself if he isn't here.*

Rúna joined us, arms wrapped around her middle. "Nothing here can tell us where he might have gone. We don't know anything about this place."

I thought for a moment, then smiled. "I expect he believes we will wait for him."

"I know that look," Eir said. "What are you scheming?"

I turned to Rúna. "Can you get us out of port after nightfall?"

Rúna tilted her head back and squinted one eye at the smoke hole in the roof, judging the arc of the sun. "It'll take some effort without the tide, but I think I can do it if we're suitably prepared."

"You two," I barked at Guðrun and Astrid, who were still sifting through the items in the hole with shining eyes. "Get all that sorted and back into crates. Find handcarts or a wagon. All of it needs to be loaded. Do it now!"

Scorched by the fire in my voice, they scrambled to it.

"I urge you to reconsider," Eir said as Liadan and Rúna moved off to help. "What if we are caught before we get to *Sea-Wolf*? Our chance to meet with Olavi on our own terms will be lost."

"You already have my answer."

Kneeling at the lip of the cellar, I pried up the lid of a small crate and began sifting through its contents.

Eir watched me with a frown. "What are you doing?"

"Ah, this will do!" I plucked a sturdy length of linen from the crate and draped it over my arm. Then I slipped off my sling and wrapped the linen around my head and shoulders.

Realization struck. Crossing the room in two long strides, Eir planted herself in front of the door. "Gyda, no. Leaving now is folly."

I motioned at Guðrun, who grimaced but passed me the sack she carried. From it, I took a handful of ingots and stuffed my coin-fold full.

"Get all this to *Sea-Wolf*," I said to Eir. "I'll meet you there before we set off."

Gray eyes hard as flint, she leaned her back against the door. "Tell me where you're going."

I huffed. "We left Nashwa and Hadiyya to the guards. I need to see if they are safe."

"They're likely dead," she said bluntly. "Or else prisoners. Our exit was not a quiet one."

Rúna plunked her crate down beside another and laid a hand over her heart. "Don't say that! The girl Hadiyya was so young. I'd hate it if they've been hurt."

"I heard no struggle, Eir," I said. "No cries of pain. We owe them, and not just silver."

Eir shook her head. "The town guards know your face now. So do Olavi's men."

Grinning, I put my hand on my seax. "And I know theirs."

"Please, just think for a moment! If Olavi is truly out for blood, then we must look after ourselves first. Forget everything else."

Heat rushed to my face. "Move out of the way, Eir."

"Gyda, listen to me."

"Cease your fucking whining!" I bellowed.

The other women halted in their movements, and Eir's face drained of color.

"*Gods,* will you undermine every decision I make?" I snarled. "You act as if I am an old woman, toothless and wetting herself, without a younger woman's hand to hold while she squats! You disrespect me, question me, argue with me every moment."

Eir's throat bobbed. "I'm only looking out for you."

I stepped closer, put a finger in her chest. "Nashwa warned us. She gave us shelter when she could have turned us over. You are looking out for *yourself,* Eir. Going to Olavi serves your own interests, after all."

Eir's mouth twisted. "I warn you. Don't make this about me."

I laughed. "You warn me? Alright. Will you fight me, Eir? Do you have the fire in your guts that requires it? Or will you speak softly, gently, like a mother to a fosterling bastard with no teat to suck?"

Stepping back, I unbuckled my seax and tossed it at her feet. There was blood on the scabbard, dried to a dull brown. "Here, I will make it easy for you. Pick that up and prove yourself."

Eir stared at the seax for a long moment. "I will not fight you," she said tightly. "This course you're following will kill you, Gyda. It will kill all of us. But I see you cannot be turned from it."

"The only course I follow is for Rán's Daughters," I said. "We make promises and we keep them. Whether they are in silver, or blood, or oaths of friendship. Since when did you become so afraid?"

"Oaths mean nothing if you are taken or killed," she cried. "You say I am afraid, and I am. There is no shame in saying it. You are reckless and selfish, and I will be proved right in the end."

"You do so love to be told that, don't you? Wise Eir! Eir of the All-Seeing and Knowing. Eir the *Seiðkona.*"

Her face changed again, because I had plunged the knife deep with that, and I relished it.

Raising my voice, I turned to the others. "*Sea-Wolf* is safe! You—all of you—are safe. Our silver is safe as well, and it is because of *me.*"

I pounded my chest with my fist.

"All of this is because of me. I killed a man today because he chose to be my enemy. I will kill more of our enemies to keep you safe. I am not afraid!"

The women said nothing. Their faces were so tired, so blank that my teeth ached with frustration. "Look at you," I said. "Like *draugar* fresh from their barrows."

"What good is any of this if you end up dead yourself?" Astrid murmured. "I think you should listen to Eir, Lady. We need you."

"Have I mishandled something," I demanded. "Have I shown myself incapable? Do I need to remind you all of the fucking *fortune* at your feet, and who it was that made it possible? Oðinn didn't shit it out, I tell you that!"

"Enough," sighed Eir. She stepped away from the door. "Just go, if you're going."

I shoved past her, leaving my seax in the dirt.

"Load all this in *Sea-Wolf* and wait for me, if any of you find that an order worthy enough to heed."

I left them, allowing the door to slam behind me.

CHAPTER SIX

"Take care of yourselves," I said, pressing the last ingot into Hadiyya's palm.

She smiled shyly, slender fingers curling over the silver. "We are safe here," she whispered. "I hope the same for you and your friends."

Hadiyya stepped back to lean against her mother in the doorway. The three of us stood in a quiet alley behind the funduq. The afternoon calls to prayer had recently finished and the streets calmed as people returned to their homes for meals and rest. We were entirely alone, and yet I could not shake off the itch of being watched.

"Where do you go from here?" Nashwa asked, her voice low.

I tucked my empty coin-fold into my belt and drew my shawl closer. "The fishing harbor. If I remember the way, it should be a short walk from here."

Strangely, her approving nod shored up my nerves. I ventured a smile, which she returned, briefly.

Nashwa sported a bruise along her left cheek that reached to her hairline. Her eye was ringed with black but was otherwise undamaged. Hadiyya's arms sported bruises as well, but she herself appeared unshaken.

When I'd appeared at this alley door, Nashwa had yanked me inside, shoved bread and a flask of wine at me, then demanded to know whose blood stained my garments. Between her and Hadiyya's anxious stream of questions, I reassured both women that I was whole, and then brought out the silver ingots. That had silenced them both.

"Were you successful in your purpose here?" Nashwa asked, a strange glint in her dark gaze.

"We were not successful," I responded, grimacing. "But I am satisfied with a hold full of cargo. My crew are preparing for departure now."

"Good, good. Better to leave this place swiftly. The tide will go out soon. You should ride it."

Feeling uneasy, I glanced down the length of the alley. A shaft of strong sunlight illuminated its end, causing waves of rippling heat to dance with the dust. I moistened my lips.

"The other foreigners should follow suit and leave your home in peace. They should never have come here."

She flipped a hand. "What do I care of them?" she said. "They came. They left. After all, my girl and I are not their prey. You are."

Skin heating, I lowered my head. "I am sorry, Nashwa, truly. We brought troubles upon troubles to your door. Such was not my wish."

"Ay, quiet yourself. We invited trouble in. This more than pays for it." She patted her middle, where more silver ingots hid.

Hadiyya brightened. "We can refurbish now, and hire more help. And we can bribe the guardsmen to leave us alone."

"Yes, my love," said her mother proudly. "Afzal can eat sheep's dung for his supper, and we will prosper."

The broad smile she wore piqued my curiosity. "Have you found an ally, then?"

Nashwa lifted her chin. "We have a friend. A generous one."

I made a bitter sound. "Be wary of generous men, Nashwa. Obligation follows them, and it carries more weight in this life than a woman's own words or blade."

Nashwa reached for my hand. "For women like us, our blades and our words must be used together. Often they are the same. Keep safe, Gyda of Dyflin. I will pray for fair weather and clear skies."

"Set aside an ingot or two," I told her. "If either of you find trouble that you cannot get out of, buy passage to Jórvík. Ask for the *Fiskwif*. I am known by the king there."

Hadiyya made a little sound of fear at the idea of that, but Nashwa only nodded.

"You carry much on those hard shoulders," she said. "Your mind is loud. Let your friends help carry your burdens. Now, go. May your travels bring you wisdom."

With a flap of her shawl, Nashwa ushered me away. And so I went, looking back only once when I felt certain they had gone inside and would not see.

As I crept down the back streets and alleys, many homes I passed were fragrant, full of families taking their meals. Quiet laughter and conversations mingled with the aroma of fresh flatbread, stewed meats, and baked fish.

I was careful as I walked, keeping to the shelter of the walls and staying out of sight of the residents. It was easy enough to avoid the guardsmen, standing on prominent street corners and near the fountains and wells. They questioned bystanders, but appeared bored and sweaty. None of the guardsmen were accompanied by Olavi's oath-men. I could only hope that if the fighters still hunted for me, they looked on the other side of town.

Had my Daughters made it to *Sea-Wolf* safely? Were they loading the hold by now?

As the heat pressed on me, my stomach shriveled like a walnut and my shawl hung damp around my shoulders. Lines of sun-faded laundry stretched overhead, providing little shade. I reached up as I passed, trailing my fingers across a linen tunic. The fabric was threadbare and soft, bleached to a gray-white, like the underbelly of a rabbit.

A boundary wall provided some relief. I leaned against the stone and wiped the sweat off my neck.

"Surtr's fire," I muttered. Dyflin felt very far off, and I'd never believed I'd miss its rain and mud.

A tiny sound drew my attention. At the foot of the wall, there was a sand-colored mouse digging at a crack in the mortar and stone, eager to get to any moisture trapped there.

"My skin will be peeling like a snake's by the time I catch the tide," I told the little mouse. "You're better off finding a hole to hide in until the sun is down."

It carried on digging.

I thought of Nashwa's wine flask and swallowed, regretting that I'd left it behind. None of the town's opulent water fountains were here on the outskirts. Even an old bucket of stale rainwater would have sufficed. At least the ocean's salt on the air soothed my tongue.

A group of women rounded the street corner, chatting and laughing as they made their way towards me. I pulled my shawl over my head and hurried on. Even with my head covered, I was an obvious foreigner. There were no guardsmen nearby, but that meant nothing when I was still covered in dried blood.

I wondered what sort of tales Guðrun would tell of this place. Certainly embellished with glory, gods, and sea-monsters. There would be no sniffling noses, stained tunics, or blistered fingers. No petty arguments either.

In Dyflin, Guðrun and Rúna used to sit near the hearth in Olavi's hall, mugs of frothing ale in their hands and laps open for the little ones to come and sit. And come they did, bringing older siblings along to hear the stories.

Eyes would grow huge, mouths would hang open, and the children would gasp at all the right places. I would perch on a bench to listen, poorly disguising my fascination. Though the real events made decent tales, the invented adventures were far more entertaining.

I chewed a flap of dry skin on my lip. It had been nearly a full year since we'd left Dyflin. How many of those children still waited for the Daughters to return with new tales? How many of them had died from disease or hunger? How many had grown old enough to hold an axe and shield on Olavi's raiding ships?

Too many. Every year, too many.

A breeze ruffled my shawl and the smell of fish guts grew stronger. I pushed on.

If *Sea-Wolf* ever returned to Dyflin, I could see to it that the smaller ones would eat. Ragnar's payment was certainly enough to spare the expense, even split six ways. And once little bellies were full, I would tell a tale or two of my own, if they could endure my vulgar descriptions and lack of eloquence. A skald would be better suited, or one of the Irish storytellers. Those were never in short supply, and most were eager to take a shiny coin for a song.

With my fortunes changed, I could refit *Sea-Wolf* properly, with new tackle and a strong sail. Perhaps I would have it dyed a brilliant scarlet, or even indigo. Wouldn't that be a brilliant thing to see?

I tripped over a stone in the road and wrenched my arm trying to balance. I yelped as pain crackled down to my hand.

"Gods, what a stew of shit!"

Damn this folly. It was stupid to dream in this far-flung town. In Dyflin, there would be no hearth, no tales, no skald, no songs. Because there stood no hall in which I would ever again be welcome. Fuck Dyflin, and fuck Olavi.

I knelt in the dirt, refastening my shoe with clumsy fingers.

"You troll-cursed idiot," I mumbled.

I didn't see the sack until it slipped over my head and a fist hammered into my temple.

CHAPTER SEVEN

I went down hard. Disoriented, screaming, furious, I thrashed against my attacker.

"Rancid bitch, stay still!"

His breath was hot in my ear. With a knee shoved into my spine, he wrenched my arms back and bound them with rope. As I fought and howled, he dragged me upright. His sun-wreathed outline was visible through the weave of the sack over my head. He stood as tall and broad as a ship's prow. Too big to fight.

"Who the fuck are you?" I struggled in his grasp. "Get your troll hands off me!"

"This is for Eskel." He struck me again, a blow like an iron hammer to my belly.

I folded over, a groan sticking in my throat as my lungs spasmed.

He laughed. Then a new pair of hands grabbed me by the shoulders, dragging me off the road. I kicked at nothing but gravel and air.

"Come quietly or there will be more of the same," he told me.

I know this voice. My breath came in quick gasps. I couldn't fight, couldn't see anything. There was the sound of a latch and the creak of a hinge, and stark fear filled me. I pulled against the man, digging my heels in so that he stumbled. Cursing, he released me long enough to smash his fist into my cheek. Blood filled my mouth.

"You bastard!"

"Ho, listen to how she bleats," said the first man, somehow already inside the house. "Should we gag her?"

My captor shoved me towards him, and I tripped over the threshold. The bigger man caught me and spun me around, holding me against his front.

"Let me go, pig-shit!"

"She must want to die," he crowed. "Are you sure he wants her kept and not killed, Lord? Can we not just drown her?"

The second man shut the door and threw the latch. "Do that and you'll drown after her. She's mine to bring in, and I'll have my justice from her flesh before then."

Hearing him speak again, my heart stuttered and the sweat on my skin turned to ice. *It can't be. Helgi? His ghost?*

The big man made an angry sound. "But what about Eskel? He was a friend."

"Eskel was stupid, and he deserved what he got."

Fingernails dug into the flesh of my upper arms and squeezed. "Then I'll take my justice from one of her whores instead!"

"You shit-brained dogs," I snarled. "Where are they? Where are my Daughters?"

"Play nicely with us and maybe you'll find them."

A finger dragged down my cheek. I twisted and bit through the fabric of the sack, satisfied to hit knuckle.

The man screamed and shoved me off. "You bitch!"

The knot in the hemp rope was loose. Quick as lightning, I pulled my wrists apart, then ripped the sack off my head, just in time to watch as bloodied hands closed around my throat like an iron vice.

The big man shoved me against the stone wall, pressing close, his breath hot and rank on my face as he squeezed.

"Try not to kill her," sighed the other man. "Break her if it makes you feel better, but don't kill her."

He was watching us, a small, hard smile splitting his face.

Not Helgi, I thought dimly.

Black dots floated at the edges of my vision. I clawed at his forearms, but soon my fingers lost their nerve and fell away. The big man's face twisted with concentration. He was so close I could count the lice in his beard.

Not like this. Please.

A new, third voice reached me as if through deep water. "Heimarr, if your dog kills her, Father will gut you."

A beat passed, then an unhappy grunt. "Let him go, Uffe."

The pressure on my neck released abruptly and I collapsed, coughing and retching into the dirt.

"Bastard," I croaked.

No ghosts had caught me. These were Hákon and Heimarr, the two remaining sons of Olavi. I was fucked, and I knew it.

I thought of *Sea-Wolf,* floating vulnerable in that small fishing harbor. And the silver. Had the Daughters already secured it? Or had they been caught? I imagined Olavi sinking his grubby hands into my future like a snake sinks its fangs into prey, and felt sick.

"Get up, woman," Hákon said, though he made no move to help me.

His brother turned to him, red-veined nostrils flaring. "Why the fuck are you here? I'm the one who found her. I'll bring her in."

"You pig-shits are lucky I found *you* before the guardsmen," Hákon responded. "Afzal is ready to strip the skin from our hides. He wants the lot of us gone by tomorrow."

"We were handling it, Lord *Stáli*." The big man, Uffe, bowed to Hákon, then tossed a rude gesture at me. "But this she-wolf fought harder than you said she would. The Jarl can't fault us for her own fucking stupidity."

Heimarr smacked Uffe upside the skull. "Don't wag your tongue at my brother, half-wit!"

As the eldest son, Hákon *Stáli* was the Jarl's heir, and so held authority over Dyflin's oath-men. Though Uffe's loyalties clearly rested with Heimarr, he sported a thick silver Jarl-ring around his left forearm. He shut his mouth and dropped his gaze to the dirt.

"Apologies, my Lords," he mumbled.

"Fuck the lot of you," I rasped, and all three turned their scowls on me.

Trembling and sweating, I picked myself off the ground and took a moment to orient myself. The dwelling we occupied was cramped, barely large enough for the four of us to stand without our heads hitting the rafters. There were no beds, no windows, and no hearth beyond a smear of black soot in the corner. Even the little table shoved against the far wall was cracked and had no stool with it. Whoever lived here had not been home for a very long while.

Uffe, Hákon, and Heimarr were between me and the only door, and each of them were armed and wearing leather *brynjur*. I had no escape and no weapons beyond my wits and my words.

I straightened my spine and cleared my aching throat. "It took two Jarl's turds and a great wet shit to catch an unarmed old woman? How embarrassing."

"You should feel honored, *Fiskwif*," Hákon replied, half-smiling. "Not many of the Jarl's enemies deserve the launch of his best dragon ships. The men even cleared a bench on *Dreki* for you and your crew. You'll have the best view on the way back to Dyflin."

I frowned. Dyflin? Did that mean Olavi wasn't here himself?

Heimarr grunted. "This bitch is getting a chain on her neck and a soggy arse in the hold. If she doesn't drown in piss and seawater first, that is."

Uffe laughed at that, and so I chose him as my first target.

"Hey, pus-face, you ever touch me again, I'll rip out your bollocks from their sack."

Uffe ran his tongue over cracked lips and grinned. "You hear that, Lords? She wants to touch my balls!"

"How about I feed them to the gulls? And when they vomit them up again, I'll feed them to you."

Uffe didn't like that. His face turned red and his chest heaved, and he would have lunged at me had Hákon not stepped forward.

"Swallow that shit you spew," he said, blunt finger leveled at me. "I just saved your neck, and it wasn't out of charity. You killed one of my men today. Threats won't make you any friends here."

"I don't need friends," I spat. "Where the fuck is my crew? What did you do to them?"

A furrow between his brows appeared. He backed away, strangely formal again. "We haven't yet found them. If you kindly tell me where they hide, I swear they will not be harmed. You have my word on that."

"Piss on your word! Take it and shove it up your arsehole."

"All of you will be returning to Dyflin," he snapped, composure gone. "The only question is if you'll be chained together like thralls, or free to row like the rest of us. It's your choice."

I bared my teeth. "I won't go anywhere with you goat-fuckers. If Olavi has business to settle, let him search me out himself. I don't answer to his overgrown brats."

"You arrogant bitch!"

I whirled on Uffe. "I think your bollocks are too good for the gulls. Maybe I'll send them to your wife for her porridge."

While his cheeks blew like a forge bellows, I turned back to Hákon.

"Where is Ragnar Grettisson? Did you kill him? He was a free man. Used to be one of your father's sworn *drengr.* That would be murder, you know. Not fair."

Uffe found his voice. "You killed Eskel. I should knife you like you knifed him, and *that* would be fair."

I hawked in my throat and spat a blob between his feet. "Who was Eskel to you? Your bed-slave? Is that why you're so heart-sore over it?"

A grin split his beard and a dark glint came into his pouched eyes. "Ragnar is dead. I killed him in the street and threw his corpse into a midden like rotten meat!"

He started laughing and heat rushed to my face.

"You lie!"

Heimarr made a guttural sound and laid a hand on the head of his axe. "Enough of this," he said to Hákon. "Give the hag to me, brother. I'll get her to comply."

"You pukes look just like your brother Helgi," I sneered. "Right before my blade found a new home in his gut-rope."

The slap I received for that rattled my skull and reopened the cut in my mouth. I grinned bloodily at Heimarr. "Another!"

Hákon caught his brother's fist mid-swing, and the glare he wore could have stripped the barnacles from *Sea-Wolf*'s hull. When he spoke, his voice was deadly soft.

"Get yourself under control."

The muscles in Heimarr's neck bulged and spittle gathered at the corners of his mouth. He struggled, but Hákon refused to release him until he dropped his fist and stumbled back.

"Take a walk, both of you. Out." Hákon jerked his head at the door.

Heimarr held his brother's gaze for a defiant heartbeat, then grumbled a vile curse. Kicking the door open, he let Uffe pass first. Then he turned and pinned me with a glare.

"This is not finished, *Fiskwif,*" he said raggedly.

"I'll take that as a promise," I responded, though my skin prickled at the cold rage in his face.

These shit-stained cowards, I thought.

But the Jarl's absence proved a poignant truth to his sons acting as his hounds. Without a master, dogs turned feral. Vicious. There were no chains to keep Hákon and Heimarr from ripping me to pieces.

Hákon stood staring at the door, as if uncertain his brother wouldn't come charging back through it.

"Ah, finally alone," I said after a moment. "I never took you for a romantic man."

He whirled, more violence in his face than I'd expected. "Don't think you're safe, *Fiskwif,*" he barked. "You will comply, or I'll make sure your journey is as unpleasant as I can make it."

His chest heaved.

Slowly, I backed away. When my legs bumped against the lip of the old table, I figured this was a safe enough distance from the reach of his sword. We regarded each other with the same narrow-eyed suspicion.

"So Olavi sent his favorite hounds all this way to fetch me," I said carefully. "What a cunning trick. Certainly the skalds in Dyflin will sing their tall tales of it."

I knew what Eir liked about him; Hákon was a handsome man, even when angry. He was tall, like his father, and well-formed in limb and sinew. Beyond that, among all the *drengir* of Dyflin, Hákon had a reputation for being clever and fair-minded. Men followed him and enemies feared him. But his emotions tended to overrule his reason, which could prove useful to me.

He said nothing in response, but I noticed the vein in his temple pulsing. I tried again.

"I suppose it was your idea to bribe this town? Oh, how *honorable,* Hákon. Your father must be so proud of you."

Still nothing.

When I lifted my hands, he stiffened, then relaxed when all I did was run my fingers over the column of my throat.

"I can count the lumps that *bak-rauf* gave me. Seems as if the hounds' teeth ruined the hare for the stew. Better throw the hare back in the bush, eh?"

Now he bristled. "Shut your mouth, woman."

I smiled. This was too easy.

"Have anything to drink," I asked.

He blinked. "What?"

"I'm thirsty."

"So is a fish."

We stared at each other.

I sighed, leaning back on my hands. "So what now, Hákon? Is the Jarl looking to bargain?"

The big muscle in Hákon's jaw flexed. His shoulders were tense, pressed back so that his chest was tight as a drum.

"I think you'd like to kill me," I observed. "But you won't. It's beneath you. So, Hákon, why are you here? Surely there are better things to do in Dyflin, like drinking ale until you piss yourself or smashing Irish heads. Your talents are wasted fetching a feeble old widow for your father."

Now his jaw bulged with the effort to keep his anger behind his teeth.

"Ah, I see," I said, clicking my tongue. "Olavi has no lack of thralls. You never could go against your father. Unlike Helgi. He—"

Hákon cursed and took two heavy strides forward. "Do not *dare* speak of Helgi!"

"Hákon *Stáli*, named such because he is as strong as steel. The elder brother. Always loyal, always scraping the shit off his sire's boots. A weapon to be sharpened, used, and eventually discarded when it breaks."

He went taut like a shroud-line. "I may not kill you, goading witch, but I could take your tongue. Sheathe that blade before I lose what patience I have."

I straightened and bared my teeth. "I half-raised you, *boy*. We are not family, but you owe me your respect. So does your father. Where is he, hiding inside some midden pit?"

"No more talking," he rasped. "Now you listen."

"Go on, then," I said haughtily. "What do you want?"

It took visible effort to master himself. "Tell me where your crew are hiding," he said firmly. "I swear to send my own men to make sure they're protected. Let us make this as easy as possible."

"And if I refuse?"

He tapped the scabbard hanging from his waist. "I could kill you now. It's what they want and that is your fault for stirring the shit. If I leave here with your head in that sack, they'll be satisfied."

"Who, those two troll-turds?"

"Not just them," he said. "All my men. Eskel was popular. He was stupid, but they liked him."

I settled my arse on the table, crossed my legs in front of me, and inclined my head. "If you're trying to persuade me to take your offer, you're doing a piss job of it. I won't willingly return to Dyflin just for Olavi to kill me there."

"Ah, Gyda. Your death is not what my father wants, even if I wouldn't mind it. I hate you for what you did to my brother. My sense of justice demands it. But my need to understand is greater than all of that."

This confession surprised me. I examined Hákon for some hint of trickery, but his expression was open and guileless. I decided I would focus on the first thing he'd told me.

"So, if not my death, what does Olavi want? To sell me as a thrall? To torture me?"

Hákon looked away. "He wants you and your women returned to his control."

It was such a simple and absurd answer, I choked on a laugh. "He never had control of me, not even when I sailed for him. Rán's Daughters never depended on his generosity. We freely chose our service, and freely withdrew it."

He didn't respond, but the rapid drumming of fingers on his thigh showed there was a great deal more running through his skull.

I searched for what to say. Hákon had revealed a weakness to me by sharing his desire to understand Helgi's death. I was his enemy, and he was a warrior. Such a confession was a considered move, not an accident. Which meant he wanted my side of things as long as it carried the truth he searched for.

"You want to know why I killed your brother," I said. "I'll tell you if you listen."

Unprepared for this, he flinched, then covered it with a shake of his head. "Speak."

I took a steadying breath. "Helgi earned his death," I began. "Ragnar challenged him to *holmgang*. They fought. Helgi lost, and then refused to concede even though Ragnar let him live. He went for Ragnar with an axe when his back was turned. It was a coward's strike, a thing without honor."

I paused, aware of the pain rising in Hákon. His fists clenched and his eyes closed.

"So you stepped in and killed him," he said roughly.

"I would have done the same for anyone," I said. "If it had been Ragnar, I would have killed him too. I tell you this because you wanted the truth. There is more. Will you hear it?"

Hákon nodded.

"Do you recall the guest of your father who was found murdered last summer?"

"Ishraq," he said, brows rising. "The emissary for Córdoba. I remember."

"Ishraq was Ragnar's lover. Helgi killed him for jealousy."

Genuine surprise overtook his features. "Jealousy? Of Ragnar?"

"Jealousy of me, though he didn't know it then."

I stopped. Hákon's attention was mine now, and he stared at me hungrily.

"Explain," he said.

"Through Ishraq, your father brokered a trade deal with the Emir. It was meant to be secret, but negotiations took many months. News of it reached Helgi in Jórvík. As Master of Trade, such an agreement would have multiplied his wealth and influence. So he traveled to Dyflin on the pretense of a family visit. In truth, Helgi sought to bribe Ishraq and turn the deal in his favor. When Ishraq refused, Helgi murdered him."

"How can you know all this?"

"Ragnar was Ishraq's bodyguard, and a convenient scapegoat. But Helgi gloated when confronted."

Hákon turned away and dragged a trembling hand down his beard as he pondered this. "So that is why they fought that duel," he murmured. He paused, then looked at me again, searching my face. "But I could never reckon what caused my brother to encounter your ship at all."

I waited, hoping he would solve the riddle himself.

"Helgi left Dyflin to go after *you*," he exclaimed, angry again. "Not Ragnar."

I tilted my palm. "A little of both. Because of my lucrative dealings and reliability, your father chose Rán's Daughters to deliver the first goods to Córdoba. Ragnar knew this. He fled the same night of the murder and hid on *Sea-Wolf*. He figured his story might save the deal, but only if he told it to the Emir himself. Helgi pursued my ship to silence all of us. The rest you already know."

Hákon looked away, unable to speak for several moments. When he recovered, his expression was full of bitter grief.

"My father would never tolerate such a coward for a son," he said hoarsely. "You saved his reputation, and that of our family. He never told me any of this. He allowed me to believe you murdered Helgi over nothing."

I grimaced. "This is exactly why your father will not let it rest, and why he wants Rán's Daughters back in Dyflin. I did what he could not. He loses honor if he doesn't publicly blame and punish me. But neither can he kill me without losing self-respect."

Hákon's blue eyes clouded. "I am Olavi Sharp-Spear's eldest son. His heir. Even knowing these things, even knowing Helgi's nature, I am not capable of letting go. He was the youngest of us. He was difficult, but we loved him."

"Is Ragnar dead, Hákon?"

That took him aback. He looked away quickly. "I don't know," he said. "But there may be something I can give you. A story for a story. No more than that."

A flare of hope kindled in my belly. "Go on."

Hákon walked a little, thinking over what to say. Afternoon

sunshine poured through the cracks in the little door, the only source of light in this little house. Dust motes danced through its beams like stars over the water. Hákon ceased pacing and cleared his throat.

"Ragnar hid from us as soon as we anchored in the bay. His capture wasn't a priority, but I knew if I waited long enough, he'd lead us right to you." He paused, half-smiling to himself. "The poor fool, I've never heard of a man so unlucky. Well, despite my rather generous bribes, you were seen entering an inn. Ragnar left his hiding spot to warn you. I sent Uffe and some others to follow him. But even injured, he was canny enough to lose himself in the streets. The others went back for you, but Uffe split off. If he did kill your friend, this is the first I've heard of it. He is Heimarr's man more than mine."

"If Ragnar is dead, Uffe will pay with his own life," I growled. "You should know that."

Hákon waved that away. "A story for a story, as I said. I wouldn't put it past Uffe to lie."

I chewed on that. Even if Ragnar was alive, there was nothing I could do for him now. My focus needed to remain on myself and my Daughters. Thus far, Hákon had not mentioned *Sea-Wolf* at all, which implied my ship hadn't yet been found, but that could change quickly. Disused or not, a fishing harbor was difficult to miss in a coastal village. Every moment I remained trapped here, the greater the risk to my ship, my silver, and my Daughters. I needed Hákon on my side.

A sharp knock on the door stole my chance to speak.

"Come," said Hákon, and Heimarr ducked through the doorway. He was alone, and streaming sweat.

"The town guards are useless goat-turds," he said to Hákon. "Afzal pulled them back. Whoreson said we sail the morning tide or he'll burn the ships. There's no sign of the women. I sent Uffe to gather everyone else on the strand. I say we take this one and leave." He jerked a thumb at me.

Hákon dragged his beard through his teeth, then touched the hammer hanging around his throat, a gesture I had not seen before.

"I won't leave Eir or the others," he said finally.

My heart rose to my throat.

"Afzal is a crow-pecked bastard," I said quickly. "You've already spent a king's sum to keep these people quiet. He's using threats to ask for more, isn't he? He won't stop there."

"You shut your lying hole!" Heimarr gnarred, but Hákon squinted at me.

"What do you care, *Fiskwif*?" he said carefully.

I straightened and folded my hands on my knees, holding their gazes. "Olavi wants to make an example of me," I said. "But the two of you managed to make a bloody mess of it. You can't risk more violence in the town, or not only will Afzal burn your ships, he'll bring the Emir's garrisons from up and down this coast on your heads. Seems to me you're in a tight spot and need a better option. I can help with that."

"I won't listen to this troll's piss!" grunted Heimarr, but he watched me with a hawk's glare, alert and hungry.

Hákon touched his hammer once more, then dropped his hand. "What do you suggest?"

I smiled, knowing I'd hooked them both like fish.

"It's very simple," I said. "Let Olavi win. I'll sail away from here in peace with my crew. *Sea-Wolf* need never be seen in Dyflin again."

Heimarr and Hákon both stared at me, eyes bulging round as eggs. Then Heimarr swore, and Hákon threw back his head laughing until his eyes streamed.

"Thor's balls, you must think us fools!" He wiped his face. His chest was heaving and the grin he wore was terrible. "No one could say you aren't crafty. That was as brazen a chance-taking as I've ever heard!"

Heimarr scowled and tugged on his leather *brynja*. "She's nothing but a Loki-tongued shit-speaker. Brother, let me throw her bones in *Storm-Serpent*'s belly. That will silence this bleating until we get them all to Dyflin."

"I meant every word," I said, sliding off the edge of the table and pacing forward. "It is a good plan."

Hákon's brows climbed to his hairline. "I take back what I said. You aren't crafty, woman. You're just arrogant."

"I'd like to think so," I said, affecting a shrug. "What is there to talk about? We all get what we want, do we not?"

Now Hákon's features turned suspicious. "How is that?"

I cleared my throat and put out my left hand, palm up. "Here, Olavi cannot bear to allow Rán's Daughters to roam about, reminding all Miðgarðr of—of what transpired," I amended, feeling Heimarr's glare on me. "My proposal solves this. I will take *Sea-Wolf* and go north. Birka, or perhaps the Orkneys. Rán's Daughters will stop trading, and Olavi can claim to the world that he sank us off the coast of al-Andalus or found us dead on a beach somewhere. He gets his justice either way."

I paused, opening my other palm. "Now, you—both of you—can take your men home. No one needs to die today, and no one needs to know either. We all leave, and this business is done." I closed both fists and dropped them. "All that is left for me is to disappear."

"And how the fuck is that justice?" Heimarr said. "You walk away like nothing? Fuck that!"

"This is not painless for me, toad," I said hotly. "I lose my home in Dyflin. I forfeit my trade, my reputation, and my position. All I will have is my ship. I will be nothing but a ghost."

He snorted and began to speak, but Hákon made a noise, catching his eye.

"I would speak with you," he said, and the pair of them stalked off to huddle and whisper like jackdaws in an oak tree.

I waited, arms folded to hide my irritation. I had them. I knew it by the way they stole glances and fiddled with their beards and belts as they talked. The sons of Olavi were thinking things over, and that meant I had won.

So why did my belly writhe and the back of my neck stream with sweat?

"Say I agree to this," Hákon said suddenly, leaving the corner. "What guarantee do we have that you won't continue trading and sailing under new names or a new patron? Such as King Sigtryggr, hm?"

"Sigtryggr?" I said.

He grinned at my expression, knowing he'd caught me off-guard.

"Oh yes," Heimarr said. "We know very well about your business with Jórvík these last months." His voice ran smooth like oil and just as thick. "The king has been made aware of how he housed a pack of murderers, and how the Jarl of Dyflin breaks shits like him who shelter his enemies."

I stalked forward, hissing, "Sigtryggr was never a part of this! I swear, our trade deals are dissolved. We will not return there."

"And you have been known to lie, *Fiskwif,*" Hákon said. "We need a different sort of assurance from you."

Anger and dread curled around the cage of my lungs. I looked between the brothers, suddenly uncertain. What else did they know? Did they know about Ragnar's hoard? Had I gambled too much?

I fought down the metallic taste in my throat. "What, then? I have nothing left to give you."

"Oh, but you do," Heimarr said.

Hákon nodded. "We need something more than words to bring to the Jarl. Hard proof, so to speak. You may follow whatever troll-cursed tides you wish, and the others may also have their freedom to venture out with you." He paused, a smile tugging his mouth. "Or return to Dyflin, if they choose."

I started to sputter, but Hákon had not finished.

"The sight of *Sea-Wolf* anchored at our father's quay in Dyflin is your best chance at convincing him you're dead. Give us *Sea-Wolf,* and you may go on your way unchallenged."

White-hot rage shot through my heart like a spear's blade.

"You shit-eating whoresons," I cried. "I will *never* give you *Sea-Wolf!*"

"I told you, brother," Heimarr said smugly.

Hákon shook his head. "The Jarl requires *something,* Gyda."

I backed away, fists clenched. "After all I've done for him, after my own husband lived and *died* as his oath-man, he cannot require this of me. *You* cannot. You have no honor, you pig-shits! Troll-cursed pus-cocks!"

Unmoved, Hákon spread his hands. "This is the best we can offer.

There is a bench and an oar waiting for you on *Dreki* if you'd rather tell the Jarl all this to his face."

Blood roared in my ears. A cold sweat coated my face and neck. I choked on my fury and wracked my brain for something to say, but there was nothing. *Nothing*. My freedom or my ship? They were one and the same. I could no easier choose my fighting arm from my shield arm.

Chuckling, Heimarr turned and made for the door with an easy, careless gait. He paused with his hand on the latch and looked over his shoulder.

"Just kill her and be done with it," he said. "The sea-bitch will never bargain. I'm going to *Storm-Serpent.* The tide is running and I mean to catch it. When you get done wiping her blood and shit off the floor, who knows? Maybe her crew will scatter like rats from their holes. Easier to catch them that way."

Distaste twisted Hákon's features, but he waved his brother off, and we were alone again.

He put his hand on the lobed pommel of his sword.

"Well, *Fiskwif*? What is your choice?"

I stood there, trembling, the earth rolling under my feet like Ragnarök had come and the gods were dying.

I was nothing without *Sea-Wolf.* It was my life. Every scrap of reputation and standing that I had scratched from the flesh of this world. *Sea-Wolf* was *mine.*

"What would you choose?" I demanded. "Tell me that, boy! When you have lost everything else, what choice would you make?"

"I cannot choose for you."

"Tell me, Hákon. Say it."

He held my gaze. "I would choose death," he said. "To live in obscurity, without honor or glory, without a legacy? Without a family? I would rather die than suffer such a Loki fate. At least there is some honor in death if Oðinn favors you with a good one."

"Legacy and family," I spat. "As if you had to work for any of that."

He had no response.

I turned away, thrusting my hands into my filthy, salt-crusted hair. *Think, you shit, think!*

I stared at the wall. It was featureless, plastered and painted a muted color. *That* would be my life. Everything I had strived for, every hurt I suffered, every indignity I endured—none of it would mean anything without *Sea-Wolf*. Not even the power of Ragnar's silver could make such a life bearable.

"No," I said, and Hákon frowned.

"You must choose. It was your proposal. Or do you agree to return to Dyflin with us?"

"No," I repeated.

My hand went to my belt, to where my seax usually hung. If I did choose death, would Hákon allow me to die with honor? Or, to please his men, would he dump my corpse into the ocean to sink down and join Helgi in Rán's halls? Or would I simply feel the cold steel across my throat and withering shame as I shit myself in the dirt?

Here, in this empty house, the Norns had spun the web of my fate and it was threadbare.

Well, fuck them.

I had fought my way out of the stinking fish guts and muddy streets before, and I had done it alone. I could do it again.

I turned back to him. He watched me, expression empty of all mercy now. I had played into his game like a fool.

But he had also given away far more of himself than he knew. Every time we'd spoken of my Daughters, of their fates, his cheeks had flushed and his jaw muscle jumped. Just a little. Just enough to betray that he cared far more about their welfare than he let on.

And knowing what I knew about Eir's feelings for him, I didn't believe he gave a horse's shit about Astrid, Liadan, Guðrun or Rúna.

Could I really do this?

Nausea boiled in my gut. Iron bands wrapped around my chest. My mouth went dry as stale bread.

"Hákon," I said, voice first wavering, then strong again. "I have a counter-offer for you."

CHAPTER EIGHT

The sun crossed the vault of Ymir's skull and hung fat over the horizon.

Encircled by jagged cliffs and a rocky beach which sloped sharply down from the town's walls, the bay was wide and shallow. Looming at its center was a curved, serpentine prow-beast.

Dreki, the Jarl's own warship. Built two decades ago, it was a battle-hardened dragon of power, deadly swift and vicious. More fearsome than anything else on the waves. Njörd himself would be jealous. I knew I was.

The ship was a flurry of activity. Two dozen of Hákon's oath-men scurried between the benches, readying for the voyage.

True to his word, Heimarr had made a head-start for Dyflin, taking *Storm-Serpent*, Uffe, and his half of the crew out to sea. When Hákon and I crossed the strand to see him off, he'd been silent, unimpressed that I'd shown up unbound and unafraid of him. Soon after, he'd vanished around the headland and the weight of his resentful stare lifted from me. Good riddance.

There were a few hours of daylight left. I needed to hurry if I wanted to get underway before the moon rose. But not yet. Not until I'd seen the Daughters. I owed them that.

I waited on the end of a short timber pier, observing *Dreki* and its crew with a critical eye. By my count, three lines had been tied too loose, and another four stretched taut enough to snap with a good gale. I shook my head. These oath-men were no sailors, that was clear. Not my ship, not my problem.

Sea-Wolf still floated at the small fishing harbor on the other side of town. As part of the bargain between us, Hákon had provided an allotment of oath-men and sent them to secure the ship for voyage. Once ashore in the destination of my choosing, the crew would disband and return to Dyflin. At my own expense, of course. Hákon seemed to think it was the height of generosity on his part.

Watching the sun sink low behind wisps of cloud, I wondered if the men had reached the harbor yet. What would they make of *Sea-Wolf*'s hold, packed with goods and crates and sacks hiding a fortune beneath its deck boards? If any of them took it into their foolish heads to snoop—well, into the water they would go, and no excuses made. Rán might even enjoy such a tribute in her name.

Heavy footsteps stalked up the pier and halted behind me.

"They're here," said Hákon.

I closed my eyes. There was bile in my throat.

"If you wish to speak with them, do it now," he said gruffly. "Or don't. I doubt you care what they think."

Carefully schooling my expression, I turned to face him. "I care."

His blue eyes were cold and sharp. The fingers of his right hand twitched. He was angry again, and rightly so.

"This is a low thing you've done, *Fiskwif*," he murmured. "They don't deserve this."

"It takes two parties to bargain."

"It does," he replied. "But you have made me the wolf among the sheep with this. My honor is shredded and it sickens me."

I huffed. "I don't think anyone will worry much over your *honor*, Hákon. Least of all Eir."

He bared his teeth. "Don't goad me. I will not forget this day, and neither will those women. When you leave these shores, I never want to hear your name spoken again. You are a *coward*, Gyda *Fiskwif*, and you ruin all the lives you touch."

"And you are the man who brings his father justice. Is that not what you wanted?"

"So it is," he said stiffly. Then he drew a hand down his face and took a breath. "Gyda Eyvindsdottir, in exchange for your crew, those who call themselves Rán's Daughters, I acquit you of your grievous offense against my family. As payment of my brother's life-price, you forfeit your possessions, your status, and your reputation as a merchant. Your ship remains yours. You are free to roam any port of your choosing. That is my word as the son of Jarl Olavi Sharp-Spear, and it is binding."

"The Daughters, Hákon," I said as he turned to leave. "You will guarantee their safety in Dyflin? I won't have them mistreated because of Olavi's spitefulness."

Hákon made a strangled sound, shoulders bunching with anger and insult. A flush crept over his cheeks. He opened his mouth, ready to strike back at me.

I drew myself up, daring him to say it.

But then his face shifted, becoming haughty and hard like the steel he was named for. There was nothing of the open-hearted youth I had once known him to be. So long ago.

He clenched his jaw, turned on his heel, took three steps, then angled his head to spit in the sand beside the steps of the pier.

"I may be a bastard, but I am not cruel," he said viciously. "I swear they will be looked after. Send them to *Dreki* when you're done."

He strode off without looking back.

Only then did I turn my gaze to the small group waiting at the far end of the strand. They stood near a small boat tethered to a jetty which would take them to *Dreki* and on to their new lives in Dyflin. There were two oath-men, guarding them closely. And five women. Rán's Daughters. No longer mine.

I crossed the beach. The gravel and sand crunched under the leather of my shoes. My breath came shallow, tinged with the vegetal scent of salt and seaweed.

I halted a spear-length away from them. I swallowed, struck silent and suddenly uncertain.

The oath-men, one broad as a horse and the other rangy and scarred, backed away, busying themselves with undoing the knots that tied the little boat to the jetty.

I scraped a tooth against a sore spot on my lip. Perhaps I should go, leaving whatever words I wanted to say for another time, when hearts were not so raw.

Rán's Daughters were a pitiful lot. Guðrun and Rúna stood together, their hands gripped tight and dried tear streaks marking their faces. Beside them, Liadan sat on the edge of the jetty, legs dangling over the water. Astrid lay in her lap, her eyes swollen and red-rimmed. Liadan stroked her hair and didn't look up.

Eir stood furthest away, half-turned. She wore a linen shawl the same color as her eyes: gray as storm-cloud. She was serene in profile, staring across the bay and out to the sea beyond. I could hardly tell if she even breathed.

Certainly, Eir bore the worst of it. We had once been as close as sisters, or closer. Widowed women, facing this world of men with fists raised and hearts thirsty for freedom.

Regardless of my hopes, or how even now I intended to return to Dyflin and secret all of them away from Olavi's clutch, none of that mattered; not here, on the stony shore of al-Andalus. There might be no coming back from this. Would it not be kinder to leave the Daughters as they were than to dig a spear-point into this wound?

I shifted my weight from one foot to the other. "I, ah, wanted to see how you were before we sail," I said.

Rúna simply stared at me, and Liadan continued stroking Astrid's hair. Eir did not move at all.

Guðrun was the first to speak. "Why the fuck are you here? What do you want?"

"Just to talk," I said. "Give an explanation. Nothing more."

"Funny how lies come so easy to you," she responded.

Rúna sniffed, then turned her face away. "I have nothing to add to that."

"We don't want you here," said Eir. She still faced the sea. "Leave, Gyda. You are not welcome."

"Will you not allow me to explain?" I said, taking a step closer. "Please. This is not what I wanted for you, but I had no choice."

Liadan raised her hands from Astrid's head. *You see this girl?* she signed. Her movements were controlled, but her face expressed all the tumult she felt. *She is broken. This is what you do, Gyda Fiskwif. You break things. You break people. All for your own gain.*

Her hands dropped, covering Astrid. Protecting her.

"I am sorry," I said softly. I put my hands out. "Please understand. I swear to you —"

Eir turned. "Fuck your swearing," she said savagely. "And fuck you."

Now my hackles rose. "Do you think I wanted any of this? Hákon would not bend. Rán's Daughters are—,"

Eir lunged, and again I was cut off, this time by her striking my cheek.

My head filled with white lightning and scarlet heat radiated from my face. My cut reopened and filled my mouth with blood.

When I could see again, Eir was a vision of trembling rage not two paces away.

"Your explanation means nothing," she spat. "Your oaths mean nothing. You are faithless, cruel, silver-hungry and selfish. Never have the gods put me in the path of someone as repulsive as you."

The words hung in the sultry air, demanding answer, but I had none.

Guðrun and Rúna kept silent. Liadan did not lift her hands from Astrid's hair again. All their gazes brimmed with reproach and betrayal.

I sagged. "Unworthy I may be of forgiveness, but I swear, I did what I could for your security and fair treatment. You will be looked after in Dyflin, Hákon assured me of it. I just want you to know—you were mine, all of you. My Daughters."

Eir wrapped her shawl around her shoulders and stepped away. "You have no Daughters here," she said. "Go back to your ship."

"Eir, please."

"Go and spend your silver," she continued. "Lick the boots of Sigtryggr in Jórvík. Enjoy your freedom. I hope it gives some meaning to your barren, lonely life."

A hot wind kicked up. Eir moved to the jetty. She peered out over the bay, quiet for a long moment. The two oath-men lingered beside the boat, glancing between all of us awkwardly, unwilling to rush their female charges when they were in such a state.

"When I am Hákon's wife," Eir said finally. "And one day *Jarlskona* in Dyflin, you will be nothing but a memory. Soon after you won't even be that."

I stared at her.

"His *wife?* Eir, what are you talking about?"

"Did you really think you were the only one with secrets? He is a good man."

I took a step back and gazed at all of them.

"Is this all, then? This is how we break, after all our years together?" My voice cracked and faded. No one would meet my gaze. My words were nothing now but bird shit falling on the stones.

I turned to go, and as I did my eyes locked with Hákon. He stood on the main pier, and his expression was odd as he looked at me. It was almost sad. No, not sad. He pitied me.

You got what you wanted, Olavi, I thought bitterly. *I am humiliated. Without a home. Without family. As dependent on your goodwill as I ever was.*

There was a sound behind me. An intake of breath.

"Is that *Sea-Wolf?*" said Astrid.

"Lord," came a yell from up the slope. "Lord Hákon, something has happened!"

Deadly cold snaked over my skin. Those were oath-men, my crew, waving and calling. They were pointing out at the bay, past *Dreki.*

Hákon saw them and turned to the water. Then he turned to me and began to run.

"Fiskwif," he called. He stumbled. Righted himself. Cursed. "Gyda, your ship!"

I knew. Before I watched the silver hoard I'd sacrificed everything for vanish, I knew. Before I watched unknown thieves pull on *Sea-Wolf's* oars to carry my ship out of the bay, I knew. Before Hákon reached me and the cry of pain I made shattered the hush across the water, I knew.

Sea-Wolf hit open water. The sail bellied out and caught the wind. Soon, my ship was gone.

For a long time, I watched the darkening horizon. Even after *Dreki* set off, chasing the rise of the moon, I watched, alone and silent at my place on the back bench.

Sea-Wolf had been stolen, and I was going to Dyflin.

PART TWO: DYFLIN

Two months later

A cold dawn. The rain had returned. Thick, fetid air hovered in the rafters of my home, crushing me into my straw pallet. I listened to the drumming on the thatched roof and stared at a long crack in the wall.

This house had been my husband's work.

When we'd come to Dyflin with Olavi all those years ago, Jörund had shaped this house's frame, its doors and posts and even the sleeping platforms running parallel to the hearth. I had woven the wattle and daub for the walls, packing everything with clay and animal dung so it would be water-fast. Then we'd dug the midden and lined the threshold with paving stones. When the house was finished, we'd lived here for a twelve-month.

But then Jörund had drowned, his little fishing boat leaking because of old tar in the joints.

The crack in this wall appeared a month later. I had left it, and every time I returned to port it had grown longer.

A rooster called outside. The wheels of a cart creaked through the mud as it drove past my door.

I could not bring myself to rise this morning. I traced my fingers over the crack, feeling the rush of cold air on them.

Those years ago, when our door was finally hung on its hinges and the statues of the gods were set on the lintel to watch over us, Jörund had taken a clay pot and buried it beneath the northwest foundation stone.

The pot had a stopper of pine-tar and cloth. We'd filled it with silver ingots, dirhams, rings, bracelets, shining jeweled brooches. All my husband's shares from raids long past.

I had admired Jörund. He was a lover of peace, born on a farm tucked in a quiet valley in Gautaland. His father had fostered Olavi as a favor to his jarl. When Olavi succeeded him, Jörund followed. Anywhere his foster brother led, Jörund would go. That is how we came to Ireland, newlywed and ambitious. As a young wife, I pushed Jörund hard, hungry for the glory and reputation that came from being married to the Jarl's strongest oath-man.

Jörund hated it. Every moment. Every raid. For him, the treasure we'd buried was a reminder of death. But, I'd reasoned, he was an axe-man, a sworn warrior among his shield-brothers. Blood and loyalty. It was a life we chose together.

Eventually, it became too much for him.

Jörund concealed our wealth deep, far from prying eyes and grasping hands. And then he went inside and hung up his axe on the wall. I wept, knowing he would never take it down again.

It was a thing of rust now, still on the wall, a reminder of my obscurity and loneliness.

He drowned. I wept. And the very next week, I'd commissioned the building of *Sea-Wolf*, using every last scrap of hacksilver inside the pot to pay for it.

And now?

The Norns weave strange fates, indeed.

CHAPTER NINE

The man standing in my house dripped muddy rainwater. Worse, he'd tracked in pig shit.

"Get out," I mumbled.

"You reek of spoiled fish and rancid wine," he said. "A river bath might suit on this lovely day, or would you prefer my bucket? I promise, it's not as cold."

I peeled open one eyelid. Late morning light streamed through the warped cracks in my door, and the rain had lessened.

The man in my house was silhouetted by shadow, and though there had been a hint of laughter in his voice, he dangled an iron-banded bucket from his right hand.

"I will shear off your balls if you dare," I told him.

He scoffed. "With what? You can't reach anything from there. You'd have to get up, and I'll have reached my goal. The question is whether I get to enjoy the sight of you soaking wet." Grinning, he stepped closer and held up the bucket.

"Don't threaten me. You know what comes of that," I said, then yawned and burrowed my pounding head back under the scratchy wool blanket. "I will rise shortly. I had no sleep until the cocks were crowing. I need rest, Hrœrekr, not a chiding mother."

There was a silence, long enough that I reckoned my guest had found his senses and left me.

I began to drift off again, warm and wonderfully drowsy, lulled by the last evening's ale and the rain on the thatching.

But then there was a grunt, followed by an icy, stinking deluge of slimy water.

I came up sputtering and cursing a foul streak. The man whooped with laughter.

"Shouldn't have called me that name," he cried. "But there, job finished. I'll be off now."

He dropped the bucket and backed away. I reached for the closest weapon, and his laughing turned to surprised shouts as half-filled cups of ale flew past his head.

"You shit," I hollered. "Troll-cursed bastard goat-fucker!"

I threw a stool. He dodged it and it clattered against the daub wall. Putting the table between us, he leaned on it with bright mischief in his face.

"What is my name, Gyda?"

"Shit-licker!"

There was nothing else to throw, so I gripped the table's bench to heave it. But I stumbled with the weight, falling arse-first into a smear of pig filth.

His eyes went wide. "Gods, you're still drunk enough to drown a shark!"

I was a pathetic, sodden heap of shit, mud, and tangled hair. But I rose on wobbling legs and faced him with my chin up.

"And so what if I am?"

Finally sobering, he looked me up and down, brows raised and mouth pursed. "It is not even midday," he said. "What are you hoping to achieve in your ale-soaked bed? That you can drink and sleep better than Thor himself? Come now, this is pathetic."

"Watch yourself," I snarled. "I'm still well able to rip the beard off your insolent face and feed it to you."

"Enough, Gyda!" He slammed his palms on the table, shattering a crock of fish bones. He gave a high-pitched yelp, effectively dousing any reaction he'd hoped to elicit.

I clicked my tongue and scoffed. "Idiot."

He stared at me, and I stared back.

"Fine," he sighed, dropping the act. "I may be an idiot, but you're the chief of them. This is why we're friends."

Righting the upended stool, he planted himself and held up his left hand. Blood seeped from a gash at the base of his little finger. "You see this? Ridiculous. Both of us."

I moved around the table and grabbed for the hand, yanking harder than necessary and drawing a hiss from him.

"Hold still," I ordered. "There's a bone in you."

He muttered some comment of a nature that I chose to ignore.

Pinching the little fishbone between my fingernails, I drew it out and dropped it to mingle with its brethren amongst the broken crockery. Then I took a linen rag from the rafter and wrapped it around his bloody palm.

"There," I said, stepping back. "The cut is shallow. You'll be fine. Now get the fuck out of my house, Ruarc. You stink of pigs."

His mouth, always quirked, curved into a deeply satisfied grin.

"Ah, so you do remember my name."

"Don't start again."

He flexed his fingers. "Not a bad job, but it still hurts like my grandmother stuck me with her eating knife."

"So get young Dúri to kiss it for you," I said.

A pink flush crept up his neck and his eyes narrowed like a cat's. "Stifle that wheezing, woman." he said crankily. "Do you want me bollocked? The ears in this fucking town grow through every wall."

I gave his lap a pointed glance. "When it comes to Dúri, growing ears are the least of your worries."

"Horrible woman," he cried, shooting to his feet. "Troll-wife! I should leave you to waste away in your—," he paused, glancing around my little house to find an appropriate insult.

"Troll-cave?" I finished for him. But I was smiling, and after a moment he smiled too.

"As you say." He rolled a shoulder, somewhat bashful. "And anyway, Dúri is finished with me. He's gotten married, the disloyal shit."

"Bad luck," I muttered. My attention was waning; my head felt stuffed with sheep's wool and my belly rumbled sourly. The pitcher of ale on my table promised oblivion. If Ruarc left, I could finish it and return to the sweet warmth of dreamless sleep.

"Bad luck. You could call it that." Ruarc hunched forward on the stool. "To be honest, I think it's the Jarl's meddling. Can't keep his crusty fingers out of everyone's business."

I had a chest at the foot of my sleeping platform that held fresh garments, provided I had any. When was the last time I'd gone to the river to wash? I swatted a pile of soiled things from the top and retrieved two faded pieces of fabric. Holding them up to the light, I grimaced. A tunic and a pair of trews, both threadbare and ill-fitted. No leg wraps, and no woolen socks either. But better than my damp underclothes.

Ruarc was still talking. "It's for the better, in any case. My Irish friends outside Dyflin say I have to marry by *Jól* or they'll throw me back to Olavi as a thrall."

"Marry? No, they wouldn't do that to you," I said. "You earn them too much silver. Make up that hearth, will you?"

I began stripping to my skin with no hesitation, and he turned away hastily.

"Gods, woman," he said. "Warn a man before you expose yourself!"

"You're the one who invaded my private home. Your antics split my head. Get to that hearth."

Muttering, Ruarc dropped to a squat and fed two pieces of dry wood into the hearth pit. The fire hissed and smoked and sparked to life.

"Do you have anything fresh to eat in this troll-cave," he groused, sitting back on his heels. "Or have you picked every perch and bream in the city clean of flesh?"

I yanked on my tunic and belted it over my trousers with a strip of linen. "Tormenting me gets you nothing, save maybe a boot to your arse. If you're hungry, leave."

"Can't a man look after his friend?"

I retrieved two cups from the floor and set them on the table. I filled both with ale and held one out. "Have a drink," I said, a little kinder. "I am awake now, and sober for the moment, so you've done your duty for the day. Why are you still here?"

Ruarc rose from his crouch and eyed the cup warily. "Actually, I'd rather we take a walk. Sounds as if the rain has lifted. Fresh air will bring out the merchants and visitors. There are bound to be a few you haven't interrogated yet. And several I haven't bribed."

The hammering increased behind my temples. I pinched the bridge of my nose. "Do I have a choice?"

"No." He jabbed a finger at my pile of dirty garments. "Bring those. A good scrub in the river will take that disreputable stench off."

I waved this absurd suggestion away and drained my cup. He

watched warily, as if he half-believed I might chuck it at his head again and go back to snoring. I was sorely tempted.

"Nothing but ghosts and regret in this troll-cave anyway," I said casually, setting the cup down. "Might as well slog through the mud and shit."

Ruarc's smile reappeared. "There's the *fiskwif* I know! Come now, shoes on. Wear something warm over that pitiful tunic. And I'll lead. Can't have you stumbling around Dyflin like a drunk on your own."

Dyflin in early winter was as dismal as it was filthy.

The rain had stopped, as Ruarc promised, but the sun was threatened by thick, roiling clouds from the east. We walked on reed matting, picking our way slowly because most of them had been swallowed by the rising mud and animal dung.

"I'd forgotten what a fucking midden this place is," I muttered.

Ruarc walked beside me. He gnawed on a heel of bread, swiped from a stall set up at the end of a street. "Higher ground won't be any better," he said around a mouthful. "Breathe through your mouth if the air offends you so much."

"It's not the smell," I said. "I'm used to that. It's the damp. The cold. Like Hel herself pissed on this town and it never dried out."

"You are a delightful walking companion," Ruarc said.

"So fuck off and leave me to my delights."

He shoved the last of the bread into his mouth, chewing and swallowing it nearly whole, like a child.

"Ah, if I did that, what sort of friend would I be?"

"Hmph."

"Who do you think we'll see at the riverbank?" he said, unaffected. "Certainly the Jarl's errand-boys will be there." He scanned the alleys as we passed, eyes never resting on one thing for long. With his long nose, it made him look like a hawk on the hunt.

"Don't worry so much," I said. "And slow down. Your pacing is making me dizzy."

"Then it's a good thing I'm looking out for you. What if you fall?"

"I don't need a guardsman."

"No, you need a leash," he said dryly.

At my narrow expression, he shrugged.

"We've been doing this for weeks, Gyda. I think we're starting to draw the wrong kind of attention. There are only so many merchants who will entertain us without offense. We've run out of the patient ones."

"What are you saying, Ruarc?"

"I'm saying the Jarl knows you're asking questions. If he knows, then everyone knows, and there are some who don't like you as much. That's why I'm here."

I laughed and slowed my pace. "You think *you* will be able to keep them away? I've seen that little knife you keep in your belt. It might be pretty enough to impress the merchants' sons into bed, but it's useless in a fight. And anyway, even if you had a proper blade, no one would care. You stick out too much for anyone to mistake you for a fighter."

He'd placed a protective hand on the ornately carved knife, but when he heard my last words he frowned. "I stick out?"

"You do," I said. "Like a swan on a battlefield. It would be a *niðingr*-fight to kill you. Shameful."

He went quiet. We walked on.

Ruarc was the only child of a minor Irish lord, an obscenely wealthy but unremarkable one who had been dead for years. His mother was a cousin of my husband. I never knew her particularly well, but Ruarc had been a fixture in my life from the early days of my marriage. As a widow, she'd moved far from Dyflin and joined her husband's people. Ruarc's Norse name, Hrœrekr, came from her, though he steadfastly preferred the Irish name.

His silence as we walked made me wonder if I'd hurt his pride, but I did not care enough to apologize. I had spoken true, and better he heard truth than simple flattery.

Ruarc spoke like a northman, but dressed and behaved like an Irish noble. To outsiders and visitors, he appeared no different from any other free man in Dyflin. But to the ones who lived in these streets, his origins could not be more obvious. Today he wore a fine sky-blue tunic with yellow trews. His cloak was lovely soft wool with silk tablet embroidery and fastened at his right shoulder with a large silver brooch. It was a show of wealth which many would envy, including me.

Even as I barked at the boy, I worried for him. There were many who wondered what Ruarc's presentation said about his true loyalties. No lord held his oath. He owned no land or title beyond that of his dead father, and that was enough for him. He carried no real influence with the Irish factions outside Dyflin. He had no slaves, no servants, and no housekarls sworn to him. Ruarc was as free an agent as there ever was. If he had any ambition at all, he might present himself as a power to contend with. But he was happy as he was, and that confounded me. All of this, of course, made him an anomaly in Dyflin, and inspired no confidence in either the Norse or Irish camps.

Perhaps that was why Olavi chose him often to carry messages of business and trade to the Irish lords, and the Irish lords sent him back just as often with messages of their own. There was little use for Ruarc beyond being a bridge between the two factions. It was good enough that he brought everyone more trade and wealth. As long as each side could halt their infighting, that was.

And here Ruarc stood as my friend, an ally when I had no others and deserved none. With his broader loyalties always in question, he seemed to want to prove his true fidelity—to me. I dearly wished he wouldn't. I loved him for it nonetheless.

"I may not be capable as a warrior," Ruarc said after a while. "But you speak rightly; only fools would risk killing the Jarl's favorite broker. My father's people would take it badly. An attack on me is an attack on the Irish. Olavi knows that, and so do his housekarls."

"All the more reason to keep your nose out of my business," I said.

He frowned. "It's a bit late for that, no? Your business is my business. I promised I would help you find *Sea-Wolf*, and if that means acting as bodyguard, so be it. I'd like to feel useful as a man sometimes, you see?"

That surprised me. I glanced at him. The shadows in the hollows of his face had grown deeper. "Now you're talking shit, Ruarc."

"I'm not," he said, voice softening. "I need to marry. Olavi offered me a Dyflin-born woman from a wealthy Irish family. Someone that he chose because it would keep tensions to a minimum between our peoples. It's a good match."

"There are tensions between our peoples all year," I said. An ox's dung pile steamed in the middle of the street. I stepped around it. "It doesn't matter how many trade agreements, treaties, or marriages there are. Over the whole of my life, I've watched how peace is promised always and procured never. It hasn't been that many winters since Dyflin was won back from the Irish kings. It won't be long before there are more battles, more deaths, and more kings rising up to take up the standards."

"So everything I do is fruitless?" Ruarc huffed. "I might as well marry. I can make an heir, then go off and die in a battle somewhere. My family will get my name and my wealth, and Dyflin gets its peace for a little while. At least my life will be for something." His laugh had a bitter bite.

"You don't mean any of that."

"Don't I?" He caught me by the shoulder and planted himself in my path, spine straight and strong like a spear-haft. "Remember, Gyda, I *chose* this," he said. "Whatever you may think of the likelihood of peace-making, you can't deny that there is growing trade with the hinterlands. It is possible to live and work together. As my parents did, and as so many others do. I can do my duty as a man. Whatever the outcome, right now I represent hope for Dyflin and the rest of Ireland."

"You are one pebble in a rockslide," I said bluntly. "A pebble that represents broken promises and pain. Don't mistake me, Ruarc. I am not a *völva* who sees what the Norns have spun. There are many more in Dyflin who have the same dreams and can do the same duties. Olavi and King Guðroðr want peace and prosperity as much as the Irish. But you must understand that just as there are those who have scores to settle with me, there are those who would not find it a terrible thing to settle their grievances over your corpse. You have to be ready. Keep your hand on that knife of yours but stay out of the business of peace-making."

Ruarc shook his head and stepped away. "Fuck you, Gyda."

We'd come to a timber gate. Beyond was a short dirt track that led to the riverfront, and already I could hear the screams of seagulls and the stench of fish guts. My belly tossed and I hastened my steps. Better to finish this business and go back home. Perhaps I wouldn't drink so much tonight. A clear head would do wonders for my mood.

Ruarc fell behind as we passed under the gate arch. I would have continued on without notice if he hadn't made a frustrated growl in his throat and stopped.

"You know what your problem is, *Fiskwif*?" he said.

Rolling my eyes, I turned to face him. "I have a pounding in my head worse than Thor's hammer on a giant's skull?"

"No, it's that you contradict yourself constantly."

"What the fuck does that mean?"

"Your advice is troll-shit," he growled. "First you say I can't fight off the fuckers, but you also say I might have to. So which is it?"

I threw up my hands. "Both! Neither. I don't know anything now. I am an old woman with no brain and no sense and you should leave me to my muttering."

We glared at each other, two monuments buffeted by streams of people eddying along their way to the river.

Ruarc's green eyes were narrowed, his mouth thin and slanted. It gave him a wry, scornful appearance when he was angry, and an impish one when he was not. Right now, his ire was palpable. But past that, his youth was more evident.

Poor, young, *stupid* man.

A desolate, spiteful part of me wished that he would turn and leave, saving himself like all young men do. I could drown in my own tumult in peace. Why should he bear any of my impotent rage at a world that was not fair and never would be?

After a long moment of staring each other down, a glint entered his eye and his shoulders loosened.

"I know one thing is certain," he sighed. "You need a protector. It's true, you are an old woman. You have a good brain, but you're alone in the world, and your reputation is not what it was. The power you had is gone, Gyda, and I am the only one who wants to help you gain a little of it back. So be kinder to me. The gods know I need kindness."

"I'll bear that in mind."

We walked on, silent again.

We followed the track. Dyflin's river, called *An Ruirthech* by the Irish, rose to greet us from behind the flood-defense walls.

Dyflin was never quiet, even on water-logged days. Fishmongers yelled their catch, children darted through parents' legs, and seagulls wheeled overhead looking for morsels to steal. My ears ached with the cacophony.

We were not a large settlement compared to many, but the area was densely populated. Houses and animal byres were packed in rows, as close as possible and often overlapping. There were open middens and hearths and wells and outbuildings scattered in a chaotic organization that was as claustrophobic as it was pungent. The settlement itself sat on a peninsula, nestled between this river and another, which flowed around and bellied into a great pool of dark water, from which Dyflin took its name. With the convergence of these two waterways, Dyflin suited itself perfectly for shipbuilding, trading, slave-markets, and defense. Dyflin was not Jórvík, true, but it was as lively and prosperous a city as any other.

Ruarc halted beside a fish-monger's stall and brought out his purse. In his palm, he counted out three pieces of hacksilver and laid them on the table. The stall-woman handed over a parcel of dried herring and we went on our way.

"So," he said, handing me a strip to chew on. "Who do we approach first? Ketil the Rus with the boil on his chin and a half-sunk tub of moldy furs? Or Ingrid Grettisdóttir? She might have fresh news, I hear her thrall recently returned from a journey to Chester."

"Neither," I said. "We've exhausted them both. Today, we speak to the dock-master."

Ruarc's fist clenched around the herring. "Ásl? You're not serious."

"I am."

"Why, Gyda," he sputtered. "Why would we do something so stupid? That turd-licker will go to Olavi as soon as the silver drops from our fingers."

I tore off a piece of fish and gnawed on it. The salt was wonderful, a tonic for my ale-thick tongue. "Let him go. You said Olavi knows we're asking questions. It stands to reason that Ásl has been told to expect us. Which means his answers will be false. So, we look in the direction opposite of what he says."

"Why ask him at all if he lies?"

"Why does Olavi care about our business?" I countered. "*Sea-Wolf* is still my ship. I own it. I owned the cargo on it. Some fucking arse-pebble stole it. It is within my rights to search for it."

Ruarc made an irritated sound. "You won't keep your head down the way he wants, so you're poking the hornets' nest to get a rise. I understand the urge, particularly because it is you. But why Ásl?"

"Is there a reason we shouldn't see him, Ruarc?"

That made him flush pink to the tips of his ears. "No! No reason that you're thinking of. It's only that I often do business with the man and he hates the sight of my face."

"So you're concerned he will be unfriendly," I said, smirking. "Your need to be liked is precious. Shall I get you a teat to suckle on as well?"

"Gyda, don't torment me. You may not care whether you make friends in this town, but my livelihood—,"

"Hush." I patted his shoulder. "You are so easy to rouse. I will see him alone if that makes you happy. You won't even be mentioned."

We'd come to the end of the street. It dumped out into a large oval space, with various water-front storehouses on the left and an alley full of animal pens to the right. Knots of people milled around, visiting stalls or drinking cups of ale together. Livestock bound for slaughter stood shivering in a byre at the far end. Vacant brown eyes rolled and spindly legs stamped at any human who dared come near. One animal, a strapping ox with enough meat on him to feed a longship of warriors for several weeks, lashed out with his teeth at a thrall who came too close.

"Not too keen on his fate, that one," Ruarc muttered. "I hope his death will be quick."

"You soft-heart," I said fondly.

When we passed a building with its doors gaping wide, his hand went to his mouth to stifle a gag. "Agh, what's that smell?"

"Blood and shit," I told him. "Thralls do the slaughtering there. Makes this entire quarter reek like a *blót*."

"All of Dyflin smells that way," grumbled Ruarc. He eyed the remaining strips of herring warily before stuffing them into a pocket in his tunic. "Either this or a midden. I've never been down this street. Why are we here? I doubt we're in the market for any pickled ox tongue before we darken the door of the dock-master."

"Before we see him, I need to speak to someone else. How about you scrounge us a few cups of ale? I'm as dried out as the herring after all that salt."

Ruarc's shoulders sagged, but he heard enough in my tone not to argue this time. Off he went, and I was left to myself.

A group of people, mostly craftsmen, stood nearby talking and passing each other bits of amber and glass beads. In the middle of this gathering was a gaming table, the reason for their betting. Two gray-bearded men sat opposite each other, playing *hnefetafl*. One man, the older of the two judging by the deep sunbaked crevices cutting his face, made a move that elicited curses and gasps all around. More bets changed hands as his opponent tugged his beard and cursed at being thwarted.

I craned my neck, catching the eye of a diminutive woman who stood at the shoulder of the winning player. Her eyes widened at the sight of me.

I jerked my chin to the left, and she bit her lip, giving me a shake of the head.

I understood her hesitation; what person in their right mind would go off alone with Dyflin's most disliked castoff? But she owed me, and it was time to do business.

I walked toward one of the storehouses, then motioned again, more insistent. After a moment, she followed, unnoticed by the others.

"What in all of God's creation brings you *here,*" the woman hissed, shutting the wooden door behind us. "If my master notices me missing, I'll need something to show for it."

The gloom of the storehouse cast her face in shadow, but I still caught the hungry glitter in her eyes as I produced a fine antler comb from my belt.

"Give him this for his trouble," I said.

When she reached for it, I tightened my hold. Her hunger turned to uncertainty as she looked up.

"You had better have what I asked for," I murmured. "Or this is the last you'll get from me."

"I've got it," she said.

I released the comb and she hastily hid it away and brought out a small purse. She tipped it into my palm, its contents jangling musically.

"There's all of it," she said. "Some dirhams, and Saxon coins. Nothing from Jórvík or Dyflin, as you said. Though I still don't understand why that matters."

She peered at me expectantly, but I pressed my lips together. The value of the coins didn't particularly matter, but ones of foreign make were prized in Dyflin. They gave the bearer status as one who went out into the world and came back with wealth and stories and reputations behind them.

Ásl never traveled, being a man of high nerves and little belly for sailing. He envied the merchants who came and went, wearing their exotic fabrics and swilling expensive Frankish wine. These coins would fill his purse as well as loosen his tongue.

The thrall hummed when I wasn't forthcoming. "These bits were not easily come by," she said reproachfully. "My mistress went to great pains. Some merchants needed their coffers fattened with extra crates of barley or mead. Others needed rather more—ah, persuasion. Not always without violence. One of them lost his ear for the way he spoke to my mistress after too many cups of ale and a joint of lamb." She shuddered and ran a hand over her shorn scalp. "If my master had heard his words, all this would have gone to pay that louse's life-price."

"Such a thing never should have happened," I said, horrified. "I never wanted either of you to put yourselves in danger for this."

"Your trade had better be worth our efforts, *Fiskwif*. If we are discovered helping you, the Jarl's favor falls away, and my freedom with it. This is my last winter as a thrall."

"You won't be found out," I said. Then I pulled out the final piece of our deal: a gilded brooch inlaid with a garnet. It had been a gift from Liadan, once.

The woman's intake of breath was loud in the stifled space.

"A comb for your trouble, and this for your trade," I said. "Your mistress will wear this brooch and be the envy of all Dyflin. And you'll stand proud knowing it was all thanks to you. It may even buy your freedom sooner."

"Indeed it will," the thrall gasped. "She's never had so fine a thing."

She reached out, gently caressing the brooch, its golden edges, the red stones set in the center. "It is a wonder. It's yours, like the other baubles?"

I took her hand and put the brooch in her palm. "Yes," I said, my throat thickening.

All of my bribes had been paid this way, and this was the last piece of any value that I owned, save for my seax hidden at the bottom of my chest. And that would never find its way into the hands of another. Not ever again.

Eir had given it back to me, on the voyage back to Dyflin. She said nothing about it, and I hadn't thanked her. Our debts to each other were paid.

The woman's fingers closed around the brooch and she peered up at me. "What do you do this for, anyway? Selling off all these treasures like a queen going into exile. Is it because you lost that ship?"

"How do you know about that?" I said sharply.

"Oh, everyone talks." She leaned in and sniffed. "I hope you aren't spending everything on ale and beer, but I suspect you are."

"Enough," I said, stepping back. "We're finished here. Go back to your master, and if he gives you grief, give him that comb. If not, keep it for yourself. Sell it, maybe. Thank you for your services, and I wish you joy and prosperity when your freedom arrives."

She went to the door, muttering some rebuke that she was too afraid to say aloud.

"Wait," I said, and she froze, her hand on the latch. "Would you do me one last kindness?"

"God's eyes, do I have a choice?"

"Will you seek out Ásl the dockmaster and send him to the alehouse near the amber merchant's?"

She went quiet, and I grit my teeth to keep from pressing. If she refused, I'd have to do it myself, and that would waste daylight, and another day would be gone. Another day without word of *Sea-Wolf.*

"I will do this," she said. "I know what it is to be alone. But then I will do no more. God go with you."

CHAPTER TEN

Ruarc found me in the same place he'd left me. By then, the *tafl* game had finished and the table was cleared away. The gamblers milled about, trading their winnings on cuts of butchered meat and fish, or sulking over their losses around a barrel of beer.

"I had to walk four streets over to find ale of any quality," Ruarc groused. "That barrel there is sour. You should be grateful." He handed me a cup and I took it, downing it in one gulp.

"My business is finished," I told him. "We've got a meeting at the amber merchants' alehouse. Ásl will come to us."

Ruarc's russet brows, having lifted with my drinking, came down in a scowl. "We're going to an alehouse? Why not just wait for your drink, then?"

"Because I was thirsty now," I said.

Midday came and went, and we found ourselves on a long bench in front of a cheery hearth. I was two cups deep into a jug of ale and enjoying it.

"This is good stuff," I said, and Ruarc dropped his forehead to the table.

"You're going to be too drunk to talk," he moaned. "I should never have agreed to this."

"Ah, Ruarc, you've been at every other meeting. What's one more?"

I was speaking too loudly, but I didn't care. I felt light, as if made from ale froth and honey. Though Ásl would arrive when he felt like it, the hope of real progress lifted my heart. It was like fog clearing after a storm and leaving a glass-like calm over the sea.

"I thought I didn't have to be here," Ruarc muttered.

"Your support is much appreciated," I said cheerfully. "We might finally have a true heading with Ásl. At the least, a new lead to pursue."

"You think you can gather a lead from the crumbs he drops?"

Ruarc's mouth twisted. "I don't understand how you can reckon truth from lies. It's like trying to find garnets in shit-piles. You're more likely to find cherry pits."

I laughed. "Even Loki-knots can be unraveled if you have enough patience and just as much guile. Ásl is bound to have heard something from the Córdoban merchants."

Ruarc shook his head. "They've already left, Gyda. Two days ago. If Ásl knows anything, what makes you think it'll be about *Sea-Wolf?* And if it's not about *Sea-Wolf,* then what do you plan to do?"

"Ruarc, please. You're nagging me worse than my—," I choked on the last word, covering it with a quick gulp of my ale.

Ruarc looked down, picking at the joint of lamb in front of him.

I never mentioned the Daughters. Never thought of them, if I could help it. It brought pain like my seax straight through my gut. I hadn't seen any of them since we'd arrived in Dyflin two months before, though I knew where each of them resided now. I could have visited, learned how they were faring, tried to explain myself again. Instead, I chose to stay away. They didn't want to see me.

Ruarc knew better than to ask, or speak of them, though he loved them like they were his own sisters. In a way, they had been. But that was all over now.

I drained my cup and reached for the pitcher. Ásl would arrive soon, and it was best if I kept myself sharp. Ale would give my tongue the smoothness I needed. I drank the cup down and lifted the pitcher once more.

"I wouldn't," said a man's voice.

I froze, every muscle tight in an instant.

Scowling, Hákon Olavisson swung his long legs over the bench and settled himself next to Ruarc, whose spine went straight like a spar.

"You know why I'm here," Hákon said. "No need to gape like thunder just came out your arses."

I forced looseness into my muscles and cracked a grin. "Hello, Hákon. Don't you have a wedding feast to prepare?"

Reaching again for the pitcher, I filled my cup and slid it over. His fingertips fluttered, but he didn't touch it.

"Congratulations, by the way," I said. "Eir will make you a fine wife. But be cautious, Hákon, she likes the spearing of men more than she likes a man's spear."

Ruarc's face turned the hue of a fish's belly. "Shut *up*," he hissed.

"Don't forget you have an invitation," Hákon said smoothly. "The feast is tonight. Naturally, you are expected to make an appearance."

The way he said it made my blood rise. I folded my arms and leaned back. "So this is how you show hospitality now? With veiled threats from your master? Still Olavi's dog, even while he calls you heir."

Hákon leaned forward. "I would be happy to stay, casting insults back and forth until we're both shredded and stupid from drink, but I'd rather get back to my *wife.*" He paused and raised his brows. "And I think you would rather get back to selling shit and bribing shit-shovelers."

"You bastard."

He tilted his head, smiling a little. "My father's patience with you is not endless. So this is my advice to you: *Sea-Wolf* is gone. You would be wise to move forward."

Under the table, I pressed my fists into my thighs. How easy it would be to strike his arrogant face. But if I did that, any leverage I might have would be lost.

"It is my right to search for what is mine," I ground out. "The thief is free, and I cannot keep my pride while they live. Olavi can't limit a free woman's pursuit of vengeance."

"If *Sea-Wolf* is under sail, someone will see it eventually," Hákon said. He reached for the cup and sipped it, making a face when the ale hit his tongue. "Don't mistake my warning for threats. My father is inconvenienced by your meddling, but other matters press him, and you are but a bothersome flea in his beard. I am not here as your enemy. Not now, anyway."

"*You* sought me out here, with your warnings and your axes." I nodded at the corner, where a group of five oath-men sat drinking, trying hard to blend with the crowd and failing spectacularly. They kept stealing glances, fingers on their weapon-belts. "Why bring your dogs if you aren't aiming to tear flesh?"

Hákon spread his hands. "I come with no weapon. They follow because it is their oath." He placed his palms on the table and leaned closer, lowering his voice. "Gyda, please take heed. If I could change what happened in al-Andalus, I would. But I cannot. Neither my father nor Dyflin would have accepted anything less. Your blood was all these people slavered over for months. They have no love for you right now, and even less when the merchants complain of harassment. I'm here because…well, I am not your friend, but I can be an ally. Allies give counsel."

"You have a habit of never coming to the point, boy. Spit your words or fuck off."

He moved back. "Very well. Ásl the dockmaster is not coming, because he's in front of my father moaning about you. You're wasting your time."

"And why should I care about Ásl?" I scoffed. "He's in Olavi's purse anyway, so he's useless to me."

Now Hákon's choler rose. "Don't play games. You think I don't know every merchant, every traveler, every official you've bribed and threatened and cajoled these last weeks? No one has any information because there is none to be had. Not yet, anyway."

He turned to Ruarc, scowling. "And don't think you have escaped my notice either, Hrœrekr. If your Irish patrons knew what mess you've entangled yourself in, intimidating their merchants, I should hate to think what they'd make of your loyalties."

Ruarc's crooked mouth thinned and the color returned to his face. "We've done nothing wrong," he said, voice thin as a reed, but Hákon turned back to me.

"How long do you think until someone realizes how vulnerable you truly are, *Fiskwif*? There will be a knife in the ribs while you lie reeking in your drink. You'd be too drunk to notice you're dead."

"Fuck your false concern, and fuck your father's obsessive control! I am not sworn to him."

He shook his head. "Are you such a fool to think that he has some need for your loyalty? Thor's balls, woman, Jörund was my father's brother. How does it look if his widow is left to rot and waste her life away? You have been forgiven much, Gyda, but now you are being reckless and stupid. *Sea-Wolf* is gone. Dyflin is your home now, whether it loves you or not. You should treat it that way."

The noise of the alehouse rose to a clamor in my ears. I had no words, only the hate in my stare, and so that I gave to Hákon, as fierce and as hot as it burned.

Perhaps he saw it, because he cleared his throat and rose. "Ásl is not coming. The other merchants will not speak to you anymore. Your silver has been spent in vain. *Their* loyalty is to Olavi, and to Dyflin. Your loyalty is to yourself only, and there is no honor or pride in that. They know it, and we know it. I urge you, for the love my wife once bore for you, and for my own regard, find a new path. This one leads to ruin."

His men rose from their benches and followed their lord out the door.

Grasping the pitcher, I stood and hurled it after them. It shattered on the door, staining it dark with the ale.

"What now?" Ruarc said softly.

My head spun. Blood and anger sloshed through my veins.

"Now, we send Olavi a message."

When I was a child in Norway, I had watched a longship burn. The fjord had glowed like a dragon's nest. Flames reflected off the deep water and leapt to the sky, where the night swallowed them. By dawn there had been nothing left, no mark on the water to show where the ship had vanished.

The ship had been an offering. The gods demanded sacrifice, said the *völva*. For better raids. For richer plunder. For fewer deaths of our young men.

It hadn't worked.

Now, as I held a torch to the furled sail of a *byrding*, a wolf's smile split my face. No, not a wolf's. A shark's.

I was wrath and destruction and rage, but I was not devastation. There were other places within the walls of Dyflin, other ships, all packed with meat and grains and easy to burn. But *this* ship…burning it would send Olavi the message I wanted.

Stay out of my way. The sea is cold wrath and without pity. And I am a Daughter of Rán.

Like a shark leaves blood in the water after feeding, I would leave the rest of his vessels and his storehouse untouched.

Each of the three light cargo ships berthed at Jarl's Quay belonged to his household, and each bore supplies for the week of celebrations following the wedding feast. In each of the *byrdings'* holds, there would be fine cheeses, casks of ale, chests of bottled Frankish wine. There would be barrels of rendered fat for the lamps. Silk runners for the tables. Garlands of dried summer flowers. Only the best for the Jarl.

The fire caught in the sail, and Ruarc and I stood on the sand and shingle to watch the embers dance.

"What have you done, Gyda?" Ruarc breathed. The planes of his long face writhed with shadow.

The newly-landed crewmen had scattered throughout Dyflin. Like a feeding frenzy, every man would drink and fuck and doze off their long journeys, as they always did before slogging to the back-breaking work of disgorging their cargo. How often had Rán's Daughters done the same?

One young boy barely into his first beard had been left to watch over this quiet stretch of riverbank. Ruarc, face covered with his cloak and knife in his hand, offered the poor frightened lamb his big silver clasp if he went off to drink himself to sleep. That was all it took; the boy pranced off, his eyes shining with silver and belly aching for ale.

How many of the crewmen would piss themselves for fear of Olavi's wrath? When the goods were delivered to the hall, would they lie about what was missing? Would they beg his mercy for their foolishness? Would Olavi feel the sting of losing something without knowing who had taken it from him, the same as I ached for the loss of *Sea-Wolf* every day and every night?

I waited a moment longer, glutting myself on the sight of the devouring fire. The heat was delicious on my skin. It was like bathing in a hot spring, scouring away all the weakness, all the sickness I bore inside.

"You were right," I whispered. "It is time to leave my grave mound."

"What was that?"

I turned to Ruarc. "I said let us leave. This won't go unnoticed for long and we have a feast to attend. We are late already."

And so as the stars began winking in the sky, we put the ships and the fire to our backs.

CHAPTER ELEVEN

The feasting hall rose from the dark, a haven of light and warmth.

"Now, isn't that a pretty sight," the wagon driver said. He was a grizzled man with thick-veined hands and large ears. Sitting hunched over clutching the reins, the light gave him the appearance of a troll driving us to Muspelheim.

"Oh, thank the gods," Ruarc wheezed. "My backside aches."

"When doesn't it?" I said, and he tossed a handful of barley at me, scattering it in all directions.

"Don't be mucking about with my goods, hear me?" growled the driver. "By all the saints, I should have made you walk."

The wagon bumped and rattled in the ruts of the road. We'd hired the man at the town gates as he'd loaded the last of his grain sacks. Chests heaving like bellows, we came upon the wagon like two ghosts in the dark, scaring his ox and provoking the man to look us over like we'd crawled out of a midden.

"Everyone of any worth has gone to the hall tonight," he'd groused. "You ain't the first of the rabble to ask for a ride, and ye won't be the last." He leaned towards us, sniffed the air, and made a face. "And ye smell of grease and smoke! Ruin the barley, that will. The sun might rise before I make my delivery as it is. Lord Jesus forgive me, punctuality is a virtue I am not blessed to possess, and my patron is not disposed to mete his grace to his vassals when his breakfast table stands empty. Get your sorry selves away, I'll not stop for the likes of you."

In response to that, I gave the man five full dirhams of silver, Ruarc gave an antler comb, and there had been no more fussing. The old man shifted his sacks of barley and cereal grains, and Ruarc and I settled in the bed of his wagon for a long, jostling trip down the pitch dark trackway leading outside Dyflin to Olavi's hall.

"Do you think we've made it far enough?" Ruarc whispered. He was looking past me, back towards the river, and I knew he looked for the fire.

I saw nothing more than the usual ambient glow of the town. If the *byrding* still burned, the sight was hidden from us.

"We're well away," I said to him. "Don't dwell on it."

I found the farther I got from Jarl's Quay, the less real my actions felt. Had I truly done such a thing? Burnt a ship full of food? What if my precautions went awry, and other ships burned, or houses? What if others were caught in the fire? Thralls? Innocents?

I shoved those thoughts somewhere deep. *Trust yourself.*

Olavi would learn of the offense in due time, but first, I would enjoy his hospitality. The ale in my blood lingered and I craved more of it.

"Boundary wall," creaked the driver. "Now, off, the pair of you, and send up a prayer to whatever heathen god you serve that my patron sleeps through the morning."

He snapped his reins, and the animal took off at a trot into the dark, leaving us at the foot of a small hill, with Olavi's hall looming over us.

"He was a right shit," I told Ruarc. "I hope that comb you gave him was worth less than a rock in his porridge."

As we started up the sloping pathway, Ruarc stiffened and clutched my arm.

"There are oath-men everywhere," he hissed.

"It's the Jarl's son's wedding," I said dryly. "It would be strange if there weren't oath-men everywhere."

He shook his head. "I don't think we should be here, Gyda. Not now."

I reached up, taking his face in my hands. "Look at me, Ruarc."

He did, though there was a tremor under his skin.

"You sweet boy, if we behave as if we are guilty, we attract attention. If we act as if we know nothing, we pass as any other guest. You are a man of standing in this city. Act as you normally would, and no one will notice how nervous you are."

I did not release him until he swallowed and nodded.

This hall officially belonged to Dyflin's King Guðroðr, though Jarl Olavi had the use of it because the king spent most of his time raiding or gallivanting about with Sigtryggr in Jórvík and Northumbria.

The hall itself had seen many gatherings over the years, both for my people and for Ruarc's. Weddings between high-status folk were common events, as were visits from foreign dignitaries and ambassadors. Though my words were meant to reassure Ruarc, they gave me no such comfort.

The last time I'd been inside this hall, I had received a great honor. Olavi gave me his trust, his respect, and the Córdoban trade deal. My fate had been spun by the Norns into something favorable, something grand and glorious. But then came the murder of Ishraq the emissary, a stowaway appeared on my ship, and my fate had changed again. I could not say it was for the better, though the memory of Helgi Olavisson with my seax in his gut still brought me a glimmer of pleasure.

Ragnar owed me nothing, and yet I felt somewhat resentful of him. Wherever he was, alive, or dead in some Córdoban ditch, at least he was free.

"Guests of the wedding?" A dark-haired man bundled in wool and holding a spear stood beside the great doors. He looked us over, bored already. Next to him was a stool with an empty ale-cup and a plate of bread crusts.

Ruarc straightened. "Guests, indeed," he said confidently.

"Names?"

"I am Lord Hrœrekr mac Ceallachan, mac Rumann, and this is Gyda, widow of Jörund, who was cousin and foster brother of Olavi Sharp-Spear. We were invited by Hákon Olavisson, the groom."

The man's eyes widened at our names, but his gaze went to me, curious.

"You have a lot of gall showing up here," he said. "On your own shoulders be it. Go on." He waved us through.

Both outside and inside the hall, masses of people heaved and buzzed like a hive of wasps. Men stood drinking together, already too far into their cups. Some gathered in circles of three or four, tossing carved stones on the floorboards in patterns and slapping each others' backs when they landed cleverly.

Married women sat on benches gossiping with friends and feeding their little ones from platters of bread and fruit. The children would be sent to an early bedtime, bundled up at the far end of the hall, separated from everything by a removable screen. Across from that was an antechamber where the Jarl and his family members slept. A long shelf above the door held the carved wooden likenesses of Oðinn, Týr, and Freyja, all stern-faced and glaring.

Hákon and Eir were inside this chamber, making themselves ready for the wedding rituals. Olavi might likely be with them. When the time came, the family would enter in a procession, taking their seats on a high platform that had been built at the head of the great hearth in the middle.

From this place of honor, they could see everyone, and everyone could see them. Eir, as the bride, would be admired, envied, and asked for her favor throughout the night. Hákon would preen and smirk, drinking his nerves away until the time came to take his bride into the antechamber to finish the ritual.

I would be sure to avoid the platform and its performers entirely.

Ruarc and I were borne along by the crowd. Tables had been set up everywhere in long straight rows, along with benches and stools and smoking braziers. Young women and thralls moved through the aisles like agile minnows, balancing plates and serving bowls.

With a word of thanks, I grabbed a large mug from one passing tray, and was pleased to discover mead. I sipped it, relishing the cool sweetness on my tongue.

"Olavi always knows how to host a good party," Ruarc said, lifting his own mug. "Though I'll need a lot of this to enjoy myself." He tilted it back and drank greedily.

"You won't find a lack of it," I said, smiling. "With luck, it'll cover many of your indiscretions."

"What does that mean?" A flush came to his cheek.

I shrugged. "Go on and have a good time. I won't be staying long, just enough to show that I was here, and then I'll make for home. Meet me tomorrow by the river, and we'll see how things are with Ásl."

Ruarc put a hand on his neck, uneasy. "How things are," he repeated. "You know, I'd rather not, if it's all the same to you. More pressing is the fact that we don't know our next move. We have no leads. No allies. And we just committed an act that could get both of us expelled from the town, if not killed outright. Gyda, I think Hákon was right. It may be time to put this endeavor to the side. At least until spring. There's bound to be more news then."

I pretended his words were swallowed by the crowd.

"Drink," I said. "Eat. Savor the festivities. We should enjoy ourselves. This is a wedding, after all."

"Gyda," he pressed.

Irritated now, I lowered my voice. "If you're still fretting, stop. You are not the one who set the fire."

"Unbelievable," he muttered. Straightening, he took a deep draught of his mead and stretched on a weak grin. "Fine. If I am to enjoy myself, it will be with a plate of food, more ale, and far less belligerent company."

"Less belligerent, but rather more *stimulating,* I'd wager."

I winked at him, and a deep flush colored his cheeks. He whirled and strode off, but whether or not he'd counted on vanishing into the crowd, his path was thwarted. A short man with a great bushy mane of black hair and scrawny arms leaned back on his bench as Ruarc brushed past.

"There you are," the man belted, a smile cracking his weathered face and beard. He was Irish, but spoke our tongue well. "I'd hoped you'd be here tonight, my boy. Come, come! My wife and daughter are so looking forward to meeting you. My future son-in-law!" He stood, clapping his hand firmly on Ruarc's shoulder and steered him away.

Ruarc tossed a panicked look back to me.

"Have fun, my friend," I called. "Come see me in the morning if you're not too thick from drinking!"

His reply, if he made any, was lost to the roar of the crowd.

At any other time, gatherings like this would have stripped good humor from me like the skin from a snared rabbit. But tonight, the mug of mead in my hand held a kind of *seiðr*. Its magic flowed over my tongue with the taste of juniper and infused my blood with happiness.

I wandered the rows of tables. So many people. So many neighbors. So many who knew me, or who had known my husband. I would have called them friends at one point. I drifted, noting as their gazes slid away from mine, their smiles and nods of greeting aborted as they realized who it was walking among their tables.

Oaths of friendship, of fellowship, meant nothing after all, and I cared little for the slights. Oaths were just words, spoken amongst shield-brothers because they were expected, and when expectation is replaced by apathy, by the span of too many years and too many battlefields, how could anyone take offense? Especially when the shield-brother in question is dead and his disgraced widow is nothing but an old woman with too much ambition and a taste for killing noble sons.

Remember your fire, I thought to myself, and a smile touched my lips. *Remember Helgi.* It was power that I held, not disgrace, and they all knew it.

They look away because they fear for their own sons.

A rare space at the end of a bench opened and I claimed it, shoving away a skinny youth with an overfilled ale horn and an amorous glance for the girl serving ale nearby. His glance turned to a vehement scowl for me.

"Slow serpents make poor suiters," I told him, wedging my legs under the table. Still glaring, the boy slouched away and the girl bobbed her head in gratitude.

I raised my mead to her and drank.

The evening felt charged, as if Thor rode the lightning and Freyja blessed the thunder. And this was only the start of the celebration. Wedding feasts went on for days, even a week. People would come and go at all hours, and Jarl Olavi was expected to host them all.

By now, the burnt cargo barge would have been discovered. The merchant would be on his way soon, hauling the untouched goods and remaining food, trembling in his wagon because he knew Olavi would be embarrassed when guests ate their way through what was already on these tables. Dyflin expected more and could never be satisfied.

Every bite of bread tasted like honey and every morsel of flesh filled my belly with warmth. The bodies at my table howled their laughter. These people I did not know, and they did not know me. It was a gift, this anonymity. A moment of utter relief, like the shelter of a sun-gilded bay after a month of freezing seas.

A blast from a horn interrupted my dreaming.

The crowd quieted as a grizzled old gods-priest, a goði, walked out of the antechamber. Behind him, in procession, walked Eir, Hákon, and Olavi. Heimarr was not with them, and I wondered if he'd bothered to show up at all.

"Hail, my Jarl," shouted a man at the end of my table. Hearty cheers, toasts, and calls of celebration and admiration filled the air. The goði led the way onto the platform, a dour expression on his wizened face. He wore a coarse linen robe belted with a length of woven cloth. From his belt hung hundreds of strips of metal, which clinked like bells as he walked. Behind him, Eir and Hákon beamed like sunshine, their hands intertwined as they reached their places on the platform.

The seat of prominence in the center of the table was a large, high-backed thing of yew, carved with figures of beasts and draped in fine yellow silks. This was King Guðroðr's seat, though tonight, it would be Jarl Olavi who filled it.

The Jarl stepped up to the platform and raised his hands for quiet.

"We are here this wondrous night," he began. "To witness the joining of my eldest son, Hákon *Stáli* —."

At this, there was more raucous cheering, and men pounded their plates and cups and ale bowls on their tables for their lord's warrior son.

I covered a sneer with my cup, which at some point had been refilled with more mead.

I had never found Olavi as well-favored or handsome as his sons. Age rendered him round-bellied, droop-eyed, and without hair on his head. But as a tall man in a room of tall men, he commanded attention. Beneath a scarlet tunic, his shoulders spanned wide from years of oar-pulling. Thin scars marked his knuckles, reminders of his many raids and battles. Great tufts of coal black and ash gray hair sprouted from his chin and reached to his belt. He smiled, waiting for the noise to dissipate.

"As I was saying—we are here for the joining of my son to Eir, daughter of Sigmund and Bergthora. Widow of Bjarni Bitter-Tongue, an oath-man who served me loyally. Hákon and Eir, a suitable match!"

More cheering, lusty whistles, and toasts. Eir smiled wide, a blush painting a pretty shade on her cheeks.

She had not seen me yet, and my bench was far enough away to draw little notice. But I saw her clearly, and she was altogether changed.

Whether a new life in Dyflin had treated her more kindly than our seasons at sea, or if she had taken special care for this event, she was radiant. She wore a dress of night-blue wool that suited her well. The neckline and wrists had been embroidered with silver weaving—a skill I never learned, but knew Eir performed with enjoyment. Over the gown, her apron was made of a fine silk, colored a deep red that shone in the firelight. Two brooches fastened the apron's shoulder straps, and each was crafted with interlacing snakes of gold wire and onyx eyes.

Her hair had been plaited in two pieces, and both were wrapped in ribbon and turned around her head to form a wreath. Between the braid-knots were pins of bone and amber, with serpents of the same style as her brooches.

I stared at her like a stunned sheep. Her hand clasped Hákon's, and when she turned her smile on him, it was one that I had never seen her give another person, not even her first husband.

This was not the Eir I knew. This Eir had become a wealthy woman of renown, and appeared before Dyflin's people not as a Sea-Norse, crusted with salt and burned to shoe leather, but as a goddess. A true Daughter of Rán, or of Freyja herself.

Olavi spoke again. "Before we begin the wedding rituals, let us honor our absent king and my middle son Heimarr, who is away in Jórvík on his father's business. A toast to their health and success!"

I turned to my neighbor, a Dane who was verging on sleep from the amount of ale he'd ingested, and toasted the king. A shame Heimarr was in Jórvík, or I would return the blows he'd dealt me in al-Andalus. I wondered if his oath-man Uffe was with him. I still owed that one a blade in the gut for Ragnar.

"Now," boomed Olavi. "Lend your ears to my skald as he sings of how my son won his byname—Hákon Steel!"

Amongst the cheering and pounding of tables, the beat of a drum rose. A small man took his place at the foot of the great hearth, facing the platform. He was Irish by his dress and features, but he wore Olavi's silver arm-ring. Bowing, he struck the drum skin, building the rhythm quickly. He turned to face the cheering hall and began to sing. His words and his music beat in my breast, melting together with the cheering of the crowd.

The evening wound on. A new bowl of bread and stew was placed in front of me, and so I devoured both, washing it down with ale.

At some point, the goði stood and spoke, though his speech flowed together and turned to mist in my ears. My bones were liquid. The hall sunk and rose, a vessel of gold and blue and green and brown, the hues of the sea. A ship to carry me to oblivion.

A while later, a stool was brought and set up on the high table. Hákon helped Eir onto the table, and she climbed onto the stool, standing so all could see her. She was a gleaming, rosy-cheeked goddess robed in shadow and flame, a vision of something which this world had only caught small glimpses.

The goði walked a circle around the table, chanting as he went, his hailing of the gods becoming the only sound echoing through the hall. A shallow bowl appeared, full to the brim with bright blood taken from an animal. The goði dipped his fingers in the blood, then flicked them at Eir. Her dress and apron would be spattered from the neckline to the hem. Sacrificial blood to cover her in the blessings and favor of the gods. I remembered how my wedding dress had stuck to my skin, warm with gore and reeking of slaughter and *seiðr*.

Eir lifted her arms over her head "Thor!" she cried. "Vár! Freyr! Freyja! All the Æsir and Vanir! Look upon me now and bless me."

The people gathered called out the same, and the sound was deafening.

"Will my husband give me his hammer?" she asked. "Will he give me his sword and his spear? Will he give me the key to his home, so that I may be his shield and his hearth-guard?"

Hákon stood and pulled himself up onto the table to stand with her. She turned to him and he took her hands.

"I give you all of this," he called out. From his belt, he took a hammer - a simple blacksmiths' tool, meant to represent *Mjöllnir*, the lightning-bringer of Thor. He held it up and the crowd hushed.

"I give you all this," he called out again. "I give you this hammer and I give you my seed, so that our marriage is fertile and our children are strong." He lowered the hammer and gave it to Eir.

She held it to her chest. "I accept this," she said, her voice ringing through the quiet. "And I accept you, Hákon *Stáli*, as my husband."

Hákon beamed, the people cheered, and something dark uncoiled inside me.

With a curse, I gave up my seat and shoved my way through the screaming crowd and out a side door into the night air.

CHAPTER TWELVE

The world had blurred into a smear of colors and shapes. I made it halfway to the latrines when a muffled, angry cry stopped me.

Closing one eye, I swayed and looked around. No foxes, or cats that I could see. But then, I was as drunk as Thor and bursting for a piss. It would be a long, dark walk back to Dyflin alone. Better to leave soon, before Olavi heard the news.

I continued on my way, only to stop again when another sound broke the night's peace. A woman was yelling.

"Freyja's tits," I muttered.

This path led behind the hall, and further along to my right stood the brewing-shed, and to the left a large cookhouse. A continuous stream of people passed through the buildings and back up the path towards the hall, hurrying to replenish ale pitchers and platters. The ones coming towards me were not in distress, though a permanent scowl of harassed aggravation was on all their faces.

"You Irish witch," came a woman's voice again from the direction of the cookhouse. "You've befouled the stew!"

At the corner of the cookhouse, a knot of thrall women had gathered to take a break from their duties. They sipped cups of beer, which they quickly hid as I approached.

"Who's back there," I demanded, stomping like an old steer. I was slurring.

"You'd best leave it alone, Lady," said one stout-heart, casting a knowing glance at the other women, all older than her. They gasped audibly and winced when I stepped closer.

"You're new here," I said to the brave girl.

She was stocky, with deeply tanned skin. Her black hair was shorn to her scalp, which was customary for thralls in some households. Her accent was Frankish, though she spoke Norse perfectly. Her gaze was unafraid.

"Begging forgiveness, please," the girl said. She clasped her hands in front of her and bowed her head. "I meant no disrespect."

I waved that away. "Speak, child. You have nothing to fear from me."

She hesitated, looking to her companions again for support, though none was to be found there. "It's only that you shouldn't trouble yourself with that noise, Lady," she said. "It's nothing."

I laughed. "And why not? Is there some fearsome troll with a club waiting to bash your brains in? No? Then I'll take my chances."

I pushed past her and the others, who hissed their warnings and urges to leave it.

"Oi," I yelled as I went around the corner of the cookhouse. "I need to piss and your shouting is—,"

My words died in my throat.

There were two women, one facing me, the other crouched and facing away. Both were near a fire with an iron cauldron over a grate. The sides of the cauldron were streaked with something nasty and crusted: the remnants of an overflowing stew.

The standing woman I vaguely recognized. The other I could never mistake, even from the back.

"Liadan!"

"Stupid thrall," the woman snarled at her. "I'll have you beaten. Get up! Bring me that ugly face, I'll drown you myself."

Liadan held her right arm close to her body. She raised her other hand and moved it rapidly. The woman advanced on her, a large iron ladle in her fist.

"Don't you fucking dare," I shrieked, rushing forward. Startled, both women swiveled to face me. "Do not touch that woman if you value your hands, Asny!"

Asny's fingers tightened on the ladle. She was one of Olavi's hearth-wives, the dozen or so noble women who oversaw the hosting, feasting, and hospitality of the hall. Most of them I knew in passing. Some I even liked. But Asny had never been counted in that number.

"You're that wretched sea-hag," she said, narrowing her eyes as she took my measure. "I heard you were dead. And anyway, this matter does not concern dirty fishmongers. Make yourself scarce, you stink of brine."

I halted beside Liadan and offered her my hand. "Get up," I said. "Don't kneel for this cow. She won't hurt you."

Liadan signed something at me hastily as I helped her rise, protesting even as I took her forearm to run my fingers across the injury. She jerked out of my touch, pressing the arm tight against her middle and scowling.

I sighed and stepped back, keeping the sting out of my face. "Your arm is bruised, not broken. You'll be alright."

Asny snickered. "What are you, *Fiskwif*, some kind of honor-hero to thralls? It's too late for that. Your reputation is already written in shit. Or fish-guts, perhaps?"

The eyes of the other women were on us, all of them thralls, and Asny turned on them next.

"What are you idiots gawking at," she bellowed. "Is this one of your lot? No wonder she's useless." She turned her glare back to Liadan. "Why don't I have one of the men beat you? I can promise their arms are far less gentle than mine."

"My Lady Asny," said the girl from before, stepping up beside us. "Lady Liadan is not a thrall. She's a guest of the Jarl. You shouldn't treat her this way."

"Don't bother, girl," I told her. "Leave Asny to her shrieking and get my friend something to wrap her arm with."

"How dare you," Asny hissed at the girl. "Once I've dealt with these *karlkonur*, I'll have your nose for speaking back to me!"

The girl shrank back from this, and I felt Liadan stiffen. It was a terrible insult.

Asny saw her reaction. "Oh yes," she sneered. "I know about you two. Wearing trews and making war like men. Did you fuck like men too? Which was the mare and which the stallion?"

Liadan replied, her hands moving jerkily, punctuating every word. Asny, of course, could not understand. But I did. I gave Liadan a smile, and she ignored it.

"Don't you cast your *seiðr* at me, witch!" Asny raised her ladle.

For an instant, I wished I'd left this matter alone. My lower belly burned for the latrine. Liadan was more than capable of fighting for herself. I'd seen her disarm far stronger opponents than this fool, even when caught off guard. She'd have Asny on the ground as quickly as gutting a fish—which is what she had told her. Would it not be wiser for me to step away? There was still time to keep my presence here unnoticed. I could find another corner, another cup to wallow in until oblivion took me. None of this was my business.

But if I let Asny find out for herself what Liadan was capable of, this encounter would turn into a fight, and that would draw far more attention than I was comfortable with.

I caught Liadan's eye. *Wait,* I motioned, hand by my hip.

Her expression tightened, unhappy with my interference. But she dipped her chin.

"You're conspiring together!" Asny's voice pitched up. "Don't cast your Irish *galdr* on me!"

I growled. "Shut your mouth and step away before I befoul the stew with your severed tongue."

Asny flushed at the threat. "I'll be going straight to Olavi with this. Just wait, *Fiskwif,* you'll get yours."

Her feet shifted and her shoulder dropped, the action almost imperceptible. Almost.

Ah, well. I was drunk, after all, and wisdom had never been a quality I bore. When Asny moved, no one could claim it was I who had started the fight.

I caught Liadan's eye and nodded. A ghost of a smile reached her lips.

The hearth-wife's jaw flexed and her arm drew back, ladle poised to come down like a hammer. That same instant, Liadan danced forward, knocking the ladle from her grasp with ease. It clanged against the cauldron, then fell into the coals of the cook-fire with a hiss.

"Shit!" cried Asny.

The thralls behind me stifled their laughter.

Embarrassed and turning red, Asny cursed and reached out to claw at Liadan's face. It was a bad choice. Her scream cut the night as Liadan's fist connected with her nose. The crunch and gush of blood choked off her cry, and she stumbled back, clutching it. "I'll kill you, witch," she sputtered.

"What in the name of all the gods is happening?"

All of us started and whirled around, fists at the ready.

"Eir," I blurted, stunned by the vision of her.

She stood illuminated by the torches, their fire reflecting off her embroidery and jewelry. Dark stains of ritual blood dappled her garments. She was like a Valkyrie, full in her wrath. The hairs rose on the back of my neck.

"Incredible," she said, gray eyes like iron as she raked them over me. "Of course I would find you in the center of some scuffle. Crashing my wedding, Gyda, *really*?"

My gut tightened like a vice.

"Tell me what happened," she demanded, turning to Liadan and Asny. "Why is my father-in-law's hearth-wife bleeding so profusely?"

Asny lurched forward, spitting blood and snot. "This bitch ruined the—,"

"Not you," Eir told her coldly. "Go ahead, Liadan."

Liadan lifted her chin, then signed the events, clearly and concisely.

Evidently, Olavi himself requested Liadan to oversee a handful of servants in the cookhouse for the evening. Liadan was not a thrall, not anymore, but she was a single woman, and single women were obliged to work during feast-time. She had accepted the task, happy to avoid the crowded party. Instead of servants, she'd found Asny, drunk in the cookhouse. Unaware that Liadan was now her overseer, and unwilling to find a way to understand the way that she communicated, Asny had assumed Liadan was just another slave, and dismissed her.

Two angry, flaming spots appeared on Liadan's cheeks as she told all this, but she continued, her hands strong as they told her tale.

The stew in the cookhouse had run low. Liadan went in search of a fresh batch to replace it. She'd found Asny snoring against the wall, deep in drink. The cauldron had overflowed, the stew burned to a crisp in the bottom. Liadan took up the ladle, hoping to find any salvageable portion. That was when Asny woke and tore the ladle out of Liadan's hands in rage, twisting her arm and shoving her to the ground.

"That was when I came upon them," I said as Liadan's hands paused. She nodded and dropped her hands to her sides, inclining her head to Eir.

Eir's expression had remained tranquil throughout the story. "I see," she said. "Thank you, my friend."

Asny, looking between all of us, scoffed. "*How* can you see? This woman can't even speak! You're going to believe whatever she's telling you over Olavi's favored hearth-wife? This is ridiculous."

Eir eyed here. "Careful, Asny, you are hardly the favored anything. This woman is no thrall, but a dear friend of mine. A *free* woman, and a guest of the Jarl. You are just one hearth-wife among many. Replaceable."

Asny gaped at her, struck wordless.

"Even if Liadan had been a thrall," Eir continued, her jaw tightening. "Your treatment of her is an insult. Not just to her or me, but to Hákon and the Jarl. I doubt they would care to hear how you insult them, nor how you neglected your duty. How many guests will go hungry because of your failure, do you think? Shall we inform them?"

Asny's nose had ceased gushing, but she put a knuckle to it anyway, turning away with a deep flush. "Forgive me," she forced out. "I was taken by foolishness. It won't happen again, my Lady."

"Just go," Eir said softly, and so Asny did, disappearing around the opposite corner. She did not bother to look back. I imagined finding her later, when Olavi's oath-men were not so near, and smiled to myself. I would see how much gall she had then.

Behind Eir, the women's faces were smug. They'd never say aloud what they thought of Asny, but I felt proud of their naked disdain nonetheless. She would never again have their respect, or their obedience.

"Young one, step forward, if you will," Eir said.

The brave thrall stepped forward, surprise crossing her features at Eir's notice of her. Instead of bowing her head and fumbling, she met Eir's gaze directly.

"You have done well," Eir told her. "You've earned my praise and my thanks. I shall ensure a measure more respite for you and your friends over the coming winter feasts, and I will see if I cannot nudge the Jarl's hand towards freedom by next *Jól*."

The girl's mouth dropped open. "Lady, your kindness is too much! I did nothing!"

"Hush, child. It is not kindness, and I will not hear your protests."

The girl stepped back, wonder replacing her surprise.

Now Eir turned to me, expression turning rigid. "Tell me what you're doing here, Gyda," she said.

"I was invited, that's what." I wobbled on my feet, still simmering from the mead and ale in my blood.

Her lip curled. "You were invited? Certainly not by me."

This rankled. My goodwill for her evaporated. "Your dear *husband* extended me the honor. Did he not tell you? He came to town today to request it in person."

"Did he?" she said mildly, though could not conceal the jump in her throat. "I shall be sure to ask him later."

"I am certain you will."

Liadan raised her hands. *This is foolishness,* she signed. *The feast still needs food, and we have wasted enough time. Take your bickering elsewhere.*

Eir once again swept her eyes over me, and it felt as if I were a sow being appraised for market.

"Invited or not, you are a wreck," she told me. "You reek of mead and your clothes are filthy. Is this how you honor the marriage of the Jarl's eldest son? Is this how you honor me?"

I scoffed. "Spare me your false outrage. Not all of us have the wonderful privilege of new dresses, fine jewelry, and a wealthy husband."

"No, some of us only have the privilege of walking through Dyflin as free women."

My breath caught. "*Free?*" I snarled. "You would say that to me? After what I've lost?"

Eir raised her chin. "What you've lost, Gyda? Tell me, exactly what would that be?"

I closed the distance between us in a moment and slapped her.

She gave a small gasp. The imprint of my hand revealed itself instantly, red as the coals in the fire on her white cheek.

"By all the gods!"

Hákon emerged from the dark like a *draugr,* red-faced and seething. Four oath-men arrived on his heels and the women scattered in terror.

"You would strike my wife?" he roared. The sharpness of his cheekbones cut through his skin as he advanced. "How dare you strike her? At our wedding feast! Your audacity and shamelessness ends now!"

Hákon shoved me back. His height and force were overwhelming. But I would not be a snared rabbit. Though my heart thundered, I planted my feet and met his anger.

"Fuck off, Hákon," I snarled. "This has nothing to do with you. Go back to your father and cry for more of his favors. Lap up his piss and wipe his arse. Did your mother never teach you to be your own man?"

Sputtering and puffing, Hákon recoiled and I braced, waiting for him to strike at me.

But then a slender hand covered Hákon's, and in an instant, he relaxed.

"I am well, husband," she said softly, though her gaze was on me. "No harm was done. This woman is not herself, and I provoked her. But she did defend Liadan from attack, and that is to her credit."

Hákon turned to Eir and touched her face, his gentleness a stark contrast to the way he'd handled me. He studied the mark on her cheek.

"Provoked or not, I would not have you mistreated so." He offered his hand and she took it with a smile.

I gaped at them, at their ease with each other. The way Hákon stared at her, like a man marvels at the rise of the sun. Did he actually *love* Eir? And did she welcome it? The thought made me want to shriek with laughter, or vomit.

"*This woman* awaits your judgment," I said caustically. "Poor, drunken wretch that I am."

Hákon raised his brows at Eir and inclined his head.

"You are no longer welcome here, Gyda," she said coldly. "Leave, and do not dare show your face to me for a good while, or I will return that strike tenfold."

"I'll leave and be glad of it," I shot back.

A scuffle within the cluster of warriors and women drew our attention.

"Let me through!" A teenager shoved into the circle of firelight, pale and panting. "The Jarl requires your presence, Lord," he wheezed to Hákon. "There's been a fire at Jarl's Quay. He will question the merchant now."

Stunned silence followed these words.

My belly writhed like a snake. If I ran now, Hákon's oath-men would be on me in an instant. But if I was quiet and careful, I could find Ruarc and slip away quietly when their attention was elsewhere. He and I could be safely in our beds before dawn.

I backed away slowly.

But then Eir lunged for my arm and pulled me forward.

"We will come with you, husband," she said. "All of us."

Liadan had chosen to remain behind, and so the rest of us followed the pale, skinny youth through a side-door set under the eaves of the back-side of the hall. Hákon and Eir went through first. I followed them, and the oath-men followed me.

We arranged ourselves inside the entryway, which served as one of the many alcoves lining the walls. This one was nearest to the Jarl's platform and gave us the advantage of observing everything without ourselves being observed by the bulk of the crowd.

The celebration was dead, of course. From the quiet whispers and the swaying of the guests, we'd missed nothing.

"It seems he hasn't announced it yet," Hákon murmured, and Eir nodded. Her face was bloodless as she stared at Olavi.

The Jarl of Dyflin stood on the platform alone, stern like a prow-beast and with forearms trembling as he leaned on the table. The high seat had toppled behind him, spilling its fine silks and furs across the boards of the platform. He was staring, eyes hard like coals, at a man that had placed himself between the platform and the long hearth running down the center of the hall.

The threat of fire meant many things in a settlement the size of Dyflin. Even a simple blaze could erupt into widespread destruction. Far beyond the loss of homes, livelihoods, and animals, fire brought death. I had only burnt a single *byrding*, but seeing Olavi's thunderous expression, it might as well have been half of Dyflin's storehouses.

The object of his anger had his hands clasped tightly in front of him and his shoulders bunched up by his ears. The man wore a fine woolen tunic, loose trews, and a waxed sea-cloak slung jauntily over his right shoulder. He was clearly a merchant, and a very frightened one at that.

I fought the smirk pulling my mouth. Rising on my toes, I looked across the sea of guests. Pale, red-eyed faces watched Olavi, anxious for him to master himself and speak. Quiet whispers rippled across the rows of tables. I couldn't see Ruarc among them. Had he fled? How much did Olavi know? And where were the rest of the *byrding's* crewmen?

"We should be with him," Eir whispered, and Hákon started, then cleared his throat.

"Father, what is the news?" he said, striding forward out of the shelter of the alcove.

People turned to stare, and then parted as he and Eir approached the platform together. I remained where I was, resenting the lurking presence of the oath-men behind me. I couldn't slip away now.

Olavi shook himself. "Ah, Hákon. And Eir, my daughter-in-law. Come and sit. We are about to hear what this man has brought us. Such auspicious news for a wedding feast."

Under the Jarl's venomous gaze, the man wrung his hands. Sweat ringed his armpits and made his forehead shine.

Hákon and Eir climbed the steps. Hákon lifted his father's damaged chair without a word, and Eir gathered the fallen silks. She handed them to a serving girl, who took them with a bob of her head before vanishing through the antechamber's doorway.

Once all was put right, Olavi waved a ringed hand at the merchant. "Speak, man, so we may all hear it."

Trembling, the man raised his chin. Soot streaked his face and beard. When he spoke, his voice was hoarse. "There was a fire, Lord. At Jarl's Quay."

There were gasps across the hall, and cries of fear from those who lived or worked in the area. Olavi raised his hands, jeweled rings winking in the firelight, and they quieted.

"A fire of what kind," he rumbled. "And does it still burn?"

The merchant shifted from one foot to the other. "We…we managed to douse it before it spread too far."

"What is the damage? Tell us, man," called one of the guests near the front, and his table-mates echoed it.

"Two *byrdings* and the storehouse have been lost," he said.

"The storehouse as well?" Hákon said, frowning behind his beard.

"Yes, Lord *Stáli,* though we did what we could," the merchant responded.

He wouldn't meet Hákon's eye, which displeased Hákon. His frown turned to a scowl.

I swayed on my feet, still dense with ale. To my reckoning, there was no evidence to incriminate me. The foolish boy who had taken Ruarc's silver brooch had probably lost or spent it, and now found himself clutching a skin of ale and sleeping in the embrace of a warm body. By morning, he'd have forgotten everything.

I had no reason to worry. None at all.

"The storehouse stands away from the water," Eir pointed out. "It shouldn't have burned at all."

"How did this happen?" growled Olavi. A muscle below his right eye twitched. "Did you not set a watchman? Where are the rest of your crew?"

"My Jarl, the men have been at sea for weeks," said the merchant. "I sent them into town to rest."

"You sent all of them?"

"No, Lord," the merchant said quickly. He wiped sweat from his temple. "I kept my five best men with me. We went to find a meal and left the last man behind to watch the quay. When we returned, the turd was gone, and fire had already taken one ship."

"Strip the fool and beat him," rumbled a man named Bragi Arse-Nose, who sat on a front bench.

Bragi fancied himself the Jarl's champion, second only to Hákon. Had he the notion, he could have reached over and beat the merchant himself without even getting up. But he was lazy, and his companions knew it. They rattled their cups to egg him on, suggesting worse things he could do.

"We were short-handed," protested the merchant. "Nothing like this has ever happened before!"

Other tables took up Bragi's threat, growing loud enough that Hákon pounded the table and called for quiet.

I covered a smile with my hand. This was unfolding better than I'd hoped. The merchant's failure was worse than a simple shirking of duty. Aside from the cost of the goods, he now owed Olavi the loss of those two ships as well as the contents of the storehouse. Had it been his own ships and goods, he could have saved face by calling the fire an accident. It would likely be a grave blow to his silver-hoard, but he might recover, as long as he kept business flowing.

But losing a patron's trust? Well, the merchant's reputation might never escape the shame of that. He would lose all standing among the other traders. Certainly, Olavi would find it difficult to find another one who was willing to take his chances without significant compensation.

My satisfaction grew as bright red smudges appeared in Olavi's cheeks.

"You idiot," he snarled. "Why didn't you send a rider for help? There are plenty here who would have come."

"The man was too busy humping the ale-wife," Bragi hollered, and even those sitting on the back benches laughed at this.

The merchant's hands flexed. With public opinion turning against him so quickly, he would drown in the mockery if he didn't defend himself. So he drew himself up, puffing out his chest and holding Olavi's gaze. But there was a tremor in his chin which betrayed his feigned bravery.

"There was no time to send for help, Lord. A scrap of sail must have blown on the wind and caught in the thatching. The ships were too far gone, so we left them to douse the storehouse. If we had stopped to send a message, the fire would have spread to the houses behind the wall. We did what we could."

I made a sound of derision, but hastily covered it with a cough. What was this arse-licker's game? Even if the storehouse had burned to the shingle, there would have been no danger to the houses. Was he trying to make the Jarl angrier?

Hákon caught my reaction. He frowned, and whatever he saw in my expression made him reach for Eir's hand. He bent to her, whispering, and confusion spread over her face. She turned to study me. I pretended not to notice.

"The whoreson doesn't respect you, Lord," Bragi called. Knuckling his nose, which was split nastily from between the nostrils to the bridge, he pushed up from his bench. Once there, he tottered, oblivious to the snickers of his friends.

"How's about I teach him some manners, eh," he slurred. "Been a while since we've had any blood sport in the hall."

He lurched for the merchant, who gave a high-pitched scream, and for a moment I thought the merchant would piss himself right there, in front of everyone.

But then Olavi cursed and stood. "Will someone get this drunken, stinking fart out of my hall," he roared.

Two stout oath-men shoved past me, and Bragi barely had time to register that it was *his* farting arse they were after. He blinked stupidly as they reached for him.

"Wait," he protested, hands up. "You lads can't take me, I've got a right to be here!"

They grabbed Bragi by the arms and hauled him back. He thrashed, and the friends who had cheered him on now hunched lower on their benches, refusing to look at him or answer his bleating for their help.

The oath-men got about halfway down the length of the hall before Bragi chose to do the stupidest thing he could have done. With one mighty shove, he flung the man clinging to his right arm into a bench. The woman sitting on it screamed, diving out of the way just as the man went over it. With his arm free, Bragi twisted, grabbing an eating knife off the corner of the table. He slashed the other man, howling some incoherent insult.

Blood soaked the oath-man's tunic sleeve and he released Bragi's other arm. "You fucking worm!"

Bragi, still clutching the knife, teetered precariously, then ultimately lost his balance and fell on his arse. He sat blinking up at the wounded oath-man.

"Fucking told you," he slurred. "I've got the right to be here."

And then he gave a loud belch, rolled his eyes up in his head, and fell back, thumping his skull against the wooden planking.

No one said anything for the span of a breath. And then the Jarl broke the silence. "Borr, bring me that shit-heap's nose."

"Yes, Lord," said Borr, pressing a hand against his wound and wincing.

Hushed curses and protests cut through the thick air, and Olavi smacked the table. "Be quiet!" he bellowed. "This is what he gets for shoving that ugly arse-hole of a face into my business!"

The protests died.

Exchanging uneasy glances, the oath-men arranged themselves. Borr's companion held Bragi down by the shoulders while Borr himself took up the knife that bit him and used it to slice through the remaining gristle of Bragi's mutilated nose. Lucky for Bragi, he was too far gone to realize it. Two more oath-men came forward and dragged his senseless carcass out the main doors. His head lolled and streamed blood and snot the whole way.

The hall remained deadly silent as Borr brought the Jarl his prize. He left the thing on the table, a gory lump of flesh that turned even Hákon a shade of green.

This was Olavi Sharp-Spear, the Jarl of Dyflin, and his wrath had been stirred.

Sitting again, his black eyes flashed with fire and his teeth ground as he weighed his next words.

"No more weaseling," he gnarred at the merchant, who was now as pale and terrified as a snared shrew. "Tell me the rest now, or I'll reconsider Arse-Nose's proposal to beat you."

The man clutched the ends of his sea-cloak, wringing it in his hands as he sought for some excuse. "Ah—my Jarl, that is—fire such as this could not have been caused by a stray ember or fallen oil lamp. It could only have been set."

Olavi glowered. "You mean to say that this blaze was purposeful?"

The merchant didn't bother to hide his relief. He bounced on his toes and nodded. "Yes, my Jarl. This was surely no accident."

Olavi rose again. "Who," he bellowed. "What whoreson would dare?"

Several guests, drowsy from the ale and the fog of hearth-smoke, startled on their benches. Even I flinched a little.

"It must have been the Irish," the merchant said brightly, too far gone to realize the danger of his words. "Yes, yes. The Irish set it! They must be jealous of your good fortune, Lord. Hákon *Stáli* is not loved among them."

You fucking fool, I thought, and the hall exploded.

Screams and protests hurled over the tables. Those who were Irish suddenly found themselves under the scrutiny of their Norse fellows. Too much ale and mead turned a hall of mirth to a brawl of bitterness. Suspicion turned to insults, then to spitting, then to smashing fists and broken teeth. Women screamed as their husbands lunged for each other with eating knives.

Fear, sharp and acrid, coated my tongue. Without my seax and as drunk as I still was, I was defenseless. Heart in my throat and thoughts spinning, I clung to a post in the midst of the chaos. This was not what I'd wanted. How did the burning of one troll-cursed boat warrant this?

An elbow struck me in the back, breaking my hold on the post and making me stumble. The rest of Hákon's oath-men surged forward, spreading into a line across the width of the platform with axes and spears brandished to keep the riot away. The merchant was gone, cleverly vanishing into the fray before anyone remembered the Jarl was angry with him.

On the platform itself, Hákon and Olavi both roared their orders. Both went unheard.

I backed away, realizing that the side-door was left unguarded. I could slip through and be back in Dyflin before Olavi even knew I'd been here.

But before I could put my hand to the latch, a flurry of movement on the far side of the hall caught my attention. From a shadowed alcove hung with a heavy drape, a man stumbled out. He was badly disheveled and sporting a blackened eye.

"Ruarc," I called, waving, but the distance was too great for him to hear above the noise of the fighting.

On his heels, another man emerged, fists balled and jaw set. He grabbed Ruarc's shoulder and spun him. Ruarc mouthed something, palms out, wincing as the man screamed something back.

Horror and realization struck.

Ruarc could be blamed for the fire. All these people knew his business in Dyflin. Every day, he dealt with the merchants and craftsmen. He oversaw trade of food and material goods with the surrounding settlements and the imports from the hinterlands into Dyflin's markets. And his father had been an Irish lord. Many of the warriors knew that, and had likely fought in battle against his cohorts.

Worse than all of that, I realized, was that Ruarc and I had both been seen near the quays today.

The man, a stranger, hauled back his fist and drove it into Ruarc's belly. Ruarc doubled over, coughing and spitting.

Fuck. Fuck!

Who was that man? Had Ruarc tried something in the alcove, and found that he'd chosen the wrong man? What if he accused Ruarc of inappropriate, unmanly advances? What if he knew Ruarc's origins and drew the attention of the Jarl?

I went cold at the thought. Ruarc would suffer, or even be killed, because of who he was and who he associated with.

I lurched for the platform, thoughts racing for something to say, anything that might save us both.

Hákon caught sight of me, and followed my gaze to Ruarc. He shifted in his seat, muscles bunching as he scowled. Eir pressed against his arm, lips moving urgently, but he shook her off and stood to gain his father's attention.

No time. I had to stop this.

"I did it," I hollered. Practiced from years of screaming over howling winds and rough seas, my voice carried. "I burned the ships. It was me, Olavi!"

Olavi, Hákon, and Eir all turned to me.

"Enough of this," the Jarl bayed over the crowd. He pounded the table, jeweled rings leaving gouges in the wood. "I said *quiet,* you fucking bastards! Shut your ale-holes and sit down!"

The line of oath-men fanned out at a gesture from Hákon, and within moments the yelling and fighting tapered off. Blood-smeared men grudgingly took their seats, nursing split knuckles and broken noses, but respecting the sharp iron of the oath-men's seaxes and spear-heads.

I cut my eyes to Ruarc. The stranger had Ruarc's upper arm clamped in a tight grip. Ruarc was ashen. He shook his head at me, but I did not acknowledge it.

"What did you say?" Olavi demanded.

I wasn't sober, not entirely, but the ale-dream had finally lifted. I gathered my courage and squared my shoulders. "I said I set the fire, Olavi."

The hall went as still as a barrow-mound.

Hákon had taken his seat again. His hands were tight fists on the table. Eir refused to meet my eyes.

To my surprise, Olavi grunted, then sat heavily in his chair. His skin took on a gray cast. "*You?*" he rasped. "You would do such a thing?"

I floundered. Now that I had confessed, I had no idea what else to say. And I had not expected such a reaction.

"I set fire to a single *byrding,*" I said hesitantly. "If I had known the flame would spread, I never would have done it."

His broad face, so familiar to me from the span of years, showed genuine astonishment. Betrayal, too, and denial. Like a small boy whose friends had left him in the woods to find his own way back.

"Why, Gyda?" he said. "Speak."

If I were clever, I could turn this around. It was a risky path, but taking it could give me something of what I needed. What I *deserved*. I just needed to tread lightly.

I took a steadying breath, then spoke, letting my voice carry over the reeking air. "What sort of Jarl treats his foster brother's wife with such dishonor?" I began. "Jarl Olavi, I did this because you have left me with *nothing*. You took my life and my honor from me. I would take them back."

His black eyes widened.

"Why do you let her spew her bile, Lord?" a man behind me groused, and his companion rattled his cup in agreement.

"Throw the troll-bitch out of here before she fills our ears with it," he said.

"I said *silence*, you fucking pus-pukes!" Hákon barked, and the men shut their mouths.

The Jarl nodded stiffly at me.

"When I followed you to Dyflin years ago," I said. "I had a warrior as a husband. Jörund was a valiant man. Many oath-men here remember him. But he grew soft and died a straw-death. I am alone. I have no sons to provide for me. No father or mother to return to. Every woman here knows and fears the consequences of widowhood."

Olavi clutched his mead-cup and a thrall rushed forward to fill it. "Get to the point, woman," he said. "This is not about my brother."

"You're right," I said, forcing a smile. "This is about your failure to care for the people you claim to love. This is about your loss of honor."

Uneasy whispers passed through the crowd.

"That is a serious claim," Olavi growled, his heavy brows furrowing.

I lifted my chin. I had to be clear. I had to be strong. I had to be canny.

"How can you call yourself protector of Dyflin when the lowest of your people cannot trust you to defend them? How can we trust you to fight for us when you strip us of dignity and property? How can we swear loyalty to you when you show no loyalty to those whose blood and toil built your reputation? You are powerful and wealthy. A great Jarl. But how can you call yourself worthy of that leadership?"

"You speak goat-shit, woman!" Hákon burst out. "How *dare* you?"

I waited. This was as direct a challenge as I could ever make, and what the Jarl said now would shift opinion regardless of how he answered. Helgi's death had not been mentioned, but Olavi knew I could reveal the true nature of that business to all present. His shame would be revealed, and that meant I held more power in this moment than he did. The only question: What would he do, knowing it?

Shifting in his great seat, Jarl Olavi made a ponderous noise. Then, very slowly, he leaned forward and clasped his hands on the table. His gaze was direct and cold, and this change of manner made me wary.

"Tell me, Gyda," he said. "Did you burn my ships and my storehouse because you wanted to provoke me? Let us speak plainly. This is because of the loss of your ship, isn't it? Harassing my merchants wasn't enough for you, eh? You had to cut me like you think I cut you."

"Answer my charge, Jarl," I barked. "I am deprived of my property, and you prevent me from seeking it. You call it harassment, but what choice do I have? I beg for scraps of news from every piss-soaked sailor that passes through Dyflin. I spent what little silver I had paying for a mountain of shit and lies!" I paused and pointed at Hákon. "Just today, you sent your favorite errand dog to kick me further into the mud. Jarl Olavi, your neglect has stolen my livelihood and my reputation. I have nothing to my name but what my anger can give me."

"Gyda Eyvindsdóttir, you are a fucking liar," Eir called out.

I stiffened.

Eir leaned forward, piercing me with her glare. "I have said nothing before now, but I cannot remain silent in light of this. It is not your ship you search for, but the silver hoard within its hold. A sum you gained for your aid to Ragnar Grettisson, whom you saved by killing Helgi."

Her words fell like molten iron over sand. Cries of outrage rose across the benches. Those who knew Helgi, who had fought with him and rowed shoulder-to-shoulder with him, called for my death. Others demanded my removal. My injury. My imprisonment.

I faltered. *Damn you, Eir!* With her words, I couldn't use Helgi's death as a pawn now. Anything I said about it would be seen as a lie, a spiteful attack against a grieving father and brother.

Anxiously, I searched for Ruarc, but didn't see him. The man from the alcove was also gone. I hoped Ruarc had slipped away and left the hall.

"You are faithless," Eir spat at me. "An oath-breaker." She was standing now, face twisted and red. Her words struck me like stones, one after another. "Silver-struck troll-wife. Untrustworthy and forsworn friend. *Betrayer*."

Spent of breath, she fell back and Hákon put his arm around her.

I stood stunned, unable to respond.

"Does she speak true?" Olavi said, low and dangerous. "By the gods, if you lie to me now, there is nothing that can shield you from my wrath."

"I gained nothing from the death of your son," I said, choosing my words carefully. "You know the truth of how and why Helgi died. As declared by Hákon *Stáli,* I am absolved of his death and the circumstances of it."

There was a deadly calm behind the Jarl's eyes. "And this silver she speaks of?"

"Only a payment," I said. "Promised to Rán's Daughters in exchange for Ragnar's passage to Iceland. He paid it only once he secured your trade agreement with the Emir of Córdoba. A duty *you* commissioned, Olavi. Ragnar fulfilled that deal, evidenced by the exports of silks and finery that now decorate your hall."

"Ragnar Grettisson was unable to corroborate this story when we encountered the *Fiskwif* and her crew," Hákon pointed out. "He has not been seen or heard from since."

"That is because Uffe Shit-Face claimed he killed him," I cried. "Where is that whoreson? I still owe him for that."

"Keep your tongue still, woman," Olavi snarled. "Hákon, how can we know any of this is the truth?"

"Gyda does speak true," Eir said. She had regained her usual composure, though her cheeks were ashen. "You know that Ragnar was a man of honor, despite the false accusations against him. The freedwoman Liadan can attest to his integrity, as can our other crewmates, though they now reside outside of Dyflin."

"I had wondered," Hákon said, turning baleful eyes on me. "What made you throw off your women, your purported Daughters, for a ship, and not even a decent one? Now, it is clear to me." Disgust wrote itself over his face, and it hurt me almost as much as Eir's matching expression.

"Don't pretend your hands don't reek of shit," I hissed. "You forced me into that choice."

Olavi cleared his throat and leaned back. "I must commend you, *Fiskwif*. Loki himself could never match your schemes for cunning and guile."

"It was never a scheme," I protested. "Only business."

The gambit was failing; my heart thumped painfully and a cold sweat coated my skin. I had risked too much this time.

The Jarl tented his fingers and stared at me over them. "*Sea-Wolf* is gone. That payment of Ragnar's is long since spent, or sunk. Such is the way of things. It was a fruitless pursuit from the moment the thief touched the tiller."

"You took everything else!" I cried. "What else could I do?"

"I took nothing," he replied calmly. "I simply gave you choices. Choices you made and cannot blame anyone else for."

"They were never choices. They were curses! Cruel tricks by a cruel man."

"You had your *life*!" Olavi bellowed. "You had my protection, my forgiveness. We welcomed you *home*, and you pissed on my mercy and set it ablaze like my ships and my storehouse. You could have burnt down Dyflin and killed its citizens, all for your fucking pride!"

I spat in the dirt, and the oath-men next to the platform hissed and lurched forward, hands tightening on spear-hafts, halting only because Hákon ordered them back.

"You forget yourself, Gyda," the Jarl said. His voice carried something dark. "I see now that I have given you far greater freedom than you deserved. I held you above other traders, placed you in greater esteem than the sons of kings. And still, you flaunt your spite. But you must remember: I am still the one that holds your fate in my hand." He stood and made a fist.

"Tell me, Gyda, have I not been generous? Have I ever, in all your years of service to me, required an oath from you? No? Well, I shall bear the consequence for this folly every time I look into the faces of my sons and remember one is missing. I have given you much, woman, because of the love I bore for Jörund, my foster-brother. But no more."

Desperation overtook me. I was beyond caring now. All I had left was ambition and gall. And the advantage of knowing what Olavi wanted most from the world. "Give me another ship, then," I blurted. "I brought you wealth before, Olavi. I can bring it again. You know my worth, and I will prove it to you. Let me swear loyalty to you. I will swear any oath you set before me. Only let me have a purpose again. Please, Olavi."

That brought another wave of anger and outcry. The Jarl looked over his people, black eyes darting from person to person. His brows drew together and he returned his gaze to me.

Of course, I knew what I demanded was impossible. I had no right to ask for anything. But I had no other way forward. It was this, or die.

Slowly, I knelt on the packed earth before the long hearth.

"I will swear an oath," I said, raising my voice over the howling crowd. "I will swear it like a man swears, pledging my life for yours. I will bring you wealth, great Jarl. I will bring you renown. I will bring you reputation, greater than before. Only let me prove it."

Olavi stared at me. The silence was heavy. My breath came in shallow gasps.

"Gyda Eyvindsdóttir," he said. "*Fiskwif* of the muddy roads. Widow of my foster brother. From this moment, you are outlawed from Dyflin."

My breath left me. "*What?*"

"You are to leave this place," he announced. "You have burned my ships, destroyed my food and property. You have harassed my merchants and terrorized my people. You have put Dyflin in danger. This is unacceptable, and I will not tolerate your presence any longer."

The smoke and heat pressed in, squeezing my bones like iron bands.

"There is a ship departing in the morning," the Jarl said. "Wherever you skulk off to, do what you will. Die. Live. I don't care. This will be my final dealing with you. If I ever see your face in Dyflin again, or anywhere in this world, I will kill you. This is the final mercy I offer you. Get out, and may Loki take you."

With that, Olavi sat, waved two spear-men forward, and watched without expression as I was taken by the arms and dragged from the hall.

CHAPTER THIRTEEN

The next morning brought a freezing dawn. The rain had returned.

I lay awake again, staring at the crack in the wall. I covered it with my hand. The length of it went past my middle finger.

Whose hands would repair it now? Whose feet would pack the earth around the fire? Who would take down Jörund's rusted axe and hang their own? Would they raise children here? Would they be happy?

The rooster crowed and I rose, numb in my bones and empty in my head.

The creak of my door announced an arrival as I packed the last of my possessions in my sea-chest.

"Ruarc, if you're here to see me off, please just leave."

"I am not Ruarc," Eir answered. "I wouldn't even know where to find him on a morning like this."

The bone comb in my hand snapped. I turned slowly, holding its pieces.

Eir showed me her empty palms. "Before you strike me, I wish to speak, and to leave you something."

I dropped the broken comb on the floor and turned back to my task. "Get out."

She sighed. "So you want to play it that way. Fine. You are welcome to ignore my presence. But be assured, I did not come to fight."

"Did Olavi send you to see me off?" I said nastily. "Don't bother. Tell him I already left. He must be anxious."

"I came for myself."

"Hmph."

Eir clicked her tongue. "I'm here because I wanted to apologize. I spoke in anger last night, and I don't wish to part with these words still between us."

I grit my teeth. I wanted to respond with something scathing, something that would take the skin off her. Instead I chose to keep my back turned. Let her make her shit-brained apology, it made little difference.

"I imagine you're as hungover as Thor," she went on. "So I will not linger. You have a ship to catch, after all."

The rain was loud on the thatching. Though the sun had not yet fully risen, I needed to get ahead of the bad weather. It was late in the season to be making a journey to Jórvík. Sailing around the Isles was treacherous at any time, but now, there could be ice fields, or gales worse than the one that had blown *Sea-Wolf* to the shores of al-Andalus.

"Speak what you came for, if you have to," I grunted. "And then leave me the fuck alone."

She snorted. "You know, I wish I could. Leave you alone, I mean. But I never could. I never could leave you, Gyda. And even now, I am here, after everything, still not leaving you. Will you at least look at me?"

With a muttered curse, I turned to face her.

Eir appeared much the same as the night before, if not a little tired. Her gray eyes had circles beneath them, but her cheeks bore the flush of a newlywed. Her dress was simple today, none of the silk weaving or fine jewelry, and none of the blood spatter. A kerchief of bleached linen covered her golden hair. Her cloak dripped on the packed earth, turning it dark.

Unclasping her bronze brooch, she hung the cloak on a peg near the hearth to dry.

"You look well," I said, and we both heard my insincerity.

"I look like the wife of a jarl's son," she replied.

We remained silent for several moments.

She bent, righting the stool I had thrown at Ruarc only yesterday, and settled herself on it with a deep sigh. "It was a good thing you did, helping Liadan last night."

"She didn't need my help."

"No," she assented, tilting her head. "But it was still kind of you to step in."

"And why wouldn't I have?"

Eir held my gaze and said nothing. I looked away first.

"You said you brought something?"

"Ah, yes," she said. From a fold of her cloak she brought forth a pouch that clinked musically. She placed it on the table. "Silver. For your journey."

I turned away. "I don't want that. Get out."

"Don't be a fool, Gyda."

"I'd rather have a pig shit in my shoe."

"Do you think I wanted this for you?" Her voice was strained. "Let me help. It's all I can do."

"Keep your pity."

She laughed at this. "You think I *pity* you, Gyda? Gods, you are worse off than I thought."

"Spit your venom or swallow it, Eir," I bit out. My cheeks burned. "I don't care what you came for. Go back to your new husband. Give back the silver and tell him to tuck it into his arse-hole."

"Would it help if I told you Hákon doesn't know I'm giving this to you?"

"Lying to him already? How honorable of you. What a happy marriage you've made for yourself."

Eir shrugged and ran a hand over the end of her braid. "We must all do what we can to survive," she said. "Not that my marriage is any of your business, but Hákon is a good man. I *chose* my happiness with him. He won't miss this silver, and I'll have done my duty to you."

A bitter smile curled my lip. "Duty. If that is what you want to call it. I would call this irony."

That tightened her jaw. "Don't goad me. Not now. I came here out of kindness, not for any other reason."

"Kindness," I scoffed. "You sound like a Christ-wife."

"Would you shut your mouth for once in your life!" She hit the table with her open palm, and the raw emotion, so uncommon for her to display, silenced me.

"I came to tell you that I would have supported you last night," she said. "If you had come to me, I would have interceded for you. Olavi owes all of us his care and generosity, as any ring-giver would.

He ignores your need because he still grieves Helgi. I understand it, but you were right to confront him."

"Fuck your support," I hissed. "That smug goat-fucking *bak-rauf* is your husband's father, Eir. Remember that. He may be smiles and charm now, but step outside his bidding and he'll nail your tits to *Dreki's* hull."

She was unfazed. The stool creaked under her as she regarded me. "You were wrong, Gyda, burning that ship," she said. "But the action was entirely authentic to who you are. Vindictive. Short-sighted. But I know you didn't mean for anything worse to happen." She paused and softened. Dipping her head, she picked at a loose piece of skin by her thumb. "It's rather remarkable," she said, more to herself than to me. "I used to envy your ability to be that bold. Maybe I still do."

"It wasn't boldness or vindictiveness," I said stiffly. "It was necessary."

She smoothed her dress over her knees. "Yes, that is what you tell yourself, isn't it? Will you say that to the family of that merchant? They may starve this winter."

Every sinew in me wanted to shake her, to make her understand. "My aim was not to hurt anyone," I said. "I only wanted to—"

Eir stood. "I know. Your actions are never *aimed* at anyone. They're only self-serving, and the collateral doesn't matter."

I hated the tears burning my eyes. I swiped them away. "What should I have done?" I said, voice thick. "Sat here in the mud and the shit and waited to die and be forgotten? Should I have gone back to selling fish, back to scraping scales and blood from my palms the rest of my life? Because I would rather have drowned, Eir. I would rather have my corpse torn apart by the World-Serpent than spend one more moment—"

She cut me off again, raising her hand. "One more moment without your ship."

I fell silent.

"This isn't about *Sea-Wolf*, though," she said. "It's about your love of wealth over all else. Your independence. Your notions of reputation and glory. You hate the trammel of what is expected of you, so you run from any reminder that you are a woman in a world that demands your submission. It hates you for your very being, Gyda, and you cannot abide its limits."

"Does our world not hate you as well?" I said. My throat ached. "Were we not sisters, the two of us? Facing the world together and shaking our fists?"

"We *were* sisters, Gyda." Her gray eyes glistened. "And that is why I cannot understand. All of this—" she swept her hand around her. "—is because of your own choices. You abandoned your family, the very ones who stood beside you with our own fists raised. Why would you choose anything but us?"

I had no answer, and any bluster I might dredge up would only serve to prove her right.

It had all been straightforward in my head: all my reasons, my feelings, my belief that my decision was the best for all of us, and that Rán's Daughters could come back together once Olavi's anger had boiled away in time. My reasons were valid and uncomplicated, and I'd held tightly to them. But laid bare like this before Eir, I could not deny that she spoke the truth. As she always did.

All of what I had done was as worthless as my husband's rusted axe on the wall.

"I need to catch my ship," I said.

Eir retrieved her cloak and fastened it around her shoulders. The pouch she left on the table.

"Use the silver, please," she said. "Make a new life. I wish you happiness."

Turning, she opened the door. A cold wind blew in. The rain was a sheet of lead behind her.

"Gyda, don't come back here," she whispered. "My heart couldn't bear it."

She shut the door, and I was alone.

PART THREE: JÓRVÍK

CHAPTER FOURTEEN

"How many?" I yelled at the man running at me down the alley.

"Twelve!" he called back.

I smacked the timber siding of the ale-house. "You sheep-brained ass! *Twelve?*"

Skidding on the paving stones, the man came to a full stop in front of me. "It was unavoidable," he panted, hands on knees.

"Thorstein, I swear by the gods I'll gut you if you get us killed."

He had no time to reply to that, because the first of his hunters appeared at the end of the alley. "He's over here!" he called, and his friends' shouting and curses grew louder, only one street over from us.

Thorstein choked. "Gods, they're fast."

Tugging open the back door of the ale-house, I grabbed him by the shoulder and shoved him through. "Go, now. Fucking run!"

Hearts pounding, feet flying, we tore through the kitchen, shoved past the crowded benches and open-mouthed ale-wives serving them, and streaked out the front door.

"Can't they get ahead of us from the alley?" gasped Thorstein, looking over his shoulder.

I was puffing just as hard as he was, but my legs were shorter, and so I kept my eyes forward to avoid tripping on the uneven road surface. "They'll have to climb the stone wall," I responded. "More likely they double back and go around. But run faster anyway!"

Our pursuers, if they had been foolish enough to follow us through the ale-house, would find it too tight a space for their numbers. The chaos we'd sparked on our flight would block their progress, at least for a little while.

"If they catch us, you won't need to gut me, I'll do it myself. It was a stupid mistake I made. Stupid."

"Tell me about it later," I panted.

We turned a corner, and three women carrying baskets for the market shrieked as we raced past.

Lucky for us, Jórvík was not like Dyflin. These streets were ancient, established in their patterns already. Founded by the Romans, the unmistakable marks of order and logic remained. It had taken me less than a week to memorize each and every turn of the old part of town, and the newer part was just as easy to navigate.

"Left!" I said.

Thorstein faltered, stared at me wild-eyed. "That goes to the Foss!"

"Just do it, boy," I screamed, then veered down a sloping track that left us with nowhere else to go but into the swirling, mud-darkened water.

Without waiting to see if he followed, I threw myself in feet-first.

The water was cold, *nasty* cold, and it assaulted me with silt and algae and decaying fish. It took everything in me to keep from gasping and drowning myself.

It had been only a week since winter's final frost thawed, leaving the waterways of Jórvík swollen with spring melt. The Foss and the Ouse cared little about warmer weather and did what they liked anyway. Right now, what the Foss liked was to freeze my bones and fill my nose with fetid, slimy water as it dragged me in its current. I kicked and broke the surface just before the tumult could smash me against a jutting timber dock. My fingers caught a post and I clung on hard.

"Ruarc," I yelled over the water. "Tell me you didn't drown, you clod!"

"I didn't drown," groaned a miserable, soggy, bedraggled bundle behind me. He had his arms around a broken stump, and I caught him by the strap of his belt before the current pulled him farther downstream.

"You are a true friend," he sputtered, wiping his eyes. "I hope you know that. Thank you, really. I needed a wash today."

I fought the urge to dunk him again.

He swiped his hand through his beard, dislodging a glob of snot. "Did we get away clean at least? Are they gone?"

I craned my neck, searching the bank. We had traveled only a short distance, but I saw no more than an old man and his wife pushing a wheelbarrow full of driftwood some yards away.

"They're gone. Probably running downstream to catch our corpses. We'd better keep out of that ale-house for a while."

He grunted. "And just as I'd made us some new friends. What a shame."

"Twelve, Ruarc? Really?" I said, releasing his belt to slap a palmful of water at him.

His crooked smile reappeared. "No doubt my guts are marked for nailing to the walls today."

We busied ourselves with getting out of the chilly water. The gray-haired couple gawped at us as we shivered and dripped and wrung out our tunics. I bared my teeth and snarled at them like a beast, and they blanched, hurrying on and clutching the crucifix amulets around their necks.

"Don't antagonize the locals," Ruarc chided. "You're already terrifying looking like a drowned rat. You don't need them thinking you're Devil-spawn too."

"I wasn't planning on getting soaked through today," I groused, twisting my hair into an algae-slimed knot. "Our shoes will need a good stretching when they dry, if they're even salvageable. We can't afford the leather to replace them."

Ruarc's teeth were chattering. "It isn't all bad," he said. Then he unfastened a soaked fabric pouch from his belt and let it sit in his palm like a leaden stone. He winked. "My winnings will more than cover what's needed."

"Ruarc, you fool," I said, patting his rosy cheek affectionately. "I should never have taught you to play *'tafl* so well. Next you'll cheat Loki, and then we'll really be fucked."

He tucked the pouch away and smiled shyly. "Don't say my name too loudly here."

I squeezed the last drops from the hem of my cloak and slung it over my shoulder. "Ah, stop fretting. No one from this quarter knows our faces from that of their favorite pig's," I said confidently. Though perhaps we were right to be wary.

Upon arriving in Jórvík at the onset of winter, he and I contrived a solution to an obvious predicament. Whereas my aging face was unremarkable and plain, much of the city still knew my name and reputation. I feared that lingering animosity from my former rivals in trade could turn into the exploitation of my poor luck. And so, to hinder this, Ruarc and I took on the roles of mother and son. He became Thorstein, a widowed fighter who put aside raiding to care for his ailing mother.

As Thorstein, he had the freedom to take charge of our circumstances without scrutiny. He procured us lodging and devised various ways to survive on what silver he could scrounge. Currently, his methods included gambling at the *'tafl* table, haggling in the markets, and an occasional scrape with those who found themselves mysteriously light on silver after crossing paths with him.

"Let's get back to the inn," he said. Then he plucked at his chest and his tunic came off his skin with a sucking *pop.* "I'm beginning to chafe. I'd like a dry change of clothes and a good meal before tonight."

He couldn't keep his eyes from crinkling as he said it, and my heart rose. "Ruarc, you brilliant bastard. You managed it?"

His wide grin was all mischief. "It wasn't just silver I took from those *bak-raufs*. I found myself a place in the king's fighting ring! Not a bad day after all, eh, Mother?"

Matching his smile, I took his arm and steered him up the dock and back onto the street. Our shoes squelched in tandem as we walked.

"Let's hope all my teaching managed to turn you into a half-decent fighter," I said. "You're going to need more than a handsome face and canny feet to get you into Sigtryggr's good graces."

His puffed-out chest deflated. "You can't ever let a person celebrate, can you?" he muttered.

"Never," I agreed.

CHAPTER FIFTEEN

On the morning of my exile, Ruarc had concealed himself in a sea-cloak and gone to the quays to board the longship leaving Dyflin. Hidden on the back bench and clutching an oar, he passed unnoticed. No one much cared or said a word against the addition of another strong back to pull us out of port. By the time I'd noticed him, we were too far out to sea to turn around.

After my initial fury subsided, Ruarc confessed he'd done it to escape his imminent marriage, and it appeared he'd nearly convinced himself of his own lie.

As for me, I felt simply grateful for his presence. Ruarc had kept me on my bench, holding my hand and becoming a lifeline as we sailed the coast of Alba and the storm-lashed Orkney Islands. Without him, I likely would have found myself in Rán's Hall, and it would not have been because of a storm.

Having him with me in Jórvík steadied me, kept me focused on my purpose. I ventured to hope I could provide the same for him.

"What is King Sigtryggr like?" Ruarc asked as we trudged up a street of newly built houses. They were well-constructed, sided with timber and arranged in neat rows. Some of the plots even sported domed ovens made of clay. Pale gray smoke rose from the gable openings and hung around like a pall on the thatched rooftops.

"You never met him in Dyflin?"

He shook his head. "Only saw him from a distance. Never spoke. My business is not with kings, it's with my people and our traders." A furrow appeared on his brow. "Or it was."

We walked a ways and I thought of what to tell him.

"Sigtryggr is a friend," I said finally. "If one can call a rangy, half-starved wolf a friend. He's a canny, savage bastard, but he has good humor. You'll impress him if you fight with your brain as well as your blade."

"No one's ever called me a clever man," Ruarc said gloomily. "I'm going to lose, aren't I?"

I stepped around a steaming pile of sheep's dung. "Did I say you had to be clever? You don't even need to win, boy. Just make him take notice. That's all we need."

Ruarc's face twisted. "If he is a friend, why can we not talk to him directly? Why go through this to get his attention?"

"He doesn't do audiences," I said. "Even living here before, I met with him on two occasions only, and both were for business. Since this is personal, we need to be in as favorable a position as possible to have a chance."

"Even your schemes have schemes," Ruarc muttered.

"Don't sulk. It makes you sound like a tooth-sore brat."

"Say that again when I'm bleeding out at your feet."

Presently we came to a street teeming with people. The area was popular for its metal-work, leather-tanning, and artisan crafts. We followed the ebb and flow of the crowd, always keeping an eye open for Thorstein's new "friends".

The clank of hammers on anvils, the rasp of files against antler and bone, and the scraping of sharp-edged tools over strips of hide brought me a certain comfort. This was a day like any other, and business went on. People were buying and selling and shouting over each other, haggling for the best bargain. And none of them cared a bit for the pair of sodden outcasts walking between them.

"I'm going to need a *brynja,*" Ruarc said suddenly, and I had to laugh because the look he wore was like he'd swallowed a live eel.

"You're up against beardless and unblooded cock-sure bairns," I told him. "The only fights they've ever seen are brawls they start in the ale houses."

His neck swiveled as we passed a table laid out with shield bosses, whetstones, strap ends, and a myriad other odd bits. The trader brayed his prices to the crowd, revealing a broken and rotting set of teeth.

"You've already got the advantage of age," I said, pulling Ruarc along. "And you've had me training you, so that counts for something."

"It's a contest for the king's personal guard," he replied. "There are bound to be warriors of every age and merit. It's expected we bring our own kit. Certainly most of these lickspittles already had some fine weapons made."

"And most likely had the silver to pay for it, too. You won't be the only one needing to borrow a shield and a blade, so stop fretting. Focus on how you'll fight instead of what you'll use. Half the game is confidence and the other half is skill. Wearing a heavy *brynja* you're not familiar with will only slow you down."

"Thorstein is meant to be a raider. If I turn up with nothing at all, it'll draw the kind of attention we don't want. Suppose someone knows my face?"

I reached up and tapped his temple, shaved earlier this week and prickly with new growth. "Remember, boy, you're a stranger here. If anyone should be recognized, it is likely to be me. I lived here for a twelve-month."

"Ah, but you're an iron-faced woman with graying hair and scrawny limbs. No one cares who you are when they see a strapping young warrior next to you." He puffed out his chest in a pitiful show of sarcasm and bravado.

I grit my teeth. Nothing I said would stop his ruminating. Any more of this back and forth and he'd lose his nerve altogether.

What I could not tell him was that the idea of seeing Sigtryggr again made my stomach churn and my hands tremble. The king of Jórvík certainly had many qualities, but friendliness was not counted among them.

Even if Ruarc managed to put up a good fight, Sigtryggr might choose to ignore us altogether when he saw me. After all, Olavi was his ally, and I was just a disgraced and exiled trader.

"Wait here," I said, abruptly breaking away to approach the last stall on the street.

"What are you—," Ruarc started, but then trailed off into a frustrated curse.

The trader was an old man with a drooping face and dirty fingernails. He looked at me vacantly as I tipped out the pitiful contents of my coin fold.

"I'll take that string of beads, those smock-brooches, the three-lobed clasp, and if you have a pair of shoes, I'll have them too."

"Not got shoes," he said, scratching his neck. "But I've got some leg wraps." He bent down behind his table and lifted a scale, setting it on the scored wooden surface before turning to rummage in a crate.

"Just the beads and brooches then," I said. "And tell me, where I could get a *brynja*?"

He straightened, a little too quickly, clenching the scale weights in his hands. "A *brynja*?" he said, suspicion clouding his features as he looked me up and down. "Why would you even need one, woman? Thinking of fighting for the king today?" He hooted a laugh.

"Never mind that," I snapped. "I have silver. More than this. Coin and hack. Do you want it or not?"

He slapped the weights into one pan of the scale. "*Brynja* can be found across the way, but don't be expecting something shiny. Everything good is sold already to the fools who think they're getting a place in the king's shield wall. Anything you find will be a rusted piece of goat-shit, torn off some poor lad with no gut-rope in him to take to Valhöll."

"Goat-shit will work fine."

I counted out my silver, and he weighed it accordingly, muttering to himself. "Never heard of a woman needing a mail-shirt, by Thor's balls."

Dire warnings aside, his own wares were nothing to gape at. The brooches and clasp were cheap copper alloy that was bent and patched. The beads were clouded glass with no design, scratched and old. Secondhand, certainly. But I needed them to fit into the crowd tonight. I wanted to appear like the rest of the hearth-and-home women, the ones who made their lives in the streets and alleys and farming fields as best they could. They were respectable and strong in their own ways, survivors. And they were invisible to the elite. With my seax and my manner, I fit poorly everywhere I went, like a troll's foot in a child's shoe. But if I wore a simple smock and kirtle, I would be seen as something average. Something tame. And that might give me an advantage when I needed it most.

The drooping man wrapped the items in a sack of filthy linen and handed them over. I had overpaid, but the silver wasn't mine, after all. I thanked the man and moved away.

"What was that for?" Ruarc hissed when I rejoined him.

"Be quiet and give me your silver," I replied. "We're getting you a *brynja*."

We came to our current residence, a small tavern nestled amidst decaying storehouses and older dwellings. Because the place was shabby and out of the way, the beds were affordable. Better yet, the owner served hot meals from dawn until midnight.

There were two rooms for sleeping and one large common space with enough tables to service a great many more patrons than actually visited on any given day. Today was the exception. When Ruarc and I emerged in dry garments, all but one table had been taken by day laborers seeking shelter from the unpredictable spring rains.

"I'm going for a piss," Ruarc muttered. As he pushed his way through the crowd, I settled myself at the remaining table on the far wall. It had a cracked leg joint and wobbled, but it was better than no table at all. I relaxed into the drone of conversation and savored the aroma of the stew bubbling in the ale-wife's iron pot. Pork, I thought. A bit of luck at last.

I mulled over the upcoming fights, and what they might hold in store for us. Ruarc's *brynja* was indeed a rusty, horrible thing, and the rings needed repair in several places. It would have to do. He wore it over a thick wool tunic and belted it so that the weight sat on his waist instead of his shoulders. When he'd tried the awful thing on, he wore it as well as any man would for the first time, that is, with a grimace and a curse. He would be slow in the fight, but if he worried less, he might focus better.

Hild, the ale-wife, set two steaming bowls of stew and two cups of ale on the table, then propped her arm on her hip.

"Interesting company you keep," she said mildly.

"What company," I said, frowning.

She jerked her thumb at the open door. Ruarc was making his way over, dark spots from rain dappling his shoulders, but it wasn't him she meant; there was another man approaching from the street corner. He stopped just inside the entry and craned his scrawny neck to look over the crowd.

"He's an important whelp, that one," the ale-wife said. "Came here looking for your fine-looking son earlier. Wonder what he's after?"

She didn't bother hiding her hungry expression as she peered at me.

"You'll get no gossip from me, Hild," I said. "Go find it elsewhere before this crowd moves off and you're left to pick rat turds off the floor again."

She huffed and moved away as Ruarc sat and reached for his ale.

"We've got a visitor," I said.

Ruarc paused with his cup halfway to his mouth. "Who?"

"Thorstein!" The young man's eager voice reached us over the noise of the crowd and Ruarc hunched.

"Shit," he muttered. "That's the boy whose place I've taken."

"And he's not alone."

My stomach dropped to my feet, for behind the boy strode two burly men, taller than Ruarc and twice as broad. They carried short spears in gloved fists and wore matching iron helmets, fine *brynjur* and round shields strapped to their backs. Another man wearing the same placed himself at the door.

"Sigtryggr's oath-men," I said, then took a swig of ale.

"What do they want?"

"You, I expect."

Ruarc turned gray.

"Thorstein, I've been looking for you," the young man said with a wide smile. It was an expression that the men at his back did not share.

"If you're looking for me to give back your place in the fight, forget it, Harleif. Take up your grievance with your father. He's the one who gambled and lost it."

The boy was not that young by my reckoning, but the lamb-fuzz on his cheek could have fooled anyone into thinking he was five winters younger. In contrast to the fully-kitted warrior escort, he wore a simple linen tunic and trews, and bore no arm-ring, though his shoes and belt were finely tooled leather. He carried a lovely little knife with an antler handle on his belt. He was the son of someone wealthy, that was certain.

"Oh, no, you're welcome to it," he said, still smiling. "I never wanted to join the king's guard. My mother put me forward because she fancies him."

"Harleif, is it?" I creaked. "Are you a friend of my Thorstein?"

Ruarc winced.

Harleif turned and blinked owlishly, as if he'd just noticed me. "Oh, you are Thorstein's mother! Arnþrúður, right?"

"That's right." I showed a little more teeth in my smile than necessary. The other patrons were staring at us.

Harleif's smile faltered, but his bow was suitably formal. "I am Thorstein's friend, yes. He saved my life a few weeks ago. Got me out of a debt that would have me dancing skinless in front of the king's high seat."

He beamed at Ruarc, who slouched miserably.

"Did he now?" I said. "What a good lad he is. One of the king's men, he'll be!"

"You have a message, Harleif?" Ruarc growled. "We're eating and you interrupted."

The oath-men shifted their weight, the grip on their spears tightening.

"A little respect, goat-turd," rumbled the one on the left. He was missing part of his nostril and cheek, and the teeth showing through the plate of the helmet were very white.

"It's alright, Osvar, he means no harm," Harleif said. "But Thorstein, you're going to have to leave that stew and come with us."

I scowled. "And why is that, child? The fights are not until this evening."

"That may be so, but all entrants are required to meet in the ring. King Sigtryggr is working them over before they fight. Culling the ones he doesn't like the look of."

Ruarc gave me a panicked look, mouth flapping. "I am not prepared," he stammered.

"It isn't a choice," Harleif said ruefully. "You've got your mail on already, and you have me as an escort. The others are getting dragged there by the rest of the oath-men."

I eyed Osvar and his companion. "You'd better go with them, Thorstein," I said. "I'll follow along after."

The warriors took that as permission. Moving past Harleif, they clapped hands on Ruarc's shoulders and hauled him out of his seat as he sputtered protests and stared at me wild-eyed.

"You'll be fine, son," I told him, rising out of my chair. I moved forward and embraced him. In his ear, I whispered. "The king doesn't know your face. Confidence and skill."

I stepped back and nodded, and the oath-men marched him off. The stares of the tavern's guests followed.

I put a hand on Harleif's arm before he could go. "Who is your father, child? Would I know him?"

The young man flinched at my grip. "My father is a sworn man, a king's guard, and I am fostered in the royal household. Now I had better go. I give you my respect, Lady."

He bowed again and left, striding out the door into the gray afternoon.

CHAPTER SIXTEEN

Sigtryggr's fighting grounds stunk of beer, roasting meat, and blood.

It was long past sunset; torches and braziers cast plumes of pale smoke over the crowd. The fighting arena was a roped off square of packed dirt and straw in the center of the space, and it was surrounded on three sides by benches and tables. In the back right corner, away from the benches and the king's silk-canopied platform, a tent had been erected for the fighters to wait in between bouts. It was inside this tent where Ruarc and I found ourselves, patching up before the next round.

"You're doing fine," I told him, tugging on the hem of the *brynja*. "This is holding up rather well."

Ruarc touched a knuckle to his split lip. "That's six of them out," he said, "but have you seen the size of the spear-man? He's big as a mountain."

"Don't worry about Thrym," I said. "He's slow. Someone else will put him down before you get to him. Now, make sure to finish that ale. You'll be called back soon."

Ruarc's hands trembled as he tipped back his cup. "I don't know if I've got more in me. That last fight was too close. I was lucky to get in that last punch. Next time won't be so easy."

"Luck had nothing to do with it," I said, tightening his belt. "That boy was too concerned with waving his father's sword about than actually using it. Your instincts were good."

He wrinkled his nose and looked away. His right eyebrow sported a swelling, red welt underneath it. "All I did was dance around. It's not enough to get the king's attention. He's bored. This is fruitless."

I shushed him. Only three other fighters shared the space inside the tent, and the rest were gathered outside to watch the current bout. None of the others were in a talking mood, and no wonder, what with the broken teeth and bloody knuckles. Ruarc looked over at the most afflicted, a young man who made small mewling sounds as his mother bandaged his finger. The thing was a horror, hanging by a strip of skin and leaking blood in a steady flow.

"He'd be better off removing it," I whispered, and Ruarc blanched.

"Stop worrying about scrapes and bruises," I told him, leaning in. "You show these maggots any weakness and they'll know how best to crack your skull in the square. Stay focused and trust my training."

"Easy for you to say, watching from the sidelines."

"King Sigtryggr hates wasting a chance for good blood sport," I said, reining in my irritation. "These trials are supposed to be brutal. All of these fighters are doing their best to maim or otherwise break each other in the most spectacular way possible without killing. As you said, six of them are out already. If you doubt yourself, you'll lose, and Sigtryggr will look right past you. Right now you're doing well enough. Keep at it."

The fighters who had outlasted the king's cull were a range of ages and experience. The more skilled men, the warriors with pale scars telling of their years of raiding, were pit against each other first, and fought every other bout. The rest were younger boys or the unblooded, like Ruarc himself.

For the first round, two fresh-faced wealthy merchants' sons had jumped around each other like birds, never actually making a strike. The crowd had gotten sick of their gutless scuffling and called for Sigtryggr to disqualify them, which he did, lazily waving his ringed hand from his high seat on the platform. The next fight was more captivating, ending with Thrym putting down his far smaller opponent with a bone-cracking kick to the thigh.

The other fights were much the same. Each bout was less about elimination and more about endurance. If a man won his fight, but left the square unable to face the next, he was made to leave. However, if a man had lost but was still able, he would go up against the next opponent, and so on. At the end, Sigtryggr would choose his favorites from those still standing. The clear forerunners would then face off. One man would be the winner, though all would gain a place in the king's guard.

I hoped my nerves could endure until then. Ruarc needed as

much belief in himself as I could give him, even if both of us knew he was in too deep.

"How will you win? Remind me of what I told you," I said.

"I need confidence, brains, and whatever bloody favor your gods decided to piss out today," he muttered. "As if any of that will help against the blood-hungry wolves out there."

I pushed his shoulder, making him wince because the bruises were already blooming there. "The crowd likes you. Keep being clever and they'll stay on your side."

He stretched his neck, masking his discomfort. "And the king? Even if I make it through, how are we going to get him alone? He's more likely to throw us out those gates and get back to his drinking."

"Keep your head in the fights, Thorstein. That's all you need to do."

I ignored his protests and ducked out of the tent to join the knot of men idling beside the brazier. We had a good view of the arena. A pair of thralls were sweeping the bloody dirt with bundles of straw and stamping it down again.

"Two amber beads on Freki," growled a man beside me. He had a swelling bruise on his cheek, and a nick on his earlobe that leaked blood into his beard.

He'd been speaking to his friend, who stood on his other side. "I'll put five on 'im," was the reply. "And my ring. There's no way old Thrym can take him down, doesn't matter how big the fucker is."

"Aw, you're useless," my neighbor complained. "S'posed to bet against me, not with me."

His simple sincerity made me laugh.

"What about you, eh?" he said, eyeing me. "You're no fighter. Got a snot-eating brat in the running? Did I crush him yet?"

"Thorstein is mine," I told him. "He'll take that Freki easy, like a shark takes a seal."

He grinned, delighted. "You hear this one?" he crowed to his friend. "She's got stones! Ha!"

The man leaned forward, scowling like I'd spat in his face. "You better bite your words before they're too much to swallow," he said. "That boy of yours is getting his brains stomped in. Soon you'll beg for a healer instead of running your mouth."

I let him see my teeth. "What'll you give me when he puts you down? Five beads and a tarnished copper ring is hardly worth more than the look on your face when he kicks it in."

That set my neighbor laughing again. I moved away as he howled and his friend cursed my back.

The fight had started already, and the spectators stomped their feet and cheered. Freki was a squat box of a man, with a neck thick as a jug and legs like posts. He bore an axe and shield, provided by the king's overseers. His opponent across the square, Thrym, was indeed as big as a mountain, and had an unfortunate overbite that gave him a rat face. His spear was nearly as tall as himself and fit snugly in his fist. The iron point gleamed.

"Begin!" came the call from the overseer, and Freki let out a bellow. They charged at each other, weapons clashing and melding with the shouts and curses of the spectators.

As Thorstein's mother, I'd been allocated a seat in the front rows with the other families. I'd refused it, having no desire to expose myself to the scrutiny of the dozen former rivals I saw in the crowd. I also wanted to keep out of sight of the king as long as I could. Sigtryggr had made his high seat at the open end of the fighting square, to the left of the tent. He wouldn't see me unless he twisted his neck to the right, which left me free to study him closely and determine his mood.

I wiped the sweat gathering at my temples. There was no going back now. Once this round was decided, Ruarc would fight his final bout. He'd better make it good.

Soapstone lamps hung from the struts of the canopy, bathing Sigtryggr in a golden light. It suited him well; I had always found him handsome, with long limbs and hair dark as soot. He had a signature tendency to squint, a trait acquired when sand was ground into his right eye during the battle for Dyflin years ago. This had earned him the Irish name *Cáech,* though no one with sense used it in his hearing.

I smiled to myself. Sigtryggr was a vain, confident shit, with all the common arrogance of a blood-hungry man in his prime. He not only expected deference and respect, he was also one of the few men I thought actually deserved it.

Up on his platform, he gave off a languorous, casual air. He sat with legs extended and cushioned on a pillow. In his fist was a cup of ale that never ran dry, because the thrall standing behind him constantly refilled it. Tonight, he had dressed well, grinned broadly, and laughed freely.

It was all for show. I knew King Sigtryggr to be a ruthless, sharp-eyed, scheming bastard. He never missed a chance to prove he was the cleverest man in the room. This strange ease set a buzzing fire in my limbs, one that had me chewing my fingernails and pacing back and forth as the fight in the square played out.

Thrym was winning. Which meant Ruarc would have to fight him. His *brynja* wouldn't stand up to that iron spear point, no matter how fast he moved.

"Put the troll-shit down!" bellowed an oath-man on the other side of the royal platform. From the benches, the crowd stomped their feet and howled.

"Freki, you limp-cock! Use that axe!" bawled the man with the bleeding ear. His humorless friend was not with him, and I wondered if he'd forfeited his wager of beads and copper ring when Thrym started to win.

A stirring at my elbow made me start.

"I'm going to die," said Ruarc pitifully.

"You keep saying that and it'll be me who kills you," I hissed.

"Won't matter, will it?"

"Are you ready? Did you choose a blade from the overseer?"

"A big seax," he said, eyes on the square. "I figure if I get inside Thrym's reach, I can cut his thigh."

"Good thinking," I said. "He's got a weak left foot."

He turned to me, opening his mouth to speak, but his green eyes went wide and he sucked air.

"Thorstein, is it?" drawled the oath-man behind me. "You and your, ah, *mother*, come with me. King Sigtryggr intends to speak with you."

Heart in my throat, I turned and faced him.

"My son is next up for the fight. Surely the king wishes to judge the winners before he conducts any business?"

The man twitched. He had lips like a fish, wet and puffy and pale in a florid face. His gaze remained somewhere over our heads.

"Thorstein has been disqualified," he said. "You are to wait for the king. Come now, or I'll have to drag you."

I turned and looked at Ruarc. The bruise around his eye was already turning black and he'd chewed his split lip open. He jerked his head, mouthing *no.*

"Fine," I said to Fish-Lip. "But allow me to retrieve some food from the tent. We have not eaten since arriving."

Fish-Lip hesitated, and I hid my trembling hands in the folds of my linen dress.

"Go," he told me. "Be quick. I will ensure you are provided ale as well while you wait."

"My thanks," I said, then turned and hurried to the tent, leaving Ruarc to stare after me open-mouthed.

Pulse beating in my head, I ducked under the canvas. There was a trestle table in the middle, piled with bandages, platters of food, pots of steaming water, and a pitcher of beer. Quickly, I sifted through the items, wrapping a heel of crusty bread in a strip of bandage before grabbing one more item and stuffing it in the sleeve of my tunic.

"Lead us on, then," I said to Fish-Lip once I rejoined them.

"Close that gaping mouth," I said to Ruarc, taking his arm. "You're not fighting Thrym. That's luck, hey?"

"I feared you were leaving me behind," Ruarc muttered. He sat at a table with his head cradled in his hands. His left knee bounced, drumming a quick rhythm which made the splintered floorboards squeak under his foot.

We were kept waiting for Sigtryggr within a bare room inside an empty storage building. An iron brazier burned in the corner, its smoke wafting out of an open gable. I paced in front of the brazier, sweat dampening my dress and underarms. "Even if I had left you," I said. "I wouldn't have got far. So moaning about it doesn't make anything easier."

"Would you stop wearing a path into the ground?" Ruarc barked. "It's driving me mad."

"Do not speak to me that way, boy. What's the matter with you? You're quivering like a rabbit in a snare."

"What is the matter?" he cried. "The matter is I would very much like to be drunk and lounging by a roaring fire, not stinking of blood and fear and someone else's puke. You said the king was a friend, Gyda. What exactly are we doing here?"

"Sigtryggr is a friend," I said defensively. The weight of his stare was accusatory and uncomfortable. "He must have seen me. Perhaps he wants to be certain everything is as it should be."

Ruarc clicked his tongue and looked away. His knee returned to bouncing.

"You didn't have to fight Thrym. That should be of some comfort," I said, but it lacked conviction.

I plunked into the chair opposite him, and reached for the heel of bread I'd retrieved. Fish-Lip had not brought us the ale he'd promised.

"It's stale," Ruarc warned, but I ripped off a piece and chewed it anyway to spite him.

He shifted, bringing his ankle up as if to force his knee to be still. "Suppose the king does not throw us out on our arses?" he said. "What happens then? How can you be sure he wants to help us? Will we swear an oath to him? I can't do that, Gyda. I have duties in Ireland. By now my mother must know of my absence, and I can't imagine what my bolting has done to the villages and people relying on me. They'll have my hide when I return." His hands, still scraped from brawling, flexed. He stared into the brazier. "That is, *if* I return. I am not so certain anymore."

"You want to return to Dyflin?" I said, the words coming out choked.

"You're not hurt, are you?" he challenged, pinning me with a glare. "You cannot expect I would spend the rest of my life chasing after your ship. I had a life, Gyda. As much as I want to help you, I have to go back to it soon."

"I know that," I protested. "I hadn't thought —"

"You never think," he spat. "You rush ahead and assume everyone else is running behind. But I can't do that forever."

I clenched my teeth and looked down at the table. He was right, of course, and I had no argument against it. Though anger and a sense of betrayal were yet sharp within me.

There was a knock at the door. It swung open, and Ruarc and I leapt up as two oath-men strode in with wicked axes on their belts.

"What is this?" I demanded. Saying nothing, the men took us each by the arm, pulling us out into the larger, main space. There was a hearth in the center and near it stood a carved yew wood table. And it was at this table that Sigtryggr, once the king of Dyflin and now king of Jórvík and Northumbria, sat waiting with a wolf's grin and a pitcher of ale.

"Hello, Fishwife," he said. "Surprised to see me?"

My tongue tarred itself to the roof of my mouth.

"Kind of you to visit," he said. "I admit, I am disappointed you took so long. Lying your way into the trials is an odd way of going about it, but you've always been an odd woman. It's why I like you."

My skin grew hot. I stammered something, but he waved a hand.

"You're going by Arnþrúður these days, is that right? This must be your man, Thorstein. Blindingly handsome, but a bit young for your taste. Or so you used to insist to me."

The king's smile was unwavering and vicious. He dangled his hand off the arm of his chair, letting his fingertips brush the pommel of his sword. Ruarc let out a terrified squeak, which made the king's smile widen.

"He's my foster-son," I blurted. "Ruarc, not Thorstein. The names are for protection."

Sigtryggr threw back his head and laughed, a big room-filling sound. "Woman, your lie is as bold as that toothpick you hide in your sleeve! I've known you the better part of my life and never once have I seen you bear any motherly affection for anyone. Your own cursed stubbornness would never allow it."

I went rigid. "If you were not the king I would slap that insult from your mouth! You know nothing of motherhood, nor what affections live in me."

Behind him, the oath-men bristled, and I pulled the knife from my wrist.

"Here is my toothpick," I spat, and tossed it onto the table between us. "I didn't think I scared you that much, king. Two bodyguards against one woman? It's offensive."

"It is a practical move," he replied. "Considering the news out of Dyflin, I thought it wise to keep a pair of solid lads near me. Much has changed since last summer. But not you. *You* are ever Gyda the schemer."

We stared each other down for a long moment. Then the hearth popped and the king leaned back and smirked.

"Why the lying, Fishwife?" he said, sitting back in his chair. "Usually, you're not the one spewing gilded turds at me. So, why is this Irish man you call your son fighting to become my guardsman?"

He sighed, coal-black brows furrowing as he looked Ruarc up and down. "A long way from home, eh? You're no warrior. Scrawny neck. Weak arms. Abhorrent *brynja,* but I can't fault you for not having the proper sense to choose a good one. Thrym would have smashed you, and you'd have deserved it."

Ruarc's shoulders bunched. His mouth opened, and I jabbed him with my elbow, swallowing the grunt of pain when bone hit iron rings.

"Don't mistake precaution for lies," I said quickly to cover it. "Jórvík remembers my name for reasons I prefer to leave at rest in Rán's hall. As I said, Ruarc is with me for protection. Making him my foster-son lends us both safety and family, two things we are in great lack of these days."

"I thought *Thorstein* was your son," Ruarc said under his breath, and I pretended not to hear.

Sigtryggr thought for a moment, running his thumb over the band of the silver ring on his index finger.

"Hmph," he said. "It is a wonder you provide her any sort of protection at all. Do you bear no lord's arm-ring, man? No oath? If you lie, I will know."

The knot in Ruarc's throat bobbed. "None, Lord," he said. "I mediate the trade between Dyflin and the villages around it. I serve no one but my people."

The king tilted his head and a gleam came into his dark, damaged eye. "And yet you entered the trials. Are you ambitious, then? In search of glory and a wealthy ring-giver?"

Ruarc faltered, and Sigtryggr gave a sly smile.

"I thought not," he said. "Fine, then. Come and sit, the both of you. I've got ale."

As he reached for the pitcher, Ruarc and I exchanged a look, then sat. When each of us had a cup, even the oath-men, I lifted mine and cleared my throat.

"To you, King Sigtryggr. Thank you for this hospitality."

"Yes, our thanks," mumbled Ruarc.

The king tilted his cup and drank lustily. The rest of us did the same.

"Now then," said Sigtryggr, giving a great, satisfied gust. He wiped the foam from his mustache. "I plan on drinking until hearth-smoke makes my eyes run like a frightened nun's piss. So you had better fill my ears to keep me awake."

I took a steadying breath. "As you rightly guessed, entering the trials was a ploy to get an audience. We're here to ask for your help."

He scoffed. "That's as evident as shit in a midden. You must need something outrageous. As long as I've known you, Gyda, you've never been a supplicant. How can your notorious pride endure it?"

Ruarc choked on a laugh.

"There is no shame in supplication as long as it gets me what I want."

My indignation made Sigtryggr smile again. "You are a wealthy widow," he said. "And you have four men alone in a room with you at this moment. Oh, how the gossips will bleat. These men are married to Christ-followers, and whomever your foster-son is fucking will likely seek a word with you. What a scandal this could bring!"

The oath-men laughed at this, but I saw Ruarc clench his fists under the table.

I nudged his foot to keep him silent. This was a goad, nothing more. I'd seen Sigtryggr use such tactics before. He loved to catch people on the back foot, get them angry before they'd even made their demands of him. And when fools were angry, they were bolder, senseless to everything but what they wanted. Those who found themselves needing something from Sigtryggr often gave up more than what they got from him. Therefore, if Sigtryggr wanted to make me angry, then he was far more interested to hear my request than he'd let on.

"Wealthy widow?" I answered. "You flatterer. If you are searching for a new wife to bear your sons, Siggi, you won't find much of one in me. I haven't had my bloods in five winters. Even then, I produced nothing but dead children with my husband. You'll have to get your whelps on some other woman."

The tips of his ears turned pink. He coughed and raised the cup to his lips again.

"If I may," said Ruarc politely. He lifted his fists from his lap and relaxed them on the table.

"By all means," said the king.

Ruarc took a sip of his ale, cleared his throat, and then cleared it again. "I am acquainted with your foster-son," he began. "Harleif. He, ah, well, he —"

"Feeble-tongued turd," growled the oath-man on the right. "You're speaking to the king. If I were you, I'd cut off my cock and bury it in shame to be such a piss stain. Find your guts, man, or we'll find them for you, and you won't like how."

Ruarc's shoulders squared like a sail-yard. Instinct sent my fingers to my sleeve, which, of course, was disappointingly empty. The men glared at each other, the tension thick as smoke.

Sigtryggr intervened before it could boil over. "Be grateful to him, Harmund. Considering your son owed me a troll-hoard for sleeping with my daughter before her wedding, I would not be so eager to judge others' manliness."

The blood left Harmund's face. He dropped his gaze and said nothing more.

Sigtryggr sighed and shifted in his chair. "So, you did my fosterling a good turn," he said. "It is no burden on me to take your silver. My coin purse thanks you for it. But Harleif's debt is not why the two of you conspired for this meeting."

Ruarc looked to me to answer.

"What you know of Dyflin is true," I said to the king. "With the exception that I alone am guilty. Ruarc had no part in the offenses I committed."

Sigtryggr's brows rose. "An admission of guilt is grounds for exile. If I refuse your petition, will you burn my ships and warehouses? Why should I take the risk at all instead of simply throwing you out of Jórvík."

I kept my gaze steady. "I had good reason for what I did in Dyflin. No, Siggi, your ships and warehouses are safe from me."

He refilled his ale and waved his hand. "Speak, then. Tell me the tale."

Straightening, I folded my hands and began. "What you see is a trader whose livelihood was stolen. Since I saw you last, I have lost my reputation, my crew, my home, and my ship. Everything I owned was thieved from me like eggs from a nest. I want it all back, and I want the snake who did it dead at my feet. That is why we came to you with hope and by the gods' favor."

Sigtryggr thumbed his eye. "And here I am, suffering from the favors of the hearth-smoke." He wiped his finger against the edge of the table. "I heard of your losses," he said. "But I have nothing to do with them or your snake. Why not take it up with Olavi? He's bound by honor to help you, isn't he?"

"I did take it up with him," I snapped. "Olavi wiped it from his hand like he'd touched shit. Then he threw me off like I was the one who did the shit."

"And did you?"

"I said I did, didn't I?"

Ruarc sucked in a breath.

"Watch how you thrust that tongue, woman," the king snarled. "Or you may find such a blade turned on you."

Teeth clenched, I cursed myself. Rashness would get me nothing. When I spoke again, my temper was bridled.

"I did not burn just any ship or warehouse," I said. "I chose Olavi's own. I burned goods meant for the wedding feast of his son Hákon *Stáli*."

I paused, but Sigtryggr was listening attentively. I went on.

"Since the theft of *Sea-Wolf*, Olavi hindered all my efforts to learn what became of it. I had no power, no say in my own fortunes. He refused to help me, so I decided I would kick him like he kicked me.

I hurt nothing but his property and his pride. If I were a man, no one would question my choices. Why is my honor worth less than anyone else's?"

"Gyda, honor is not what you're after here," Sigtryggr said. "Is it silver you want? Slaves? A raiding party?"

"No, nothing like that," I started, but Sigtryggr went on, pointing a blunt, ringed finger at me.

"Do not take my fondness for you as approval, Gyda. I have sympathy for your plight, but don't cause me to regret it by asking me to move against Olavi Spear-Breaker. He is my cousin, and he owns my life several times over. Kin and blood-debt come before any feeling I have for you. Should you ask, I will retaliate, and feel no guilt. Do you understand?"

"I am offended you would think such things," I said snidely. "As it stands, I care little for Olavi now. May he rot in his hall with his brats and his grubby hands."

Sigtryggr sat back. "You want information, then?"

Was that relief in his gaze, or disappointment?

"I want my ship," I said. "I want to know if it still sails, or if Rán claimed it. Then I want the name of the scorn-snake who stole it from me. I want his gut-rope for my rigging. I want his bones as my ballast. I want his cracked skull as my fucking prow-beast."

Sigtryggr looked down his long nose. "What makes you think I have the power to give any of that to you? There are merchants you could ask who would be of more use. Give me a description I can pass to them. Specifics. It has been a good while since I last sailed with you."

I bit the inside of my cheek. How could I describe a ship that I knew unconsciously, like the way a mother knows the shape of her child in a crowd of children? I thought of the splinters in the deck under my sleeping roll. The curve of the tiller like a dragon's tail. The oars and how they slipped into my Daughters' hands like well-known lovers.

Ruarc cleared his throat. "Forgive me, king, but we've tried that," he said, then turned to me, expression apologetic. "Gyda, there are dozens of *knarr* ships in the Ouse right now. Even if, by some Loki-trick, *Sea-Wolf* came through here, you said we couldn't do things like Dyflin. The merchants are not going to know anything. Why would they care?"

I lifted my ale and took a drink to give myself a chance to come up with a counter, but I had none.

Sigtryggr regarded Ruarc. "The man is right," he said, a note of new respect in his voice. "Yet there may be some new angle to chase. How long has it been since *Sea-Wolf* was lost?"

I bristled. "It wasn't fucking lost. It was taken."

Sigtryggr wiped his eye, which had turned red. Soon it would swell shut. "This is growing tiresome, *Fiskwif*. Answer my questions or don't. There is a feast outside where most of Jórvík's nobility are pouring mead down their gullets and drowning in it. I'd very much like to join them."

"It was at the beginning of last Autumn," Ruarc said on my behalf, touching my arm. "On the western coast of al-Andalus."

Sigtryggr nodded. "And do you have any notion of why? Or who they are? Any idea of their heading?"

"If I knew any of that, I wouldn't be here," I cried.

"Then you are asking the impossible," Sigtryggr said, smirking. "Easier for Thor to make Freyja a blushing wife."

I slapped the table with both hands. "Then what fucking good are you?"

Ruarc whispered a curse as Harmund bared his teeth and pulled his axe. The other oath-man had no reaction at all, but the gaze he sent me chilled my skin.

"I am the only good you have," Sigtryggr muttered, then sighed and scrubbed his hand over the short scruff of his beard. "Your thief could have been from Córdoba, Miklagard, Sigtuna, or Gardariki. It doesn't fucking matter. What matters is *why*, and you aren't saying. So, either tell me what you know or get the fuck out of my city."

I stared at him.

"Fine, then," he said, and scraped his chair back to stand. "Fuck you too, *Fiskwif*. Next time, enter the trials yourself. That would be far more entertaining than this."

He made it to the door with his oath-men before I choked out the words.

"I'll tell you, king," I said, standing.

He paused, lip curling. "Spit it out, then."

I shook my head. "Send your men out first. I have no wish for rumors to spread across Jórvík. My misfortunes are mine, and I'd keep it that way."

Harmund, who had opened the door already, slammed it shut. "Don't listen to this, Lord. She has nothing but troll-shit to shovel. She'd stab you as soon as you turned your back."

The king scoffed. "With what? That piss-rusted knife? Hardly more than a bee sting."

"My Lord," Harmund sputtered, but Sigtryggr made a shooing motion. "Go on, man, Go see after Harleif. Make certain he isn't rutting with the merchants' daughters while their fathers drink my mead. And send in the tall girl with the cold ham and a jug of mead, would you? Now, get out, the both of you."

Harmund cursed, and continued to curse as he slouched out the door. However, the other man hesitated, his eyes shifting from me to the king before he ducked out to join his fellow.

Sigtryggr stared after him, a slight frown on his face. "He's an odd bastard, that one," he said, then shook his head.

Ruarc clicked his tongue. "Thank the gods," he said. "I was like a mouse in a field with them glaring at me the whole time. Gyda, you're going to destroy my sanity one of these days."

"Not before I destroy my own," I muttered.

Sigtryggr did not return to the table. He knelt beside the hearth and stirred the glowing embers.

"Don't keep me waiting, *Fiskwif*," he grunted, putting another log on the fire.

I gathered my courage and approached him. Long, flickering shadows danced on the walls. I took a breath and met Sigtryggr's sharp gaze.

"*Sea-Wolf* carries a cargo of wealth and trade goods. Vast amounts of silver in ingots and coins, as well as silks, ivory, stones, pelts, and amber."

Sigtryggr stilled. "Such a *dvergr*-hoard would be cause for anyone's resentment," he said. "That is a heavy sum to offer for my trust."

"What choice do I have but to trust you?" I said bitterly. "The only friends I have left are here in this room. Those bastards in Dyflin would have had me starve and beg. And here I am, doing just that."

The king rose off his knees and stood. "I understand you better now," he replied. His gaze remained on the fire as he weighed his next words. When he spoke, his voice was low, but firm. "How did you come by this cargo? What happened to your Daughters? Tell me everything, and leave nothing out. My help comes at a price."

I opened my mouth, a lie already rising, but then a soft sound came from outside the oak door. There was a wet, grating exhale and a heavy thump, then nothing.

The three of us looked at each other for a moment, and then I brought my finger to my lips.

Keep talking, I mouthed at Sigtryggr, and he nodded, black eyes bright.

"I see your logic," he said, louder. "A ship like that is a target. Similar ships arrive in Jórvík occasionally, but they never stay long."

As he spoke, Ruarc grabbed the knife off the table and shoved it into my palm. I crept to the door and pressed my ear against it.

I heard nothing aside from the distant music and laughter of the feasting, but then there was a scrape and a muffled grunt of effort. I moved to the side so that the door would hide me when it opened.

Ruarc touched my elbow. "How many?" he whispered.

I held up a single finger. He nodded and moved back. Sigtryggr was still speaking, rattling off names and pitching his voice as if he were answering questions. Then he feigned a heavy sneeze.

The latch on the door was lifting. Whomever had killed the man outside, he was an expert hand, and swift. I wondered if he had a distance weapon, intended to eliminate his targets before someone had the sense to rush him or turn away a blade. Would it be a throwing axe or a bow? A knife?

I braced, my own knife gripped tightly by my hip. An upward thrust, and whatever the projectile was would fly too high.

The door slammed open, knocking me against the stone wall and winding me before I could react.

"Die, fucking heathen Dane," bellowed the unnamed oath-man,

exploding forward. "King of demons! Go now to your kingdom. For the glory of King Edward!"

There came the sound of a drawn bowstring, and I stumbled forward, gasping.

My knife caught the man in the armpit of his drawing arm, slipping through the joint and tearing open the delicate pathways of blood. He screamed, and the bowstring snapped, whipping my cheek as the arrow and longbow dropped from his nerveless fingers.

With his good arm, he pulled his seax and came at me. Still half-stunned and reeling, I pushed against him, grappling weakly, twisting just as he thrust his seax at my gut. Its wicked point dug into my outer hip, striking bone but going no further. I bit back a cry.

Ruarc howled, and suddenly the man was off me, slipping from my arms and falling like iron slag, his blood soaking my shoes and hem. He twitched, moaned once, and died with Sigtryggr's sword through his spine.

Ruarc trembled and stared down at the corpse, his fist opening and closing as he panted. He dropped the sword like it burned him.

"Careful with that," Sigtryggr snapped, but then, scowling at the corpse, he whistled, drawing out the sound. "The fucker shat himself. As if his indignity wasn't great enough."

I pressed my hand hard against my bleeding hip bone and toed the corpse. "When it comes to negotiations, I suppose blood and shit are as good as any other cornerstone."

"I suppose you're right," he replied, and swiped at his weeping eye.

Using the light from the hearth, I dabbed at the puncture on my hip, hissing and huffing in equal measure.

"Are you sure you're alright?" asked Ruarc. He was a lovely shade of green and sat with a bucket between his knees. He'd vomited twice, and though he'd sworn it was because of the pork stew he'd eaten earlier, neither Sigtryggr nor I could keep our contempt at bay.

"I'm fine," I told him. "Keep your head over that bucket, puke-pustule."

Sigtryggr snickered. Ruarc turned a deeper shade and ducked his head to heave.

The king had taken it on himself to put Harmund to rights, and had just finished covering him with a blanket found in a chest in the corner.

"There," he said, folding the corner carefully under Harmund's feet. He put his hand on the dead man's chest for a long moment.

"This will give him some solitude and dignity," he said quietly. "Though it's not as if reeking of piss is dignified. What a fucking waste. Harmund was a good man."

While we all recovered, I weighed up the consequences of all that had transpired. It seemed Sigtryggr had secrets of his own, and that could prove to be good leverage if I were careful enough.

I chewed on the possibilities as I inspected the wound on my outer hip. When I'd twisted away from the thrust of the seax, nothing beyond the flesh had been damaged. Further hindered by the layers of my dress and apron, the cut was shallow, seeped slowly, and would scab well. Wound-rot was unlikely, though always a concern.

The slice across my cheek, however, stung like a sea nettle's hundred arms had gripped my face and called down Thor's lightning. I prodded the raised wheal with clean fingers, and they came away bloody. I'd have to smear my cheek with honey and hope it wouldn't scar.

"So what do we do with this fucker?" Sigtryggr said. He dragged the bowman's corpse one-handed towards the hearth by the ankle. A smear of blood clotted the dirt. Sigtryggr dropped it in front of the hearth and Ruarc cringed.

"You have two rivers," I said. "One of them will suffice."

He grinned. "That I do. And plenty of stones. But if I had my way, I'd nail his hide to the door of the minster church as a warning," he said.

Ruarc wiped his mouth with the back of his hand. "What about Harmund?" he rasped. "Harleif should know what happened to his father."

"My foster son will know what he needs to know, and nothing more," Sigtryggr said, surprising us both with his ferocity. "None of this leaves here. Do you hear me? Nothing."

"Oh, calm yourself, Siggi." I tossed my bloody rag into the fire and went to a side table that bore a bowl and water pitcher. Once my hands were clean of blood, I dried them on my ruined apron skirt. "Ruarc and I know very well how to keep secrets. Same as you, I'm thinking."

His scowl was dark and full of warning.

"There's nothing to hide anyway," Ruarc said. "Harmund's killer is already dead."

The despondence in his voice struck me. This was the first life Ruarc had ever taken. I realized he was trembling, staring at his hands like they were foreign things. I moved towards him awkwardly, thinking to put a hand on his shoulder. But he stood and made for the door with his bucket before I could touch him.

"Even so," I said, turning to Sigtryggr. "Your people should know of this. What if you had been at the feast? He would have killed you in front of all your guardsmen, and no one would have stopped him. Your safety is under threat."

"Do you need a reminder who is king in this city?" Sigtryggr bellowed. "You will say nothing, or it will be your tongues I nail to the minster door. Those crucifix-kissing whoresons seem to have forgotten their place, and I will not have you undermining my authority."

Ruarc froze with his hand on the latch, but the king's words had been for me.

I folded my arms and stared back. "Don't think you can cow *me*, Sigtryggr. It isn't gossip you're worried about. You're in the kind of trouble that makes people want to kill you. No amount of intimidation is going to make me let that go. So tell me, or shove your kingly threats back down your throat."

Sigtryggr's jaw flexed, and his swollen eye puckered. "Think very carefully what you say, Gyda. You cannot unsay it."

I sneered. "You were never going to help us, were you? All your warnings, your goading, your so-called blood-debt to Olavi. It's all sheep's piss, isn't it? You lying fuck."

"Sheep's piss?" he sputtered. He paced forward, fists clenched.

A raging man was a familiar sight, and I felt neither fear nor pleasure at it. I met him half-way, stepping so close I could smell the ale on his breath.

"You won't hit me," I said. "Your honor is too precious to strike someone who speaks the truth. Sheep's piss, that's what all this is."

"Don't dare speak to me of honor," he snarled. His pulse beat fast in his neck and sweat beaded his upper lip. But there was something other than anger in his face.

I stepped back and took a breath. "You're terrified, Siggi."

He stilled. The lack of denial was a confirmation, and so I went on.

"You've got unrest, king. Men who hate you. Men who want you dead. That oath-man mentioned Wessex. That Horse-Face King Edward is involved, isn't he?"

Sigtryggr jerked a nod.

"Ragnvaldr was your predecessor. He swore an oath to Edward, but when he died Edward demanded yours." I stepped back and kicked the bowman's corpse. "This one was trained. Silent as a nun's fart. Got a place in your ranks too easily. That means others will come, and you don't know if you can hold them off."

"You know just how to burrow into a man's balls and bite, don't you?" Sigtryggr said.

Then, dropping to the ground like a child, he stretched out his long legs towards the fire.

"I can't argue with you," he said reasonably. "So come, sit. We'll talk."

Dumbfounded, I hesitated. He reached for my wrist and pulled. I hit the ground with a *hoomph*. He leaned into me.

"There we are," he said, then waved at Ruarc. "You may also have some insight to this pig-wallow too. Sit your arse down. But toss out that puke first, it's making my stomach roil."

"And the blood and corpses aren't?" Ruarc said in a high voice. But he did what was he was told, then sat with the bucket within reach.

As the heat from the fire and Sigtryggr's body seeped into my limbs, I found myself relaxing. Muscles that had gone stiff from the aftermath of the fight unspooled.

The king, by contrast, had his knees pulled up to his chest. He rested his forearms on them and the firelight reflected off his rings. He was every inch an imperious king and a scared child.

"Go on and tell me, Siggi," I murmured, bumping his shoulder. "Let us help each other."

He blew through pursed lips. "You're right. I'm fucked. Ragnvaldr left me an inheritance of shit. Wessex seems to expect the agreements and treaties will hold, but it means Jórvík must be tamed. Broken like some broodmare."

"Surely Edward doesn't expect you'll swear fealty," Ruarc said, brows raised. "You're stronger than Ragnvaldr was, and you have more allies."

Despite never ruling, Ruarc had been a landowner and a trade broker long enough to understand how oaths and peace treaties between kingdoms should work, and what happens when one side presses their case over the other. It was a good question, and Sigtryggr nodded.

"Not fealty as such," he said. "Complete submission. Ragnvaldr and the other rulers—Strathclyde, the Scots, the Northumbrians—they all came to an agreement with Edward. Much of it still holds, though true peace is as rare and fleeting as ice in summer. If I give in, Jórvík would be a thrall to Wessex."

"What are Edward's demands, then?" I asked.

Sigtryggr shifted, agitated. "He wants me to pay him."

The absurdity of this made me laugh before I could catch it. "*Pay* him?"

"The fucker wants silver," Sigtryggr said, spitting the word. "That Christ-following whoreson wants every bit of what Jórvík has. I tell you, if my foot were made of silver, I'd give it to Edward and put it where he deserves. Then when he shits, men will call his arsehole the richest wealth-giver."

"Jórvík is wealthy enough," Ruarc pointed out. "Trade is strong. You have connections all over the northern seas and with Dyflin. Tax the foreign merchants and give Edward a healthy appeasement."

"I thought of that, but it's the principle of the thing," Sigtryggr said with a shrug. "My spies say Edward's coffers are low. Mercia isn't an easy mistress, and he's unpopular because he put his sister's daughter in a nunnery instead of letting her rule. He thinks to use my resources to keep hold of his seat in the south."

He paused, raising his head to look at me before miserably confessing: "It's all this, and I raided Deneport before I took the kingship. Edward wants revenge. He wants me to shame myself for him like the rest of this bloody island."

I leveraged off the ground with a grunt of pain. "So Edward sends his demands, you refuse them, and on it goes. So he sends someone to stick an arrow in your arse. How long until Edward sends someone else? How long until he targets your daughters or your lovers or guardsmen? The longer this feud stretches, the more blood spills."

"I do wish you well in finding your ship," the king said, smiling bitterly at me. "You see I've got more pressing matters."

I laughed. "The only thing I see is that you're a moon-faced *boy* who wallows and stares at his cock like it's going to offer a solution."

"I've found a great many things are solved by my cock," he said dryly.

I yanked him up, and he sputtered and protested as I took him by the shoulders.

"Are you a child or a king, Sigtryggr?" I demanded. "Your grandfather the *Beinlausi* would spit on you if he saw you like this."

He shoved me off him with a curse, and so I stepped forward again and slapped him across the face.

"This is a negotiation, not a battle. Get yourself under control."

His hand went to his livid cheek in shock. Then his expression shifted to blood and rage.

"You have the gall of a troll, *Fiskwif*," he snarled. "You expect my help after this? I could kill you both instead and no one would mourn."

"A bowman got within an arse-hair of you, king. That is reason enough to help us. We own your life now."

Sigtryggr's stare was feral, but my words hit their mark. He said nothing.

I took a steadying breath. "One portion of my silver," I said, straightening. "You help us find *Sea-Wolf,* and you can forge a dozen gleaming feet to shove up Edward's arse."

"And let me join your guard," Ruarc blurted, and the king and I both turned to him with open mouths. He flushed. "You need a man close who knows what happened here. I am not a fighter, but I am a good judge of people. I'll keep watch for treachery and a way to counter Edward."

Sigtryggr opened his mouth to answer, but there was a gasp at the door, and something shattered on the ground.

"Oh," said the young woman, tall with dark eyes and a braided rope of black hair over her shoulder. She stared at the bloody corpses. "Oh," she said again.

All the air left me in a rush. "Hadiyya?"

CHAPTER SEVENTEEN

The night had grown long teeth. The feast was long finished and a miserable, chilling rain fell. I stood sniffling under the eave of a doorway while Sigtryggr lifted the dripping canvas off a pile of firewood and took a stout piece off the top. He held it to the flame of a hanging brazier. Once the tip had a strong burn, we went out into the rain and darkness.

I had left Ruarc to look after Hadiyya, who was in rather a state after encountering two blood-soaked corpses. She'd seen and recognized me long enough to give a ghostly smile before dropping in a dead faint.

Sigtryggr and I squelched through the mud between buildings. The torch hissed and popped in the king's fist, filling the absence of conversation. Soon, we halted at one door out of many in a row of small outbuildings at the very edge of the royal complex. There was a sturdy latch on the door. No smoke escaped the gable of the pitched roof.

"These two keep to themselves," Sigtryggr said. "They're a pain in my kingly arse, you know. Showed up one day filthy and as weepy as a nursing cat with no kittens." He pounded on the door. "You awake in there? I've brought you a gift!"

There was a rustle inside and my heart thrummed. The door swung open. A woman appeared, wreathed in a swath of red and gold silk.

"Nashwa!" I cried, then lurched forward to grasp her. She returned the embrace, arms tight around me, warm and fierce and enveloping like a winter fur.

"Gyda, Gyda," she murmured. "*Subhan'Allah*, it is a joy to see you, but I cannot breathe."

I released her and stepped back, unable to hide my broad grin. "Your presence is a welcome gift, dear woman," I said, using her language.

"And yours is as well," she said, returning the smile. "Though, you look as though you have been in a slaughter! What has happened to your face? And your dress? Are you hurt?"

"Don't worry for me," I said, covering the welt on my cheek with my palm. "I am whole enough."

Sigtryggr made an uncomfortable noise. "Ah, I see I have misjudged you," he said to me in Norse. "You know this woman and her daughter very well? Perhaps I should not have kept them from you so long." He flushed a little.

Catching my expression, Nashwa turned to the king with a click of her tongue. Her Norse was confident and clear: "Your capacity to judge anything rightly can be considered a wonder of the age."

Sigtryggr's brows rose and he sniffed. "A king cares not for the opinions of foreign nuisances."

"This nuisance has much more to say! Bend your ear, boy, and I will educate you."

"What can an old troll-wife teach a king, eh? I ask you that!"

This bickering had a dull edge, no real heat to it. I let their barbs volley back and forth, simply content to see Nashwa whole and safe.

"I saw Hadiyya," I said, cutting off one of Sigtryggr's more colorful lectures. "She looked well. Strong."

"Ah, that girl," Nashwa answered, pulling her silk around her. The rain had stopped, though the deep-night chill grew. "Despite this one's negligence, we hold each other up as well as we can." She nodded at Sigtryggr, who scowled.

"I may be distracted," he said imperiously. "But let it be known I strive to be a good host. I have fed both of you sufficiently, kept you warm, and provided you protection from my own household when you go out."

His chest puffed as he said all this, and Nashwa poked at it.

"If you are the measure of a good host, I would hate to meet any other of your kind," she said, and he deflated.

"That is unfair! I have done more than most would. You and your daughter are strangers. With no husbands or servants accompanying you, it is my right to be wary. I could have turned you away."

Nashwa scoffed and uttered something that made me chuckle.

"What does she say?" he demanded.

"Does it matter?" I replied. "Nothing you say now can change her opinion of you."

"Say it anyway. A man has a right to defend his honor."

I looked at Nashwa and she nodded, eyes creasing as she held in her smile.

"She called you a bloated goat, and that you drink ale like an infant drinks milk. I tend to agree with her, old friend."

Sigtryggr blinked for a moment, shifting his gaze between the two of us. Then, thrusting the torch into my hands, he turned on his heel.

"If you insist on such rudeness, then I'll be in my hall," he barked, and stalked into the darkness, muttering and pulling at his short beard.

"That one feels a particular sort of way for you," Nashwa said to me. "There is a shyness that shows when you look away from him. You call him friend, but there is more."

"Perhaps on his side," I said, bemused. "Though I'd reckon calling him a complicated ally would be a fairer explanation."

She smiled, but the shake of her head belied her doubt. "Yet he strives to impress you. All this makes him easy to mock."

"It certainly does," I said, laughing. "By the gods, Nashwa, I am happy to see you. Tell me, are you well? I mean, truly well, beyond your simple needs? How did you come to be here? Jórvík is a long way from al-Andalus."

She took my hand and patted it. "We will speak of all things," she said, "but I would hear first how you came to be so bruised. That king is not responsible, or I would expect him to be a corpse."

"He isn't," I assured her. "In fact, it was for his sake I won these cuts and bruises. But I am bound by confidence not to speak more of it."

Her brows drew together. "Then I will give you the same counsel you gave me: be wary of generous men. Sigtryggr is a man like all others. He is unreasonably sure of himself and full of stupidity. Do not shed more of your blood for him."

A few spear-lengths away, a door creaked open. The sound of a groan and a stream of fluid reached us.

"Shall we find the great lodge?" I said, swiftly taking Nashwa's arm. "My arse is freezing off and there is much we need to tell each other."

Nashwa allowed me to pull her along, sparing one longing glance for her little dwelling and the warm bed inside it.

"It is a tale of two parts," she said, sighing. "The telling will take some time. My stomach gnaws at me. Let us share bread and tea and I will make you a good story to bring the dawn."

The hours waned as Nashwa and I spoke. Dawn was near; the first of the birds trilled softly, cautious as the stars faded from the sky.

Sigtryggr and his family had retired to various side rooms long ago, leaving their guests to manage alone. Ruarc made a valiant attempt to stay awake, but exhaustion overcame him. He slumped against a wall, snoring lightly with his head pillowed on the edge of the ale barrel. Hadiyya had also found herself a bed under the eave timbers.

She had not spoken a word to her mother of what she had witnessed in the storage building, and I surmised Ruarc cautioned her against it. Her wariness and his avoidance left me apprehensive about the corpses. Sigtryggr strived to appear unconcerned and had drunk himself into silent brooding before slouching off to bed.

Nashwa and I were the last awake. We sipped tea and warmed ourselves at a table near the fire, too absorbed in conversation to sleep.

Her tale was not a happy one, and bitterness radiated from her as she told it.

Not long after we had left the shore of al-Andalus, Nashwa and Hadiyya were driven out of their home. She spoke of her brother, how he and many others had been called away to join the Emir in Córdoba city. In his absence, their rival Afzal seized his opportunity. His loyal guardsmen came to the funduq and took it from Nashwa by force.

"You spoke no lie when you told me a man's word has more power than a woman's blade or tongue," she said. "Before he departed, my brother paid Afzal off with the inheritance of our father and mother. *Hadiyya's* inheritance." Her voice dropped; by its darkness I knew that should Afzal appear before us, he would die that same moment.

"That swine took everything. He is the wealthiest man in the town, and no one spoke against him. My daughter and I left with two chests of clothing and valuables, along with the silver you gave us."

"Could you not go to your brother in Córdoba city?" I asked.

Her dark eyes flashed, irate at the idea. "And do what there? He lives with the soldiers. We have no home, no way of earning our place. I would never force Hadiyya to marry for my sake. May a curse fall on my head should that ever be so!"

She continued with her tale. A Frankish trader with a cargo for Ireland made space in his ship, and so they had traveled alone, with no knowledge of what they might face on arrival. They landed in Limerick and spent the worst of the winter there. When the weather permitted, they made their way to Dyflin, hoping to find me.

"Why Dyflin?" I said, astounded. "You had no possible way of knowing I was there."

Her expression was sly. "I will tell you all my tale, but you must be patient."

By the time she and Hadiyya arrived in Dyflin, I had been cast out for weeks.

"Olavi was a fume of smoke when we arrived in his grand hall," she said, laughing.

The others had just gone to bed, and she gained confidence with the privacy and the warmth of the hearth. She let her scarf loosen around her as she relaxed.

"We were two strange, foreign women, clutching silver in their hands and with words of praise in our mouths. Only the praise was not for him. It was as if your Jarl's gods had come from paradise to pass their judgment against him. What did you do to him, Gyda? It must have been something truly savage to turn that man's face as red as the Córdoban sunset."

I hid my grimace in my mug of tea. Her words, though meant in jest, had an edge as sharp as her gaze. There was much she held back.

"To his credit," she went on. "Olavi did extend his hospitality for a time. But we had no protection. No benefactor. No guarantee of safety or self-governance. Eventually, Olavi made it clear we were a burden and an offense. I began to fear. It was a fear unlike before."

The clenching of her jaw and fists told me all that she would not say. Dyflin was a city of slavery. The markets there were some of the largest in the northern isles. I thought of Liadan, and of so many others I had known and had never seen again.

Reaching over the table, I grabbed Nashwa's hand. "Listen to me, friend. I swear to you that you will be safe here in Jórvík. Nothing will befall you or Hadiyya. I will not allow it, and neither will the king."

She scoffed at me. "We are part of a harsh world. We must be harsh to survive. I will give Hadiyya a weapon. A knife, or an axe. She will learn to use it. On herself, if the need comes. There must be no more broken lives for us. Only broken skulls."

Uncertain how to respond to this, I released her, and when she next spoke, her voice had lost its vibrancy.

"A woman from Olavi's household came to us. We did not recognize her. The clothing she wore was fine, rich with decoration and embroidery. Her cheeks glowed with the radiance of the moon and held the same roundness. But her eyes—her eyes were sad when she spoke of you. Like doves in the rain."

I said nothing, though I listened with every muscle tensed.

"We did not ask Eir what happened to the other women who traveled with you, but I hope they found the same contentment, or at least a measure of the comfort she found. Eir has a new husband. A rich man. A good man, or so she says. That is a gift of heavenly grace."

"Olavi's eldest son Hákon *Stáli* is her husband," I replied. "Hardly a gift, that one."

She picked absently at a loose thread on her shawl. "She advised us to go to Jórvík. I remembered then you had told me the same."

"And so you came to Sigtryggr."

"Yes," she answered, and plucked the thread with a hard jerk. "Much good that did us. We sought you for weeks, Gyda. Not knowing if you were somewhere in the city or elsewhere. Hope cannot cling to such a thing. The king would not help us find you."

"He is a distractible man," I said carefully. "There are many duties he must bear. And Jórvík has no love for me. It is not his fault I hid behind a false name to protect myself."

"Do not defend his negligence," she scolded. "If he'd wanted to help us, he would have. He is your friend before he is a king. Let him bear that."

Chastened, I turned my attention to the fire. We fell silent, each carrying the weight of our own thoughts. Much time passed thus, for when she spoke again, I started and spilled cold tea over my hand.

"You are succumbing to sleep," she repeated.

I dragged an arm across my face. "Apologies," I mumbled. "My nights have been rather poor lately."

"Given the events of this evening, that is no surprise. You still reek of blood."

I looked down at myself and spread my hands. "I've been told it is my usual state."

She snorted. "I think more likely my tale made you weary." She raised her arms over her head, stretching her back. "Ah, I cannot not blame you. This night has been spoken to its grave. My voice will croak like a red toad's by noon."

"Weary or not, I have been a happy captive to your tale," I said. "But there is more yet to tell, I think."

Nashwa let her smile fall. She stared into the hearth, posture elegant and gaze serene.

I pressed my fingertips against the edge of my chair as I waited. I would not force her to speak or bend to my will. That was a mistake I had made once too often.

"You have yet to share your own story, Gyda," she said, rising with our empty cups. "More tea? It will be cold." She went to the sideboard without waiting for my response and filled both cups from a pitcher.

"You know as much as there is to know," I said stiffly. "My ship was stolen and I was forced to return to Dyflin. While there I greatly offended Jarl Olavi. He exiled me. And now I have met you here in Jórvík."

"Would it offend you to say I know more than you think? As much as I have kept back, you have kept more."

"If you have a question for me, ask it."

She returned and placed the cups on the table. Perching at the edge of her chair, she dangled her hands between her legs and leaned forward. "I will share what I must when I am certain you are trustworthy."

My spine stiffened. "Trustworthy?"

Her coal-black stare bored into me. "Did you think my warmth towards you was without a measure of caution? I have not known you long, but I can see you are never without your own motives."

"My joy in seeing you and Hadiyya is genuine," I said. "I have no other motive."

"No? Then tell me why you are bloody and why my daughter avoided my eye all evening? Why did your man Ruarc sit alone and stare at his hands? Why did he flinch at every noise?"

I drew back and said nothing.

"There," she said. "*There* is your silence."

"What do you wish me to say, Nashwa?" I demanded. "I am bound by my own interests, just as anyone else. You cannot expect me to share what I am obliged to keep close."

The crease between her dark brows deepened. "You are a secretive woman, Gyda *Fiskwif*. Deceptive. Eir told me much of you. She told me how her husband paid Afzal to intimidate the town. My *home*. He bribed us to refuse guests because of you. Learning this made me question everything. How could you not have known when you came to my door? Did you put my daughter in danger deliberately? Had you lied to me? You left with this man and a horde of his angry, violent friends. Then my brother wasted our inheritance and left us alone. And more angry men cast us out. I wanted to trust you, to seek you out as you had advised me. When Eir told me what you had done in Dyflin—," She paused and shook her head. "This and everything else made me frightened of you. I had to be sure of you. I am not satisfied yet."

Ruarc choked on a snore and jerked, knocking the barrel hard enough to make the ale inside slosh violently.

"What—?" he mumbled, one eye slitted open.

Nashwa gathered her shawl and covered her hair again.

I stared at her, my response caught in my throat. I had nothing in my head, nothing in my gut.

Ruarc settled on the chair beside me. He knuckled one eye. "It sounds like you've made up your mind," he said to Nashwa, half yawning. "I heard the end of your story. You say Eir told you everything. Did she also tell you *why* we did what we did?"

He enunciated his words, sounding like he had taken an active part in it all. Like he had followed me willingly instead of suffering under my coercion, my actions of anger and spite. I pressed a hand against my gut.

"She did not share that," Nashwa answered him, "but I am not a fool."

He leaned forward. "If you are no fool, then no doubt you recognize Gyda is a woman who suffers no fools. And she does not take any decision lightly."

"Did I ask your opinion, child? You are not the one whose honesty I question. Instead, I think you should question why you follow a woman who asks you to kill for her. Oh, yes, I recognize the look of one who has ended the life of another for the first time. I know this because I have seen the same look on my brother's face. And now you bring my daughter into your secrets. Do not tell me who this woman is. Ask yourself who *you* are."

Ruarc paled and fell back in his chair.

"You burned a ship," Nashwa said, turning back to me. "And threatened the safety of many. I can guess why you did it. One hour in Jarl Olavi's company tells me enough. What I want to know is this: When you stayed in my home with your women, did you know of his involvement? Did you know Afzal's guardsmen and Olavi's warriors would come to my door and beat me and my daughter? Did you know, and did you allow it to happen?"

I held her gaze. "No," I said firmly. "I did not know who was responsible until after they arrived. I would never have put you in danger willingly. I came there to meet with an ally, and believed it was safe to do so. That is all. I swear to you."

She leaned back in her chair and shut her eyes. The skin around her mouth sagged.

Exhaustion washed over me. "I burned Olavi's ship because I was angry," I said quietly. "Anger has followed me all my life, Nashwa. It brings only ashes and dust, but still I carry it with me. Because of it, everything has been ripped from my hands. And so the anger grows. I have misused my Daughters. My ally and friend is dead. I have brought my own life to ruin."

I held my hands up, spreading my fingers wide. "I bring rot to everything I touch. I push those I care for to the edge of hate. I demand what I do not deserve. I destroy what I wish to save. There is nothing I cannot manage to mangle. I am hard. I am spiteful. I am a schemer. I am as unyielding as a glacier. My husband loved me, but I could not love him. I bore children who did not live. My Daughters were the family I chose, the only ones I loved, and I betrayed them."

Nashwa said nothing, only studied me with her shining black eyes.

I covered my face with my hands. I had never revealed myself like this to anyone. Not even to Eir, who had been more than a sister once.

Ruarc placed his hand on my shoulder. "You are not alone, Gyda," he murmured.

Get a hold of yourself, I thought, setting my teeth and straightening to meet Nashwa's gaze.

"You are wise in your distrust," I said, "but know that I would never willingly bring an enemy of mine to your door. I am sorry for causing you to doubt that."

Nashwa dipped her head. "All praises to God, I am satisfied," she said in her language. Then, she reached out and took both of my hands in her own. Gaze leveled on mine, she spoke again in Norse, her voice firm and urgent. "I share this with you now, knowing that you are a woman of worth and integrity. Your ally lives. Ragnar Grettisson is in Córdoba with my brother. He is whole and well, my friend."

The weight of this crashed on me all at once, and a choked curse escaped me, making her frown.

"Baldur's beard, Ragnar Goldmane is alive?" Ruarc looked dazed. I didn't know if he'd ever met the man, but was certainly familiar with his reputation as one of the Jarl's favored oath-men. "That is news I'd never have expected."

Nashwa pulled back. "Is this not good news?"

"No, no, this is wonderful to hear," I said, a little breathless. "But, *how,* Nashwa? I was told he'd been killed. There was no proof, but after so long without word from him, I thought there could be no chance. How do you know this?"

She gave me one of her cryptic smiles. "The man turned up on my doorstep the night after you left. He was more than half dead, with a badly broken ankle and bruised from head to feet. He had been beaten so terribly that I thought it certain an evil spirit had come to my door. He croaked your name, shoved a gilded bracelet into my hands, and fainted on my threshold. There was no turning him away after that."

"The bloody arse," I said, smirking at the image this conjured. "He was always entitled."

She pushed her shoulders back in mock outrage. "Entitled is too kind a description! The man is as demanding and voracious as the Emir himself, blessings be upon him."

Ruarc and I both laughed.

"Tell me, Nashwa, do you know of a way to get a message to him?"

"The king may know of a ship bound for Córdoba," Ruarc said, picking up on my excitement. "You want to ask him to join our search, don't you?"

"He might be as eager as we are," I replied, mind already racing with the possibilities. "Ruarc, this is real hope. He could be the key to *Sea-Wolf*. Think of how many ports he could search!"

Nashwa looked at us both quizzically. "Are you speaking of your ship?"

"*Sea-Wolf* must be berthed somewhere," I said brightly. "With Ragnar in al-Andalus, we cover many more ports than we can now. That way, we'll have a higher likelihood of finding it."

Her hand went to her mouth. "Gyda," she said. "I thought you knew. Your ship was stolen by one of Olavi's men. The same man who left Ragnar for dead. His name is Uffe."

"I think you've killed it," Sigtryggr said dryly.

"Not dead enough," I grunted, and walloped the prow-beast again. The oar shaft warped and shivered, making my bones ache.

I stood with Ruarc in Jórvík's muddy shipyard. The morning sun had burned to noon and now I was drenched in sweat and fury. The king had arrived moments ago with two of his bodyguards, loyal warriors, verifiably not sent by the Horse-Faced king of Wessex, by virtue of the hammer talismans hanging from their necks and Sigtryggr's silver oath-rings adorning their brawny arms.

"Pus-cocked bastard," I hissed, and brought the oar down on the wooden boar's head again. A carved ear snapped off and flew into Ruarc's shin.

"Gyda, if you break everything, the shipwrights will have your neck," he said, rubbing the spot and wincing.

"It's a pitiful substitute for Uffe's fucking skull!"

"Soon, Gyda," Sigtryggr said. "I've sent Eirik Fish-Lip off to gather and ready the men. In a week, we'll be glutting ourselves on blood. You'll get your chance at his skull."

I stuck the oar blade-down in the mud and propped my hand on my hip. "Has there been any word from Heimarr?"

Sigtryggr scratched his short beard. "About that," he drawled. Crossing his arms, he leaned against a half-finished oak sternpost. "Heimarr has left the nest, Gyda. The house was empty and the hearth cold. His thralls told my men he sailed at dawn."

Ruarc sighed and scrubbed at his eyes. There were dark rings underneath them. "Heimarr must have seen you in the crowd last night. Got a scare and crept away like a worm. He must have known of Uffe's treachery. If he's pointing his prow anywhere, I say it will be to join him on the Isle of Man."

"We cannot know for certain," Sigtryggr countered. "It is just as likely Olavi called him back to Dyflin for a *blót*. He often leaves my court in spring for this reason."

Rage boiled in my gut. Snatching up the oar, I turned and scythed it at the prow-beast. The oar splintered and the boar toppled into the mud and wood shavings.

There had been no stopping me after Nashwa's revelation. Roaring and bellowing, I'd barged into Sigtryggr's darkened sleeping chamber and dragged him bare-arsed from his bed. Between the two of us, our arguing woke the whole of the king's household. Nashwa and Hadiyya fled wide-eyed out the door, followed by the children and the king's lover. Several oath-men came storming in after, spitting curses and brandishing their fists. Eventually I returned to reason long enough to learn that Sigtryggr could not deliver me Uffe's head like I demanded, for he had sent him to the Isle on trade business months before.

"The situation is unfortunate," Sigtryggr said now, mouth pinched sourly. "Had I any suspicions of Uffe, I never would have let him leave Jórvík. Heimarr vouched for him and that was enough."

"None of this is a comfort," I bit out. Throwing down the oar, I stalked to the king and put my finger in his face. His oath-men did nothing because I was a head shorter than him and, though he bore no weapon, he had his sword strapped to his hip and a steel-ringed *brynja* riding his shoulders. He looked down at me, faintly bemused.

"Uffe be cursed," I spat. "He's a troll's-arse and never does anything without Heimarr's finger leading him by the nose. *You* made that bastard Master of Trade. How could you have trusted any son of Olavi's after what Helgi did? How could you not have seen?"

"Gyda, on reflection, the king could be right," said Ruarc wearily. "Neither of us ever considered Heimarr as the culprit. Such an act threatens his father's reputation and power too much. Also, we have been in Jórvík for months and haven't crossed paths with him. Uffe could be entirely and solely to blame for this."

I ignored Ruarc. "You should have noticed my ship in your river, king," I seethed. "If they did hide it here, I half-think you did know and you lied to me."

He lifted his lip and showed a corner of sharp canine. "I would never lie to you, Gyda. I may keep things from you, but never lie. Not about something like this. If Heimarr is involved, then we will send him back to his father with his cur's tail between his legs and his balls in a bloody sack. You have my word on that. Now get your finger out of my face before I cut it off."

I stepped away, but heat rose off me in waves. *"Fuck!"* I cried, then kicked savagely at the downed prow-beast. I barely felt it smash against my toes.

Desperate to allay the situation, Ruarc said: "What I'd like to know is how could Uffe keep a *knarr* out of sight so long?"

One of the oath-men laughed. "Do ye not have boathouses in Dyflin, boy?" he said, voice rough as gravel. He was not quite Thrym's rival in size, but by the proud, chest-puffed way he carried himself, I took him to be Sigtryggr's champion, Thorkill. He wore more armrings than I'd ever seen on another: three on his right wrist and four on his left.

Ruarc's cheeks flamed. "Ah, well, yes," he mumbled, looking away. Thorkill smirked, but did not rib him further.

"If *Sea-Wolf* had been in a fucking boathouse, someone knew it," I grunted. I picked a splinter out of my fingertip and wiped it on my skirt, which was stained rusty brown from old blood. The welt on my cheek and the cut on my hip had already scabbed, and now itched fiercely. My bones ached for sleep, but my brain was aflame. How could I sleep when *Sea-Wolf* had been near my grasp? For months! My fists curled tight around the pieces of oar.

"A ship needs lookin' after," Thorkill agreed, digging a fingernail into the gap between his front teeth. He brought out a scrap of something and flicked it away. "Tarrin'. Joint caulkin'. Sail stitchin'. If Uffe took it out for work, there'll be dockhands or shipwrights who'd seen it."

Sigtryggr grunted. "Good, Thorkill. Put someone on it," he said, then turned to me. "How soon can you be ready to sail? There is much I need to set in place still. Get your affairs in order and return to me as soon as you can. We must plan before we set out."

"Ruarc and I will be with you by evening," I responded.

"I've got a different task for him, actually," the king said, then turned to Ruarc. "Follow me back to the lodge, lad, and I'll apprise you of it."

Ruarc shifted eagerly. "If you wish it, king," he said.

Now Sigtryggr smiled at me again and crowed: "I hope you remember your famous appetite for blood and glory, *Fiskwif*. Soon, we'll be hunting for troll's-arse!"

CHAPTER EIGHTEEN

The scent of blood hung on the sea-borne wind. I breathed in, tasting metal and death, and smiled.

Sigtryggr stood with me on a rise overlooking a gravel beach, where the shadows of his men grunted and cursed as they hauled his ship, *Hrið-Ormr,* out of the dark seawater.

"Smell that?" I said to the king. "Someone's caught a whale's calf, I think. Or a shark. It's a butcher's feast."

He inhaled, tilting his nose to the night sky. "They'll fill their bellies with the catch and sleep like they're dead already," he answered. I heard the keen pleasure in his voice.

The moonlight was bright and gilded the water in silver as we descended the hill and joined the rest of the men on the gravel. The king had chosen this inlet on the southern coast of the isle because it was secluded, just wide enough to conceal our company and to provide a screen against the crying wind. According to Arvid the scout, *Sea-Wolf* floated in a bay up the coast. It was guarded by a stand of two dozen tents and thirty-odd ill-prepared men. They'd never know we were coming until we were on them with knives against their pale throats.

"Someone get a fire going," hissed Freki, who stood with several men in a cluster. They watched as the strongest of their brothers heaved against the strain of the thick ropes. No doubt they were thanking the fate-spinners they had not been given that bone-cracking task.

Next to him, Red Yngvi grunted and spat a wad onto the beach. "I can't see my arse to wipe it, let alone whose neck I'll be chopping," he said.

Other than Thorkill the king's champion, Yngvi was the best fighter, and he looked it. He was a stout trunk of a man, built like the war god Týr and as flame-haired as Thor. Each of the men muttered their agreement with him.

"You don't wipe your arse anyway, Yngvi, so why do you need to see it?" Sigtryggr said, clapping the man on the shoulder. His friends laughed heartily.

"Quiet," I growled. "And no fires. The smoke will rise and carry."

"Only downwind," Freki mumbled, but he dropped his eyes to the stones.

During our voyage, all of Sigtryggr's oath-men learned the hard way not to argue with me. In fact, a week with me as skipper taught everyone that I suffered no complaints and no stupidity. I'd earned the byname *Grim-Bitch* and I carried the title with pride.

The evening had grown murky. A bank of heavy fog rolled in from the sea, strong with the scent of rotting whale flesh. Soon our little beach would be obscured from the moonlight by a cloak of cloud. Perfect for hiding, but that wasn't the purpose here. Eagerness to strike out rose off our company like steam off a horse's back.

"How far to their encampment, boy?" Sigtryggr asked Arvid.

The lad perked up. He'd been hovering at the edge of the beach, bouncing on his toes and hoping to be noticed. He was scrawny and fleet-footed, useless with ropes and oars, but a perfect scout. He'd proven himself eager to be useful, which made me like him better than the rest of Sigtryggr's men.

Arvid scratched the stubble on his jutting chin. "How far?" he repeated. "An hour, I'd say. Coast is hard in the dark. Too many cliffs. Sharp stones. Faster to take the road, King."

Sigtryggr grunted. "The road, then, and let's hope it is the shorter route. I don't want to spend the night on this fucking rock."

"A main road will be watched," I pointed out. "There's little chance we can keep out of sight for long."

Red Yngvi stepped forward and ran his tongue over his teeth. "There's only thirty of them," he said. "We're twice that. Surprise or no, their blood will whet our throats, and that is certain."

"Surprise is everything, Yngvi," the king rumbled. "I've seen a hundred raiders wiped out by twenty defenders with pitchforks and scythes."

"Preparation is the difference between success and slaughter," Arvid quipped brightly, which made Yngvi roll his eyes.

"Boot-licking pup," he muttered.

"Are you certain there isn't another path?" I asked the lad. "One less exposed? A sheep's track?"

Arvid's bony shoulders rolled as he thought about this. "Some kind of tread-way, yes. It's broken, easy to miss. Might not come out at the camp. You'll be guessing once it diverges from the road."

"What's wrong with the road, *Fiskwif*?" Sigtryggr demanded. "A pissing sheep's track? Bah!"

"It will be challenging in the dark, but it brings less risk of discovery. I would call that acceptable odds."

He scowled, but seemed mollified enough.

A quarter hour later, *Hrið-Ormr* was safely tethered and the company kitted out. I wore a poorly-fitted wool tunic and carried a top-heavy axe with a bulky shield on my back. My muscles had atrophied in the months since I'd last worn my own seax and fine *brynja*, but at least these items were sturdy, and would do the killing job just as well.

We followed Arvid as he bounded through hillocks of grass and patches of dirt. His path, if one could call it that, was little more than a wagon rut running chaotically between the sea and the road. If it indeed led to the bay, then I'd give the scout a fat garnet as a token of thanks.

"I can guess you're thinking of Olavi," Sigtryggr said, joining me as I walked at the front of the company.

"He might have refused us," I whispered to the king. "Soon as he saw Ruarc's face among your family's, he'd know it was me asking for help, not you. And he knows that Nashwa and Hadiyya are my friends. What if he threw them all out on their arses?"

Sigtryggr made a deep noise in his throat. "If that were likely, then I should have been wise enough to send a representative of my own along. For insurance reasons, of course."

I looked at him sideways. "You think I am worrying over nothing, but you haven't known Olavi these last years. Who did you send? Thorkill? He'd be the only one to stand a chance. If not for cleverness, then for sheer, stalwart stubbornness. Olavi is many things, but a master of the mind he is not."

Sigtryggr shortened his stride to match mine. "Who else would I trust to protect my household and my children? But you aren't wrong about Olavi. He is a stubborn, stupid bastard. It's why I enjoy him so much." He gave a short, delighted laugh. "But he's vain! Vain as Freyja. See, I sent a chest of pretty silks with my house-thrall, who by all arguments is the best seamstress in Jórvík. She'll have sewn him several fine tunics on the journey."

I stomped through a dark patch of weeds, and my *wyningas* caught on the thorns. "Silk tunics against a Jarl's spite. Seems a fair deal."

He snorted. "Ah, one sail is good enough. Traders come and go from this isle all the time. *Hrið-Ormr* is easy to ignore. But a pair of *drakkar* bristling with shields hanging from strakes—well, that would bring down a force of these island's fighters on our heads."

I could hear his toothy grin; Sigtryggr loved nothing more than he loved a bloody fight, except maybe a strong drink. But not me. We were strolling into a scuffle with no promise of help, and that set my belly roiling like a basket of eels.

Sigtryggr nudged my shoulder roughly. "Olavi will come, Gyda," he said. "A little late, maybe, but he'll come. Even if Heimarr is not in Dyflin like we hope, Uffe is still an oath-man, and his crew are too. What is all this but a chance for Olavi to finally settle affairs with you?"

I tilted my head and spat. "If he does come, it's not to settle affairs, but to get his fists into my silver."

"That too," Sigtryggr conceded. "I'd offer to alleviate that cost, but, well—"

"You'd be spending my silver too."

His laugh was a nasal, infectious thing.

We fell into the rhythm of walking, our breathing mingling with the company's so that anyone out in the darkness would think a puffing *wyrm* was passing by. We'd wrapped our weapons in oiled rags to keep the noise to a minimum, but that didn't matter much, for a rising wind drowned out most sound beyond that made by ourselves. The fog had thinned around the hills, and as we came to the crest of one, the stars above us gleamed with cold fire and the moon peeked out from a wisp of cloud.

"Where's that troll-cursed Arvid gone off to?" mumbled Sigtryggr. He raised a hand and the company's heavy footfalls halted.

"What is it, Lord?" whispered Eirik Fish-Lip, stumping over and squatting behind a bush to have a quick piss. "Are we close?"

Sigtryggr looked around. "Has anyone seen the scout? He's meant to show us the way, not bound off like a fucking hare into the dark."

I'd gone ahead a few paces to peer at the shrouded hills and dips in the track. "I think we've left the road," I said, pointing to the east. "See? It wraps around the base of that hill, then vanishes. We're heading northwest. Towards the coast."

"So we're close enough," said Eirik, rearranging himself. "Good I pissed now, eh Grim-Bitch? If I get killed, no one can say I soiled my dignity."

"You'll still shit yourself, Fish-Lip," cracked one of his friends. Eirik sneered at him.

Sigtryggr said nothing, but stared off into the dark as if he could peel it away.

Sea-Wolf was still hidden from this vantage, but the weight, the *knowing* of my ship's presence out on the dark water filled my brain and my lungs. I went up Sigtryggr. "See anything?"

"Smoke," he muttered. "Something's burning."

I straightened and followed Sigtryggr's stare.

"Definitely smoke," I agreed after a moment. There was nothing more than a scrap of gray wisp in the dark, hardly discernible. A breath of wind played over my skin and I sniffed. "It's meat, I think. Not a shark or whale after all. Cattle."

Sigtryggr had gone still beside me, his good eye as narrowed and creased as his bad one.

"Fuck," he burst out. "Bow! Give me a bow!"

Something exploded a distance ahead of us, a figure of smudged darkness. It screamed, threw something at Sigtryggr, then tore off through the grass.

"Ai!" screamed Eirik. "A troll! A demon! We're cursed!" He'd intercepted the projectile, which dangled grotesquely by its hair in Eirik's fist.

Arvid the scout was missing his jaw. And the rest of his body.

"The fucker's getting away," I yelled. "Kill him!"

A handful of men broke off and ran after him, but none of them were as fleet-footed as Arvid had been. His killer pulled ahead, never once looking back, vanishing and reappearing as the mounds of earth lifted and fell beneath his fleeing legs.

"Kill him!" I screeched. "He'll warn them!"

Someone handed Sigtryggr a bow, already strung. With a gust of breath and a grunt, he hauled back and let an arrow fly. The shaft whistled, its speed making it a streak in the night.

My heart seized. We were fucked. *Sea-Wolf* would be gone again, and Uffe with it.

"You missed," I said, breathless.

"I didn't."

Arvid's killer scaled a hill, his silhouette stark. He stayed there an instant, suspended in the moonlight. Then he gave a short scream and fell.

"Run, men!" Sigtryggr roared. "Over that hill, you've got a raven's feast waiting! Get me their livers and we'll make Hel a feast she'll glut herself on!"

We surged through the grass as one, over the steaming body of poor Arvid and through the furrows made by the look-out's flight.

My fingers ached with the haft of the axe and my shield bruised my forearm as I ran, but none of it mattered. *Sea-Wolf* was mine, and its thieves would fall to my vengeance.

The tents of the encampment appeared before us. We poured down the hill like a horde of screaming wraiths.

The first man I killed was still struggling to pull on his *brynja*. My axe took him in the belly, his head still caught in the bulk of the rings. He fell and I never saw his face.

The next man I killed had his helmet on and a spear in his hand. He jabbed at me, but I was nimble, even with the weight of my shield and mail. I danced to the side and thrust my shield boss into his face. His nose crunched, and as he screamed, my axe removed the spear and his hand from his wrist. Then I buried the axe in the crest of his helmet.

Around me, Sigtryggr's company infested the tents like maggots, dragging out occupants and slaughtering them in the gravel and sand while their trousers still hung about their knees.

This camp of thirty had been here a long time, growing fat and slow on fish and bread. By the number of campfires, thirty was only a part of their number. Uffe and his companions had made friends here.

With no immediate opponent, I paused to look for Sigtryggr. I found him several spear-lengths to my left. He held a sword, a gleaming beauty of a thing that I lusted after. The fuller dripped with bright red blood as he swung it.

His foe was a bulky man, a match to Sigtryggr in height, but he had nothing to defend himself with but a seax. Sigtryggr took his neck and jaw with a casual swipe.

"There are more, Sigtryggr," I called.

He wiped blood out of his eyes and grinned like a hungry shark. "Where?"

"I don't know. I haven't seen Uffe. Be wary!"

He raised his hand to acknowledge me, then pointed. "On your right!"

I raised my shield just in time.

The axe came down and my whole body juddered with the force of it. I fell to a knee, then rolled as it came down again. It was a young man, with a set of crooked teeth and a nose to match. He yelled and leapt for me as I got to my feet. I kicked the inside of his leg, managing to avoid the slice of his blade by a hair.

"Bitch!" He struggled to right himself as I put distance between us.

We were close to a fire. I kicked up glowing embers as he lunged again, searing through his tunic and scorching his bare arm. He screamed, batting the burning coals off, forgetting that I had an axe too. I used it, felling him face-down into the fire with his mouth gaped wide.

"Gyda!"

Sigtryggr wasn't where he'd been. He was farther away now, yanking his sword from the corpse of a gray-beard. I crossed the distance, leaping bodies and dodging the fighters all around me.

"Are you hurt?"

"They're coming," he panted. "And they're bringing horses."

He pointed his blade inland. A line of men on horseback carrying torches and spears approached from the road.

"Forty at least," Sigtryggr said. "They'll be here before we can pull back. We can't face that many. Not on horses."

"We have to," I said, my voice rising. "We're winning."

He turned to me, his expression grim. "*Sea-Wolf* is there on the water," he said. "You can row it out with less than a dozen men. Take eight, get into the *faering* and go. I'll take the rest and retreat to *Hrið-Ormr*."

"No!"

"Gyda," he ground out. "We cannot fight them all."

"We don't need Olavi. Siggi, *please*. I refuse to be cowed by these shits. Form up the shield-wall. We can still fight."

He hesitated, his eyes sad.

"Lord!" Nearby, one of our men emerged from a tent, dragging another man out by the hair. "Found this fucker stuffing himself in a chest. *Niðingr*!"

He tossed the warrior onto the gravel, and my rage, sudden and hot as molten iron, stopped my heart.

"*You*," I hissed.

Heimarr Olavisson looked up at me, a horrible grin spreading over his face. "Hullo, *Fiskwif*. Thought you'd be my father's bed-slave by now. Great little boat you had. So much shine. All mine now."

I lunged, a scream tearing from my throat. My axe rose above my head.

Sigtryggr moved, his fist closing around my arm like a vice to pull me back. He bellowed in my face, desperate words I couldn't hear. Spit and bile was my answer. He would not let go.

I saw only Heimarr. His shit-eating grin. The small knife he pulled from his belt. The way he got to his feet faster than lighting, stabbing Sigtryggr's man through the eye before he thought to defend himself. The man dropped without a sound, his skull a cratered ruin.

Heimarr turned to me, to Sigtryggr, his eyes on the back of Sigtryggr's neck.

I opened my hands, dropping my axe and shield, and twisted,

putting my foot through the king's legs. Confusion flashed over his face. Using every bit of my strength, I shoved.

The king fell, cracking his arm against a tent peg. He gave a pitched scream, and Heimarr's blade missed.

Heimarr went for me next, slashing before I could pull back. Quick, hot blood soaked my tunic. I lurched, holding my belly with one hand and grabbing for anything I could use as a weapon. There was nothing but gravel. Nothing but tents and blood and blurry moonlight.

Beside me, Sigtryggr moaned, his eyes rolling in his head. Blood streaked one side of his face and bone pierced through the livid skin of his arm. He'd lost his sword.

Heimarr screamed and I threw myself down as the wind of his blade whistled by my head.

A boot drove into my chest. I choked. I couldn't breathe, couldn't see. But I could feel as he kicked me again, driving my shoulders into the gravel so my bleeding belly was exposed.

"Once you're dead, I wonder if my father will make me his heir instead of Hákon? That piss-drinker never had the gall for good knife-work. When I'm Jarl, killing him and his witch wife will be like killing lambs. Too easy."

My mind was already fleeing. I waited for Heimarr's strike, wondering if the blade would enter my throat, my brain, or my lung. How long would it take to die?

The blast of a horn shattered the air.

Heimarr stood over me, panting, staring towards shore. He grinned, then bent down to my ear. "You hear that, old bitch?" he whispered. "That is your death-call. You die unloved. Alone. Unremembered. When the sea takes your rotten bones, give Helgi my best. Rán's Hall has one more cold corpse to fill its benches."

Heimarr straightened and sheathed his knife. Then he lifted his boot and drove it into my chest, my belly, my legs. My ribs cracked. My nose broke. And when he aimed for my temple, I knew nothing but the exploding black sky above and hot red blood soaking the ground beneath.

PART FOUR: IRELAND

CHAPTER NINETEEN

"You can't disturb her. This is the first she's slept in days," said the woman standing outside the door.

It was not quite dawn. The hearth had long since died to ash, and murky shadows gathered in the rafters. A pallet lay empty on the floor beside my bed.

"She will sleep again," said another, deeper voice. "We need an answer from her. I cannot delay here much longer."

"A few more hours won't make a difference," came the answer. "Leave her be. I will speak to her when she wakes."

I jerked open the door, and the two figures gawped at me in the dim light like children caught with their fingers in the honey-cakes.

"Well?" I said, voice thin as a winter wind. "I am awake now. Speak if you're going to, or fuck off."

Hákon stepped away from his wife, who had been attempting to bar the door from his incursion.

"My apologies," Hákon said formally, straightening his tunic. His gaze went to the space over my head. I huffed and wrapped the linen shawl a bit tighter around my nightclothes.

"If you were sorry, you wouldn't have bothered," I said. "Are you coming in, or will you make me wait forever?" I turned, but pain yet unbalanced me. As I wobbled, Eir grabbed my arm before I collided with the doorpost.

"You shouldn't be rising without help," she scolded. Holding tight, she led me back to the small timber-frame bed. When I sat, she released my arm like it stung her.

"How else would I have made you two to be quiet," I said. "Your muttering could have woken a *draugr* in its barrow."

Hákon crouched at the smoldering hearth and stirred the coals. "Better for you to be up and moving. Worst thing to do is recover on your backside."

"My backside is the one part of me that doesn't hurt," I snapped. "If you're making that fire, put on some water. I want tea."

"She wants tea," Eir muttered. Rising, she retrieved the night bowl from its place in the corner. When she turned, I gave her a smile.

"A bit of porridge would be just right, too," I said sweetly. "And a few slices of dried haddock if it's not too much trouble."

Hákon sucked air, round eyes darting between us.

Eir's brows rose and the knuckles of her hands turned white. I wondered if she would dump the bowl over my head. A moment passed, then she turned on her heel and marched out, yanking the flimsy door shut behind her.

It had been three weeks since the attack on Uffe's camp. The first days, I had been too hurt to care what spit of coast Hákon had run us aground. Eventually I'd learned this place was a large abandoned farmstead, a day's ride north of Dyflin. The proximity to Olavi chafed, but I had little say in the matter. Remaining on the Isle of Man was folly, especially with the threat of more pointless death. The horsemen had likely been hired from local forces, and since Uffe had not been found among the dead, it was assumed he'd fled either before the fight or rode off with them. *Sea-Wolf* was gone, too, rowed out during the attack by some of Uffe's crewmen. This was a fact I did not allow myself to linger on, because far more pressing was that Hákon did not yet know of Heimarr's treachery.

I had not decided whether to tell him. In fact, I'd told him nothing at all, and this was the most likely reason for his visit. But as much as I resented Hákon, I wasn't in any state to argue. If he wanted to drop me into the jaws of *Niðhöggr* the Corpse-Snake, no one could stop him.

It had been his silver-throated horn on the beach, calling the king's men to rally with his own as they splashed ashore from *Dreki*. Together, the two forces followed Hákon in slaughtering the last of Uffe's warriors in the camp. King Sigtryggr and I both owed him our lives, and that put me in a most uncomfortable position.

An ember popped in the hearth as firelight chased away the shadows in the little house. Hákon gave a satisfied grunt.

"You shouldn't goad her so much," he said, squinting at me. "Next time she changes your bandages, she'll use the garlic salve."

I shuddered and pressed my hand against the linen strips across my belly. The newly-knit skin underneath itched constantly, like lice writhing between the fibers. "Not garlic," I said weakly. "It'll be the vinegar one."

Eir and I didn't speak much, and what we did say to each other was never more than what was necessary. She'd been my only companion those first fragile days. Once I'd regained enough strength to sit without puking, Ruarc or Sigtryggr took to wandering in, and these visits were infinitely more cheering than cold silence.

Hákon stretched his legs out, feet towards the fire. "Show more gratitude and she'll be easier on you. Healing work is more taxing than the healing itself. It's a wonder she didn't kill you the first night."

I snorted. "If I stop goading your wife, do you think she'd forgive me?"

"Is that a serious question?"

Sighing, I moved to rest my back against the turf wall. Hákon graciously ignored my pained grunts.

"Aggravating Eir is the only entertainment I have in this shit-hole," I said. "What do you want, Hákon? Did you come to scold me like a child, or is there something else?"

Though he was a man who strove always to appear calm, the fire under his skin never remained hidden for long. As he sat there, his right foot waggled back and forth, his teeth worried some sore spot in his mouth, and his gaze wandered from the wall to the thatching to my face.

"My men are tired of sitting on their arses," he said. "They want to go home, and so does my wife. Today, you'll tell me why we should stay."

"Stay?" I said. "You surprise me, Hákon. If your people want to go, then go. You don't need my permission."

"You sent for help," he replied.

"That was King Sigtryggr," I said doggedly.

"Ah, yes, the King of Jórvík, a man with a hundred men in his own personal *fyrd*, needs Dyflin's help."

"You say that as if it is not true."

"It isn't!" Hákon reddened and dug his fingertips into the dirt. "I did not come for an argument, Gyda. Now is the time you tell me what really happened on that beach."

"Ask the king or his men."

"They're not talking, and you know that very well. Is this still about your petty feud with Uffe over your ship?"

"*Sea-Wolf* is gone," I burst out. "None of it matters anymore. Go back to Dyflin and let me handle my own affairs."

He settled back, wearing a smug smile. "You are too easy to goad, woman."

I had wanted to keep them out of it. If Hákon knew of his brother's lies and designs on his birthright, there would be no doubt he would put himself and Eir directly in harm's way. I aimed to slaughter Uffe and Heimarr the moment I could walk a straight line again. I had already killed one treacherous brother. As long as I could keep it to myself, why not kill another?

But Hákon was too perceptive for his own good. I could not walk very far without support, and Sigtryggr still nursed his broken arm. We were far from the safety of Jórvík, and needed Hákon's help for a while longer, as much as it stung my pride to admit it.

And so I sat in my sullen anger, staring at Hákon while he stared back.

We might have sat a while longer, but just then Eir ducked through the doorway, empty night-bowl in one hand and a spoon and plate of thick berry porridge in the other. She replaced the bowl then sat down next to me.

"No fish," she told me, holding out the plate. "It would hurt your cracked teeth."

I took her offering, then reached my other hand to grasp her fingers.

"Thank you, Eir," I said huskily. "For all of it."

Faint surprise made her cheeks flush. She nodded and withdrew, making space as I crossed my legs to eat. I filled my mouth with a sloppy handful of berries.

"Oh, this is delicious," I mumbled.

"Gyda," Hákon pressed.

Eir looked between the two of us, delicate brows rising. "Oh, you think she's going to tell you anything?" she said to her husband. "No chance of that. I've already tried."

Hákon dropped his head back. "It's like this every day, is it?" he said to the thatching.

"Not a word for anyone that isn't belligerent or full of scorn."

"Belligerence is my best trait," I quipped. "Did you put honey in this porridge? It's wonderful."

"Ah, this is worse than the teething bairns at home," Hákon mumbled, then rose. "So be it. If you will not speak, woman, there's nothing more to be done. I'm raising *Dreki*'s mast tomorrow. You and Sigtryggr are on your own in whatever bog you've sunk yourselves."

He went to the door. "I'll leave you with the horse, love. A walk will do me good."

Eir waved. "Actually, I'll come along. I need another moment here, so give the horse a bag of feed while you wait. It's next to the water trough."

It was the way she looked at him, tired and sad, that made me put the spoon down.

"Alright, wait."

Hákon paused with his hand on the doorframe. "Don't bait me, *Fiskwif*."

"I wouldn't dare," I said wryly. "But answer me this first: why do you care so much?"

His head tilted as he considered this. "My father's obligations are my obligations," he said. "And now therefore my wife's. We came to help because King Sigtryggr is our ally, and a powerful one at that. If the trouble is such that he sends his family and household to Dyflin for protection, then I need to know why."

"You know that isn't what I meant," I said.

His eyes narrowed like a cat's. "I plucked the two of you out of the grasp of a score of blood-hungry horsemen on a corpse-piled beach. My men fought for you. My wife has nursed you and wiped your arse and suffered your bitterness for weeks. You tell me what all this was for, woman, and don't say Uffe or *Sea-Wolf*. I could have left you to die. I still might."

I set aside my plate, appetite gone. "Will it change anything? You knowing?"

Eir frowned at the break in my voice, but if I met her gaze now I'd lose my nerve.

"Take the chance and see," Hákon said.

The skin of my neck was hot, and I scratched it. "I am—," I started, then cleared my throat. "I am *grateful* to both of you. After all that has passed, it is difficult to give anyone my trust. Or to earn anyone else's. Neither of you had reason to come to my aid, but you did. I see it, and I honor it."

"So tell us, Gyda," Eir said. "Who did this to you? Surely not Uffe. Sigtryggr said he wasn't there."

"Do you not wish to see the fucker suffer for it, whoever it is?" Hákon added, affecting an encouraging smile. "If I know anything about you, it's that revenge is the first thing on your mind."

"You will not believe me," I said. "And why should you? Not even the gods would believe me."

Eir reached for my hand and held it gently. The gesture surprised me, but I didn't refuse it. Hákon simply waited, shoulders loose and expression open.

Fuck this. Nothing left to lose, I thought, then straightened and set my jaw.

"First, you must swear to me an oath," I said.

Hákon scowled. "I will not swear anything without the Jarl's leave."

"You must swear on your own name, Hákon," I replied. "Swear you will help me deliver vengeance against my enemy as you would against any man who had stolen from you. Bring me justice as you would to one who harmed your wife. You must fight as if your own life is in danger. Because I promise you this, Hákon *Stáli*: You and Eir and all of Dyflin is in danger if we do nothing."

Eir stiffened beside me. "Gyda, what are you saying?"

"Swear to me you will fight, son of Olavi Sharp-Spear," I said. "No matter the cost. No matter the hurt. Do this for Dyflin and your alliance with Jórvík. Do this for all the respect you once bore for me."

"I swear it," Hákon said, without hesitation. "Before the Æsir and the Vanir, before the land spirits and the ocean goddess Rán herself, I swear it. Tell me."

"Surely this is madness," Eir cried. "Gyda, what is all this?"

I released her hand and slowly, achingly, I stood, grimacing as my wounds and bruises pulled. My healing ribs creaked with the effort. I met Hákon's gaze on my own two feet.

"The man who did this is the same man who sent Uffe to steal *Sea-Wolf* and my wealth. He is the same man who tried to murder Sigtryggr, King of Jórvík, and who beat me near to death. That man is your brother, Heimarr Olavisson, and he aims to kill you. When you are dead, he will kill Olavi and steal your birthright. May his name be cursed from here to the cold halls of Hel. You have sworn an oath to me, Hákon. Now this is my oath to you: I will kill your brother Heimarr or I will die in the doing of it. May Rán bear witness."

Hákon stood very still. His eyes shone, two blue-black coals in his white face. Without another word, he turned and left us.

"What have you done?" Eir breathed.

CHAPTER TWENTY

Two days later, Sigtryggr found me behind the house, sitting on a stool in the sunshine with a bone needle and a bundle of yarn.

"No Eir guarding you today, eh?" he said, leaning his long frame against a rainwater barrel. He tucked his good arm behind his back and grinned at me.

"King, if I'd wanted your company, I'd have asked for it."

His curling hair was unbound, and it fell over his bad eye like a raven's wing. He pushed it back. "You ask for nothing, woman. You demand. It's been days and I got tired of waiting for you to come see me for a change."

I tilted my face, relishing the warmth of sunlight on my skin. The summer rains had ceased in the night and there were no clouds anywhere. Wood warblers sung in the sparse stand of trees behind the outer farmstead boundary.

"How's Ruarc?" I asked.

"The same," he replied, and I grimaced.

"Don't make that face," Sigtryggr said. "I talked to him. Your first killing haunts you a while, but he's bearing up fine. Just needs time to let the blood wash off, so to speak."

"He thinks he can hide it when he's with me," I groused. "But as long as he can relieve himself with you, I won't bring it up."

Sigtryggr gave a half-smile, which disappeared when I asked: "Is Hákon still gone?"

"Eh, Eir says he'll come back with a bloody deer slung over his shoulders and in far less of a black mood. I gathered you finally told him."

"I did."

Sigtryggr whistled. "He take it like a man whose brother is a murdering coward?"

"That's two for him, now," I said, holding up the requisite fingers. "Must have given him the shits for how fast he fled from me."

We both laughed and a measure of the tension eased.

"Never got along with that one," Sigtryggr said. "He's full of himself and too cocky. Who names themselves after steel? Annoying little shit. But honorable enough."

"So he's too much like you, then?"

Sigtryggr put on a look of offense, but forgot it immediately in favor of some new thought. He peered at me like a hound after a cooked stew bone. My anxiety returned.

"So," he said. "If you won't come down to see everyone, then how about letting your, ah, women? Daughters? —I can never remember what you call them—come to see you?"

I lifted the bundle from my lap. "These are turning out well, don't you think? Might be rough, but should keep my toes warm."

Sigtryggr's nose wrinkled. "Don't dodge me. But, is that meant to be a sock? You nalbind like a girl barely learning. It's pitiful."

"You try it, then," I said, offering him the needle and yarn.

To my surprise, he straightened and reached for the lot.

Loosening the loops with his teeth, he put the thumb of his injured hand through them and pulled tight. He met my astonishment with a wink of his good eye.

"Are you certain your arm can handle that?"

One of Eir's slings tied around his neck held the arm secure. He wiggled it to and fro.

"Are you certain your head wasn't caved in when it got kicked?" he replied.

"Pff, we've got matching bruises to tell the tale. You tell me, king." I tapped my right temple. The skin there was livid, mottled with fading yellows and greens. My nose had also been broken and would heal crooked. Breathing through it was still impossible. But of all my injuries, the headaches were the worst. They came on without warning, terrible enough to leave me bed-bound and thrashing for a full day.

"I think we'll live, you and me," Sigtryggr said. There was an unusual moroseness in his tone, and it stung me with guilt.

I studied the king. He appeared as robust as ever, but there was an odd tilt to his head and tightness around his mouth and shoulders. I knew that posture, had worn it myself enough times. And I'd seen it on the Daughters more than once. This was bravado, poorly masked with jests and smiles.

"It pains you, doesn't it?" I blurted.

He shrugged. "It would, if I weren't drinking Eir's ale by the bucketful."

"Ale?" I scoffed. "That hardly passes as medicine."

He shifted, hummed, crossed one leg over the other. "She has her ways. They're effective enough."

"Are you drunk now?"

He gave me a sly, squinting grin. "Oh, yes. Blindingly."

"Liar."

He scowled. "Of course it fucking hurts," he said testily. "But it's more of a nuisance than anything else. Better the pain than the loss of the arm. A king needs all his limbs, and this king in particular. Edward would dance in his rat-hole hall if he knew where I am."

"You're as hale as a stone," I said lightly. "Broken arm or not. Edward will shit himself the next time he sees you, not dance."

Sigtryggr pursed his thin lips and focused on his work.

The needle passed through the loops of yarn on his thumb. He lifted, and one loop came off, tightening into a knot in the sock's fabric. A new loop took its place on his thumb, and the movement began again.

"Eir says I need time before I can take off the sling," he said softly. "She won't let me touch a sword. Bah, as if I ever will again."

"Despair doesn't suit you, Siggi," I said. "Look at what you're doing. That needle requires skill to wield. It may be less than a sword, but it is no less important. Take heart. You'll trade it for your blade soon enough."

He squinted at the sock dubiously. "My men can't know about this, you know," he said.

"I won't say a word. Not even to Eir. She'd have your balls for moving too much."

The smile he wore did not reach his eyes.

We remained quiet for a while. I watched Sigtryggr work. He held the sock and loops in one hand and used the other to pass the needle. Down. Through. Up. Down again. It must have pained him to sustain the action for so long, but he did not so much as wince.

I thought of what I could give him for an answer. Sigtryggr had shown me his weakness, and respect demanded I do the same.

So much had happened between Dyflin and Jórvík and that bloody beach. I still could not believe the Daughters were *here,* living in the cluster of houses at the center of the farmstead with Hákon's oathmen and Sigtryggr's warriors. After what I had done in al-Andalus, I could not delude myself into thinking they had come for me. I was past that sort of arrogance. They were here for Eir.

I looked at the king and silently admitted that there were no easy answers, for either of us.

Sigtryggr had lost half his men in our raid, a sacrifice for a cause that was not his own. And he was still here, visiting me.

"Thank you for staying," I whispered, hoping he heard all that I left out.

"Made you a promise, didn't I?" he said, not looking up from the sock.

My throat constricted. I forced the words out before they could choke me. "I can't face them yet, Siggi. What could I even say? I can hardly speak to Eir without hissing like a snake. Humility has never been comfortable for me."

He lowered the needle and looked at me then, amusement sparking in his good eye. "You can't get more humiliated than you are now."

"I can't let them see me broken like this," I replied.

He shook his head. "You're not feeling broken, Gyda. This is guilt. Two very different things."

"Are they?"

My misery did not move him. "You cannot face them because it means you have to apologize," he said. "This is not about humility. You have to put things right, or find a way to live with the silence."

I slumped, regretting I'd ever said anything. "Apologies do nothing but make you feel worse than before."

Sigtryggr lifted the yarn to his mouth and snapped it with his teeth. "Pass me a new thread."

I retrieved the ball of yarn from my basket and broke off a piece twice the length of my arm. Holding the needle in his immobilized hand, he threaded the piece through the eye, then laid the sock with the loose end on the lid of the barrel. Wetting his fingers, he rubbed the end of the new length against the old, felting the threads together with the friction. It took three tries, but once the join was secure, he began again, this time with larger movements to accommodate the longer working yarn.

"I take it back," he said finally. "You're right; apologies don't fix the damage. But action does."

I shifted, wincing as my atrophied muscles pulled. "Is this your way of apologetic action?" I asked irritably. "Nalbinding my sock?"

Sigtryggr waggled his dark brows at me. "What do I, the grandson of the great Ivarr *Beinlausi*, possibly have to apologize for?"

"Plenty," I said, serious now. "Why did you stop me? Why did you protect that spawn of a troll from me? I could have killed Heimarr then and there if you hadn't intervened."

This was tricky ground. Sigtryggr was a proud king, unused to being challenged. But it was my nature, and I had to say it, for my sanity if not my own pride.

"Heimarr is a son of Olavi," he said simply. "His death would have been on my head, not yours. I have no wish to start a blood-feud with the Jarl in Dyflin." He shrugged, as if this was not the most infuriating thing he'd ever uttered to me.

"Heimarr stole my ship and my silver," I cried. "If there is a feud, he started it."

"*Our* silver now," Sigtryggr corrected. "Gyda, the man was unarmed. Coward or not, I don't kill defenseless men. King's honor." He thumped his chest.

"Piss on honor! That goat-fucker had a knife. He killed your man and he was going for your neck with it."

Sigtryggr's gaunt cheeks dimpled. "And here I stand, thinking you'd broken my arm and cracked my skull because your blood-lust and bollocks were bigger than mine."

Despite myself, my fury evaporated and I smiled. "Siggi, that's never been a question."

He waved the needle about wildly. "That gash on your belly is from him, then? The putrid fucker!"

We were both laughing now. Clumsily, I got to my feet and gestured from my head to my knees. "All this is from him. I didn't even come close. Which means I have another chance."

"So, what you're really asking is if I'll stop you again?"

"Will you?"

He thought for a moment, closing his bad eye as he looked up at the bright sun. "Hm, no. I won't stop you. I think I may even help you try again. I'm honor-bound to see the thing through. Also, I like seeing you smile. I wager skinning the fucker like a weasel will make you smile."

And so, like the old friends we were, Sigtryggr and I rambled on for the rest of the afternoon, easy in our shared hurts and growing regard, if that indeed is what we now had.

Later, I ate a supper of cold stew and bread, then ventured out to search for Eir and the others.

The farmstead was expansive, with ancient borders lined with curving ditches grown over with grass and broken by encroaching forest. Hákon had new timber ramparts and a gate erected in under a week. A path led down a long slope to the shoreline where *Dreki* and *Hrið-Ormr* had been anchored. If I climbed atop the water trough outside my door, I could catch sight of the tips of their masts.

My little turf-sided house stood under the boughs of an old forest on the western boundary, as if hiding from the other dwellings in the center. I was happy for it, because these houses were packed cheek-by-jowl with the two combined forces of hardened warriors. I preferred the isolation of my little hut over sleeping on a bare strip of dirt floor surrounded by the fug of farts and arse-sweat.

The sun sank as I labored down the path. Though every day I walked a little farther and grew a little stronger, currently I ached in every muscle that could ache. Sigtryggr's visit had exhausted me. To support myself in Eir's absence, I had brought along my walking stick. It was a beautiful, sturdy thing made of yew. Ruarc had given it to me, and without it my arse would surely plunk into the mud and animal shit every time I stepped outside.

I stopped to catch my breath at the edge of an empty field. A fence had been put up years ago, but now the field was overgrown with weeds and a dead grain crop. A forlorn aura hung over it, as if the earth itself sorrowed. I thumped my yew stick on the fence post.

From a nearby tuft of grass, a long-limbed heron emerged, beating sun-gilded wings to catch the evening wind. From its beak hung the limp carcass of a snake, fangs exposed in rageful death. My breath caught at the portentous omen.

Ruarc reckoned this place was ancient, a hillfort built and defended by generations of his people reaching back a thousand summers. My skin had prickled when his whispers faded to reverent silence, and it prickled now.

Night would come soon to this forgotten place, vibrating with life. Life that was soft-footed and silent in the weeds. What else might I startle on my walk home?

You're being foolish, I thought, and left the empty field with its hovering spirits and its omens.

The sun vanished below the horizon as I reached the houses. Pine torches cast golden circles of light along a maze of paths. Ahead of me, a dozen men huddled together, clutching mugs of steaming broth and throwing gaming pieces into the dirt.

These men served different lords, but conversation flowed between them all with the ease of those who had no reason to fight and every reason to be friends. Some of them even waved as I passed by. I recognized Eirik Fish-Lip and Thorkill, and felt glad they had survived the raid.

My Daughters had chosen to sleep in the same turf house as Hákon, Eir, Sigtryggr, and Ruarc, which confounded me. I couldn't imagine Guðrun sharing space with anyone other than Rúna, let alone a king. But the alternative was a horde of oath-men, and what a disaster that would be.

As I mused over what I would say to them, I met Ruarc just as he was rounding the walled corner of a dilapidated animal byre. He didn't see me, his attention taken with adjusting himself in his trousers. I stepped off the path quickly before he could knock me down.

"Whoo —*oof!*" he cried, stumbling forward. "Watch where you're walking, arse-faced fool!"

He whirled with a clenched fist, then yelped when he caught sight of me in the deepening gloam.

"Oh, Gyda," he breathed. "Ah, what, er, what are you doing here?" His fingers plucked at his mussed hair and tunic. His gaze bounced off everything it landed on, including me. There was a quick, furtive rustling in the byre he'd emerged from, and it made him jump and flush a hot red. "Erm. Well, that is, you see," he stammered.

"No harm done," I said brightly, and a little too loud. "You can be my walking stick now. What a lovely evening isn't it? You can show me around."

I took Ruarc's arm and forcefully steered him back the way I'd come.

"Thank you," he whispered when we reached the head of the path. "I owe you for that rescue."

"Don't thank me yet," I said. "We've still got an audience."

More men had gathered in a well-lit area in front of us, where a cauldron bubbled and Red Yngvi spooned heaping gobs of stew into bowls. Sitting on stools and dry patches of ground, they were devouring their suppers like they'd never had a meal in their lives.

"Shit," squeaked Ruarc. I veered us away, shambling between two turf houses and then under a washing line that had been tied between the posts of another walled animal shelter.

"This is as good a place to hide as any," I said, leaning my aching bones against one of the flimsy walls. "But we should move on soon. Which one of these is your house?"

Ruarc didn't hear me. He braced his hands on his hips and blew out a gusting breath to the sky. "That would have been embarrassing," he said. "You don't think they noticed me, do you?"

"Hungry men see nothing but the cauldron in front of them," I replied dryly. "Ruarc, do I even want to know who you left back there?"

"Assuredly, you don't," he said quickly. "And I don't need a lecture."

"I wasn't going to give one."

Turning in a circle, Ruarc rubbed his arms and grimaced like the dark scared him. Little night insects darted around both our heads. Their wings were minuscule, tiny iridescent scraps of silk. One landed on the tip of Ruarc's nose and he batted it off.

"How long until it's safe, do you think? These beasts are feasting on us and I hate them."

With a groan, I straightened and limped forward. "They're not the biting kind. Let's go. I hear someone and I don't have the stamina to deal with them."

"Wait," he sputtered, eyes widening as he finally looked at me. "Don't tell me you *walked* here? All the way from the forest?"

"Did you think I flew?"

He smacked his forehead. "Eir will have my liver for her beer! I was meant to bring you a meal before the sun fell!"

"I'm not hungry, just sore and cross. Now let's move or I'll tell her you cracked my ribs again."

"You shouldn't have come all this way, you can barely stand straight."

"Walk with me later if it makes you feel better."

He tugged against my grasp on his arm. "It won't make me feel better! Gyda, please!"

"You sound like a nagging grandmother," I told him. "Are you going to bring me to the house or do I have to keep using this little twig you gave me?"

"Who's the grandmother?" he muttered darkly, stumbling along as I led him away.

CHAPTER TWENTY-ONE

Ruarc brought me to a house that had been built into a natural rise in the landscape. Like the other dwellings, it was made from turf and thatched with dried grass. The entrance was sunken, and someone had left the door open. As soon as we stepped over the threshold, we were enveloped by the aromas of baking bread and savory stew.

"Hákon brought home that deer," I whispered.

Ruarc blinked. "Hm? What was that?"

I shook my head as I limped inside. My legs ached to the bone, and the walking stick had chafed my palm where I grasped it.

At first, our presence went unnoticed. A cheery hearth burned in the middle of the room, encircled by fur-draped benches and stools. No one tended it at the moment, but I caught the lilt of Astrid's humming from behind a woven reed screen on the far side of the room.

But it was near the screen on the back wall that I spied Eir standing with Liadan. Both were turned away from the door, though I could see them both in profile. I halted my advance, struck by what I saw.

Liadan's left arm was slung around Eir's middle, embracing her. It was a touch she had never endured, much less initiated. Her other hand caressed the lower part of Eir's abdomen gently, and her face was split with a beaming smile. Eir matched it.

She's with child. The realization entered my heart and hung there, suspended in equal amounts of pain and joy.

Ruarc saw the look on my face and followed it to the source. "Ahm," he muttered. "I think I'll leave you to this. Need to see where the king's gone off to. Won't be back soon."

He backed away, and it was the sound of the door closing that broke the spell. Eir's head snapped up and Liadan's arms fell.

"What are you doing here?" Eir stared at me with a mixture of shock and a small amount of fear. Liadan stepped quickly away.

I limped to a stool and lowered myself onto it, groaning in relief as my backside came to rest. "I came to see all of you," I said.

Astrid appeared, drying her hands on her apron and blowing hair out of her face. "Is that the men? I just need to take the bread from the coals and —" Her words cut off as she saw me. "Oh." She dropped her apron.

"I'm not here to start trouble," I said. "I thought we could talk,"

Eir squared her shoulders and strode forward. "Guðrun and Rúna are asleep," she said firmly, tilting her head towards another partition. "Now isn't the best time. In fact, there is no best time. You shouldn't have come."

"I'm here now," I replied. "I can wait until they awaken."

"Those two never come out," Astrid said. She had recovered from her shock and now moved further into the room. "I've barely seen them since we arrived. Not even Ragnarök could get them out of bed."

The girl had grown since I'd last seen her. Not in stature, but in womanhood. There was a new confidence to her, something she'd lacked before. She caught me studying her and glanced away.

Liadan joined Eir beside the fire. *Will you eat with us?* she signed. *The men are out. We will have privacy.*

She took the bench opposite and awkwardly smoothed her dress.

"Thank you, Liadan," I said. "If none of you are against it, I will eat."

Eir chewed her lip, gray eyes swimming with unspoken feeling.

"I wish you would sit down," I told her. "Expectant mothers need rest. I am happy for you. Deeply happy."

She scoffed. "I am sure you are."

"You will make a good mother," I said. "And Hákon will be the best of fathers. Certainly the proudest."

"And how would you know?" she demanded, pale cheeks reddening. "You know nothing of us! *Nothing*."

Astrid and Liadan both covered their mouths, surprised at this outburst.

"You are right," I whispered. "I'm sorry. I do wish you well, Eir."

"Well, then," she said awkwardly. "Your good wishes mean little to me. If you truly wished us well, you would not have extracted that troll-cursed oath from my husband. What are you really here for, Gyda? Another chance to twist the knife?"

I did not respond. Her distrust was well-founded, after all. Why should she expect it to be different now?

"The child within me is a fragile thing," she said when I didn't speak. "Hardly an ember. Hákon doesn't know, and I will not have his ignorance broken. It would rip his mind in two pieces and distract him from the path you've set him on. Distraction kills, and I will not be a widowed mother. Do you hear me? Not for your sake or anyone else's."

"I hear you," I said, holding her gaze. "I will say nothing of it to him. You have my word."

She huffed and turned to Astrid. "Is that bread finished yet, or are you going to burn it?"

Astrid flinched, and Liadan's hands caught the hearth-light, signing: *Leave the girl be, Eir. Your anger is not with her.*

"It's alright," I said. "I can leave if you'd prefer to eat alone. Ruarc claims he's happy to suffer walking me back. I can't make it alone this time."

"You *walked* here?" gasped Astrid in much the same manner as Ruarc. Her eyes widened. "You're half-dead and you *walked?* You're madder than Oðinn!"

"I think you might be right about that," I said, smiling.

Eir, by force of will or by her intrinsic nature, allowed better sense to take over. Her name, the same as the goddess of healing and mercy, fit her well. "Right," she said, coming over to me. "Up. Let me look at you."

With an effort, I stood, biting back a yelp as my ribs creaked and my belly wound pulled.

"Headache?" she said, detached.

"Not today."

"Any bleeding?"

"I haven't checked."

She sniffed. "When did you last eat?"

"Before sunset. Stew and bread."

She nodded, then looked over my healing bruises and prodded

my crooked nose. Finally, she gestured for me to raise my skirt, then bent to inspect the dressing across my belly.

"No blood. Any sharp pains?"

"None." I lowered my skirt. "No infection, either."

"Good." With that over, she settled herself on the bench next to Liadan. She crossed her legs at the ankle and waved her hand. "Let's talk."

Astrid had removed the bread from the coals and allowed it to cool while Eir examined me. Now, her knife scraped rhythmically across a wooden board, slicing each of us a portion. The sound made my mouth water.

"If you've come bringing excuses or pleas for help, forget them," Eir said. "We are here because Ruarc asked for us. I have looked after you, but now that you're healed, this is the last tether binding us. When I am finished with the king, all of us will go back to Dyflin. Back to our lives without you."

I nodded, then spread my hands, palms outward. "As you see, Eir, I have brought nothing but myself," I said. "No pleas. No excuses. No gifts or food. Myself only."

"Why come now?" she demanded. "And why at all? You could have stayed in that little house by yourself and not bothered. We would not have missed you."

This made me stiffen. "Eir, you could have left me to die on that beach. It was a straw-death, with no renown and no glory. A death I've deserved a hundred times."

"You don't owe me a thing, Gyda," she said firmly. "I don't want the pledge of your life-price, or anything like it from you. So if that's what your aim is, stop now."

I shook my head. "That isn't it. As I said before, I would like to speak."

I waited, and when no one protested, I began. "By the gods, I owe all of you everything. But first and foremost, I owe you an apology, and then a vow, made on the very life you returned to me. Not a vow of silver. A vow of honor, enforced by action."

Unimpressed, Eir turned away. Astrid also did not cease her slicing, and Liadan only gazed into the fire.

I searched for what more I could say. I would say anything if they might believe in my sincerity. Whatever I said, it had to be the truth, and no more or less than that.

I cleared my throat, determined to try again, but a rustling behind a partition stopped me. Two faces appeared, round-eyed and flushed from the warmth of their bed.

Guðrun yawned expansively. "By Freyr's balls and Freyja's tits," she said, her eyes watering as she squinted. "Look at the state of you."

"Hello, Gyda," Rúna said, smiling shyly. "It is good to see you up and around."

I rose slowly and bowed. "The both of you as well. I'm grateful you came out to see me."

"You should be," Eir said.

Guðrun and Rúna came around the circle of benches and sat alongside Liadan. Astrid handed out bowls of venison stew and fresh bread. Then we ate, none of us speaking.

Though my bowl was still half-full, my belly would hold no more and I lowered it. "Before I say what I need to say, could you share with me what happened to each of you?" I said. "After al-Andalus?"

Conflicting emotions crossed their faces at this request. I saw annoyance, regret, grief, and not a small measure of hostility.

Guðrun hid her face with her bowl, slurping the dregs noisily. Rúna clenched the bread in her lap so that it crumbled. Astrid alone looked directly at me. She bit her thumbnail.

"I know of Eir and Liadan," I ventured. "From before I left Dyflin at the beginning of winter. But I'd like to hear from the rest of you. Please."

"It doesn't concern you," Eir said, but Astrid cleared her throat.

"What you did," she began, voice wavering, then growing in strength. "Giving us up like that. *Abandoning* us. It was the worst thing you could have done to me." Her face softened. "And also the best."

Liadan's brows rose in surprise. Guðrun forgot her bowl and stared. There was a streak of broth on her upper lip, and Rúna wiped it away with her thumb.

"I haven't spoken much about it," Astrid shrugged. "But since we are all together, why not now?"

She paused to take a bracing breath, then began. "After we arrived in Dyflin, Jarl Olavi sent me back to my family's farm outside the town walls. After the way I'd left, running away in the night to join *Sea-Wolf*, I was certain my father would beat the life out of me when I came back. I was terrified in that wagon. Frozen like I'd been kissed by a glacier."

"What happened?" Rúna said gently.

Astrid blushed a little. "My mother wept as my father beat me into the mud with the same rope he used to beat the thralls," she answered. "And then he put me to work. I mucked the animal pens, cooked the meals, and tended to the children while my father rutted with my mother. I had to boil my infant sister's shit-rags. I wasn't allowed to speak or sing or walk anywhere alone."

She paused, took a small bite of bread, chewed it, and went on. "I remembered why I had run away. Somehow, on *Sea-Wolf*, our hard life made me forget how much worse it could be. And so in my heart I thanked you, Gyda."

"Why the fuck would you do that?" I said, aghast.

"Because you gave me a path to freedom," she replied, lifting a slim shoulder. "Returning to the farm helped me find that path. I learned it from you, every day. Every voyage. And so one night, while my father farted and belched at the family table, my sister threw a handful of fruit at him. She laughed. Of course, being off his bloody head with drink, he reached over and smacked her out of my mother's arms."

Guðrun swore, the muscles in her neck flexing. The others gasped. Liadan's fingers trembled by her mouth.

"She broke her tiny arm, the poor love," Astrid went on. "So I picked up my eating knife and ripped open my father's throat. I told my mother she was free of him, and that she should take the children to Dyflin because Olavi is now obligated to care for them. In the morning, I set the thralls free and gave them a bit of silver I'd scrounged. My mother had nothing to say against it. My father died of a farm accident, and that is all."

We all stared at Astrid, and she looked back, her gaze open and guileless.

"Your lovely soft hands are killers now, girl," Guðrun said, and Liadan nodded, eyes misty.

"We're proud of you," said Eir, and Astrid grinned.

"You should never have had to endure that," I said to her. "If I had known Olavi sent you back there, I never would have allowed it. I am sorry you had to raise the knife yourself."

"You would have allowed it," Astrid countered with a shake of her head. "Then, I mean. But I don't think so now."

My belly tightened, but she went on.

"If I hadn't killed my father right then, I'd have done it later for some other reason. He deserved it. Being one of Rán's Daughters taught me that in this world, we need to fight for what we deserve. Freedom means getting bloody sometimes. I've accepted that now. I think we all must accept that."

Without thought, Eir and I exchanged a glance full of concern and instinct. It was an old habit, and Eir flinched at it.

I turned quickly to Rúna and Guðrun, saying: "And the pair of you? I hope you had better fortunes than Astrid."

Expression full of anguish, Rúna looked up at Guðrun. "Not so much," she said, and my heart fell.

Liadan thumped her chest and I turned to her.

They do not speak of it, she signed. *Their families separated them. Rúna was to be sold to a trader from Kaupang for ten sheep. When Ruarc arrived in Dyflin, we sent the families a messenger, using a difficult pregnancy as a ruse. When Rúna and Guðrun arrived in Dyflin, it was the first time they'd seen each other in months. Is it any wonder they spend every moment together now? This reprieve will end the moment we leave this place.*

I shut my eyes. "I never wanted this," I said. "But I did this to you. I bear the responsibility to end it."

Pushing myself upright, I hobbled over to Guðrun and Rúna. Taking their hands, I looked into their faces. "I swear to you, I will use every skill in my possession to appease your families. You will not return to them. Nor will you be sold to Kaupang. I owe you this. I'll see it done, and Rán claim me if I don't."

They withdrew their hands, saying nothing because words could not convey what they felt.

I turned to the rest of them "What I did in al-Andalus and what I did in Dyflin are unforgivable things. I earned my exile, and I earned your hatred. I will not seek your trust or your forgiveness. Apologies mean nothing. Explanations are pointless. The only thing I have to offer is the regret of a mother and a promise to do better."

"You are not our mother," Guðrun put in sharply, and the others agreed.

"I know. But I always loved you like a mother. I called you my own. I sought your welfare and your successes. You were—you were all I had. But in the end, I chose myself over you. I thought long on what to say, and thought of only this: wherever I go from this place, I will carry all of you with me. And I will never choose my ambitions over those I love again."

They exchanged wordless glances, and then Eir spoke.

"Words and oaths and love are all well and good," she said flippantly. "But you mentioned action. Is this another of your schemes?"

Her suspicion rankled, and I forced myself not to bite back. "No schemes, but you should know all my business. King Sigtryggr has pledged to help me retrieve *Sea-Wolf* from Heimarr and Uffe."

At that, Guðrun, Liadan, and Eir shot to their feet, hands flying and voices rising with indignation.

Not again. How dare you?

"Another pile of pig-shit, this is!"

"You'll never change, will you? I should have left you on that beach!"

"Let her finish, all of you!" cried Rúna. She yanked Guðrun's arm roughly. The bigger woman fell back to the bench, sweating and heaving and blustering. Liadan put her hands over her face and sat, shoulders trembling.

Eir remained standing, a flush of rage blooming down to her collarbones. She pierced me with her glare.

"When I face Heimarr again," I said, voice shaking. "Either he or I will die. If it is my fate to die, then Sigtryggr will take up the task. When Heimarr is dead, *Sea-Wolf* belongs to all of you. I have asked Sigtryggr to make it so, and he agreed. There are no other claims. No schemes."

Stunned, Eir lowered herself to the bench.

I continued. "Half of the cargo, if Heimarr hasn't spent it all on hired men, is Sigtryggr's. The remainder belongs to you and Ruarc, though I haven't told him."

"What about you?" said Astrid. "How will you survive if you give away such a fortune?"

"I will find my way," I said. "As I always do."

Rúna made a small noise of concern. "But how is all this to come about? You can barely stand. How will you fight Heimarr? And what about Hákon? You're speaking of murdering his brother." She looked at Eir, fingers clenched in her lap.

"Hákon and Sigtryggr are discussing plans this evening," Eir responded. "An agreement must be struck before anything can proceed. Neither of them have returned, so I assume they have yet to agree."

"But Hákon agrees that Heimarr must die?" I said.

Eir's face twisted. "For Olavi's reputation and his own, my husband concedes that his brother must face justice. He wants to bring Heimarr back to Dyflin if he could, to face the Jarl and Dyfln's law-speakers. Heimarr has not yet done anything to offend his father beyond murdering the king's oath-man."

"He also tried to murder the king," I interjected, and she nodded.

"I believe Heimarr must die," she said. "If not for Hákon's reputation, then for his honor. Axe or exile will do. I also prefer to prevent King Sigtryggr from starting a blood-feud of his own with us because of it."

We all shuddered at the thought of that.

"Sigtryggr considers Olavi his friend, not just an ally," I told her. "But there are many in Jórvík who would call the king a coward if he didn't declare a blood-feud. He is bound by honor and obligation to see this through to Heimarr's death."

Eir's shoulders sagged. "I suppose we will know more when they return," she murmured.

As if the Norns had listened and spun fate to favor us, a noise beyond the door drew our attention.

"Beer," called a ragged voice. "I'd trade every fucking ship in my rivers for a single fucking mug. Tell me you've got some. Eir!"

A tall man staggered in, green-faced and sickly in the light of the fire.

"He looks worse than you do, Lady," Guðrun snickered at me. "And he didn't get his brains stomped."

Eir rose. "King Sigtryggr. We were just speaking of you," she said coolly.

CHAPTER TWENTY-TWO

"For a healer woman, you've got a touch like a troll," Sigtryggr said through gritted teeth.

Eir tucked the end of the new bandage and stood from her crouch. "It isn't my touch that pains you. It's your sobriety. You need a new sling. Did you drop this one in the latrine? It's putrid."

She tapped his forehead like a naughty child, and Sigtryggr cursed at her, first in Norse, then in English, and again in Irish. Even Liadan couldn't wipe the grin from her face after that.

"Is that tea ready?" Eir said.

"Here it is." The girl ladled a steaming concoction of boiled willow bark into a horn cup and passed it over. When Eir held it out to the king, he snarled at it.

"I don't want fucking *tea,* woman! Where's that beer?"

Patience flagging, Eir loomed over Sigtryggr and glared at him as hard as he did at her.

"It's gone, you toad. You drank it all. You'll have to wait for more. Drink the tea and you'll forget about the beer."

He sniffed it. "What's in this one? Some vile root and sour piss?"

On it went for a long time, Eir fighting to get the king to settle while he groaned and pinched the bridge of his nose and turned so green around his mouth he could have passed for a river fish.

Guðrun and Rúna had taken themselves outside, claiming the need for fresh air and a long walk after having slept all day. They strolled out the door with their hands clasped without shyness, confident the dark would shroud the true meaning of their intimacy. Liadan followed them out, not announcing where she was going or when she would be back. Eir made no comment on it, so I said nothing either.

Sipping my own cup of Astrid's brew, I looked on from a bench, thoroughly enjoying the spectacle. Astrid had certainly put something stronger than willow in the tea. It warmed my belly and sent the bone-ache to the distant reaches of my mind. There was pain still, but it was locked behind a veil of hazy smoke.

"Just drink it, Siggi," I said cheerily. "And then tell us all your news."

His bad eye rolled around to me. "I don't think I like you very much right now," he said, then heaved his supper onto the dirt floor.

Abandoning politeness, Eir sidestepped the puke and grabbed Sigtryggr's tunic at the nape of his neck and pressed the rim of the cup to his lips. "Drink," she ordered. "Or I'll slip something worse into the next batch of beer and you'll be shitting yourself for days."

Obediently, the king drained the tea to its dregs.

"There now," Eir said, plucking away the cup and letting Astrid refill it. "Once that settles your belly, tell me all that my husband spoke of with you. If you leave anything out, that special beer will do for you. Understand?"

Sigtryggr nodded mutely then reached for the cup again as soon as she set it down. I snickered.

"Gyda," Eir barked, making me flinch. Hot liquid splashed over my hand.

"You get yourself to your bed soon. Crawl if you have to. With the state of this idiot and your flapping fish belly, the two of you will have less luck against Heimarr than a rat against a viper. Where is Ruarc and his wagon? I ought to give *him* the shit-beer for slacking his duties."

This was a side of Eir I'd seldom seen. On *Sea-Wolf*, she had always been collected and focused, calm even with shattering waves and lashing winds. Now—and really, since the night of her marriage—her words and movements were harried, as if she sensed the teeth of a wolf nearing her throat.

"I met Ruarc on the way," I told her. "He'd been delayed by a trip to the latrine, but I assure you he deserves no scalding from *your* tongue."

Sigtryggr, who had tilted his cup again for the last rivulets of tea, choked and coughed. I raised both brows at him and he dropped his gaze like a stone.

"If you want another, just say so," chided Astrid. She snatched the cup from his good hand and refilled it from the cauldron.

"My thanks," the king said, sipping carefully. "This is good. Works quickly."

"Wonderful," Eir said. "Now, what has my husband said about his goat-shit of a brother?"

Sigtryggr stretched his long legs out towards the fire and crossed them at the ankle. "Why ask me and not him directly?" he whined. "I am no skald to be singing the tale."

Eir kicked his feet and he drew them back with a snarl.

"You've got a short memory," she said. "King of shit-trousers and midden-stink."

He bared his teeth. "If you weren't the wife of my friend's son, I'd have you thrown into the Foss for speaking to me that way. I've done worse for less offense."

"Ignore him," I said. "He says things like this because they make him sound like the great Jarls of old. Strong, deep-minded and bloody men he cannot even hope to drink shoulder to shoulder with on the benches of the All-Father's hall."

Sigtryggr threw me a black look while Eir and Astrid both snorted their laughter. I returned his look with a broad, satisfied grin.

"About my husband, then," Eir said, still smirking. She gave his cup a pointed glance and nod. "What did you talk about, and where is he now?"

The king's fingers curled tight around the cup. "*Stáli* is with his men tonight. Drinking and eating and boosting their morale. They were nervous when he left, so he reckons showing his face will ease them. Anyway, he and I did not come to an agreement."

Eir's brow furrowed. "How can that be? Are you not of the same mind?"

Sigtryggr heaved a weary sigh, as if the whole world contrived to make itself a burden specifically for him to bear. "Hákon *Stáli*, son of Olavi Spear-Breaker, thinks it is wise to keep his father ignorant. He prefers to be the fox crouched in the thicket, waiting for the right moment to pounce."

"And your preference?" I said.

He showed me the tip of one glistening canine. "I would rather be the wolf driving my prey into the teeth of my allies so that we can tear and rend flesh together."

"You don't think Hákon is hesitating because Heimarr is his brother, do you?" Astrid put in astutely. "That won't earn him the confidence of his men."

Eir and I exchanged another glance, and this time neither of us looked away.

"Neither will murdering a brother," I said. "It would be wise to see if Heimarr drops his guard. Right now, he's hiding with his friends. There is no point in hunting him or Uffe."

"Actually, the girl is closer to the mark," Sigtryggr said, then drained his cup again and wiped his beard dry with the back of his hand. His cheeks were rosy.

"I am?" Astrid smiled.

"My men suffered a blow on that beach," he replied. "With—," his voice cracked, and he cleared his throat. "With half of them dead, the remainder see no merit in chasing after one ship, let alone a man whose father is renowned across Ireland and Northumbria. They aren't invested. Most of them want to go home. The same is true of your men, Eir. They've known Heimarr for years and are reluctant to fight him."

The blood in my heart slowed. "I cannot ask more from your men," I said reluctantly. "But you have suffered loss and I cannot be responsible for more. I won't hold a grudge if you deem it better to send them back to Jórvík."

His long fingers tapped an unconscious rhythm against the horn cup. "Don't question me, woman, it's beneath you. I already told you what I wanted. Wherever I go, my oath-men follow. That is their duty."

"What of your other troubles in Jórvík?" I pointed out. "Heimarr means little to you. You could simply demand the life-price of your men from him and be done. You have far more pressing business at home."

He turned a new sort of gaze on me. The shadow of something blood-hungry had coiled inside him, and it chilled the marrow of my bones.

"Miss my chance to flay the fucker from navel to nape?" he growled. "The dream of Heimarr's blood has already taken hold of me. No. I will not return to Jórvík. And I will not lose out on a hoard of wealth fit for a hero's mound. How else am I to shove my silver-gilded boot up King Edward's bleeding arse-hole so that he shits it back out?"

This, delivered with all the malice of some preternatural thing slinking beneath the trees, brought no humor to any of us.

After that, there was nothing left to say about the matter, and so we turned to the fire, transfixed with the living flame and all the promised destruction in its molten heart. I thought of the omen I'd witnessed, the bloody snake in the heron's beak. A *völva*'s prophecy, or a curse?

The night deepened. The four of us spoke for hours, then dozed. Sigtryggr had his head tilted back, snores rising from a constricted throat in a shrieking wheeze. Eir and Astrid huddled together under a blanket on the floor. Gingerly, so as not to disturb Astrid as she slept on her shoulder, Eir poked a stick into the coals to coax them back to life.

"Shall I fetch a few logs?" I murmured, my voice rippling the still air.

"Leave it," she said. "Hákon will bring more when he returns in the morning. I suppose Ruarc's fallen asleep in a bush somewhere. You can stay here for the night. Take my bed. I'll watch the fire."

"I appreciate the kindness. I am fine as I am."

This was a lie, of course. My eyelids felt as heavy as lead game pieces, and the effects of the tea had long since worn off in my rusted joints. My bladder was nearing a painful capacity, but the warmth of the hearth had me in its grip.

Eir's gray eyes met mine. Half her face was hidden by the folds of her blanket, and the other half was caressed with Astrid's fine golden hair. All this gave Eir the appearance of being wrapped in a burial shroud. When she spoke, her voice was caught between a whisper and a sigh.

"There have been many things in our shared life that I found easy to fathom. Your blind ambition. Your rage. Your bitterness. Your silver-hunger. All of this I took part in. We all did. We knew you loved us, and we loved you."

"I still love you," I said. "And always will, until my bones are dust and my name is forgotten."

She went on as if she had not heard me. "What I find difficult to understand now is this new—*humility*. You are still blindly focused on your own future, but you are no longer driven to madness by it. You ask instead of demand. You apologize rather than justify." She gave a soft laugh. "The world has beaten the defiance out of you, Gyda, and I cannot say whether I welcome the change or resent it."

"It can be both," I said carefully. "*I* can be both. I am still Gyda *Fiskwif*, once of Dyflin and Rán's Daughters. I am Son-Killer and Ocean-Strider. Grim-Bitch. And I am a woman who has learned the fire in my belly is a festering cancer, consuming everything of value if I let it."

Eir returned her gaze to the fire. "I cannot offer you my heart again," she said softly. "Not as a sister. Not as a friend. Never again. You broke my trust badly enough that it remains shattered, sharp as glass."

I watched the shadows of the flames play over her and Astrid and said nothing.

Eir shifted, pressed a hand to her belly. She was thinking of her child, dreaming of what it would be, of how it would grow. The ghost of a flicker moved in my womb, a memory of what had not come to pass for me. I was not envious; I was sad. I had never coveted motherhood, not truly, but there remained an ache of what could have been. A life that I may not have sought, but one that I may have accepted. And I had learned that acceptance is often the only path left to follow.

"I will do all I can," I said. "For you, and for your family."

She nodded. "And I can be your ally," she said. "No more than that."

We lapsed into silence.

It was not long after, though long enough that I'd drifted into a light sleep, that the first of the alarmed shouts and cries of pain reached us. And a moment later, Hákon and Ruarc slammed through the door, blood-streaked and sweating.

"Heimarr is here," Ruarc gasped.

CHAPTER TWENTY-THREE

"The benches, *now*!" Hákon bellowed.

Eir, Astrid, and Sigtryggr were on their feet and dragging their benches to the door before I made it upright.

"What's happened? Are you hurt?" Eir's hands flit over Hákon's face, which was streaked with soot and sweat and a spattering of blood.

"Not me," he grunted, pulling away from her. He heaved the benches, working in tandem with Ruarc to pile them up against the door, a bulwark against the horrors outside.

"My men, *Stáli*," Sigtryggr said through his teeth, and Hákon shook his head.

He cursed, for we all heard it: the yelling and dull thumps of axes striking round shields and bouncing off bosses. Behind that was the bright, acrid stench of smoke.

"They're burning the fields," Ruarc said. "Working from the outside to here. If they reach these buildings—"

"Is there another way out?" Hákon demanded from Astrid, who stood behind Eir with mouth flapping and eyes as wide as serving trays. "Speak! Is there another way?"

Astrid flinched. "There is a panel in the boards near your pallets," she said. "It opens to a cellar. There's a passage that opens outside, behind another dwelling and close to the gate."

Hákon turned back to the piled benches and shoved them once, making certain they would stay. Then he strode past Eir to grab Sigtryggr's good shoulder. "Can you hold your sword, king?"

Eir gasped. "You're not going back out there. Hákon, *no*."

"Can you hold your sword?" he repeated.

"As well as I hold my cock," the king replied, his wolf's grin stretching.

"Good," Hákon said. "Stay with the women. No one is to pass through that door. Ruarc and I will go out using the panel. Stand guard and wait for us to return. If the gate is free, Ruarc will take all of you to the shoreline."

"Fuck that," gnarred Sigtryggr. "I won't hide in some dirt-floored hut while knife-work needs doing!"

"Someone tell me how this happened!" I said. My fingers itched for my seax, and my muscles burned with eagerness. Only the ache in my belly and the creak of my ribs reminded me I was still a thrall to my sickbed. Fury made my voice hoarse. "How is it possible Heimarr found us?"

"You can't even hold a shield, man," Ruarc said to the king. "Give me your sword. Stay here and protect my foster-mother." His gaze met mine for an instant, resolute and full of something I had never seen before. His mouth quirked in his usual crooked smile.

Sigtryggr's eye bulged. "Fuck!" Hulking away to his sleeping area, he pulled the blade from under his pallet. "You break it, I break you, Irish pup," he growled.

"If it breaks, you won't have to break me. Someone else will get there first," Ruarc replied, still smiling. "This is my duty, king, or did you forget?"

Hákon had wasted no time; he'd gone to the back of the house while Ruarc spoke and ripped down the partition. Tossing it aside like a scrap of sail, he worked to move the furniture away from the panel in the floor. Eir watched him with her lip caught in her teeth.

"Tell me what is happening," I hissed at Ruarc, taking his arm. "If you're going to be an idiot out there with a sword, I need to know why you're swinging it."

"An ambush," he said, sickness twisting his face. "They beached a ship somewhere down the coast and came around the hill in the darkness. Gyda, he's got more men than us."

"How many? Is he with them?"

Ruarc's throat worked as he swallowed. "It's the hired force. Uffe is leading them. They're not Dane or Norse or Irish or English. It's all and then some. I recognize a few from Olavi's own oath-men. Fucking traitors."

Cold gripped me.

"We had one guard at the gate," Ruarc continued. "Ottar. They killed him, and none of us knew anything until they set fire to the fields to pen us in. Most of us had no weapons at hand. We had to scramble."

"Oh gods. Guðrun and Rúna? Liadan?"

He looked away. "I didn't see them. But they know how to fight."

"They had no weapons at all." My voice was choked. Bile flooded my guts.

"Hákon," Eir cried, and the urgency in her voice arrested us.

Stern-faced, she strode across the room and bent at the foot of their shared sleeping pallet. From the small chest there, she lifted a mass that clinked and reflected the firelight. A *brynja*.

"Don't forget this," she said. "And kill the *niðingar* who dare bring their faces to your axe. Rip them apart. For my sake, Hákon. For your child's sake."

Hákon's expression changed. Like a living flame caught in stone, he spoke not a word, but took the mail-shirt reverently and lifted it over his head. His gaze never left hers.

"Find my men," Sigtryggr growled to Ruarc. "Tell them I'll come soon."

Ruarc nodded and reached for the sword, but then a sound came from beneath the wooden planking. A ridge appeared beside Eir's feet, then fell flush with the floor again.

Someone had found the back entrance.

Immediately, we fell silent, and Hákon drew his seax. He took a position behind the panel, and the rest of us moved quickly to hide behind the partition screens.

With Sigtryggr and Ruarc huddled with me, I peered through the narrow reed weave. How many enemies were there, waiting in the dark to slaughter us? I cursed my frail and useless body.

Outside, the sound of fighting ebbed and flowed, not yet dying away. Hákon's and Sigtryggr's men were giving a valiant defense. Perishing from an ambush would be a bad death, undignified and without chance of glory. This was unacceptable to blooded warriors, brave ones who had faced the ocean's storms and the spear-storms, emerging on the other side with scars as trophies and their lives as rewards.

Guðrun. Rúna. Liadan. I chanted their names over and over in my mind.

Sigtryggr growled in his throat as he listened to his men fight and die without him. He grasped his sword in his good hand, but his bad arm flexed where it pressed against my side.

"Give that blade to Ruarc, turd," I whispered. "You'll get your chance for blood."

There was a shuffling sound and a reluctant twitch from Sigtryggr before Ruarc mumbled, "I'll take good care of it."

Sigtryggr made to respond with something vulgar, but I ground my heel into his toe to shut him up.

The board lifted again, and this time, a head, greasy as the bottom of a cook-pot, poked through the floor. Tree-trunk arms followed, and a man leveraged himself up.

Hot rage flashed through me like lightning. Uffe.

His face had a new ugliness. Glassy eyes stared over a blood- and soot-streaked nose. His chest was like the hull of a barge. He wore no armor, only a tunic with a belt with a wicked, bone-handled long knife. His tendons and muscles stood out like copper wires on his neck. And he did not see Hákon.

I locked eyes with the Jarl's son through the slats for half a moment. Just as Uffe took a step forward and called, "Ready to die, *Stáli*? I know you and your whores are in here."

Hákon exploded from behind, a roar ripping from his throat and his seax falling so fast it whistled.

But Uffe was fast too. He dodged, grabbing Hákon's descending wrist and in the same movement bringing his knee up. Hákon went down with a winded *whoom*, his seax skittering across the ground.

"They're in the tunnel," Sigtryggr snarled as the sounds of more shouting reached us.

Uffe stepped back, fumbling for the knife in his belt. Quick as a snake, Hákon flung out his arm and yanked Uffe's ankle. The man went down like a sack of grain and Hákon was on him.

We boiled out of our hiding places, brandishing weapons or reaching for the nearest projectile. I had my walking stick, and this

I struck on the ground, yelling to be heard over the tumult. "Close that panel! Don't let them in!"

Hákon and Uffe grappled on the floor, kicking and punching and howling like trolls. Soon they were up again. Uffe's knife was gone, flung somewhere into a corner, but the man was built for strength, and as strong as Hákon was, he was not a match. With a vicious curse, Uffe peeled Hákon's arm off his neck and twisted around to drive his boot into Hákon's thigh.

Hákon tripped over the legs of an upturned stool and then Uffe was at him again with fists like hammers. Eir had her husband's seax in her hand. She was yelling, looking for an opening to give it to him and finding none.

Meanwhile, Ruarc had gotten a journey chest over the plank door. The steady pounding against it turned his face white. He still gripped Sigtryggr's sword in his fist. "I need something to weigh it down," he bellowed.

Astrid was already on it, hauling a massive iron cauldron across the floor. Sigtryggr attempted to help, swearing and panting with the effort of using his only good arm.

"They're going to get in," I hissed. I couldn't fight, I couldn't do *anything* but watch. I cursed every aching bone and bruise I had.

Eir was shrieking now, but Hákon's senses were gone. Nothing existed for him but his enemy, this threat to his family. He was Hákon *Stáli,* a warrior of steel and fury. He was strong and canny, without mercy. He would kill Uffe with his bare hands and revel in it.

But Uffe was winning. He had his fists in Hákon's *brynja* and yanked him around with it, smashing his fists into whatever body part he could. And he was gaining ground, backing Hákon up to the turf wall, where there would be no way for him to protect against his blows.

"Uffe," I screamed, ribs pulling painfully. "You fucking pus-headed goat-fucker! You puke! You're going to die here! Look at me, troll's-arse!"

Uffe jerked, pulling back from Hákon for a bare instant, and Eir found her opening.

She tossed the seax just short of the wooden planking and whistled through her teeth. Uffe saw my face just as Hákon dove for the blade. He came up with the seax in his fist, a roar in his throat.

But again, Uffe was faster. His face a rictus of berserk blood-hunger, Uffe brought both fists down on Hákon's right shoulder. The ball of his pivoting foot slipped, moving too far, falling off the shallow edge of the planks onto the dirt floor. Uffe shoved with both hands and Hákon fell, twisting so that he first struck his knee on the ground and then the side of his skull on the edge of the stool.

Vibrant, sheeting blood welled from his scalp and soaked the neck of his mail. For a suspended moment, he raised himself on his forearms and shook his head. Then, making no sound, Hákon collapsed.

We stared at him, at the blood pooling around his head and turning the dirt to red mud.

Eir wrenched the king's sword from Ruarc's nerveless fingers and launched at Uffe with a throat-ripping bellow. "I'll kill you! Fucking bastard!"

Astrid was with her, waving an iron ladle, a weapon as lethal as a club in her hands.

With both women advancing on either side, Uffe bolted. Leaping over Hákon's prone form, he put himself on the other side of the fire. Cursing and spitting, he hesitated, because now there were five of us and he had no weapon and nowhere to go.

"Eir, stop," I cried. "He can give us Heimarr!"

She could not hear me. I turned to Ruarc and Sigtryggr, hoping they would read my desperation. Ruarc was first, and he went for Eir. Sigtryggr stayed on Uffe.

Eir had taken up a defender's stance beside Hákon, her shoes and skirt hem spoiled in the mixture of blood and mud. She held both the sword and the seax now. Ruarc reached for her, and she stepped one foot back, swinging the sword and missing by a hand's breadth.

"Move out of the way, Ruarc," she hissed. "I'll gut you the way I gut fish."

"Just listen to us," he pleaded. "We can end this quickly. We've got him now, he can't hurt anyone else."

"You're all going to die shitting," Uffe laughed. "Just like *Stáli*."

Eir lunged for him again, deaf to Ruarc's pleas. She seethed with fury, as ignited as Hákon had been before he fell. Out of words, Ruarc caught her hand grasping the sword, but missed the seax. Off-kilter and clumsy, Eir stumbled and the seax skimmed the outermost edge of his right shoulder, ripping the fabric and flaying skin.

Ruarc screamed and fell back, holding the flap of skin tight against his wound. Dark blood surged between his fingers. Eir trembled as she stared at him wide-eyed.

"I—I'm sorry," she gasped.

Spell broken, Astrid lurched for Ruarc, pressing on his shoulder to stem the wound. "I've got you, brother. You're alright."

An urgent pounding rapped at the door. "Out! Everyone out!" Eirik Fish-Lip's voice was pained, hoarse from smoke or worse. "They're setting fire to everything. Lord king, if you're alive in there, by the gods, get to the ships now. The gate is ours. We'll fight as long as we can!" The pounding ceased with a cry and a heavy pummeling strike of iron against wood. The door and benches thrummed with the force.

"They're dying for you, king," Uffe sneered. "Every sniveling turd you call shield-brother. Do you hear how they squeal?"

Crazed and howling, Sigtryggr turned for the door, but I lunged forward and slammed my walking stick into the heart of the fire. Red-hot coals and embers cast up into the air, and five faces turned to me.

"Enough!" My voice broke. "We make for the ships. Get Hákon up. We leave no one behind. "

"Lord Heimarr will have taken your pretty boats," Uffe said. His forehead streamed with soot-grimed sweat. "If he has not burnt them already."

Sigtryggr's snarl was feral. "Let me have this crowing giant's arse, *Fiskwif*." White froth gathered at the corners of his mouth. "I'll rip his lungs through his putrid throat and make his carcass my prow-beast."

"You can have him when I'm done, king. I owe him," I replied. An angry grimace split Sigtryggr's beard, but he nodded. I turned to Eir.

"Go to your husband, Eir. He needs you more than you need to kill this man."

The glare she leveled at me was heavy and unyielding as arctic ice. The dying firelight caught the edge of her blades and the white knuckles of her fists. My heart stuttered, afraid for an instant that she wanted to fight me. If that happened, I would die. Any of us would. All of us would.

But the Norns looked on us then and favored the weave of our fates. A moan rose from Hákon. He stirred on the ground. Rising a little, he put a trembling hand to his scalp and looked at it. "I'm bleeding," he slurred.

Instantly, Eir dropped both sword and seax and knelt, pressing her hand against the wound. "Stay awake, my love. I'm here." She stared into his blood-streaked face.

"You've cocked this up, shit-licker," said Sigtryggr, staring at Uffe like he was chum in the water and himself a shark. "I can think of a few things to do with your gut-rope before the *Fiskwif* gets hold of you."

"Whoever heard of a one-armed king?" Uffe replied, grinning. "Was that your cock-hand? Is that why you sit around with old whores now? Do they stroke it for you while you weep through your squinting eye?"

"Fucking *whoreson*!" The king seethed and paced, trembling with the effort of keeping himself from tearing out Uffe's throat.

"You're stuck here, troll-fucker," I said, moving forward. Sigtryggr and I had him boxed in behind the fire. "Smell that? The thatching is smoldering. Soon this place will burn, and we'll burn with it. So talk fast."

Uffe sneered, but his breathing was rapid and his eyes darted to the floor panel and the cauldron holding it shut.

"A little flame will get this sparrow to sing," Sigtryggr said, his wolf's smile returning with all its blood-hunger and rage.

"Let the sparrow speak before we singe its feathers," I responded. "Your friends can't get in, Uffe. They left you, or else they're dead in that tunnel. No help for you now."

Astrid was bandaging Ruarc's shoulder with strips taken from her apron. Red bloomed through the linen. His tunic stuck to his sweat-slick and graying skin. Blood soaked the inside of his arm, but no longer dripped from his fingers.

"Get that cauldron out of the way," the king barked at Astrid. "And give me back my sword. I won't stand here like a pissing thrall!"

Uffe was swearing at me, describing what he would do to me in detail, what Heimarr would do. I laughed at him.

"You say a lot with that reeking hole. So tell me this, Uffe. Did you really kill Ragnar in al-Andalus? Or was that another wet turd that dripped from your tongue?"

Sigtryggr made a shrill noise of impatience, but I put up a hand to stay him. "Answer me, Uffe. Did you kill Ragnar?"

"You know I did, rancid bitch," he spat, grinning like a mad beast. "Ragnar died screaming. And so will you!"

I returned his mad grin. "Give me your sword, king."

"You're a shriveled old whore," Uffe taunted. "What's a sword going to do for you except slice your carcass into strips of dried out meat?"

"What the fuck are you doing?" murmured Sigtryggr as he handed it to me. "Cut off his balls once we're out of here!"

"Trust me," I said, dropping my gaze to the bone-handled knife he'd found and stuck in his belt.

An amused glint entered his bad eye. "Whatever you command, Lady Grim-Bitch."

I faced Uffe again, fingers tight around the sword's hilt. It was heavy, too long for my reach. I could hear screams outside. Too close. It was desperate combat now, axe and shield and blade and fist. *Guðrun. Rúna. Liadan. The ships.* Bile welled in my mouth at the image of our only escape sending ash and fume into to the sky.

"I have one more question, Uffe," I said. "Answer it well and you live. I'll even let you creep away free. But lie to me and you will burn until you wake up in the fangs of the Corpse-Snake. Where is Heimarr, Uffe? Tell me now."

Uffe's laugh was smug and ugly. "Don't you hear him? Heimarr is outside, feasting on your gutless men. Let's go and see him. He might even let you watch *Sea-Wolf* burn before he fucks you."

My fist tightened around the sword's grip. "Fine," I said wearily. "Have it your way. Do it now, Siggi."

With a lusty howl, Sigtryggr pounced on Uffe with the bone-handled dagger and stuck him in the side, tugged it out, then struck again, leaving it in Uffe's liver as he jumped away. Uffe shrieked, clawing at the handle, turning away just far enough for a clean sweep.

With a surge of strength, I swung the sword and took Uffe's head with one stroke. It rolled off his shoulders and bounced twice, landing in the fire. Blood hissed and popped in the coals and the stink of burning hair filled our nostrils.

Grinning, Sigtryggr kicked the corpse over and stomped it in the groin. The legs jerked and writhed. "That's for Eirik," he said, then stomped again. "And one for me. Now who's crying over their cock?"

"The others have gone out. We should join them," Ruarc rasped. His face was a mask of agony as he stared at me. "You said he could live, Gyda. Why?"

I shrugged and handed Sigtryggr back his sword.

"The fucker lied about Ragnar," I said. "Which means he lied about Heimarr. He isn't here. So we're going to find him."

CHAPTER TWENTY-FOUR

Ragnarök had come upon this place. We fled through shadow and smoke, slipping out of the tunnel and then between the smoldering black ash and debris that marked the ruins of burned houses. Corpses littered the paths, their faces blank and strange. It gave me a small measure of hope for my missing Daughters, for they were not among the dead there.

Led by Ruarc and Astrid, we hurried for the gate. I clung to Sigtryggr's good arm while Hákon and Eir struggled behind. Though Eir was tall, Hákon's boneless bulk against her shoulder slowed us all down.

Dark shapes flit past our group like wraiths, and through the pall of smoke it was hard to know who was friend and who was foe. When our enemies recognized us, they threw themselves forward to test their mettle, and for their foolishness they broke against the bulwark of our blades to fall away in the dark.

The gate rose before us, a smoke-veiled monument. We were alone for the moment. Moans of pain were all around us, and farther away came the last gasps of a struggle. The fight was over.

"Almost there," Eir said, her voice barely a whisper.

Hákon was in a bad way. He spoke not a word, and breathed heavily as if he'd endured a winter trek with a lung-deep fever. I could sense Eir's fear like a smothering blanket. I limped faster. I could not be weak when she needed me strong. Still, pain burrowed deep into my flesh.

Putting that sword through Uffe's neck had taken too much from me. My wound had pulled and slow blood glued the linen bandage to my belly. My ribs creaked and ached, and the beginnings of a terrible headache prickled behind eyes. But I had not been the only one to come out bloody; Sigtryggr's grunt of discomfort brought me back to awareness, and I eased the pressure on his arm.

"I'd offer to carry you, *Fiskwif*," he murmured. "As slight as you are next to me. But, ah, I seem to be rather short-handed."

"Evidently," I said, noticing the grin in his voice. "Though if you want me to laugh, you'll have to try harder."

A vibration of silent amusement passed through him, which amidst the chaos was heartening.

He'd handed me an axe the moment I emerged from the tunnel. A weapon in my fist was a great relief, but I'd realized the next moment that it had come from the skull of one of his own men, lying dead near the entrance with half his face hacked off. Too many of the king's men had died this night. Good men, his friends and brothers.

"There!" cried Astrid suddenly.

Against the gloomy pre-dawn sky, the masts of both *Hrið-Ormr* and *Dreki* stood defiant at the bottom of the hill. Unburned.

"You were right," Sigtryggr murmured. "But that was a fearsome gamble."

"Uffe likely meant to sail them off once we all were dead," I responded. "His filthy hands won't be touching anything now. Heimarr will have to take them from us himself."

"He can try," Sigtryggr said darkly.

A score of soot-grimed men held the gate, forming a final broken and exhausted shield-wall in front of it to protect the fleeing wounded. I searched for Guðrun and the others in the lines of warriors, but they were not present.

We passed the men and approached the gateway. Three figures manned it. The king's champion Thorkill stood inside the gaping archway, his great axe held in massive fists. Two others flanked him with long seaxes. A pile of corpses lay at their feet.

Without Uffe to lead them, our assailants had fallen to shambles. For the moment, no men came screaming out of the smoke to take control of the gate, and whichever fools had tried had their skulls and torsos cleaved by Thorkill's axe. Their assault was broken, Though Heimarr had not accomplished his goal of killing us, he'd sown enough destruction and death to force us to abandon this place. We were defenseless in the dark.

As we reached Thorkill, Sigtryggr gripped him by the shoulder.

"Well met, champion," he said, meeting the warrior's eye. Weary gratitude slackened Thorkill's face, and he touched bloody fingers to the hammer talisman around his neck.

"Get that sword-arm of yours strong again, Lord King," Thorkill rasped. "These fuckers are hard to skull-cleave on my own."

Sigtryggr smiled grimly. "You'll be splitting skulls and winning arm-rings from me again soon, I swear it. Do not linger here long. *Hrið-Ormr* needs you." He tightened his grip a moment, then released the man and ushered the rest of us through.

"How far?" Hákon croaked.

He and Eir were ahead now, and Eir paused to wipe her brow. Hákon was a pallid thing in the torchlight, streaked with dark blood and grime. Astrid and Ruarc had vanished down the path to shore.

"You'll need to help them," I whispered to the king. Sigtryggr's furrowed gaze had remained on Thorkill behind us. A deep frown pulled his mouth.

"Sig," I pressed, and he made a noise in his throat. Releasing my arm, he went to Hákon, and Eir gave him up reluctantly.

"He's heavy," she said, but he'd already slung Hákon's arm around his shoulders. A dangling hand bounced against Sigtryggr's injured forearm, and he smothered a hard wince.

"Like bearing a lamb to table," he said tightly. "Only this lamb is the size of Thor's chariot-goats." Renewed sounds of fighting reached us. "We need to move on," I urged, gripping my walking stick hard.

We hurried down the shore-path, but soon men from the shield-wall overtook us. The first were mostly Hákon's men, and they grimaced to see their Jarl's son so weakened. Sigtryggr nodded to each of them, his bad eye shut tight and his smile forced.

"Onward to the ships, *drengr*," he said to one man who'd stopped to help. "This one's only had his brains knocked. He's a little more stupid, but no less steel-skulled."

Sigtryggr's axe-man, Thorkill, found us again as we reached the shoreline. It had not been so long since we'd passed under the gate, but in that time, the king's champion had become altogether different.

"The last of the fuckers got me," Thorkill said to the king, pressing the bloody stump of his right arm against his belly. "And Bjarni and

Gorm. But we held that gate, Lord. Our shield-warriors fought like Oðinn's *einherjar*. Not a one of those arse-lickers will come. We killed them all and left them for the crows."

Pride and wonder passed over Sigtryggr's pale face. He said nothing, for nothing would ease Thorkill's pain. Instead, with Hákon still hanging off him, he gave his man a deep nod like a bow, and Thorkill returned it with a thin, twisted smile.

As we reached the waterline, I knew that Guðrun, Rúna, and Liadan were not with us.

An infant dawn cast the world in gray. Our ships bobbed in the surf, and already the able-bodied were tightening lines and sails to cast off. Two small boats waited to ferry the rest of us.

My belly soured. Sigtryggr now had fewer men than Hákon. Rowing *Hrið-Ormr* would be back-breaking work. No doubt we would lose the worst of the wounded.

"Our sisters are still missing."

Eir touched my elbow. Her voice did not break, but her fingers flexed against my skin, and I knew she imagined them gouging and ripping Heimarr apart. "I did not see them among the dead," I told her. The words held no comfort.

"Where will we go, Gyda?" she said softly. She stared out to sea, her eyes the same color as the plumes of smoke. "Not Dyflin. Our oath-men are strong, and Olavi is powerful, but I would not put those people in danger. Heimarr is a snake. He may not hesitate to attack Dyflin if he thinks he can win the Jarl's seat."

I nodded. "After this, he will hire more men. We need a new haven. We need time to recover and plan our next move."

"The Isle of Man?" she suggested, then shook her head. "No, of course not. He'd anticipate that."

"I thought of the bay in Alba," I said. "You remember the one? Due north of the Isle."

A ghost of a smile touched the corner of her mouth. "We beached *Sea-Wolf* there to scrape the hull of barnacles once."

"That's the one. If our sisters fled, they will hear of our survival and may even think to head there."

Drawing a sharp breath, she turned to me. "Gyda, if they are truly lost, swear to me at the end of all this, we will send Heimarr to Rán's hall with his cock in his hands and an adder around his neck. We'll show him he is not the only viper with a deadly bite."

I held her gaze. "I refuse to believe they are dead. Not until I see their corpses in front of me or hear their voices on the air, borne by Valkyries. They live, and so do we. As long as this is true, we do not stop fighting."

"May Rán make it so," she replied, and then she left me.

As the sun broke the horizon, we finished boarding our two ships, let out the oars, and left our dead behind.

PART FIVE: ALBA

CHAPTER TWENTY-FIVE

For days we sailed north, blown off course by summer squalls and pursued by sharks. They tasted blood as it seeped from the corpses we threw into the white-capped waves.

Buffeted by roaring winds, our ships drifted and lost sight of each other many times. Our sails were useless. We rowed like beasts, breaking our backs and tearing still-healing wounds. In my bones, a fierce, blinding ache had taken permanent residence. Still, I rowed until the skin peeled off my salt-crusted palms. I did not stop until Sigtryggr forced me to rest.

It was a teeth-grinding, blood-soaked voyage, one which proved how ravenous the halls of Rán and Njörd could be. *Hrið-Ormr* lost six men. *Dreki* lost five.

And brave Thorkill took his place among the dead.

His arm had festered rapidly, leaking pus and foul-stinking so that no one would sit with him against the strake as he shivered and cursed in his delirium. On the fourth day, I took Thorkill's seax and put it in Sigtryggr's hand.

When he looked at me, his gaze showed a deep hurt and anger, but he said nothing as he took the blade and went to his champion.

"Our friends in Valhalla call to me, Lord. But I fear the Valkyries will find my carcass too ruined to bear aloft. Help me, King, I beg you." Thorkill's smile was agonized, and so Sigtryggr did help, wrapping the dying man's hand around the hilt of the seax. Holding the blade together, they drew the edge across Thorkill's throat. Sigtryggr kept his grip, even after Thorkill ceased jerking and trembling.

I had never seen the king shed tears. But after Thorkill went over the side to Rán's hall, Sigtryggr huddled under the prow-beast with his face out to sea. He spoke to no one.

The next morning, Rán's wrath-darkened waves dissipated, leaving us a sail-filling breeze and a clear, cloudless sky. By afternoon, the dark outline of Alba's rocky coast rose before us.

We beached our ships on a narrow strand by the light of the moon, and once our canvas tents went up, all but a few of us collapsed into exhausted sleep. There would be enough time to build a proper camp come morning.

Hákon and Eir found me near a smoking fire, where I sat in huddled conversation with Sigtryggr.

"Where is Ruarc?" Eir said to me. "He should be a part of this."

I peered up at them. Hákon was a ghostly, bruised hulk in the firelight, and though he stood on his own feet, Eir was near enough to catch him if he fell.

Some vital part of him had been lost; his tunic hung from his frame like a filthy rag on a line. It should not have been possible in so short a time. A vague chill went through me, one that whispered of mound-dwellers and carrion birds. I shook my head clear of such thoughts.

"The boy's asleep there," I said, nodding at the canvas tent set up a length away to the right. "Ruarc has the least experience rowing of all of us. With his arm still skinned like a goat-shank, he's dead to all but the pain in his dreams. Let him be."

Eir crouched and picked up a sliver of broken driftwood from the shingle. She snapped it and crumbled the splinters into the flames. "Wake him."

Sigtryggr grunted as he rose. "I'll get him," he muttered.

Hákon remained standing, and the weight of his glare pressed on my shoulders. I shifted uneasily

"Can this not wait for morning?" I said as the king emerged with Ruarc in tow. "Whatever plans you're fomenting will hardly spoil with a few hours' sleep."

"We do this now, Gyda," Eir replied, and I frowned at her.

Sigtryggr resettled himself on my right, but Ruarc stood, blinking, and stared with as grim a face as a man at his execution.

"What's happening?" he said, wincing as he rolled his bandaged shoulder. "We aren't underway again, are we?"

I motioned, and he reluctantly folded himself down in the space to my left. I handed over the remains of my bowl. "It's oats," I said when he eyed it. "Nothing more offensive than that. Not even a bit of milk to cut it."

Ruarc took a bite as hesitant and scant as a bird's, then tucked in gratefully.

Eir and Hákon had brought their own bowls, and so for a time, there was nothing beyond the snapping of the fire, the snores of the camp, and the scrape of wooden spoons.

There had been no point planning anything while we rowed for our lives. Even when there had been a stretch of calm, Sigtryggr, Ruarc, and I were too spent to do anything but crouch in the shade of the prow and wrap bandages around our blistering hands. But now, there was no putting this off, no matter how dearly I wished to find a spare tent to stretch my aching bones in.

"King Sigtryggr," Hákon began, setting aside his bowl. A thin restraint hung about him, as if there was nothing he'd like more than to throttle someone as soon as the chance presented itself. "Let there be no misunderstanding between us. If you choose to take your remaining men and leave now, I will not hold it against you. You have done your part, and now this has become a family matter. I release you of obligation. Return to your people. We remain allies and friends."

Sigtryggr snorted and spat the evidence into the fire, where it hissed on the coals. "You've got the bollocks of a steer, and the brains of one, too, *Stáli*. Family matter. Bah!"

Hákon's jaw tightened. "If it is a question of payment, I will fill *Dreki*'s hold with double what Gyda promised you and send it up the river to your doorstep when all this is settled."

Considering the fragile trust between us, and the deep, angry flush creeping underneath the grime on the king's cheeks, I reckoned it was a prudent time to intervene.

"It isn't silver we're after, Hákon, or at least not only that," I said quickly. "This is now as much about our vengeance as it is honor.

Heimarr assaulted us all, and you cannot deny us satisfaction. Before the attack, you might have made such an argument, but not now. Not with all we have suffered."

Ruarc made a noise of agreement. "Heimarr is a tempest of the sea," he said softly. "A fume of anger that will not be blown away save by spilling his blood. There can be nothing that takes precedence over that."

Surprised by the lyrical words, I stared at Ruarc, but he had his eyes closed and his teeth grit together.

Hákon growled. "I know who my brother is, and I know he will come for blood again. And again. As many times as it takes. But what will you do, king, if he comes for Jórvík? It would be little effort for the wealthy Master of Trade to demand the throne in your absence."

"And what will *you* do when he comes for Dyflin and your father?" replied Sigtryggr coolly. "And when he kills your wife and unborn heir? Jórvík is nothing to him, *Stáli*. He wants the Jarl's seat because it means he's beaten you. What better way to secure his own legacy than by destroying yours?"

Hákon did not outwardly react, but I saw the way his fingers twined with Eir's on his knee.

Expression like stone, Eir spoke. "You lack fighting men, king. Something Heimarr makes up for ten times over with the promise of Ragnar's silver. Even now he may outnumber our forces. You would be wise to take my husband's offer to leave."

"Silver which he stole," Sigtryggr scoffed, thumbing his eye. "I have a claim on that hoard too, you know. Those who put their hands to it are stealing from me, and so will lose those hands."

"What is a hoard if not already stolen wealth?" I said dryly. "Anyone with that sort of shine got it by killing, thieving, raiding, or getting paid by their lord to do the same."

Sigtryggr sat back. "The *Fiskwif* has lost her edge in her dotage," he said petulantly. "Heimarr kicked you too hard. I liked you better when your ambition was as sharp as my own."

"Who said it isn't? I just think ambition should be honest."

"Could we return to the matter?" Hákon demanded, shifting forward into the firelight.

A sheen of sweat grazed the angles of his face, and a large bruise darkened his temple. His eyes were as hollow as deep pits. I knew the look well, for I'd often shared it. Pain would soon overwhelm him and he would require his bed until it passed.

I looked to Eir, and she met my gaze with a slight nod; she had already noted his suffering.

Hákon spoke again. "Think hard of what you're after, king. If your pride costs me the chance to put my brother in his place and remove the stain on my family's honor, I cannot say what may happen to our alliance."

At this, Sigtryggr whispered a curse. Then he reached out and hauled Hákon to his feet by the collar of his tunic.

"What are you doing?" cried Eir, surging to push them away from each other, but Ruarc put himself in her way and she shrank back, afraid to hurt him again.

Remaining seated, I didn't even attempt to make a protest. It would have gone unheard anyway.

"Try again, man," the king snarled into Hákon's face. "I am not the pup of some slack-jawed old bitch. I will rip your tongue from your throat if you threaten me. My men have bled and died for you, and now my champion rolls in Rán's hall with the bracken and the corpses. Don't test the reach of your rage against mine."

Sigtryggr held him there a moment, then let him go.

"Loki take you," Hákon said hoarsely, drawing a hand over his pallid face. "If this is the path you are determined to follow, then your folly is your own."

Sigtryggr grunted and sat again. He brought out a knife and began to pick his fingernails, as if what had just occurred was nothing more than a fart in the wind.

"Please sit," I told the others. "We must turn to recovering our strength. Plans and schemes are better forged when we are whole."

Hákon turned to Eir. Her clouded eyes roamed over his face, but she did not touch him. Ruarc returned to my side, stifling a groan as he settled.

"You are a man of action, Hákon, not words," I said. "I urge you to remember your friendships as well as your alliances. Heimarr will seek to break us if he can, because unity is our best weapon against him."

Sigtryggr made a derisive noise, and so I plucked the knife from his blistered fingers and tossed it away.

"Pay attention."

Shifting one knee upright, he dangled his good arm from it. "I *am* listening, Grim-Bitch," he said with a scowl. "Talk."

Courage gathered, I stated: "We stay here on Alba no longer than a full wane and rebirth of the moon. We heal and we grieve. We also wait for word of Guðrun, Rúna, and Liadan. If they survived, they may gather allies of their own and come to find us. This bit of coast is known to Rán's Daughters as a haven."

Sigtryggr's subtle shake of the head showed his doubt, but Eir responded first.

"We will also send a message to the Jarl," she said firmly. "By now, he will have heard of the attack, and perhaps sent men to investigate the estate. He knows Heimarr is ambitious, but does not yet understand the extent of his treachery. After all, it was *Uffe* who carried out this ambush, and Heimarr may yet go to his father crying of betrayal and unjust treatment."

Hákon, Sigtryggr, and Ruarc all scoffed at such a notion. "Pettiness is never beyond the reach of arrogant men," I muttered, lifting a stick to stir the fire. A red-gold flurry of embers went up. "So we ask for Olavi's help. What then?"

Ruarc sniffed. "He sends out another ship full of spears and we smash Heimarr with it? No, Olavi would never condone any plan that ends with the death of another of his sons."

"Particularly if *you* are involved in it," Sigtryggr put in with a smirk. I glowered back at him.

"That is undoubtedly the way of it," said Hákon. "If you are looking for his oath-men to fight for us, look elsewhere. Outright slaughter is not in my father's best interest. He'd sooner address the issue his own way."

"Such as a public hearing and exile," I said, shuddering with the memory of my own outlawry. "But surely that cannot be your own intention? Heimarr tried to slaughter you in your bed, and you mean to capture him?"

"He is the son of a jarl, not a nameless goat," Hákon replied with a lift of his brow. "My reluctance is not born of a desire to spare his life, Gyda. Heimarr will die, but I would have it on my terms, and no one else's."

Sigtryggr snorted, but I thought it a mark of progress that Hákon appeared resigned to our intention to remain. "Ah, how can we know Heimarr is readily found?" Ruarc queried. "He could be entrenched with his mercenaries in any stinking shit-hole now."

The king gave a small hoot of laughter. "That pig-fucker is too arrogant! He's able to strike in whatever direction he pleases from his camp on the Isle. He wouldn't give up such easy routes of attack so quickly, even to hide."

"He's likely shored up the defenses," Hákon said gravely. "And should he retrieve Uffe's ship from Ireland, he will have at least three vessels in his command. Not yet a fleet, but our own ranks lack enough strong rowers. We are outmatched, and any delay could doom us."

We fell silent, each of us trying and failing to unravel the bleak truth of this.

Then Eir lifted her chin. Turning to face Hákon, she said: "I still believe a message is a worthy idea. There are oath-men in Dyflin more loyal to you than to your father. They've known you as a capable leader, and a far better warrior than Olavi. Call on them, and they will answer."

This was an utterly unsettling thing to declare. A son commanding men who were not sworn to him was tantamount to defiance, and even outright rebellion. Hákon could be seen as claiming himself Jarl, and Olavi would never ignore such a challenge. I braced for Hákon's outrage, yet to my consternation, he merely inclined his head to his wife.

"An oath is a powerful thing," he murmured thoughtfully. "It binds us. Requires us to fight and die to uphold it. Demands our families, our flesh, and our minds. But above all, oaths demand sacrifice."

Hákon paused. When he looked at me, fire reflected in his eyes.

"You have always over-valued your freedom, Gyda, to the

detriment of those around you. But I recognize you have sacrificed it for the sake of all of us now. It may be the only noble thing you've ever done in your life. How can I find fault in that? Perhaps I should follow suit. I will send a message to Dyflin, and whatever consequence falls upon me, so be it."

Eir reached for his hand and he grasped it. "My words earlier were unwise," he continued, shifting his gaze to Sigtryggr. "To have Jórvík's king by my side, I would count it good fortune. What justice may yet be found is made more worthy when achieved with an ally. Now, let us rest and grieve for our dead. Once we are strong again, we will unite and rip our justice from my brother's broken corpse."

Then Hákon reached for Eir, and she grasped his hand and rose with him. I stared at them open-mouthed.

For a moment, the son of the Jarl was the image of his father in his younger days: a leader at the peak of his strength and wisdom. A warrior unflinching in the face of violence. A man ready for the task of killing his brother.

"We will speak more in the morning," he said. "My wife and I are going to bed. Thor himself is swinging his hammer inside my skull. May we all find a measure of peace tonight."

Together, Eir and Hákon ventured into the darkness between the tents. When no more could be seen of them, Sigtryggr made a noise in his throat. "*Stáli* makes a better king than I," he murmured. "Not one of us deserves him."

Then Sigtryggr straightened, took a breath, and met my gaze with a sudden, strange intensity that quickened my pulse.

"Will you walk with me a while?" he asked. "I have much I would say to you. Much that cannot wait."

Taken aback, I hesitated, turning to Ruarc as if it had been him the king meant to ask for, not me. But Ruarc smiled gently. "Go on," he whispered. "It's you he wants."

And so I rose, following the king and the sound of the whispering surf.

A bright moon gilded the flat-topped hill. Sigtryggr and I sat together in the dewy grass, brushing our fingers through the silver blades and pretending neither of us wanted to speak first.

A painful lump had taken residence in my throat. I plucked a stalk of coarse turf and twisted it in my hands, deliberating how best to break the silence.

Sigtryggr breathed softly, for once unaffected by the ever-thrumming drive in his body. Only his gaze was restless now, and it flit from my face to the grass and then to the spread of canvas tents and gentle lace-capped waves beneath us.

Sighing, I put my hand over his, and felt a vibration pass under the warm skin.

"If you're hoping I'm a *seiðr*-wife who can read the cast of bones and hear the thoughts of gods and men, you'll be disappointed. You wanted to speak, Siggi. I am listening."

A smile turned up the corner of his mouth. "Always a spear to the guts with you," he said fondly.

"I know no other way to be."

He looked down. Our bodies touched at the knee, and our fingers had somehow intertwined.

"Then there is no other way for me than the truth," he said. When he looked at me again, there was hope and no small amount of fear in his moon-gilt face.

"For all the years you and I have shared together, there has never been a hearth-fire that burned brighter for me than yours. Gyda, I want you as my own. It's a terrible, fierce ache, and it has never left me."

Slowly, gently, I raised my hand to his face. The rasp of his dark beard was soft under my fingertips. "I know. And you're a fool for it."

He swallowed hard. I did not remove my hand. After a moment, he gave a little nod.

"Would you tell this fool if you shared in his feelings?"

"No," I said, and this strangely seemed to cheer him; his smile returned.

"I suppose that's enough."

Taking my hands, he brought them to his heart and held them.

He was warm under my touch, and solid. His heartbeat felt strong: a vibrant and drumming vigor that defined him as a man and as a king.

His voice lowered and took on a note of regret. "Tomorrow, when my wits and pride have returned, I likely will be very angry with you," he said. "I may not know how to call you friend either. Give me time. I will strive to get past this. Just as you have the right to reject me, so I have the right to feel it and grieve it."

"I am sorry to hurt you, Siggi," I said. "This is not your doing. I am simply not as others are. My deepest heart is for myself alone. It is all I know. It is how I am."

Sigtryggr released my hands and sighed. "Just as well," he said. "I should count myself lucky you haven't gutted me and fed me my own stinking shit for speaking these things."

"Now you are being unfair."

"Am I?" He looked at me miserably. "I've brought so many of my warriors to their deaths. The ambush proved I am a weak, useless king. An unreliable leader. And now I've told you I want you, with nothing but shame to offer. Of course you wouldn't want me. What a mooning turd I must seem."

"I never said I didn't want you," I said, and then I leaned forward and pressed my lips to his.

He gave a small, surprised growl, and then returned the kiss, grasping me hard to him like I was the edge of the cliff he dangled from.

For a time, careful of our pains, we helped each other forget our griefs and our exhaustion. He gave generously and I returned in kind. We warmed each other under the stars and the moon and the open sky.

And after, when we crept down the beach to our separate tents, we spoke not a word and let only a brief clasping of hands say all that was needed.

CHAPTER TWENTY-SIX

Days passed. A week. We set our encampment on the elevated plateau between the water and surrounding woodland. To our west stood promontories of rock and high cliff faces. For the moment, we were safe from attack by both land and sea.

The food stores on the ships were scant, limited to porridge and hardtack, but we found bounty in the waves. With little effort, we harvested more than enough seaweed, pollack, dogfish, and flounder to fill our bellies and ease our pains. One morning, three of Hákon's men whooped and cheered as they hauled a sleek, thrashing ray up the gravel with only a bone hook and line. Such a catch was exceedingly rare in these waters, and the three basked in the glory of it for days while the camp feasted on the beast's meat.

A month had soon passed and true summer found a deep foothold. Long hours of sunshine gave the camp a lightness of spirit. Wounds healed and strength returned to many. But not every hurt could be repaired, and not everyone shared in the lightness.

To pass the time, I continued to allow Eir to treat me. Once I could walk consistently without support, she set forth a regimen of exercises to follow. I trained with wooden swords, lifted cargo barrels, and swam in the sea between two points of rock for hours until I could no longer float. It was a grueling, agonizing punishment, but the drills did their work; after a fortnight I could run and the ache in my ribs became less debilitating. The slice in my belly healed in a jagged, red line. My headaches diminished, too, though I still had yet to go a span of several days without one.

Hákon fared worse. His pain increased in frequency and severity. The first week after landing, he remained inside his tent with Eir. The men took this abandonment badly. The fight had been demoralizing. Grumbling and malcontent grew among the men until eventually, two of the young ones had the poor judgment to gripe about the lord's "womanly frailty" near the shitting holes at the edge of camp. Squatting over one such hole, Hákon had overheard, and since that day, those fools were charged with the digging of new holes and covering of the old ones.

Against Eir's pleading, Hákon left his tent the same day and put himself where he could be seen by the entire company. His face a bloodless mask, he sat rigid and sweat-soaked on a stool in the sunshine. He never complained, and refused to eat more than the morsels his wife prepared him. When he did speak, his words were cross and biting. Those men who tested his patience or grumbled too loudly soon found themselves with loathsome tasks. More than five men sported cracked noses from backhanded blows given by their wiser brothers. Soon, none of them questioned Lord *Stáli*, though this was more from skittish fear than respect.

The Jórvík men kept out of the entire business, saying nothing but watching with wariness.

Eir's anxiety grew. She would not speak of it, no matter how I pressed her. Even when the stirring of the child inside her belly brought a rosy bloom to her skin, the joy leached from her. Hákon suffered every day, and so she did as well.

When the time came to fight, I hoped Hákon would remember his mettle.

Fortunately, not everything was bleak. Word got around the camp that *Dreki* carried a sizable store of beer in the hold. To all of our surprise, it was Astrid who took on the initiative, retrieving three casks on her own before others even thought to try, and then she refused to cede control of them.

Drunk and wanton, Astrid found ferocious pleasure in the arms of Sigtryggr's brawny fighters. She proclaimed that Jórvík's offering of male beauty was far superior to that of Dyflin's. Such remarks might have brought out violence. After all, men who had been thrown over often said and did foolish things. Fortunately, a particular rumor wormed its way throughout the camp. It told of how the fearless Astrid Knife-Edge had handled her bastard father, and how her many jealous lovers would meet the same fate should they anger her.

After such rumors, her lovers were content to engage her attention without fighting amongst each other. What good was fighting, they reasoned, when a man could be happy fucking? It had nothing to do with her wicked knife, of course. The rumor settled deep and strong, just as I'd hoped it would when I spread it. Astrid thanked me, and then forgot her gratitude by the next day and the next cask.

The ability to seek oblivion was enviable, and it was no surprise why Astrid sought it: Guðrun, Liadan, and Rúna had not yet surfaced.

Every day, as the sun rose, I climbed the little hill to watch the horizon for a sail. Many ships traveled this coastline, but none landed. Were they merchants? *Drakkar* raiders? Travelers returning to their home shores? I created a thousand stories for each one that crossed the water, and none of them became my Daughters.

I interrogated the camp. Had anyone seen three women in the fight? Had any been left behind? Had anyone escaped that were not among us or among the dead?

No, they told me. No women. No wounded.

And Thorkill was dead, unable to tell if he'd seen three women escape through his gate.

I refused to let reason cloud my fool's hope, and so I watched the horizon every sunrise, waiting for the sail that would bring my Daughters home to us.

Ruarc joined me on the hill sometimes, watching in silence.

He was not the only one short of words; Sigtryggr had not spoken to me since our night together. He would give me a nod when he came to Eir's tent for treatment, and conceded to spar with me when no other partners could be found. But my attempts to make conversation went unanswered. *Good morning* elicited no response. The only words he did speak were in the company of Hákon, Eir, and Ruarc when we planned and argued over how best to take on Heimarr when the time came. Even then, the king's words to me were polite, forced, and shallow.

His recovery progressed well. Inactivity had atrophied his sword-arm, and the limb had a tendency to swell if left unbandaged long. Despite this, Sigtryggr trained steadfastly, perhaps to bury the words he yet lacked the courage to say to me.

Until he found a way to move past his hurt pride, there could be no easiness between us. I could not force him to it, and I had no wish to try.

In all of this aching hope and sorrow, Ruarc's solid presence was my sole comfort.

This morning, as every morning, I waited in the dark on a stony mound, watching the sea for the first rays of sunrise. When its golden fingers warmed my back, I knew Ruarc would bring me a bowl of porridge and sit with me.

Near my left knee, a little grass mouse groomed its whiskers. I studied it, absorbed by its silken gray paws and twitching white fur. When my stomach growled, it fled, and Ruarc snorted a laugh behind me.

"What a tiny, gutless thing," he said. "I feel just the same out here in the dark." He plopped down and handed me a spoon and a steaming wooden bowl.

"Careful," he warned. "Eir just took that off the fire."

I shoveled the porridge, too delighted to heed the burn. "Where did you find honey?" I groaned. "Oh, gods."

Ruarc's smile in the gray light was as cheerful as always. "What can I say? I know where the bees like to hide themselves."

I had the bowl emptied in four bites. "Any left?" I said, swiveling around.

In the middle of camp, Eir was a slight figure standing beside the cook-fire. The sun had not yet risen, so the firelight cast her in a forge's glow. With vigorous strokes, she stirred to keep the porridge from sticking to the iron pot. Beside her was Astrid, who clutched a bowl with one drooping hand. By the jerk and wave of her other hand, it was clear she was yammering on about something. The outrages of her current lover, most like. It was too far to see the hungover circles under her eyes, but I knew they would be there.

"No one's awake yet," Ruarc said. "So if you want more, I'd be happy to go down and refill your bowl. For the price of one kiss." Grinning, he offered his cheek for payment.

"Not happening!" I shoved him away. "It's fine, I'll get something later. The balls on you, honestly."

He laughed, but did not comment.

For a time, we watched the water. The half-moon still glowed faintly, and the final stars winked out. A heavy cloud was blowing in from the east, bringing with it summer rains.

"How does Hákon fare?" I asked, picking at a loose fingernail. Ruarc sighed.

"The same," he said. "Writhed and moaned all night long, though this time I think it was because of his wife. I need to move my tent away. I'm losing too much sleep."

I rocked, bumping his knee with mine. "You'll lose sleep no matter where you put your tent. I heard you had a visitor a few nights ago, the same one you had last week. Be more careful, Ruarc. If I'm hearing it, so are the others. Be safe."

I didn't see him flush, but the deep rumble in Ruarc's throat told me he could not deny it.

"I'll have to have a word with Eir about discretion," he murmured.

"And what of Sigtryggr?"

His mouth quirked. "He won't speak to me if I bring you up, but I think there's progress to be made. He laughed when Astrid told a story about how you dangled a stowaway over the side of *Sea-Wolf* by the ankles."

"That was Ragnar," I said. "And he deserved it."

"He surely did," Ruarc replied.

Gradually the sun warmed our backs and gilded the hilltop.

"How much longer, do you think?" Ruarc knuckled his nose, then wiped the evidence on his sleeve. "I don't have the stomach for all this gloom and despair. There's talk in the camp, Gyda. The men are restless."

I swallowed. "We aren't ready. Not yet."

Ruarc rose and brushed the dew from his trousers. "Then you'll have to convince Hákon of that. I overheard him tell Eir he means to demand Sigtryggr make ready to leave."

I looked up in alarm. "You could have lead with that!"

Shrugging, Ruarc turned to stare down the hill. "If you want more time to wait for the Daughters, make that damn king forgive you soon. He is still our ally, and we need him on our side. Don't rely on patience anymore. We may be forced into action whether we're ready for it or not."

I pushed off the ground and tightened my blanket around my shoulders. "It wouldn't be the first time," I said. "Hákon is one obstacle, but don't doubt Sigtryggr's ability to hold a grudge."

Ruarc smirked. "The one thing I do not doubt is your ability to overcome the odds. You'll convince them. I know that in my bones, or may the gods take me."

I took one last, lingering look at the empty ocean, then followed Ruarc down the hill.

By noon, the camp was a flurry of activity. Tents were taken down, fires put out and buried, and casks rolled and bumped down the slope to the shore. *Dreki* and *Hrið-Ormr* leaned on the gravel, bellies open like flayed fish.

"You cannot do this, Hákon. We need more time."

"It's already done, woman," he told me, turning away to bark more orders at the passing man carting a bundle of tent pegs.

We stood under a sailcloth canopy, one of the few structures yet standing. Ruarc was misinformed; not only had Hákon spoken to Sigtryggr already, but an agreement had been struck between them.

We would depart on the afternoon tide and make for the Isle of Man. The route would bring us to Heimarr's encampment on the western coast in the dark of night. An ambush to answer an ambush.

It had been Hákon's idea, and in the time I'd been here arguing, he held fast the belief that a swift strike would break Heimarr's defenses like a hammer on brittle iron. He would be lazy, Hákon maintained. Lazy and negligent and unsuspecting.

I thought it a shortsighted, stupid gamble with no hope of success, and told him so, but without Eir present to back me, my protests fell on uncaring ears. Ruarc also had abandoned me early, haring off to find Sigtryggr, so I tried another tactic.

"How are we meant to trust your plan when you never consulted us?" I demanded. "Neither Eir nor I agreed to this. Whatever Sigtryggr told you, he's bluffing. We must wait for our messengers to return from Dyflin. We must wait for the Daughters. We are not strong enough, Hákon. Do you hear me? *You* are not strong enough."

"You think I haven't considered all this?" he snapped, then winced as his skull pained him. He put a fist to his temple. "Fuck! I am *done* with waiting and shitting and sleeping on some troll-cursed spit of land for three corpses and an imaginary fighting force. They're *dead,* Gyda. No one is coming to our aid. It's all a lie. A language you are fluent in and should have recognized!"

"Even if it is a lie, what choice do we have?" I cried. "We cannot face Heimarr with our number, and you know it. We'd be striking a wasp's nest."

Hákon sneered. "So we suffer a few stings. He won't notice until we've burned his hive to the ground."

I smacked the edge of the trestle next to me. "You think you know what he is, but it is *you* who are the fool!"

My voice cracked on the last word, and the knot of oath-men waiting nearby shifted uneasily.

Hákon fixed me with a dark stare. "Careful, *Fiskwif,*" he growled. "My patience with you is spent. If you cannot see the hand of friendship right in front of you, the next thing you will see is the mast of my ship as it leaves you behind on this shore. Don't test my word on this."

"Sigtryggr would not allow it," I retorted. "I don't know what you said to win him over, but he would never agree to this without a contingency. We lost half our force the last time! He wouldn't risk such foolishness now."

"You talk a lot about what I wouldn't do, woman," said Sigtryggr, ducking under the canopy. I gaped at him, struck by his appearance.

He'd kitted himself out for departure and for battle, with his sword at his hip, a seax on his waist, and a round shield strapped to his back. A broad strip of linen bound his forearm tightly. Three of his men stood at his back, faces blank as he approached us.

"*Stáli,*" he said. "I've loaded my surplus oars on *Dreki* to replace those that snapped in the storm. We are ready to launch at your word."

He would not look my way.

"My thanks," Hákon told him, and gestured to his own oath-men.

"Round up the others and get them sorted for leaving," he ordered. "Leave nothing behind."

Sigtryggr nodded to his retinue, and all of them went off together, though a few looked me over warily before leaving.

"Sigtryggr, you cannot mean to join this attack," I said. "You know we can't prevail. This is folly."

Finally, he did look at me, and it was distant. "We cannot wait another month for something to happen," he said. "We are not exiles. We must return to our families. Some of us have livelihoods that demand our attention. Some of us have duties, and enemies to slay."

"Like Edward?" I blurted, and his teeth grit.

"Sigtryggr, please," I said before he could speak. "You made me a promise. I call on that promise now. If that must end our friendship for good, so be it."

A spasm passed over his face. "You will have your ship and Heimarr's life," he forced out. "But the rest of it matters little. A king does not wait for help to come to him. He goes to seek fame, finding it in battle or in death."

He said this last bit to Hákon, not to me, and I saw the small nod Hákon made in response.

"You are both fools," I said. "Heimarr will slaughter us all and shit on our corpses."

Desperate, I turned to Hákon. "Heed my words, Hákon *Stáli*. Your father will know what a *niðingr* your brother is, and what a fool you were to face him alone. He will lament your wasteful death. Heimarr will inherit all your wealth and all your glory. He'll marry Eir and raise your child, if he doesn't kill them outright. Your name will be forgotten, but his will be remembered as the surviving son of Olavi Sharp-Spear."

Hákon's body had lost its healthy bulk in the last weeks. He was a husk on his way to ruin, but at my words, strength and anger tightened his limbs. I had gone too far.

"You *bitch*," he hissed. Spittle flew from his mouth. "You scheming, poison-tongued shrieking bitch."

My fingers flexed. There was no taking this back. He would leave me here, and it would be over. All my efforts, my sacrifices, would be for nothing.

A high cry reached us, half-scream and half-sob. Hákon, Sigtryggr, and I turned to see Astrid fly down the slope to the sea. Eir raced after her, skirts gathered in white fists.

Another voice cried out at the top of the hill. "They're here," Ruarc called, pointing to the horizon behind him. "They've made it! The Daughters have come."

CHAPTER TWENTY-SEVEN

Miserable, I huddled in the prow of *Hrið-Ormr* and counted the splinters in the soft, raw flesh of my palms. The calluses I'd earned from years of rowing required constant ripping now if I was to properly work an oar. As midnight turned to pre-dawn, Liadan had removed me from my bench and took over. Embarrassment tightened the back of my neck, and grew worse as she endured the labor into the early hours. What kind of Daughter of Rán was I, who could no longer row without blistering like a lady of gentle birth?

"Be ready," Sigtryggr called to us softly from the tiller, barely audible above the grunting of the rowers.

The coast of the Isle lay slumbering before us, a shadowed mass of stone against a black horizon. I inhaled and savored the brine and the salt and the sea-wrack on my tongue. The pain in my palms was nothing. Gyda Grim-Bitch would be no gentle lady. Even if I did not row, I was ready. A long seax hung from my waist and I wore a well-fit *brynja* under my tunic. The king had also provided waxed sea-cloaks for everyone to keep the spray and salt off. And between our feet we'd hidden leather-wrapped axes with their handles out for easy grasping, as well as spears with freshly-sharpened blades. The fight was coming, and we were hungry for it.

Beside us, *Dreki* rode the water like a true sea-dragon, its oars like a dark forest rising and falling with each cresting wave. Built for war, Hákon's *drakkar* was all power and speed, and gods, was it beautiful. The ship flexed through the swells, sleek and canny and without fear of the dark grasping depths beneath. As much as I loved *Sea-Wolf,* my *knarr*'s bulk could never ride the whale-road as smoothly or as effortlessly.

Dreki and *Hrið-Ormr* aimed for Heimarr like twin spears for the hide of a boar. He would be blind to our coming. We burned no torches. No moon hung in the sky to reflect off our sails and helmets. Dawn's golden light would arrive too late to save him.

Guðrun and Rúna shared an oar in front of me. I watched as they pulled the spruce shaft, marveling at their power. Liadan had my seat with Astrid. Eir was aboard *Dreki* to watch over Hákon.

My Daughters were *here*. Together. All of them, safe. It was a gift I'd nearly given up as lost.

Astrid and Eir had raced to the beach to intercept the fishing skiff, in whose prow Guðrun stood bellowing and waving at us.

In that first instant after Ruarc's heralding, my heart sputtered and leapt like flame. When I saw them through the vale of tears, hope gave way to radiant joy. Guðrun, Rúna, and Liadan plunged into the surf and splashed ashore, wreathed in smiles and browned by the summer sun. The six of us, Rán's Daughters, were reunited in tears and tight embraces.

It seemed Thorkill had another deed to carry with him in death. Early in the assault, he had come upon the women in the smoky dark, cornered by a knot of Heimarr's monsters. With no weapons, they were certain to die. With one sweep of his great axe, Thorkill had cleaved the tops of the enemies' skulls and ushered them through the gate to safety. He had guarded that gate well. Better even than we had known.

The Daughters fled into the darkness. Afraid to face more enemies unarmed, they'd kept away from shore and hid in the forest until after the last cinder burned out. Unaware of our survival and flight, they found lodging in a fishing village down the coast. It took a week for the truth to reach them.

"We came as soon as we could," Rúna had said. "And brought as many men as the village could spare."

Guðrun nodded, clapping a firm hand on the shoulder of a wizened old fisherman who appeared to be the patriarch of the ragged troop. They'd brought ten individuals, aged between fourteen summers to eighty-four. None of them bore swords, but the leather-toughness of their hands and muscles showed they were no strangers to oar-work.

Put us to the task, Liadan signed, her expression grim as the winter sea. *Let Heimarr feel the bite of our blades.*

Ten fishermen and two ragged, wounded companies against an unknown number of Heimarr's fighters. It was all we could hope for. Hákon and Sigtryggr would not be swayed, and so we'd sailed within the hour.

The sea rocked us like a cradle. Ægir and his wife Rán slept, or else concerned themselves with some other unlucky ship riding the swan-road. The wind died as we went south, and so we rowed. This was considered by all to be the most direct route to shore and to the blood-letting. Muscles flexed, sweat coated our skins, and our hot hearts strained in our chests. Even I, as angry as I had been, was infected by battle-eagerness. *Sea-Wolf* floated out there in the dark, anchored off-shore and waiting for my hand to steer it once again. Feeling the tiller in my blistered palm again would be a salve to both body and heart.

Sigtryggr steered us, his eyes and mouth barely visible under his hood in the gloom.

"Aki," he said in a low, carrying voice. "Any fires out there? Any movement?"

Crouched to my right, Aki hummed in his throat. The sky had not yet begun to lighten, and Aki was a man with a gaze as keen as Heimdallr, the watchman of Asgard. He leaned over the prow-strake and squinted through the dark at the shoreline. I heard the knot in his throat bob. Each of us waited with breath held and muscles tight.

"I see three fires, Lord," he said. "Ah, four. No movement. They've settled down."

"Only four? That can't be right," I said. Rising up on my knees, I looked out.

"Your old woman's eyes can't see past the nose of the prow-serpent," said Ruarc, who stepped over a coiled rope to join us. "What about that, Aki? See that reflection there?"

He pointed to starboard, and Aki shifted his gaze.

"That is a ship," he affirmed. "Well spotted."

My breath caught. "Is it *Sea-Wolf*?" I stood, pushing Ruarc and Aki away. I searched the darkened sea, seeing nothing but vague shadows and movement.

Ruarc took my arm and raised it, adjusting the angle as he did. "Use your fingers as a guide," he murmured. "Adjust for the motion of rowing."

I peered down the length of my arm, and hissed. "I see it!"

The shape was nothing but a vague ghost, but the ripples emanating around the hull gave my ship an unmistakable profile.

"That is *Sea-Wolf*, no doubt," I whispered, and lowered my arm. I wouldn't lose sight of it now. "Anchored at the mouth of the bay. But where is the other ship?"

Sigtryggr left the stern and thumped forward, picking his way between the sea-chests. "Heimarr would not leave his prize undefended," he said. "No movement on shore, Aki? What about the ship itself? What can you see?"

Aki looked to Ruarc, and together they leaned over the strake, whispering to each other.

I turned to Sigtryggr. "What is it you're thinking?" There had been a subtle shift in his voice when he spoke.

"I'm thinking we take *Sea-Wolf* and flee," he replied.

My blood rose and I touched the borrowed seax on my waist. "We're so close now. We could do it."

"Less than ten bodies aboard, Lord," said Aki.

"We could take it," Sigtryggr said to me, then paused and cleared his throat.

"What? You have doubts?"

"We should confer with Hákon," he answered. "With so little movement on shore, I suspect there could be another stronghold for the larger force."

"Why does that matter?" I sputtered.

"Better not to plunge your cock without looking to see if it's a woman or a pig."

I bit my thumbnail, thinking this over. As much as I burned for my ship, caution must rule. "Let's call them over, then."

With a quiet order, the oars rose out of the water and we slowed. *Dreki* followed suit soon after. It took a few tries, but finally our tethering line landed with a thump on *Dreki's* deck. We drifted and our two hulls thumped and shook, a commotion that made us wince with the loudness of it. But there was no reaction from shore or from *Sea-Wolf,* and we breathed easier.

Hákon and Eir appeared at *Dreki*'s strake. Both dressed as we did—in waxed cloaks the same color as the sea.

"*Stáli,* Eir," Sigtryggr greeted them. "Fortune favors us. *Sea-Wolf* anchors just there." He nodded to the barely visible bay and coastline. "Heimarr's own ship appears to be gone, or else hidden. The bulk of his force must be entrenched elsewhere. This camp is as good as deserted."

"It is a field ripe for harvesting," I said eagerly, stepping forward. My body thrummed with excitement.

"We mean to take the ship and get away before dawn," Sigtryggr clarified. "But we want your opinion before we make our move."

Hákon blew through his lips and considered this.

His hesitation made me itch. "There could be no better chance than this," I pressed.

Sigtryggr bumped my shoulder.

"Strange," Hákon said finally. "Why would Heimarr leave his prize sitting in the open?"

"Do you think he returned to Dyflin?" Eir asked.

Hákon shifted his weight. "I doubt it. Heimarr is too much of a coward to face our father until his rage has cooled."

"So he is hiding," said Ruarc, coming to join me and the king at the strake.

"Or hunting," I suggested. "He has messengers of his own. He may have heard of our position in Alba, and is on his way there now. We could have easily missed his ship in the dark."

Sigtryggr grunted. "Any of these possibilities are sound. But why leave *Sea-Wolf* behind? He would need it for an attack."

Guðrun snorted from her bench. "It's not as if *Sea-Wolf* is a ship built for raiding," she said acerbically. "It's a tub with bent oars and too many holes to plug. A bit like Astrid."

Sigtryggr's crew rumbled in quiet laughter at that, Astrid herself included.

Rúna spoke up then. "*Sea-Wolf* is a good and sturdy ship, but of course Heimarr wouldn't have used it. That would be risking the silver. He'd be a fool to bring it with him."

"He could have stowed it in the camp," offered Ruarc. "It makes sense to leave a smaller force behind to guard it while he's off chasing us with a greater number. *Sea-Wolf* makes a good deterrent should any fool come along to sniff around."

Hákon made a noise of contempt.

"There is an alternative," Eir said. "Someone else has already run Heimarr off. There are many who'd like to get their hands on a silver-hoard like that. If he's been flaunting it and hiring mercenaries, he made himself a target. Maybe to his own men."

The implication of this was not lost on me, and I scowled. "*Sea-Wolf* is worthless to Heimarr. If your theory is true, then Heimarr could have already gone to ground with the hoard. We've lost our chance."

"For now," Hákon confirmed. He flapped his cloak and tightened it around his shoulders. "Why else would Heimarr leave this place undefended?" he said. "Thinking of it, I'd wager nothing but force would make his stubborn carcass move. Not even the possibility of gutting you properly."

"A comforting thought, but I am not the only one he's thirsting to gut."

"All the more reason why his plans might have changed," Ruarc said. "He lives to gut us another day."

Ruarc meant it to reassure me, but I shook my head and stared out over the water.

"Some thread is missing in the weave of all this," I said softly.

Dawn was coming; *Sea-Wolf* was more visible now, and as I stared at it bobbing in the water, a new resolve came over me.

I turned to the others. "We cannot know what is true and what is not. Standing here flapping our mouths like fish won't help. All that is left is to wait for Heimarr to return for it."

"You said it's worthless," Hákon said incredulously. "Why would he return?"

"Your brother is a vindictive shit," I replied. "My ship may be lacking in value, but he knows it galls me to see it in his possession. He'd never leave *Sea-Wolf* behind for long."

Bracing my hands against the strake, I looked at Ruarc and Aki. "How many bodies aboard? No more than ten?"

They murmured their agreement.

I let my voice rise. "Hardly a formidable number against us, wouldn't you agree? Wouldn't *all* of you agree?"

There were noises in the benches, a rustling as warriors leaned against their neighbors to whisper together.

"You think Heimarr expects to return," said Eir, catching on. "So even if he has been driven off, he must send someone back for the ship. Or even the silver, if he's hidden it on shore."

Sigtryggr growled. "Wherever the fucker is, he's left his nest unwatched. I say we rip it from him before he knows it. Kill him another day. What say you, *Stáli*?"

Hákon, with his men whispering at his back and a blood-hungry king at his front, did not speak. He looked to Eir, then past her towards the coast. He studied it for a long moment.

"It would be simple enough to do this," Eir said. "And we must think of what happens after. Why should we wait for Heimarr to return? Is it not better to leave him with nothing? No *Sea-Wolf*, no silver, no camp. He'd be left with what he has on his own. His force will desert him without guaranteed payment. This will force him back to Dyflin to beg for mercy. He would be disgraced and exiled. No lord or jarl would take him in. Such humiliation would be just punishment for his crimes."

"No," said Hákon firmly, then he cleared his throat and spoke louder. "No. If we leave Heimarr alive, this is all for nothing. I will be Jarl in Dyflin one day, and I would not have it said that my honor falters when it comes to sentiment."

I watched Hákon, standing straight and tall as a spear as he gripped Eir's hand. My anger with him burned still, but in that moment I understood him. Hákon *Stáli*, with his heart of steel.

Heimarr was a danger. Not only to us, but to Hákon's family, his oath-men, and all those who depended on him for safety and provision. Sigtryggr had the right of it: *A king does not wait for help to come to him.*

Ruarc touched my shoulder. Behind him, Liadan, Astrid, Guðrun, and Rúna watched me. Fire filled my heart.

"We take it, then," I said to Hákon. "We take *Sea-Wolf,* and then the camp. We lay a trap for Heimarr, and then we kill him."

"We kill him," Hákon echoed. "Brother he may be, but Heimarr dies today, and so my grievance with him."

Sigtryggr pounded the strake and roared. "Oath-warriors! King's men! How would you like to rip the throats out of the fuckers who killed our friends?" Then he threw his head back and howled, long and resonant. His warriors did the same, and even Hákon's men joined the noise.

Gooseflesh erupted over me as my Daughters' voices rose and merged. Ruarc howled last, and the vibration of all our voices shook the decking under my feet.

My ears and chest filled with something I had not felt in a long time—power. We were wolves of the sea. We were children of Rán. We were blood-hungry and silver-struck. And we would take back our destinies with our fists and our teeth.

"Oars out!" Hákon roared.

Our tether was cut, our blades sliced the water. We flew towards the shore like sharks chasing blood.

If only we knew what waited for us in the dark.

CHAPTER TWENTY-EIGHT

The dawn birds wheeled overhead as we pulled against the current. Their screeching calls mingled with the panicked shouting of doomed men on shore and aboard *Sea-Wolf.* Small figures ran to and fro across the beach, dousing fires before donning gear and weapons. I counted fewer than twenty men.

On *Sea-Wolf,* the square canvas sail rose to the crossbeam, unfurled, then sagged to one side, bellying because the fools on board did not know the *knarr* the way the Daughters did. The way I did.

I bared my teeth to the salt and the spray. This barking fear would only sweeten their deaths when I stepped onto *Sea-Wolf's* deck once more.

Finally. *Finally,* I would sway with the waves and follow the trace of whale-roads beneath my feet. I would steer with the wind and chase the spanning skies. I would defy Rán herself and battle the deep cold ocean, fight the calling to sink down to her corpse-hall and shark-dens. With *Sea-Wolf,* I would once more become arbiter of my own fate, and the sea would roar to greet me as an equal. Finally, I would be ready.

My voice was loud, my grasp on the prow-beast tight. "On! On! Break those oars or I'll break your backs!"

Hrið-Ormr shuddered and groaned as we hauled.

Sigtryggr's wolf-heart had taken him over. He snarled and grinned at the tiller, his knuckles bone-white on the handle. His bad eye streamed with tears, but fire lived in his gaze and in his blood.

Nearby, *Dreki* slid across the water, a sleek, monstrous serpent, its prow-beast a gaping maw of fang and darting tongue. Eir stood at the mast. Her pale hair streamed like a banner of white gold. One hand rested over the swell of her womb and the other curled around the haft of a long axe. The men straining on the benches pulled for her and for Hákon, their lord.

My heart expanded. I drew my seax and lifted it to the sky, letting loose a keening wail which rose and fell like the chaos of a hurricane.

My Daughters, Liadan, Astrid, Guðrun, and Rúna, took up the cry. We sang of death as the first rays of dawn rose over us. The sound rang in the ears of the poor bastards on *Sea-Wolf.* The blood drained from their faces and their hands trembled as we tacked up alongside. Our song was replaced by their screaming.

When my seax sliced through the first man's throat, I was home. My blade went through his flesh like a fish through water: with barely a ripple and without sound. He fell to the deck twitching.

The rest fought back with desperate fury. Guðrun's nose cracked against the fist of one, and soon after he lost that fist when her axe took it. Then his head split, spilling his brains across the forward deck. Guðrun snatched up the severed fist and stuffed it in her shirt, a trophy to hang from her belt later.

At my flank, Liadan was a whirling storm. Her opponent, backed against the mast, screeched a curse and lashed out with a kick. She caught his foot, wrenching it hard and cracking his hip out of joint. Then her blade went through his gullet and her fingers, those slender deft fingers, reached into the gash and tore out his tongue. Astrid howled her laughter, and in the sound I heard a madness akin to Sigtryggr's.

Ruarc called encouragement from the deck of *Hrið-Ormr*. He was with Rúna, watching us ruin Heimarr's men one by one.

They had covered over my cargo-hold with decking. I danced over the blood-slick planks and joined Astrid in the stern. Together, we took the balls and part of one leg from a tall man who thought he could repel us with a broken oar. The artery in his leg spurted and sprayed us, and I swiped the blood from my lips like a filthy kiss. Astrid put out his eyes and soon his bleeding and his weeping ended in a wet gurgle.

There were two others near us. Young, not more than fifteen summers. Hardly the wisp of a beard on their faces. Rage had not yet fully blinded me, and so, seeing them huddled against the gunwale white-faced and terrified, I halted and lowered my seax.

"Where is Heimarr?" I demanded.

"*Niðingar*!" screeched Astrid at my side. "You gutless worms!"

They cowered at my feet. I recognized their faces. Sons of Olavi's oath-men. Betraying their Jarl for the promise of stolen silver and false glory.

"Tell me," I bellowed. "You are children, not warriors. Don't give an honorless turd your loyalty. Tell me where he is or your scrawny bones will go to feed the Corpse-Snake."

"The Snake wouldn't even lick the eyes of these two troll-spawn," spat Astrid.

Behind us, Guðrun bawled. I did not turn, but the sound of the last man's skull cracking under her boot was unmistakable. The boys shrieked and covered their heads.

With a curse, Astrid lunged and hauled them up, slapping their faces and yanking their hair to force them to look at me.

"Tell me now, or meet my seax," I said to them, but they were paralyzed, wide eyes streaming and noses dripping. They stammered wordlessly. And then there came a shift to their faces, their gazes sliding past me to the horizon. The twist of Astrid's mouth just before I heard it.

"Gyda! Gyda, the ship!"

Ruarc's voice was shrill, anguished. I turned, every sinew in my body taut with dread.

There were four ships in this bay, not three.

From the north, a new vessel rode the sea around a spur of coast, sailing hard to the wind, coming on fast.

Dreki yawed, oars plowing frantically away from its intended route towards shore. They would be the first to meet the oncoming vessel.

My heart and lungs stuttered in my chest. Of course. Heimarr. The shit had hidden from us in the dark, and we had not seen the trap. *I* had not seen. I should have thought. I should have *known.* I was a fool.

There would be little time. *Sea-Wolf* was not equipped for a sea-battle, and even with ten extra bodies, *Hrið-Ormr* was short of hands. Sigtryggr could not spare enough men to row both ships efficiently.

Across the expanse of water, dawn sun flashed off *brynjur* and axe-heads. Garishly painted shields lined the strakes on both sides of the enemy ship. Heimarr had at least forty men on his benches, likely more.

Bile rose in my throat. Behind me, there was a gurgling scream and a heavy splash, and another anguished cry that cut off with a second splash. I did not look. A moment later, Astrid grabbed my elbow and I felt the wet heat of fresh blood on her hand.

"We need to get off this ship," she hissed in my ear.

I could not move. I had found him. Heimarr.

He stood at his prow, holding aloft a wicked iron hook attached to a rope. His attention was fixed on *Dreki,* on Hákon and Eir. I did not need eyes to see the hate in his face. He meant to slaughter them.

I rushed to *Sea-Wolf*'s strake and screamed for Sigtryggr.

But the king had seen everything already, and had cut the tether connecting us. He hauled on *Hrið-Ormr*'s rudder, yelling curses and orders at the men as they scrambled to push away. The wind had whipped up, and so followed the waves.

We rose and fell with the sea. I licked salt from my lips.

Heimarr was nearly on us. Aboard *Dreki,* Hákon's warriors had taken up their blades and shields. Well-matched as they could be with Heimarr's fighters in capability, I could not say the same for strength. Even at this distance, I saw Heimarr's men did not carry the lean, hungry angles that ours did. This would be a vicious, grisly fight.

"We need to row fast," Sigtryggr called to me, but *Hrið-Ormr* still floated too close to us. Our oars risked tangling and snapping.

"We won't catch them in time, Lord King," yelled Red Yngvi. "Heimarr has the wind!"

This was true, and Heimarr used his advantage well. His vessel prowled for *Dreki,* swift and eager for the hunt as a fox in the coop. There would be no intercepting him.

As we scrambled to make space for the oars, Heimarr's metal claws flew and thumped on *Dreki*'s deck-boards, catching on gunwales and thwarts. The vessels groaned with arrested momentum, then collided in a splintering, smashing storm. Men leapt from their benches, blades and shields and axes slavering for the first bite of flesh. "Whoresons! Fucking troll-cursed cowards!" I screeched.

The cries of the dying rose from *Dreki* to the sky.

I spied Eir with Hákon in the stern. She still gripped a blade, but Hákon was pushing her, shoving and yelling as he moved them both away from the fight. She struggled against him.

Sea-Wolf's planks under my feet shook as multiple heavy bodies landed on deck. I started, hand tightening on my blade.

Ruarc heaved for breath. "Put us on the benches. We'll catch these pigs!"

Rúna stood next to him, and accompanying them were four of the fishermen. They had run the oars from *Hrið-Ormr* to join us.

As I gaped, Ruarc pressed me. "Gyda, give us your orders!"

Snatching an oar from between the thwarts, I brandished it. "Fasten everything," I said. "Dump the corpses in the water. I don't care if you break your backs, you pull these oars like the gods themselves are whipping you."

Even as I gave the commands, I knew we could never be fast enough.

Astrid, still watching *Dreki,* cried out and I whirled, heart in my throat.

Hákon was at the strake, lifting Eir over it. His face was a mask of pain and effort. She was screaming, pleading with him, and when she dropped from his arms into the sea, sobs wracked his shoulders. For half a moment, he reached out to the water, as if regretting letting her go, letting his child go. And then he turned to greet Heimarr as his wife kicked against the pull of the cruel water below.

My voice broke. "Get to your oars, *now*!"

Hrið-Ormr had pulled ahead of us by several lengths. A good current caught them, bearing them along swiftly despite the lack of wind. Sigtryggr grabbed a man from his bench and put him on the tiller, then went for the bow strake. Two others were there already, a coiled length of rope between them.

The king yelled for Eir, waving his arms. She bobbed in the water, white-faced and grim, but still strong. She waved back at the king. Borne on the swift current, it wasn't long until *Hrið-Ormr* drew close enough. Sigtryggr threw the rope, but with the power of his muscles diminished by his injury, the line fell too short.

Cursing, he reeled it back as Eir kicked and struggled against the current. She was far, too far. Her head sank, then broke the surface again. My heart beat so hard I heard it in my ears, felt it behind my eyes.

"She's going to drown," I yelled. "Rúna, take the tiller. Guðrun, Liadan, get the sail down. Pull those oars, men!"

"The sail is useless, Lady," Rúna called. "They cut all the lines before we boarded!"

My crew struggled, unable to find a rhythm. Guðrun directed the fishermen, cursing and snarling as they fumbled the stroke and pull. *Sea-Wolf* lurched under me. My fingers bit into the strake to keep upright. I had to see. I had to *see.*

Hrið-Ormr drifted, the pitching hull obscuring the expanse of water. Eir was gone. She was *gone,* and I was going to vomit. *Please, Eir. Please fight.*

And then, Sigtryggr stretched, leaning far over the side, held by his two men. Eir's face flashed above the water in a swell, then her long arms appeared, reaching and waving. With a shout, Sigtryggr caught her by the wrist and dragged her on board.

Eir's skin was pale as the clouded sky above us. Her sodden garments plastered to her body like a grave-shroud. She clung to Sigtryggr. He tried to turn her, tried to sit her on a bench, but she would not heed him. She stared over the water at *Dreki,* transfixed by the fury ripping through her husband's men.

Ruarc grabbed my arm, startling me. "What do we do?"

"*Dreki,*" I croaked. "Look."

His breath hissed as he realized what was happening. "What madness possessed him?" Ruarc trailed off.

Unfathomable madness it was, for Hákon and Heimarr faced each other, neither man wearing their *brynjur*. Whether shedding it as a show of masculine strength, or sheer cockiness, the consequence was that they both were no longer entirely whole. Hákon stood in the thwarts by the mast, his left flank soaked in blood. His back had been laid open to the ribs, and his torn tunic flapped in the wind like a scarlet banner.

Heimarr bled also, though his hurt was less. He bore a shield in his left hand, and it had protected him from Hákon's axe as it came down across his body. Only his face showed a weeping graze across the cheek. His eye was swollen shut. In his other hand was a sword. Against Hákon's axe and seax, he was well-defended.

"Hákon is strong," Ruarc said shakily. "He'll win this fight. He has to."

All across *Dreki*, the combatants were matched man-to-man. While we had been plucking Eir from the sea, a war worthy of the ending of the gods had broken out. Hákon's force was outnumbered. Warriors of both parties slipped in their own gut-ropes and fell bleeding to the deck. Men I had known for years, and men I had never met. Men who hated me or respected me, or had called for my death. Men who cared for nothing at all but the lure of Heimarr's promised silver. Men who dwelled now as equals in their throes of dying-struggle, reveling in battle-joy and frenzy. The raging bellows of pain winged over the water.

I looked for Eir again. She gripped *Hrið-Ormr*'s bow strake like she wanted to leap back into the water. Sigtryggr held her fast.

Under Rúna's expert hand, we came abreast of *Hrið-Ormr* once more. Luck or the gods favored us then, for a hard breeze rose, filling our sails and carrying us towards the stink of iron carnage, the squeaking slippery shit and piss of the dead and dying. We were near, almost near enough to join the butchering ourselves. A little further.

"Hákon!" screamed Eir. There had never been such fear in her voice.

At the sound, Hákon jerked, stumbling and catching himself before Heimarr's sword could sweep his knees. His shoulder struck the mast and he howled. So much blood sheeted his flayed back that any fresh welling was invisible. Another distraction, and Hákon would go down.

Heimarr came again, and, recovering, Hákon brought his axe down against his brother's shield with deafening force. The seax met the sword, locking the two of them together.

Acid filled my throat. Hákon had meant to get Eir away, meant to give us time to escape, but there would be none of that now. "Be ready," I called hoarsely. "Let's give these goat-fuckers a feast of steel!"

Sigtryggr raised his fist and roared. I joined him with all the strength and confidence I could muster.

Then I turned to Guðrun on the bench. She dripped with sweat, and her teeth ground hard as she pushed forward with her oar and hauled back. Her muscles steamed.

You were right, old friend," I told her. "*Sea-Wolf* is not ready for such a blade-storm as this. So let us take a ship that is ready."

She grinned as broadly as a shark. "You mean Heimarr's."

"Take a few from *Sea-Wolf* when the time comes. The rest of us will attack *Dreki* directly."

"By the gods, do you hear what you're saying?" Ruarc rowed behind Guðrun, a sickly flush shading his face. Vomit puddled in the thwarts by his feet, but still he pulled as hard as the others. "Don't be foolish. We need every blade here. Tell me that isn't the plan!"

I ignored him.

"*Gyda*!"

I went to Rúna. "Steer for Heimarr's ship," I ordered. "He has left it unguarded, and we should remedy that."

"But they're tethered together," she protested. "We're outnumbered. They'll overwhelm us."

"I know the risks. Do it, Rúna."

She grimaced, shaking her head but adjusting her grip all the same.

We could take it. I knew we could. With Sigtryggr's support, we could cut the lines to *Dreki*. Heimarr and his men would be trapped aboard. Facing all of us, he would have to submit, or die. We were nearly upon them.

Liadan jerked suddenly, faltering in her rhythm. She made no sound as she shot to her feet. I was beside her in a moment, checking for wounds. But she put a trembling hand to her mouth, her eyes filling and spilling over as she pointed to *Dreki*.

I looked, and all the world darkened.

Beside *Dreki*'s mast, Hákon was on his knees, no axe or seax near him. His fists pressed to his temples. I could not see his face for the flood of red pouring from his nose, soaking his beard. He was screaming.

Heimarr stood over him, sword a jagged broken thing and slick with blood. He mouthed something to Hákon, then stepped forward, clasping his brother's shoulder as if embracing him. He looked into

Hákon's face for a long moment, then shoved the broken blade through his throat.

A shattering, tormented wail went up from Sigtryggr's ship.

The ghosting breeze brought me back to the world. It was like waking after a winter-long slumber, or a decade in the grave.

"Oh gods, what do we do?" Rúna moaned. "This cannot be. Gyda?"

I could not speak. I had no words. Sigtryggr was yelling something at me, but it was lost in the roaring in my ears. He fought his tiller, foundering in the rise and fall of the sea. The current had left us.

"Lady, tell us what to do!" Rúna's hand grabbed my own. Her skin was cold as ice.

"Sigtryggr," I rasped. My lips tasted of salt. "Get us alongside the king."

"Sigtryggr? Why him?" Astrid appeared, obfuscating the dark hole of my vision. Grabbing me by the arms, she leaned in and searched my face. "You ordered us to go for Heimarr's ship. That is still our purpose."

Out on the water, the killing continued. I could not bear to look and did not need to. Eir's desolate weeping was enough to know how the tides were flowing.

"It is pointless now," I said dully, shaking Astrid off. "Get back to your oar."

"But we have a clear heading," Rúna said. Her face was bone-white and tense, her hand on the tiller a fist. "Heimarr's ship is undefended. We can still take it."

"Have you no ears?" I barked, and Rúna recoiled. "Get us close to the king. I will not repeat myself."

"Don't listen to her, Rúna," Astrid said. "Just keep to the current. We're close now. We can finish this."

Heavy weights pulled on my limbs. I wanted to lie down. I wanted to sleep and wake to a world that was not altogether changed.

Hákon was dead. The son of the Jarl I'd served for most of my life.

The son I favored as a boy and respected as a man. The one whose brother I slew and whose other brother I had yet to face. We had never been kind to each other, but we had been friends, or something like. And Eir…

I covered my face with my hands. A trembling took hold of me, beginning deep in my guts.

"Gyda, please," whispered Ruarc. He had drawn close, but did not touch me. If he had, I would have screamed.

"If you fall to pieces now, it's over," he said. "I am sorry. I am horribly, deeply sorry. But you *must* be strong. If you cannot lead us, then at least let us see you stand tall. Do not let Heimarr take more from you." He stepped back.

I lowered my arms to my sides. "This venture is over," I announced. "All of you, listen. When we come alongside, you are to join the king and sail with him back to Jórvík."

Ruarc jerked in shock. Curses and protests erupted on all sides.

"Thor's hairy arse we will!" Guðrun bellowed, and it was echoed by Liadan with furious signing.

Have you lost your mind, Fiskwif? Send us to Hel instead!

Even the fishermen joined in the dissent.

"I am not asking! And I will suffer no rebellion. You can all swim back to land yourselves if you like. Get off my ship."

"You fucking *coward,*" Astrid hissed. She shoved Ruarc out of the way and came at me, fists balled and teeth grit. "You cannot do that to us! Not after everything. Not after this."

"I am yet the master of this vessel," I spat. "I can cast you off it when I choose."

Rage rose off her like heat. "So you banish us, and then what? Face Heimarr all alone? You idiot. You stupid, foolish woman."

"Sit down, Astrid. This is my choice and you will heed it."

"Fuck that. One man dies, and you lose your nerve? Gyda, *Fiskwif* of the whale-road and Grim-Bitch, now a weeping faint-heart?" She hurled a glob of spit. It landed on my boot. "You're a fool!"

"And you are a child who knows nothing. Shut your hole."

Guðrun rose from her bench and planted her feet in the thwarts. "The girl is right. You are a fool."

"How dare you do this? Do you see out there? Look at what's happening. *Look.*" Astrid pointed. Against my judgment, I looked.

Heimarr stood before a great number of kneeling and bound men. My stomach dropped. Hákon's fighters numbered half of what they had been. The rest were corpses or too wounded to be anything but the bundles that Heimarr's men were dumping into the water as food for the sharks.

I swallowed bile and shut my eyes. Hákon could be among these corpses.

"He's taking *slaves*, Gyda," Astrid said softly. "How dare you send us away?"

Her breath warmed my skin. When I opened my eyes, she was close enough that I could count the freckles on her nose. Eir had done the same so long ago, pushed in so I could not attend to anything but what she needed me to.

In Astrid's eyes I found not fury, but pain. The force of it shamed me.

"I am a fool," I said. "For bringing you here. For all of it."

"We are not leaving *Sea-Wolf,*" Guðrun gnarred fiercely. "Neither I nor Rúna. We stay."

Liadan thumped her bench in agreement. *I have always known it is better to be foolish than to be weak.*

I looked to Ruarc, hoping he would understand, but he looked away.

"You see?" said Astrid. "You're outnumbered. If we have to mutiny in order to go gut that pig-fucker, we will."

My throat burned. "My heart cannot bear to lose you."

"And what of our hearts?" Astrid countered. "Heimarr will scrape the skin from your bones. Giving yourself over to him is selfish. There's no honor in it. No vengeance."

"Certainly no wealth," Guðrun remarked.

"I don't care about honor," I cried. "And fuck vengeance! There is no honor greater than all of you. No wealth more precious. Leave me to face my fate. Even if it is selfish, it is a fair price for the many wrongs I have done you."

"Shut your flapping gums, woman," said Guðrun. "Look, there!" She leaned over the strake.

The morning sun rode the horizon behind us, casting long reflections on the waves. But west, beyond the bay, out in the open ocean, something gleamed.

"Are those *sails*?" gasped Ruarc.

"Two of them," Guðrun answered.

My breath caught. "By all the gods."

"Who is it?" Rúna's voice was half-worry, half-hope. "More of Heimarr's dogs?"

"It's Olavi," I said, breathless. "No one else is wealthy enough to dye their sails that shade of blue."

"He's always been an ostentatious prick," Guðrun cracked. "Liked him well enough for that. If you're going to be a prick, show it off."

Liadan shook in silent laughter.

Astrid was frowning. "Our messages reached him, then. But why send two ships?"

"Olavi has just lost another son," he said. "This changes everything. Heimarr is now the heir. If Olavi's ships are full of spearmen—" He didn't need to finish. The implication was obvious. Once Olavi learned of Hákon's death, his rage would know no limit.

I bit down on a sore spot in my cheek, thinking quickly. "Rúna, how fast can we get *Sea-Wolf* around the coast?"

"Surely you're not thinking of running?" Astrid demanded.

"And why not?" said Ruarc. "As much as this galls us, Jarl Olavi would never ally with us against his heir. We are not prepared for this fight."

Astrid's expression hardened as she turned back to me. "I don't care what fate you think you deserve," she said. "This decides it. We aren't running. There is no better place for you than with us. And there is no better place for us than with you. We are yours and you are ours."

"We sail with you, Gyda," Guðrun said. "For death or ruin."

"Death or ruin, Lady," repeated Rúna. "Whatever comes over the horizon. As it has always been for Rán's Daughters."

Death or ruin, signed Liadan with a sharp nod.

"Why not for luck and silver? Much less heavy things." Ruarc followed this with a familiar, crooked grin.

"Revenge is no longer yours alone, Gyda *Fiskwif,*" Astrid said, laying a hand on my shoulder. "It has not been so for a long while. Eir would agree, and she now has more need than any of us for vengeance. We are here by our own wills to finish this saga, and by Rán and all her Daughters, we shall finish it."

Liadan pounded her feet and rattled her oar.

"Revenge!" cried Astrid.

"Revenge!" howled the rest.

"Revenge!" I echoed.

CHAPTER TWENTY-NINE

The wind had whipped the sea into frothing swells and white-capped spume. *Sea-Wolf* and *Hrið-Ormr* wallowed in the furrows.

"You only need to get us alongside," I called to Rúna in the stern. "Hold fast!"

"I know what I'm doing," she bit out. A wave slammed us hard and she grunted with the strain of it.

The oar in my hands was a live thing, a vibrating spear to rip and shred the restless waves.

Hrið-Ormr straggled behind. Its larger mass and length made it cumbersome to row in seas like this. Sigtryggr's deep-voiced commands belied his fury.

I bared my teeth as sweat dripped into my eyes. "You still have that hand with you, Guðrun?"

"It's wrapped around my left tit," she crowed. "Shall I nail it to the mast? Let Heimarr see where we'll nail his cock!"

"His cock is only good for the sharks," Astrid countered. "But I'm thinking his balls should decorate our wolf-prow!"

Ruarc harrumphed. "That's too good for a scorn-snake like him, Astrid. I think you should wear his gut-rope as a belt."

The rest took up the thread as we rowed, inventorying our enemy's body parts and what they would do with them when we reached *Dreki.* As for me, I needed one thing only: blood.

I wanted it to paint my seax. I wanted to bathe in it. I wanted to lick it from Heimarr's face and spit it back into his empty eye sockets.

The battle-fire boiled in my veins, and I relished its power. Power and fire. I had been weak in the moments after Hákon died twitching on his brother's broken sword, but not now. Now, I rallied. With my friends, I would bring vengeance on Heimarr's every muscle and sinew and bone.

"Ready yourselves, you fuckers!" bellowed Guðrun.

Dreki loomed before us, and Heimarr was prepared. His men lined the thwarts and strakes, pounding their shields with axes and seaxes and short spears. They made a resonant noise in their throats, an eerie, primal sound like the boom of thunder, meant to make us quake and shit ourselves on our benches. Instead, it fed our fire.

Hrið-Ormr's men answered with fierce wolf-howls, and we on *Sea-Wolf* joined in with our own screaming fear-spell.

And then Sigtryggr sprang his trap. Red Yngvi, his new champion, yelled from the prow, war-bow in hand. "Send them all to Hel," he cried. "Loose, you wolves! Show these whoresons how Jórvík men fight!"

Bows thrummed and grappling hooks flew from the king's ship. Arrows arced over *Dreki*, and Heimarr's fighters ducked behind shields and gunwales. And while they sheltered, *Sea-Wolf* slipped past *Dreki's* stern and pulled up the far side of Heimarr's ship.

Rúna's guttural bellows of effort and final swing of the rudder made us cheer, and she beamed with sweat-slicked pride.

"Quickly now, you pig-shits," said Guðrun, standing on the narrow strake-ledge. "Get those lines cut!" She was joined in a blink by Ruarc and four men, and with hand-axes gripped tight they leapt across the space and onto Heimarr's ship, The rest of us rowed on, pulling as hard as we could to get clear.

"Row like the *jötunn*-wives you are!" I roared. We were coming around *Dreki* again, angling for its prow. With *Hrið-Ormr* at its stern and his own ship under Guðrun's control, Heimarr would be trapped between three enemies with nowhere to run.

Fresh screams tore the sky as Sigtryggr brought his promised chaos and death to bear. I could not see Eir, but I knew she would be with her husband's shackled men, freeing them to rejoin the fight.

"Here, Rúna, here! Hold oars, all of you!" I yelled, and the oarblades hissed out of the water. "Lines, now!"

With one coordinated throw, *Sea-Wolf*'s grappling hooks found purchase on *Dreki*. We hauled hard, and the two hulls kissed with a shudder. We boarded with weapons bristling in our fists and war-screams in our throats.

And we slaked our blood-thirst under the great shadow of *Dreki's* carved dragon-prow.

Dark joy sang in my veins. I found vengeance in the gut-ropes and neck-joints of all who dared to face me. The borrowed seax fit perfectly in the hollow of my hand. My *brynja* hung light on my shoulders. I bent and swayed, evading every clumsy attack as if I were a warrior twenty winters younger. I was made of molten iron, fluid and raging hot and filling the air with searing, streaking death.

My Daughters fought around me, a retainer of shrieking Valkyries collecting corpses for Ragnarök, the end of the world.

Dreki was a broad vessel, but the fighting was cramped, visceral, and brutal. Two spear-lengths from the mast, Sigtryggr fought with Ruarc and several others. Runnels of blood and viscera made a mess of the planking. The king was a black-haired blur at Ruarc's shoulder, his gleaming sword whistling through the air as he split a man his own size in half like an oak. Another came from the right, and he danced behind Ruarc, who held a short spear and shield.

Twisting just in time, Ruarc let the man's own momentum propel him onto the spear. The sharp metal point burst from his spine, and the man died with a wheezing gurgle. Ruarc kicked him off and waited for the next fool to try him.

Ruarc never fancied himself a warrior, but a warrior's heart blazed in him nonetheless.

The whistle of an axe startled me, and I lurched into Astrid as a barrel-chested fucker bore down on us. His leading foot met a pile of slippery gut-rope, making him stumble into Astrid's seax. He went down in a sprawling heap and she thrust her blade into his throat.

"Eir is with Heimarr, Lady," she said, smile frightening and stark in the red on her face. She pointed over the strake with the tip of her blade.

Hrið-Ormr's deck teemed with violence. With no space left on *Dreki* to fight properly, Heimarr had fled, spilling over to the other ship and rallying there. Eir had followed, and now, she was a vision of berserk fury. Standing near the mast, she was gore-splattered. Her golden-white hair had been bound up in a braid as strong as a reefing line. She held a shield in one hand and a bearded axe in the other. Her freed warriors stood with her facing a wall of death.

Stacked three-deep across the stern, Heimarr's men held their shields forward in a barrier seething with blades and spears. Heimarr himself screamed behind them from the tiller-bench. White jelly leaked from his empty eye-socket. The troll-son's beard bristled as he spat and cursed.

Sigtryggr's voice rose. "I'm coming for you, putrid fucker! My blade is ready to taste your coward's blood!"

He lunged for the strake, but Red Yngvi intervened, catching him by the arm.

"No, Lord! Not yet. A wall like that is a pit of slaughter with no escape. See how the Lady's men are flagging?"

He was right; Eir's remaining fighters held back with her, binding their wounds and catching their wind. Only a dozen appeared able-bodied. The rest were groaning in the thwarts or dead.

The enemy held their formation tight as a dog's arsehole, eyeing Eir warily. Heimarr lurked behind them, muttering and dragging his fist over his bloody beard.

Suddenly, Ruarc grabbed me, pallor turning sickly.

"Are you hurt?" I demanded, fear turning me cold.

He didn't answer. His eyes bulged, staring up at *Dreki*'s mast-top. Beside him, Guðrun and Rúna followed his gaze.

"Oh, *gods*," Rúna whispered, her hands fluttering to her mouth.

I looked up, sick and scared and blinded by grief even before I knew what sight awaited me.

Hanging by the neck, Hákon's ragged corpse had been fixed to the yard-arm. The bulk of reefed sail had hidden the sight from us on *Sea-Wolf,* but now, this grisly omen was inescapable.

Clotted blood and shit slicked down the grain of the wooden mast. They had mutilated him. Stripped him naked, stole his eyes and his nose and fingers and even his tongue.

Bitterness burned the back of my throat. Murdering a brother was scornful enough. But to put him on display like a butcher's wares or prize trophy? It was a savage, honorless insult.

Astrid and Liadan watched me with tears on their cheeks.

"Get him down," I choked, turning away. "Cover him, put a sword in his hand, and lay him out properly. The All-Father's Valkyries may yet choose him. The dying of this day is not yet over."

Had Eir seen this? I did not think so, or she would have long since thrown herself against the shield-wall in madness and rage.

We'd reached a stand-off, but the fighting would explode again any moment, and so I went to Sigtryggr, shoving past a knot of his men guarding his flank. He and Red Yngvi loomed over three kneeling prisoners. They had thrown their weapons down, though were not begging for mercy. It was an interesting limit to their cowardice; they must have known well that under Sigtryggr's care there would be no mercy.

The king was trembling. I worried briefly if he'd been wounded, but Red Yngvi was grinning at him like an eager youth. I soon saw why. With a loud roar, Sigtryggr scythed his sword across the throats of the kneeling men.

No battle-wound made the king shake. Such a thirst was remedied only by blood and blade-work.

As the three men fell twitching and choking to the deck, Sigtryggr's shoulders relaxed and he inhaled a deep, cleansing breath.

"Gyda," he said, bad eye rolling to me. "If I'd have been a wiser man, I might have left you to rot in Jórvík. Instead, I am a happy, foolish bastard. I prefer it."

"Hákon might say different," I said grimly.

He nodded. "*Stáli* deserved a better death. But he is dead nonetheless, and we are not. I call that fortune."

"Olavi will be here within the hour," I said.

Sigtryggr's fist tightened around his sword. "Yngvi, why the fuck aren't we over there yet? I want my ship back from that pustulant arse-licker."

"An hour." I said, holding the king's gaze. "I can do an hour."

His dark brows wove together as he tried to parse out my meaning. Then he swore savagely. "You dare too far, *Fiskwif*. This is not the plan we agreed on."

"Give me this, Sigtryggr. For Hákon's sake."

I stepped away without waiting for his reply and went to the stern strake. I watched the deck of *Hrið-Ormr* and my oldest friend aboard it.

Eir had not moved. Her gaze remained fixed on Heimarr, following his pacing movements like a falcon watching a dormouse. Her warriors waited patiently for her order.

"Heimarr," I called, my voice carried by the wind. "Heimarr Olavisson! The coward who hides behind a wall and kills his own brother. You thief in the night with no honor! What a brave *drengr* you are! Answer me, you whoreson!"

At this, Eir and Heimarr both swiveled to stare at me.

"You're a *niðingr* like your brother Helgi," I sang. "You hid from me when I raided your camp. You honor-less shit from a goat's arse! Come out from behind your wall. I'll make you scream like Helgi screamed as my knife went through his gut-ropes!"

Sigtryggr rushed to my side, hissing. "What the fuck are you *doing*?"

"Trust me, Siggi," I whispered.

My Daughters took up the task.

"You piss-soaked coward!" called Astrid. "Your stench is worse than a week-old corpse's!"

"Traitorous troll-thrall," roared Guðrun. "May Oðinn shit in your bed and your balls dry up!"

"Scorn-snake!" Rúna yelled.

Liadan signed her insult, though I did not see it. Astrid's choked laugh told me enough of its filth and rudeness.

Now the others joined in the assault of words. Ruarc's voice rose over the others, his Irish words rolling and poetic.

I let a broad grin stretch over my face. "You see, *huglausi*, there is nothing left for you! No reputation. No honor. No respect. People will know your shame from Dyflin to Jórvík to Córdoba. Your men are fated for Rán's cold halls. You have lost my silver and my ship. I have taken both like a dog steals scraps from the table."

In truth, I had no idea where my silver currently rested, but that didn't matter. If Heimarr thought he'd been robbed, all the better for my goal.

The insults had done a fine job; his men, a number of whom only present because of the promise of silver, and the rest defectors from Olavi's ranks, grumbled and shifted among themselves.

"You rancid bitch," Heimarr screamed, his face reddening. "I should have taken your tongue and your life on that beach! When this is done, your bones will rot on the seafloor!"

He raised his hand, preparing to give the order for the killing to resume, but I threw my head back and laughed as loud as I could.

"Don't you see those sails?" I called. "Your father is bearing down on us as you stand there farting out of your arsehole of a mouth! What do you think he'll make of you, brother-killer? Everyone knows he bore more love for Hákon *Stáli* than he bears for you!"

"The Jarl has more love for his favorite bed-slave than he has for you, worm," cried one of Eir's warriors, which made his shield-brothers laugh.

Heimarr scowled, then clambered up on the strake. Olavi's ships were making good use of the wind, creeping ever closer. Heimarr cursed and stepped down.

I rubbed it in deeper. "Even if you manage victory with your pathetic shield-wall, you still have to answer to your father."

Sigtryggr growled. "And to me, fucker. No matter where you go, I'll hunt you like a wolf, and I'll slaughter you like one too."

Heimarr jeered at this, but I could see his uncertainty.

"You have a choice here, Heimarr," I said. "You can hide behind your men like a snot-nosed child hides from his mother's backhanded slap, or face me. You want to kill me, turd? Then take your thumb out of your mouth and do it! Or are you no better than Helgi, forgotten and shamed for as long as the sky holds breath?" My blood rose and I slammed my fists on the strake. "Face me or be named a coward! I call for a *holmgang*! You die this day!"

Heimarr's rage and pride warred within him. As he contemplated his answer, he stared at his men. Their necks craned around to see how he would answer such a challenge.

"Accept or run," yelled Ruarc, and the others echoed similar things.

"Do you have snakes for guts? Face us!"

"Shut your stinking mouths," Heimarr roared. "I'll fight you, bitch, and I'll relish watching you writhe like the whore you are! Make the square!"

Eir's voice broke through the eager cheering across the two ships.

"Gyda! Swear to me he dies today!"

I looked across the water into Eir's gray eyes, haunted and red-rimmed. Grief tightened her mouth and new lines creased between her brows. She lowered her shield and her axe and let them clatter to the deck. She put her hands over her belly, where her child slept safe in her womb. For a searing moment, I was terrified she would demand I allow her to fight in my place. If she did, I could never deny her.

Instead, she spoke to Heimarr. "When you are dead, I will tell my son that his father was avenged," she said. "I will tell him that he has more family and more love in this world than any child has ever known. He will grow strong and powerful. He will be heir to all the deserved honor and wealth of his father. I swear this by the gods, and I swear it by the blood of my husband that stains his ship."

Heimarr snarled. "I will scrape that brat from your corpse and feed it to my dogs. Hákon's only inheritance is death!"

She turned to me. "I know you have earned this revenge, Gyda," she said. "I do not seek to steal it. Win this duel, and I shall count you my friend once more. Only once he is dead. Only then."

I shook my head. "Even when he is dead at your feet and his blood stains the leather of your shoes, we shall not be friends."

Confusion darkened her face.

"We shall not be friends," I repeated. "Nor will you be one of Rán's Daughters. You are, as you have always been, my sister in all things. I swear to you, I will win this fight."

I held her gaze, and she held mine. Then she nodded, and the promise was made.

"Enough of this fucking farce," snarled Heimarr. "Make the square!"

The memory of Helgi saying those same words brought a thrill to my skin.

CHAPTER THIRTY

We gathered for the duel on *Dreki*, our forces separated by both distrust and distance. Heimarr and his shield-wall gathered in the stern, staring as Sigtryggr directed men to clear the thwarts of journey-chests and corpses. Buckets of seawater were hauled up and cast over deck planks to wash the worst of the viscera into the bilges.

Those who did not labor kept hands on weapons, wary and ready for treachery. It was understood by all present that the thing every warrior anticipated more than the chance to kill each other, was the sight of other people killing each other for entertainment. A *holmgang* was as much a duel for honor and reputation as it was a ritual performance.

Once the deck was clear, Ruarc and the Daughters laid out several oars in a square. Eir knelt at the mast with her husband's corpse. Though her eyes were open, she saw nothing. Hákon's cold hand lay in her open palm. Mercifully, his torso had been covered with a length of spare sail when he was lowered.

Olavi still approached, but the wind had changed. The two vessels were far enough that we could not yet see the occupants individually, though the glint of the mid-morning sun off iron shield-rims and spear-points told us they had come prepared for battle.

The rules of a *holmgang* varied from clan to clan. Here, in this sea of blood and vengeance, we on *Dreki* agreed the parameters of this duel were obvious without anyone stating them: If either fighter steps a single toe out of the square, that fighter forfeits. They will be forced to kneel, like Hákon was made to kneel. And then they will die by the blade of their enemy.

"Are you ready?" Ruarc murmured, pulling the arms of my *brynja* to adjust the fit. "You can name a champion, you know. There would be no shame in it. It may even be expected, given your injuries."

I did not answer, and so he bent to retrieve the helmet he'd chosen for me.

It was a dented, simple thing, lined with leather and wool and made for a youth. It would do well enough, even if it was a little tight.

Ruarc and I stood apart from the others in the shadow of the prow. With the helmet still in his hands, he hesitated. His face was tight and pale, and his tongue darted to moisten his flaking lips. He had prepared an argument, evidently, and so for his own sake I let him make it.

"Name me champion," Ruarc told me. "I cannot promise you victory, Gyda, but I can promise you I'll get one good hit on him before he downs me."

The knot in his throat bobbed as he swallowed. "Sigtryggr will step in after that. We've agreed on it. You don't have to fight Heimarr yourself."

Putting my hand against Ruarc's white cheek, I smiled.

"My dear boy, you are not my champion and never will be," I said. "So tell me, where are you wounded?"

He flinched and inhaled sharply. "I am not—,"

"Don't lie to me, boy," I said. "You smell like a charnel house, you're splattered in blood, and I know it's not all yours, but some of it must be. You're standing upright, so it's not a fatal wound. Not yet. Where is it?"

"Right ribs," he said, defeated. "It's just a graze. Not even as bad as my flayed shoulder had been. The bleeding's stopped."

"Well done," I said. "We'll make a *drengr* of you yet. But you think you can hold a sword or an axe with your fighting arm against your chest like a broken-winged bird? Don't be foolish."

I grabbed the helmet from his hand and plunked it on my head, tying the thongs under my chin.

"Gyda, please," Ruarc said thickly. "I do not want to see you bleeding and broken on the deck. Not today. Not ever. Just let me do this."

Sighing, I bent and touched my forehead to his. When I spoke, my voice shook.

"I may not have borne you of my body, Ruarc, but you are as much a son to me as if I had. I love you. You must let me fight."

I stepped away before he could respond and made for the square.

"Sigtryggr, where is your gods-kissed sword?" I called. "If I'm going to die, I want to hold that shining beauty."

The king, standing with Red Yngvi and a knot of other men, left them and approached with a savage glare in his bad eye.

"You break my sword, I break your head," he growled.

I scoffed. "You've broken my head already with all your empty threats. Either you'll get this back with Heimarr's blood staining it, or mine."

"A fair bargain," he said, then offered me the scabbard hilt-first. I reached out to take it, and he pulled back slightly.

I narrowed a glare at him, expecting him to spout the same nonsense Ruarc had.

"Gyda," he began, then stopped. His gaze softened, and in his face were a host of arguments and pledges. Instead, he settled for: "Make sure it is his blood, yes?"

He offered the hilt again and I took it, mustering as much of a smile as I could offer. I attached the scabbard to my belt, on which also hung my seax and a smaller knife. Saying nothing more, Sigtryggr stepped back, outside the boundaries of the square.

Men already clustered around the edges, packing together like fish in a net for the best vantage.

"Lady," said Astrid softly. I turned to see her approaching with Liadan, Rúna, and Guðrun.

In her arms, Liadan held an iron-rimmed shield white-washed with lime. Red dragons twisted and knotted themselves around the iron boss, so many that there was no untangling their tails and heads.

Next to Liadan, Astrid held a drinking skin, and Guðrun and Rúna held each other's hands.

"Eir said to give you this," Astrid said, gesturing to the shield. "It is one of Hákon's. She could not leave him alone yet, you understand."

I took the shield from Liadan and hefted it. "It's a beautiful, solid thing," I said. "Must have been costly."

Liadan signed, her hands precise expressions that told me more of her feelings than her voice could have.

Eir wishes you fortune and the battle-strength of Tyr. You must win this fight, Lady. Win it for her.

"I will win for her," I said firmly. "And all of you. For death and ruin, eh?"

"For death and ruin," Guðrun and Rúna echoed softly.

Liadan inclined her head and signed the same.

Then Astrid stepped close and held out the drinking skin. I lowered the shield and leaned it against my lower leg.

"Mead," she told me. "The finest available from *Dreki*'s stores. I kept it away from the others. You are in greater need of it now than anyone else."

I would have rather the skin held fresh water to soothe my dry throat, but I conjured a grateful smile.

"Mighty Thor drowns in barrels of mead before he rides into battle. Such a fine drink can only bring me luck."

Unstoppering the skin, I drank deeply, relishing the honeyed sweetness as it spread over my tongue. When I was sated, I passed it back.

"Better I keep my head tolerably sober, or else I might lose it too soon," I said, laying my finger beside my nose and winking.

Rúna gasped, and Guðrun tightened her hold on her lover's arm.

"We said everything what needs saying," she rumbled, shifting from one foot to the other. "You've got us at your flank, Lady. Naught else to do but watch you hand Heimarr his bollocks and then his own head. So get on with it."

Remember the promise you made to Eir, Liadan signed. *Heimarr's bollocks come first, but his head is for her. Don't lose, Lady. Take care, and be quick on your feet.*

"Yes, yes, alright," I said. "Stop fussing, all of you. Today is not my death-day. Go stand with the others and watch Gyda *Fiskwif* get down to the bloody work of killing this goat-turd."

The women backed away, and there was nothing to do but to face my enemy.

Standing amongst his men in the stern, Heimarr cut a fearsome figure.

He wore a *brynja* of polished rings which sparked and gleamed in the sun. Under this he had several layers of linen and wool for padding, and on his shins were iron plates sewn onto leather strips. A helmet of hammered iron and bronze protected his skull. It was a gorgeous thing, skillfully forged with a serpent's head down the nasal guard. More ring mail draped from the decorated cheek guards and the back of the helmet, so that only his hateful, burning, one-eyed stare showed in the whole of his face.

These were enough to frame Heimarr as a formidable opponent, but his weapons were what made him truly fearsome. Along with his shield, he'd chosen a large, broad-headed axe with sharply curved horns. Even if I avoided getting my shield-rim hooked and pulled down, he could still use his leverage to take off a limb with one sweep. I would have to be fast on my feet and canny in movement. He was bigger than me, and I hoped that meant he'd be slower, too.

Heimarr strutted into the square, chest puffed out like he thought himself a god among giants.

"Your shoulders are drooping, arse-licker," I said to him. "And your eye! You really should wipe the bird shit out of it. Oh, it's gone? What a shame. Sit down! Rest easy, boy. Surely you have a champion to fight in your place, such an honorable and valorous lord as you are!"

My side of the square jeered and mocked. Shouts of *"brother-killer," "niðingr,"* and *"dung-eating rat!"* flew around, but the men on Heimarr's side said nothing. No defense or answering jeers went up, and Heimarr felt it keenly.

"Fucking whoresons," he spat, though his voice was drowned out by renewed shouting.

He whirled on his men. "Disloyal dogs! I should take your bollocks and feed them to the sharks. My silver is wasted on the likes of you."

"Don't you mean *my* silver?" I said. "Of course it's wasted on them, Heimarr. They know they're never getting their shit-stained hands on it, and neither are you."

"That haul is *mine*," he hissed.

I spread my arms. "Then try and take it."

My friends pounded their feet and cheered, and Heimarr's men finally joined the noise. I'd been correct, then. Their loyalty only extended as far as the certainty of greased palms.

Heimarr and I began our dance, leather soles scraping the planks as we paced in a circle, eyeing each other for infirmity or weakness. Our allies called our names and stomped and yelled out clever insults. His gaze and mine remained fixed on each other.

I knew what he saw: a mere woman, long past her best, lacking strength and bearing weapons unfamiliar to her. I was old. Easy prey. But I had years and experience on my back, and I was hardened by age, not decayed. I could still tear gut-ropes from corpses and empty throats of blood and breath. Heimarr was not the first bastard to have size and strength greater than mine, and if the gods willed it, he would not be the last.

I had one advantage, and that was speed; I was lighter and more agile, though limited by the weight of my painted shield. If I could not adapt to it in combat, then speed and agility would be useless for the effort needed to lift my arm.

With this limitation, Heimarr frightened me more than a venomous snake in the dark. I would need to stay close, harrying him like a swarm of flies on a corpse.

I watched him as he watched me, and both of us knew he had the better odds.

"That silver was forfeit the moment I caught you in al-Andalus," Heimarr snarled, still circling. "I found it. It's *mine,* you pustulant whore."

"What a boring insult," I said. "If that were true, your father's complaints with me would be far less frequent!"

The laughter from that pricked and he cursed, knowing he'd opened himself to the mocking and there was no taking it back.

"Olavi will be with us soon," I declared. "Shall I fall to my knees and make him a happy man right here on the deck, Heimarr? Your mother would weep if she weren't a rotten corpse! Or maybe it would make her moan!" I made a rude gesture with my free hand towards my breeks.

"Grim-Bitch! Grim-Bitch!" roared several men. Their stomping feet made the deck planks shake. Sigtryggr bellowed my name, and I raised my shield-arm to take in the glory.

Behind the serpent's-head nasal, Heimarr's face turned dark. With an explosive lurch, he came at me, axe raised and whistling its death-song.

We collided hard, shield boss smashing against shield boss. The haft of the axe hammered against our touching rims. I hadn't gotten the sword out of the scabbard in time, and when I tugged it now, it would not come. My grasp was wrong.

Heimarr shoved forward, pinning my shield against my torso and arm. I couldn't strike back, and neither could he without making space. His breath reeked of decaying teeth and dried herring.

I twisted to free my arm and he broke away, raising his axe again, and I did not waste the chance. It arced down just as I danced away. He missed my left shoulder by a hair's breadth.

"You're slow, turd," I taunted. "Overfed from your father's table scraps. Lazy!"

With my hand free now, Sigtryggr's sword slid out of the scabbard like silk. It caught the sunlight as I aimed for that decorated helmet. Heimarr's shield met the blow and his axe bounced off my iron boss. The bones of my arm rattled, but the limited force of the swing told me he didn't have enough power with just one arm. He'd need to drop his shield for a truly destructive blow.

"No space for the killing, is there?" I jeered, lightly dancing, shield up and sword ready. "I'm faster than you. Older than you. *Wealthier* than you."

"You fucking hag, I'll make you beg for death!" Heimarr lunged and struck my shield with his. Though I kept my feet, he came on again, hard and fast, axe repeatedly hammering into the riveted planks of my shield. He thought to tire me enough to drop the shield, or force me over the edge of the square.

But I had fought duels before him, and I knew the trick. Under the barrage, I led our movements, pivoting on the balls of my feet, so that we turned in a half-circle and never neared the boundaries.

He howled in frustration, relenting long enough to deliver a blow to my shield that sent a white-hot flash up my wrist and arm.

I refused to give ground. I pushed in again, seeking any soft spot, any weak point in his mail.

Suddenly, his shield dropped and the butt of his axe came up, catching my right thigh in a bruising blow.

I howled, side-stepping clumsily as all feeling left the leg, and for the first time there was true space between us.

For a moment, we paused to gather ourselves. Sweat trickled from my brow and down the nape of my neck. My *brynja* pinched under my sword-arm and I tasted acid and salt. Heimarr's helmet was dented at the right temple, and the connecting links of the cheek-guard had come loose, leaving half his face exposed and the mail sagging.

"You're fast, but you're weak." His breath came in ragged pants. He tugged on the hanging piece of the cheek-guard and the mail came off, broken links dropping on the deck. He tossed the piece outside of the square.

I stifled a curse as feeling rushed back to my throbbing leg. I was trembling with fatigue. If he'd wanted, he could have hammered me just then, could have brought the axe down to cleave my shield, but instead he stood there glaring like a boar in a trap.

"I've dealt you a few bruises and you've dealt me the same," he said. "No blood drawn yet. I see no reason why we can't settle things between us here."

I spat a fat glob between his feet in answer.

"I'll let you take your troll-cursed ship," he said, ignoring it. "Call it a consolation. Follow Jórvík's mad king back to berth and I'll say we're even."

"Fucking turd," I snarled. "You're afraid!"

"Coward!" Astrid hollered. "Bloodless whoreson!"

The insults and epithets came fast now, from his side as well as mine. Heimarr's expression did not change, and that gave away more than if he'd lost his temper again.

I regarded him with a smirk. "Ah, I see now. You think if you stall long enough, your father will fight me for you," I accused. "Let me sail away with Sigtryggr and Olavi might think we started this war and ran off. You think to set him after us like a hound on a snared badger."

"Rip his teeth from his skull," roared Sigtryggr. "Give the fucker something else to chew on besides his own shit!"

And perhaps I could have raised my sword in time and done just that, but the corner of Heimarr's mouth twitched, and it took every ounce of speed I had to get my shield up as he hauled back and threw his own at me, flat like a disk. It spun and bounced off and then he was on me again, his axe flashing and sparking as he brought it to bear, two-handed this time. I ducked out of its path and slashed low, blade biting into the axe's haft but not touching him.

He grunted with the movement, leading foot flexing as the weight of his swing pulled him further than he'd prepared. He adapted with a turn, following the arc of the swing and redirecting it around his head to swing again, never letting it rest.

Heimarr was skilled with the axe, and I realized he'd planned for this. He'd wanted me to think he was unbalanced, wanted me to watch his shield rather than how he moved. But he'd overexerted himself. Though his force had me backing up and lunging to get out of the way, his gasps were loud and wet. His shoulders trembled with every high swing. His feet dragged. Soon his blows would lose their power, and then I would have an opening.

But I was also tiring. Hákon's shield was not overly heavy, but the size was a hindrance. With each glanced-off blow or graze, exhaustion numbed my muscles and my arm lifted slower on the next round. I couldn't get close enough to strike with my sword. My clenching teeth creaked in my jaw.

Grasping the axe-haft at the butt and the middle, Heimarr cried out savagely as he made one final, overhead swing.

My shield broke apart. Painted splinters flew everywhere, and I yelped as some embedded in my forearm, sharp and thin as needles. Blood welled hot and thick. But I was *free.* I threw down the broken pieces and drew my seax, a feral scream in my throat, and went for Heimarr like a wolf.

The axe had bitten the deck planks. He tugged it hard, freeing it the moment I reached him. He caught my two blades against his haft.

"A sword," he cried, spittle hitting my cheek. "Get me a fucking sword, you bastards! A spear!"

My blades were living things in my hands. The blood in my veins sang, soaking my sleeve and filling my nose with hot lust. I would have *more.* More!

Heimarr caught every blow, angling his axe to protect his body. I could not break through, could land no blows on flesh. But then his defense opened on the right as he met my sword on an upward strike. The edge of my seax shrieked across his *brynja*.

Shuddering, backing away, he ripped off his helmet and threw it to the side. "Hold," he yelled, lifting his axe above his head.

Sweat and blood soaked his hair. He wiped the strands out of his florid face. "A fucking sword, *now!*" he bellowed. "Give me something!"

I was grinning like a lynx and snarling, my blades bright in the sun and deadly-sharp. My legs ached with the urge to launch at Heimarr while he was unguarded, but the terms of a *holmgang* must be fair. A combatant had the right to call a hold, and to change weapons if they chose.

"Gut him," roared Guðrun. "Rip his belly out and feed his shit to him!"

"Bleed him, Gyda," called Ruarc, and it filled me with pride to hear it.

On my right, a movement caught my attention. Sigtryggr held another shield, a smaller, plainer one than Hákon's had been.

Beside the king, Eir stood straight as a spear, her form as still and quiet as the rest of the crowd was chaotic. She watched me with an unnerving intensity.

Sigtryggr raised the shield a little, and I shook my head. Though he scowled at me, he put a fist to his chest—a gesture of respect and recognition, one warrior to another.

"Useless dog!" Heimarr shoved the man who had offered him a hand axe, though he kept the axe despite it. Someone else stepped forward with a sword, which was an ugly thing with a notched blade. With these in hand, he and I were now an even match.

He swung a few times to get the feel of the blades. "I'm going to enjoy seeing your gut-ropes splayed out," he said, grinning.

"Do you think they stink as bad as your breath, pig-shit?" I shot back. "Come and find out!"

He came, and the crash of our blades startled the gulls perched on the strakes.

As I parried and spun, the frenzied howling of the crowd was like the croaking din of carrion-eaters. The gods were here, riding with the Valkyries over my head and glorying in the fight. Would I earn their favor? Or would I draw their wrath?

With a burst of effort, I ducked under a whistling sword blow and opened the top of Heimarr's fleshy, unprotected forearm. Blood soaked his sleeve instantly, and in retribution, he struck my shoulder, a blow which might have shorn off my arm if the sword's edge had been sharp. Instead, the blade shuddered off my *brynja* rings, leaving nothing but the bloom of a bruise and a deep ache.

Fresh gore streamed from Heimarr's eye socket. Dried blood crusted in my fist. We blocked as many blows as we gave and none of them were enough.

And then Heimarr threw himself at me and broke my nose with his skull.

Spitting blood and snot, blinded by pain, reeling, I tripped over his outstretched foot. My weapons left me. Heimarr loomed above, sword and axe raised for killing.

"Honor-less whoreson!" I gasped. "Cheater!"

With a burst of effort, I twisted and kicked. My boot connected with his groin. He shrieked, dropped the sword, and doubled over.

I rolled to my feet. I was dizzy from pain and fatigue. My eyes streamed. Heimarr was still howling, but he came up again fast, swinging his axe, and this time I could not get out of the way.

The blade hammered into my side, poorly angled and lacking power, but still the edge bit through my *brynja* and thick tunic to taste the marrow of my ribs. My throat tore with my screaming.

He hauled back, readying himself again. I couldn't breathe. Another blow would kill me. Desperate, I lunged, and his front teeth broke under my fist. The axe spun out of sight.

Stunned and spitting shards of teeth, Heimarr backed away to recover. I did the same, clenching my arm tight against my bleeding ribcage. The bones were broken again. My flesh burned. Blood streamed through the smashed rings of my *brynja*. Maybe the wound was fatal. Maybe not.

"The sword, Gyda!" Sigtryggr's voice broke.

I cast my eyes over the deck, finding the blade just as Heimarr did. We lunged for it and crashed together, fighting and flailing and scratching.

My chest was agony and ruin. Rolling, I reached for Sigtryggr's sword, my fingers brushing its shining hilt. But then a crushing arm snaked around my neck. I thrashed, clawing at it as the pressure built and crushed my throat.

"Be still and die, woman!"

Heimarr punched my wound with his free hand, and my vision turned white. I couldn't breathe.

Do you hear that, Fiskwif? said a voice in my head, watery and fluid like waves tumbling the sea-wrack on the ocean floor. *Listen. It is the tide of your life, flowing out of you. Flowing like the river of your blood. Will you follow its current? Will you travel the sea-road to darkness?*

An image floated before me. In a hall of water and coral, I saw my body chained to an anchor, my flesh eaten by crabs and my filmy eyes turned up to the surface, where the sun shone over a place I would never reach again.

A woman stood behind me, her teeth as sharp as a shark's and her fingers as webbed as a seal's. She held a net in one hand and the key to my chain in another. She watched me passively, and I knew her to be both merciless and kind, as cold as ice and as nurturing as a mother.

"Gyda! Get up, Gyda!"

The voice stole into my mind. The image shivered, then grew strong again.

"Gods, *get up*! Get up, you ass!"

"Lady, please!"

Astrid. Ruarc. Rúna. Guðrun and Liadan. Eir.

I jerked, shattering the illusion and coming back to myself. With a tilt of my chin, I filled my mouth with fabric and flesh and bit down as hard as I could. Fresh blood flooded my tongue, and Heimarr released me with a curse.

Choking on air, gasping, I threw myself for Sigtryggr's sword and took it up.

"This is not my death-day," I rasped, standing, whirling to face Heimarr.

He had also found his sword. He was on his feet again, mouth a cavern of broken teeth. "I will piss on your corpse," he slurred at me. "Whore-hag. Mother of troll-spawn!"

Around us, the cheering and cursing faded to shallow noise. My mind reeled. My guts churned. My veins boiled like a storm, threatening to rise up and drag me to oblivion, drag me to Rán's hall where she waited with her chains and her net and her ice-cold fingers.

"This is not my death-day," I said again. "The gods are watching."

Heimarr swayed unsteadily. "You're done, bitch," he panted. "Yield yourself. I'll make it quick. A knife to the gut and over the side. Just like you gave Helgi."

I trembled violently. Wound-pain and blood loss tilted the world. My breath came in agonizing heaves.

I met Heimarr's gaze. In it, I saw his triumph. I saw his arrogance. I saw his cowardice and all his ambition. I saw Hákon's death and I saw Sigtryggr, lying broken and bleeding on the beach. I saw my Daughters, led away to become thralls and corpses and worse.

In Heimarr's face, I saw myself. I saw who I had been, and who I would never be again.

"Fuck you, *niðingr*," I said, and with a guttural yell, I ran at him. His axe came for my skull, and at the last moment I moved, catching the blow with my left arm, shrieking as the lower part of the blade split the skin but missed the bone. My other arm, my sword arm, flowed like water and I shivered as the rings of Heimarr's *brynja* parted under the blade. It went through mail, tunic, and flesh, and I followed its ruinous path until the length of the sword jutted from

Heimarr's back and his mouth was next to my ear. In this embrace, his lips moved, and I heard nothing but the frothing of blood and air.

We went down together, my legs giving up their last strength as my life-tide flowed like the currents of the sea-roads into the dark.

Time passed. Or perhaps it didn't.

Above me, wreathed in shadow and white as a gull's wing, Eir's face floated. Her mouth moved, yelling something I could not hear.

I am sorry, I thought. *I have stolen your vengeance.*

She turned to someone else beyond, speaking urgently. My sight faded.

Numbness crept up my fingers and feet. Something sour coated my tongue and I wondered if it was blood and fluid from my lungs.

So, this is my death-day after all.

There was fear, lurking somewhere in the back of my sluggish mind, but mostly, there was curiosity. Would Oðinn send a Valkyrie? Would she deem me worthy of the Hall of the Slain? Or would she refuse, leaving me to be devoured by Niðhöggr, the Corpse-Eating serpent who coils around the roots of Yggdrasil?

Something pressed against me and I hissed. Eir again. I closed my ears to her voice and allowed myself to float in the black and silence. It was pleasant here, if not as warm as I would have liked. A dream of winter before the dawn of spring.

Years ago, when I was a child, my mother told me of a goddess who was half-dead and half-living. *'Niflheim is her realm,'* my mother said. *'And it is a place of ice. Ice and cold mist.'*

Would I awaken there? Or was I fated for Rán and the crushing depths, the hall of coral and the iron chains?

A searing, grinding pain yanked me from the void. I arched my spine and screamed.

"Grab her! Hold her down!"

The world and all its roaring chaos crashed against me and I was *alive.* Cursed and agonized and broken, but undeniably alive.

Something warm touched my lips and then left.

"Bite down, *Fiskwif*," said a male voice.

A knife scabbard shoved between my teeth. My skin prickled and I realized I was bare to the sky; my *brynja* and tunic were gone. My arm was bandaged already, though fresh blood stained the linen.

I spit out the leather. "What are you doing?"

But Eir did not answer.

A spearhead, red-hot and hissing steam, touched against my side. For the second time, my vision turned to lightning as I howled. This time, I did not slip back to the easy embrace of unconsciousness.

My flesh burned, my blood boiled, and the wound closed. When the blade lifted, the heat did not. Tears soaked into my hair.

"More bandages, now," yelled Eir. "And a clean tunic!"

"She is shaking," Sigtryggr said. He was on his knees to my right, his gray face a savage mask of ash and rage. He held my hand like a smith's vice. Blood stained his lips.

"More bandages," Eir said again. She wiped her hands on the skirt of her dress, already bloody from battle and made bloodier from her work on me. "The shaking will pass," she told him as strips of linen were brought.

"She could die from it."

Quick as a snake's strike, Eir snatched Sigtryggr's face and brought hers close. "Who is the healer here, king? Seal your mouth and be useful or fuck off."

She released him only once he nodded, though the glare he wore was as savage as her own.

"Someone fetch fresh water," he snarled as Eir turned back to the bandages.

I squeezed his hand. "It's not bad," I croaked with a weak smile. "Hardly a tickle. Like a flea in a troll's armpit."

His lip curled, though his gaze remained sharp on Eir as she ripped the linen strips into thinner ones.

There were other figures gathered, and with my wits returning, so did recognition. Ruarc knelt at my feet, holding my ankles together.

Astrid's hands flashed over my head as she passed Sigtryggr a skin of water. He put it to my mouth and I sipped hesitantly.

She smiled as I drank, though it did not reach her eyes.

Nearby, Liadan, Guðrun, and Rúna were a barrier of flesh and boiled leather. Six of Eir's fighters were with them. Blood-streaked blades bristled like the spines of a sea-beast as they faced the clump of whispering, fidgeting men in the stern. Heimarr's fighters.

With their leader lying dead a spear's-length away, they had no purpose but to wait for judgment and, more than likely, thralls' chains.

"Olavi," I said to Eir. "Is he—"

Ruarc's hand tightened around my left shin. "Olavi is here. He's bellying up to shore now. We're to gather on the beach."

"Does he know?"

Sigtryggr made a noise in his throat and his bad eye pinched. This of course stole any comfort the answer may have given.

"He knows what has happened," he said tightly. "Remember you have allies now, aye? And sworn men to enforce it. We will speak for you."

I shut my eyes and fought the rising sickness. Olavi's sons were dead, and again I was the cause of it.

"Raise her up," Eir ordered.

It took Ruarc and Astrid several tries to get me sitting while Eir wound the bandages around my torso. I bore the pain throughout, though I kept my eyes shut, embarrassed not so much of my nakedness in front of several dozen men, but by my vulnerability. I was wounded and weak. Nothing would stop a well-aimed knife from an enemy.

Once my head and arms were thrust into a clean tunic, Ruarc lowered me down and I breathed easier.

Eir bent forward, gently moving my hurt arm onto my chest.

"The cut was bad, but not bone-deep," she said, breath warm and sweet on my face. "You might still lose it to wound-rot. We need a good salve to keep it healthy, and honey for the burn, but I've done what I can for now. You foolish, stupid woman."

She did not smile, but this felt like the kindest thing she'd ever said to me.

"Can you stand?" Sigtryggr asked me, and Eir looked at him in alarm.

"Right now, there is more blood on the inside of her than the outside," she said sharply. "I'd like to keep it that way. She's staying down."

"I won't be on my arse in front of Olavi," I told her. "He'll shove a spear in my gut from pity alone, as he should."

I looked at Sigtryggr, and he nodded grimly. When I bent my legs, Eir cursed.

"Gods! Not even on your deathbed will you heed sense. Fine. If you strike your head on the beach-stones from fainting, woman, I won't patch it up for you. Stand up yourself, if you must."

Stubbornly, the king pushed in and offered me his arm as leverage. One groan and hiss and curse at a time, I stood, my legs trembling like they were made of the jelly sitting atop day-old stew.

"Do not drop me, Siggi," I warned him. "You've seen what happens to men who lose their grip on me."

"Lose hold of a she-wolf? Would never dare," he murmured, the ghost of a smile on his blood-flecked lips.

Ruarc took the space at my other side and nodded stiffly to the king. His hand brushed my shoulder, letting me know he would be mindful of the wound in my ribs.

"Are you alright?" I asked, remembering he had also been hurt.

"We're a matching pair, the two of us," he replied, tone wry. "But I think you've come out the worse for it, eh? You're a quivering, bloody mess."

I scowled. He was right, much as it stung me to hear it. "My chest aches like a troll stomped it. I'm bruised to runny pulp."

"I thought you were gone," he murmured, grimacing. "Lying there bloodied and pale as a sheep's fleece on the deck. The Christ-folk speak of wonders they call miracles. I wonder if I haven't seen one today."

I scoffed, wincing as it pulled on my ribs. Embers of light danced in my vision, and I leaned heavily against Sigtryggr.

"Have pity on the boy," he said to me, a slight flush creeping into his cheeks. "It is a hard thing for a man to see a woman soaked in the dew of slaughter when he might have prevented it."

"Insulting me already, the both of you," I whined. "Stop sniping and worrying. You're as bad as Eir."

"There's plenty of time yet for dying," Eir said, jerking her chin towards the shore.

Not far off the gravel shoreline, two ships lurked in the shallows, sails furled and masts stepped. Waiting for a reckoning. Waiting for me.

With the gods' favor or with their chaos, before the sun's setting I would know the cost of the path I'd chosen.

"I am ready. Let us follow the threads of the Norns' weaving," I whispered.

CHAPTER THIRTY-ONE

Eir shared once that *Dreki* had been Olavi's wedding gift. She'd declared that, rather than generosity, the act was a declaration of confidence and favor in Hákon, and thus a test. By passing his flagship to his eldest son, Olavi conveyed his expectations of him. The heir must take on the sire's position at the tiller, so to speak. Hákon had not been heir only to Olavi's seat, but to his reputation, so long as he could prove himself worthy of it.

Whatever Olavi's intentions had been, they were no more, for that same heir now lay stiff and cold before his sire in the mid-day sunlight, wrapped in a bloody shroud of canvas next to his brother, who had killed him without mercy or honor.

Olavi did not speak when his children were brought before him and laid on the salt-crusted gravel.

With his tall, broad-headed spear in his fist and a shining mail shirt under a cloak of dyed wool, the Jarl looked like Oðinn *Hjaldrgoð,* god of battle, who brings frenzy and whose eye beholds all the doings of the nine realms.

Jarl Olavi, much like Oðinn, had come with a thirst for war.

Our forces gathered up the strand, in a cleared area bordered by sagging canvas tents and cold fire-pits. Heimarr's shore watchmen were gone, fled into the hills, and only fate knew if they'd be seen again.

Eir and Sigtryggr arranged themselves closely in wings: Hákon's warriors led by Eir to the left, and Sigtryggr and his ranks to the right. I stood in the center of both, with my four Daughters and Ruarc, who supported my sagging frame on his arm. The pain of being upright made me tremble, and I strove not to burden Ruarc too much for it. If Ruarc suffered, he gave no hint of it.

There was another host present, lining the camp perimeter near the shoreline; it was clear they were of an entirely different order than the rest of us, for these men were from Córdoba.

Black-bearded and bronze-skinned, the warriors wore polished helmets and iron *brynjur,* which were remarkable enough for their pricelessness. Warriors had to either earn them from their lord, loot them from a corpse, or spend their hard-won silver. Yet every man, to the very last, sported a set.

However, their garments made the greater impression. Each wore silks of goldenrod, scarlet, and malachite, and around their shining helmets were wound scarves of the same. Their beards were neatly braided with beads of gold and amber. In their firm grips, long spears caught and reflected the sun, a glimmering forest of death. But most spectacular of all were the swords hanging from every belt.

It is as if the Emir of Córdoba himself has sent his personal army, signed Liadan next to me, astonished.

"They can't be from the Emir," Rúna whispered back. "Or not entirely. See their wrists? Arm-rings, like oath-men. How strange."

"Do you think they're here because of Nashwa?" Ruarc said, craning his neck. "I don't see her among them."

"Make no assumptions," I responded. "Much as I'd hope Nashwa reached her brother and Ragnar from Dyflin, it may be just as likely the Jarl called in his own favors."

"You don't think Olavi is here to fight us?" Astrid said, hands resting on the axes in her belt as she sized up the foreign company. "I wouldn't mind gutting a few more fish today."

Ruarc shifted his grip on my arm. Two deep furrows had appeared between his ruddy brows, and a frown pulled his mouth into a more crooked shape than usual.

"What is it?" I whispered, following his gaze.

In the open space between our forces, there was a huge, gnarled hunk of ancient oak. The thing appeared carved from a stump and shaped in a vague approximation of a throne. Yet more proof of Heimarr's seething desire to be seen as powerful. It was a pretentious, filthy eyesore. Of course, Jarl Olavi himself occupied the seat now, which did not much improve its appearance, but did lend a certain ominous ferocity.

Behind him, five retainer men gripped spears and finely decorated shields. They were tall and broad, Olavi's best fighters, chosen as his most trusted bodyguards. The rest, some thirty-odd *hirðmen,* stood in ranks five men deep. These were the brothers and fathers and uncles and cousins of the warriors making up Eir's number. In stark contrast with the Córdoban men, Olavi's ranks bore shields painted with a simple coat of the same color that dyed their sail. They each had wicked seaxes strapped above their groins, though only a few bore swords.

"Do you think the silver hoard is hidden somewhere close?" Ruarc muttered, keeping his voice down so the Daughters would not overhear.

I frowned, taken aback by the question, for he'd not previously shown much interest in it.

"*Sea-Wolf*'s hold was light and its draft high in the water," I replied. "Whether it's here or buried elsewhere, I suspect Heimarr wanted it easily found. Why do you ask? Coin fold feeling light?"

Ruarc didn't answer. Sunlight glinted off the hammered bronze clasp on his tunic collar, reminding me that he needed no wealth, as he had plenty of his own. I waited, trusting him to pull the stopper of his thoughts when he'd gathered them.

After some moments, he shook his head. "I want to say it's nothing, but really, it's that I never imagined Olavi would appear on the horizon like some swooping war god on a battlefield. And with our Córdoban friends watching like a flock of vultures, I feel uneasy."

"Are you afraid he'll force you back to Dyflin and marry you off?" I said. "Don't worry, you're safe from that at least. Sigtryggr's got a claim on your oath now."

"Don't make light of such things," he scolded, then drew his lip between his teeth and squinted across the space between our forces. "I know Olavi well. Perhaps not as you know him, but I fear his greed may yet outweigh his sorrow. He may try to claim our hoard, Gyda."

"He might."

Turning back to me, his stare was direct and unnerving. "Or he may demand the life-price of his sons. This time, I don't think you'll be as lucky as getting exiled. Olavi is out for blood or silver. More than likely it's both."

I said nothing, for I had been chewing the gristle of similar thoughts for a while.

Just then, Rúna grasped Liadan's arm and hissed. "Look! He's going to smash them, I know it!"

I attempted to rise on my toes, which only brought on a wave of dizziness, and I tightened my grip on Ruarc. Even with a full skin of mead in my belly and wounds bound tighter than a drum, spots danced in my vision, only receding when I could breathe normally again.

Each of the four men who had carried Olavi's dead sons up the strand now stepped back, avoiding his dark, probing stare. This was because these men were shit-slimed oath-breakers, and to face the lord who'd held those oaths was akin to facing their own deaths. One of them looked ready to vomit.

"Get back with the others," snarled Guðrun from the front of Eir's line. She'd been given charge over the rest of our captives, whom she stood over with a glare as fierce as a troll's. Meekly, the four obeyed her, shackles clanking as they trudged through the dried seaweed and stones back to Eir's ranks.

Olavi watched them go, his only reaction being a tightening of his ringed fist around his spear-haft.

"Why doesn't he speak?" Astrid murmured.

The answer came as Sigtryggr moved forward. As the king of Jórvík, he outranked everyone present, and it was his duty to begin the dealings.

"Olavi Spear-Breaker," he announced, opening his arms wide. "Old friend. I am glad to welcome you on this neutral shore. You have my gratitude for your patience; my oar-benches have thinned these past weeks."

The trailing warriors at Sigtryggr's flank had made a sad attempt at a shield-wall. Though steered by brawny Red Yngvi, the formation was barely two men deep. With the surviving fishermen and half a dozen oath-men left to look after the other ships and the wounded, Sigtryggr had but a paltry number under his command now. It was a humble display for a king, even shameful, and he felt it keenly.

Sigtryggr strode forward to meet the Jarl, setting his spine arrow-straight and face in granite. His sea-cloak was flung over one shoulder, hooked by the shining pommel of his beautiful sword. Expectations were expectations, after all.

His voice carried. "Olavi of Dyflin, we gather to speak of these events and to dispense what justice there is to be had. As king of Northumbria and Jórvík, I declare that all in attendance are free to speak in their turn."

He inclined his head and opened his hand to Olavi.

"Sigtryggr, king," acknowledged the Jarl. His words rumbled across the gravel. "Much time has passed since we last met. As things stand now, I cannot repeat your welcome."

In his controlled voice, I recognized the tight clamp Olavi had on his rage. Soon, that clamp had to break. He had undoubtably seen me, though he had yet to acknowledge my presence. I was content to be ignored as long as it lasted.

"I confess, Spear-Breaker, your welcome is nothing to me," Sigtryggr said, a hint of wolfishness tugging his mouth. "I did not look for your sail, yet here you are, bringing warriors like a younger man seeking fame on a raid."

He turned to the Córdoban ranks and swept out his arm. "And trailing after you is this decorated company! Who is your lord, and could he move his silver-gilt arse into the open, if he pleases?"

For a moment, no one moved, and Sigtryggr scowled. "Do any of you whoresons speak Norse?"

A man, thin-shouldered and with a narrow, bearded face bearing more than a passing resemblance to a goat, reluctantly stepped forward from the line of shining men.

"I am Farajj ibn Ahmad ibn Hasim al-Fakhri," he said in a heavy accent. "We have come at the behest of one who has pledged his support, King of Jórvík."

Sigtryggr grunted. "Ah, how fortunate, Farajj the Goat," he said. "Truly the gods look on our ragged lot with favor. Whose behest, then? Whose support?"

The Córdoban man's expression did not change, but a new tension entered his voice.

"You shall call me Farajj al-Fakhri if my name is too long for your godless mouth," he said politely. "We remain a separate party in your dealings here. Our role is not for you to meddle in."

I stiffened as angry grumbles went through the king's ranks, but instead of reacting, Sigtryggr turned to Olavi and hooked his hands into his belt.

"How did you come upon these wet turds, Olavi?" he asked. "When *Stáli* sent off his message to Dyflin for help, I don't think he expected you to bring all the worms from your arsehole."

That brought laughter from Sigtryggr's men and the Daughters, and two red spots appeared on the Jarl's weathered cheeks. But still, he did not elaborate.

"It seems kings in these lands rely on insults rather than wits," Farajj al-Fakhri declared. "I've come to understand how your men are little more than a blood-stained pack of rabid dogs."

"Save your air, you forge-bellows," Sigtryggr snarled. "If you claim to be a warrior, I've seen better ones in the Christ-houses with toothless, doddering old goat-swivers for priests. Whoever heard of a rich arse-welt with a name as long as my cock?"

"Enough!" Olavi pounded the butt of his spear into the gravel. "My sons lie dead at my feet and you are squabbling like hens in the scratch!"

Sigtryggr grimaced and closed his hand around the pommel of his sword. "You forget, Olavi. I am here out of courtesy, not obligation. I might have left your sons to the sea and returned to Jórvík without a backward glance."

"That was low of him," Astrid muttered, and Liadan thumped her chest in agreement.

"Can't blame him, though," Ruarc put in. "We've got two fresh mobs of thirsty blades facing us, and he's responsible for what happens now."

Shifting my weight and wincing, I added to this. "Eir may have charge of her husband's oath-men now, but they were Olavi's first."

Astrid dragged her teeth over a split lip. "So if he calls them to him, we're on our own." For a moment, she looked just as she once had: young and frightened and impossibly vulnerable.

I sucked in a breath as a jolt of pain went through my chest. "I won't let that happen," I said to her, though it barely meant anything. It was my fault we were even on this beach, after all.

"I am less and less convinced Nashwa sent for Ragnar at all," Rúna said, coming over, brow furrowed in concern. She put a gentle hand on my shoulder. "Lady, we may do well to get you back to *Dreki* and leave these puffed-up cockerels to their crowing. You look ready to collapse."

I opened my mouth to agree with her, but Sigtryggr and Olavi, who had been arguing all the while, momentarily fell silent.

Uneasiness gripped me. Jarl Olavi no longer stared at Sigtryggr. Now, he glared at me, straight through like a blade.

"Don't be afraid," Ruarc muttered darkly. "He'll have to get through me first to hurt you."

"I had heard you threw in your lot with the fire-starter and son-killer," the Jarl announced. His teeth were clenched behind his beard. "Are all the years of our friendship worth less than the shit on my boots, king? Not only do you flaunt your failure today, you spit in my face."

Sigtryggr released the pommel of his sword. "We are friends still, Olavi," he answered smoothly. "But you are wrong to blame the *Fiskwif* for this day. She has done you a service, and you know it well."

Olavi's lip curled. "A *service?"*

"I have brought your sons to you as a gesture of good faith, Olavi," he replied. "As your ally and, indeed, your friend, I offer you my sorrow. Hákon *Stáli*, heir of your house and eldest son, died well-deserving of his byname. Oðinn All-Father welcomes him to the Hall of the Slain with open arms and a horn of heroes' mead. Hákon will feast and await the day that you, his sire and lord, may join him."

It was a fine speech, and if Olavi heard any of it he might have taken issue with the exclusion of Heimarr, but as it was, he cared not at all. For the first time, he looked directly at the bodies on the gravel before him.

"My sons," he said, and a horrible, twisted grimace stretched over his face. "My sons are dead, Sigtryggr. You have brought me bloody corpses in place of my boys. Tell me, how has this happened?" He looked up, tears spilling from his coal-black eyes. "How is it that all my children are dead?"

Sickness coiled in my gut. Olavi's grief was a raw, ruinous thing. Sigtryggr gave him a partial bow, which was a gesture of great respect to a man considered lower than him, as well one who had thrown insults moments before.

Olavi's breath hitched on a sob and he shut his eyes, drawing into himself.

Our gathered companies remained silent. Those with children of their own touched hammer amulets and knife hilts, as if cold iron could ward away the same ill-luck, should it come prowling for their own families. A Jarl and a father sorrowed openly before us, and there were no words of comfort for a loss such as this.

And then, with an explosive curse, the Jarl surged to his feet with his fist tight on his spear-shaft. "Come out, *Fiskwif!* Show yourself to me. Where is the murderer of my family and the catastrophe of my house?"

Olavi's retainer men tensed at the outburst, their war gear jangling as they put hands to their weapons.

"I see you," he bellowed. "Come forward. Face me."

A hand touched my elbow, making me startle. Pain bloomed over my skin and I sucked in a sharp breath. I had forgotten Eir. She bent and whispered urgently in my ear.

"Let me speak for you, Gyda. He means to demand his vengeance. But I am Hákon's widow and I carry his grandchild. He must listen to me."

I put my hand over hers. This offer cost her to make, and I dearly wanted to agree to it. But Ruarc guessed where my intentions bent and spoke for me.

"Olavi will do as he will," he said. "It is his right as their father. Gyda must accept whatever he says." He paused, swallowing hard, then set his jaw. "We all must. Even if that means more fighting."

"Fuck that," she exclaimed, but I shook my head.

"It's alright, Eir. I am capable. No one touch me, I do this alone."

Throat dry as bleached bone, I let go of Ruarc's arm and moved, limping awkwardly. Every muscle felt wrung dry and pummeled like tanned leather. But I would face Olavi on my own legs and in my own strength.

Olavi's black eyes followed my slow progress. When I finally halted beside Sigtryggr, trembling and sweating, he spoke.

"My sons are dead, and yet you live," he said, voice carrying. "Tell me, Gyda *Fiskwif*, how is it that the threads of your fate are woven in this way? How is it that the gods favor you over me?"

"I have no answer for that, Lord," I said. "No one here does."

His lip curled. "Once again, you face me with the blood of my sons staining your tunic and your hands. You dare say this to me?"

"It is Heimarr's blood she wears, Lord," called a bull-necked man from the knot of prisoners.

Guðrun kicked him with a snarled curse, and he threw his shackled hands up.

"She stole his life like she stole Helgi's!" he shouted. "We are your men, Lord. Defend us against these goat-swivers!"

"You shut your rancid mouth, dog," roared Red Yngvi, for though he was a man of Jórvík, the bull-necked arse-licker had killed several of his shield-brothers in the ships.

"Murderer," cried the prisoner.

And then, with a shriek like a spirit in a fen, Guðrun pulled her axe from her belt and brought it down. Red sprayed from the ruin of the man's bull-neck, and he fell, twitching, onto the gravel.

Outraged cries and curses ripped through the Dyflin host, and Guðrun faced them, spreading her arms wide, axe-blade dripping gore.

"Anyone want to speak for this oath-breaking fuck?" she roared. "This coward who died with less honor than a mud-wallowing pig? Come and fight me for him!"

Of course, no one took the thread of that up, for who wanted to be seen defending a man who would have been sold as a thrall or killed anyway? Even so, anger simmered throughout the companies.

"Your women are full of glorious spite, aren't they?" Sigtryggr said, wolf-grin pulling his mouth, but I ignored him.

"I am no murderer, Olavi," I said, lifting my voice as much I could. "It is true, I killed Heimarr. We fought the *holmgang*. He lost.

I put a sword through him. I did this not for my own gain, but to carry out justice."

Olavi's knuckles whitened on the haft of his spear. His other hand flung a gesture at the bodies in their bloody wrappings. "You call this justice?"

"For Heimarr, yes. From the shores of Córdoba to the thwarts of your flagship *Dreki,* he has murdered, thieved, and schemed worse than any *hrafnasueltir*. When I challenged him, he accepted of his own will. His fate is his own doing."

"You lie!" Spittle flecked Olavi's beard. He took two steps forward, halting when Sigtryggr moved to my right.

"Think well, Olavi," the king warned. "There are worse things than being called a raven-starver, and there is yet time for you to join your sons beneath a shroud."

That brought renewed shouting and curses from all sides. Such a threat was a brazen thing, especially from a man who could call on fewer than two dozen warriors to fight for him.

Across the stretch of rocky beach, fire-blooded fighters rolled their shoulders and stretched their necks. A few loosened blades from scabbards and axes from belt rings.

The Córdoban men, however, stood passively, as if all this was nothing but the simmering of a stew pot. What did they care if the rest of us killed each other over blunt-tongued insults?

Fuck. No more of this, I thought. *No more.*

Between Olavi's men and ours, violence hung thick in the air like a swarm of corpse-flies. If it erupted, there would be no turning from death. We all would bleed, and the gods would glut themselves on it.

I could not fight. I wore a sling and my body was a dry husk, crackling from pain and exhaustion. There was a seax sheathed on my belt, but what use would it be? In the crush of a shield-wall, I would be ripped apart in moments. I was worse than useless; I was the spark on the tinder.

"Hákon *Stáli* fought with honor," I declared, moving gingerly away from Sigtryggr. He could not protect me from this. "No braver warrior have I seen in all my years, Olavi. He has brought your name and house a legacy that can never fade. Take comfort and be proud of him."

"What good is honor when Hákon lies dead before me?" the Jarl said fiercely. "What good is legacy? You have slaughtered my kin and taken everything from me. My future. Every hope I carried. You are nothing but a curse. A plague that destroys and spreads chaos and rot everywhere you trod. You look half-dead already. I should put my spear through your gut-rope and finish you off."

For a heartbeat, I expected him to do just that. But then Eir appeared beside me, gripping my elbow hard and nailing Olavi with a stare as baleful as a shark's.

"You are wrong," she said to him. "It is Heimarr alone who bears the guilt for these crimes. You know this well, or my husband's pride in you was misplaced."

Olavi's grizzled brows knotted together, but the sight of her seemed to steady him. "I know it well, do I?" he responded. "This one-eyed king said the same. Hmph. I know this for certain, woman: your loyalty is as changeable as Dyflin's weather. How odd that I find you standing with these sea-urchins. Your husband is barely cold. Could you not wait a day before throwing him over for this pus-stinking outlaw, this traitor?" He flung a hand at me. "Did she not betray you at the first opportunity?"

"You speak of loyalty?" Eir drew herself up to her full height, which was a full head taller than him. "I know more of loyalty in my span of years than you've ever farted on in your Jarl's seat. I know more than all the men you lord over. My *child* will know more of love and of loyalty than you. If I did not pity you, Olavi, I would find it contemptible in a man with such a reputation as yours."

None there who watched her could deny she held herself well as she scolded him. Dignified and haughty as Freyja herself, Eir was a marvel, the noble queen and wife of a man who could have been king, had he lived long enough to seek it.

Olavi's eyes bulged. "Your *child*?" he sputtered. "Hákon's child?"

She spoke again, words carrying over the crash of the surf. "You came with a war-band and a ship full of strangers. Why is that, if you are only here to bully and blame your failures on a wounded and weary old woman? Go home and sit in your stink and your shame if that is all your bluster is good for."

"How *dare* you say such things to me?" he cried. "After taking you in like a daughter! I'll have your tongue torn out!"

"Give us the order, Lord," called a man in Olavi's ranks, bristling with his spear and shield. "We'll bring you all their tongues, the fucking dogs!"

"All this has come about because of Heimarr's treachery," I said. "And *your* folly. You blinded yourself to the rot within your own walls. If I must bear a part of the blame for these deaths, then the rest of it must lie with you."

"The *Fiskwif* speaks truth, Lord!" called a warrior from behind us. "Heimarr killed Hákon with his own blade! We saw it!"

Two more men joined in, bolstered by their fellow's courage.

"I saw him mutilate Hákon's corpse and hang it from the mast," declared one.

"The turd took us as thralls, Lord! All of us, your sworn men of Dyflin," reported the other.

Man after man stepped forward to relay their accounts. After all, Hákon had been their brother as much as their leader, and they had loved him deeply.

Astrid joined in next. "The coward Heimarr is not worthy of any name but Brother-Killer and Dung-Worm!" she shouted.

"We stand with the Grim-Bitch!" called Red Yngvi.

Olavi's men, leashed tight and itching to be let loose, snarled and stamped as more of their shield-brothers took up the account. Even the prisoners on their knees were howling their own defenses.

Olavi was oath-lord, and these corpses were his sons. Reputation is everything. It is the thing a warrior lives for and it is what bears them to *Valhöll* in the arms of Valkyries when death comes. With these accusations wafting like the stink of pig-shit, soon that stink would cling to Olavi and never leave. Trust in a leader, once broken, is impossible to earn back.

Olavi pounded his spear butt into the ground and screamed his insults, but the uproar drowned him out.

"Let us gut these whoresons," hollered a man in the rear of Olavi's shield-wall, louder than Thor himself. "Send us forward, Lord!"

The Daughters surged then, flanking Eir and I in a fighting wall of our own. Guðrun wielded her still-bloody axe and Rúna held a spear. Liadan brandished a seax and shield, her words now made of sharp edges and death. Astrid had her axes. Sigtryggr drew his sword, and Ruarc appeared at my side, holding a shield.

"Shield-wall!" Eir's command was as loud and piercing as a thunderclap.

"No, no, stop this!" I cried.

A mass of heaving men coalesced, pushing us back behind them to make room. They smashed their shields together, overlapping them in a pattern as tight as strakes on a sleek war-ship.

"Get your arses in the wall, you pus-stinking filth," hissed the king to his retinue. His other men were already filling the gaps, and those without shields remained behind the line, prowling with blades.

I was knocked forward by a straggler seeking his own fighting position. My wound burned like fire. Ruarc caught me in his arms. I clung to him, gasping.

Sigtryggr turned to the foreign line of warriors, in their silent ranks with their forest of spears shining.

"Will you stand with us, Farajj al-Fakhri?" He raised a fist. "You declared your lord's support. We have need of it now."

"We will not join this fight, king," Farajj called back. "We have no quarrel here. Kill each other if you must, but we will not take part."

"Fucking whoresons," Sigtryggr growled, then whirled, grabbing his shield from the man carrying it. "Come on then!"

He pounded his sword hilt against the rim, and Red Yngvi raised a war-cry beside him, joined by the rest. And then Olavi's men howled, attempting to drown them out.

The sound rattled my head and filled my belly with bile. The beach would turn to a savage struggle soon, with shit and viscera and shattered bone trampled under our feet, and none of us coming out whole.

I screamed for the king, but my voice was lost in the chaos.

Ruarc had me by the shoulders, pulling me back, away from the shield-wall. "Get out of here," he gasped. "Hide yourself somewhere. I'll come for you when it's over."

"No, stop. Ruarc, listen to me." I tugged on his sleeve. I was swaying, dizzy, exhausted. Pain screamed through me. "Get me to Olavi. I can stop this. We still have a chance."

Ruarc's eyes went wide. "Are you mad? We need to get you away from here, Gyda! He will *kill* you."

"Is that not worth preventing a slaughter?" I demanded. "My life is nothing. Please, Ruarc. This must end. Help me end it."

Tormented, agonized, he held my gaze for a single moment, and then lifted his voice in a howl. "Sigtryggr!"

This time, the king heard.

"Shut your fucking mouths, you dogs! Shut up!"

The roar and pounding of blades and shields diminished, and Ruarc walked me forward, pushing between the ranks.

"What are you doing?" Sigtryggr hissed, storming to grab us.

"We cannot fight them and win," I told him. "I have another way. Let me speak to the Jarl."

His face drained of color. "Don't be a fool," he started, but I reached for his cheek and he stilled.

"Trust me, old friend," I said. "Please."

Sigtryggr stared at me. And then: "Olavi," he yelled. "A parley! The Grim-Bitch wishes to speak!"

I tugged on Ruarc's arm and we moved on.

Eir and the Daughters watched me, pale-faced as I labored. But they did not try to stop me. Eir shook her head, mouthing a protest, but I looked away. I could not stop now.

The gnarled stump was gone, tossed aside in a heap on a canvas tent. The corpses were gone too, and I hoped Hákon at least had been treated with more respect.

Olavi's shield-wall filled the open space, rank after rank of iron bosses and sharp blades. As I approached, they stiffened, ready with their spears and seaxes to cut me down.

"Put down your sticks, children," I told them. "I'm here to talk, not make you piss your breeks."

There was laughter behind me.

Olavi had retreated into the protective knot of his bodyguard behind his men, and I saw the top of his bare head over the rim of his painted shield.

"Anything you have to say is goat-shit in my ears, woman."

"This is foolish, Olavi," I said. "Do you see a weapon in my hand? I cannot even walk without assistance. Do you think I care a pig's fart for any of this?"

"What is it you want?"

I took a breath. "I want to surrender."

"What?" Ruarc hissed, his muscles jerking underneath my grip. "That isn't what you said!"

"Gyda, no, you can't!" Astrid cried, and this was repeated by Guðrun and Rúna. Their protests buried inside my skin and cut me deep.

"Finally accepted your fate, eh, troll-wife?" sneered a man in the front rank.

"You'll look much better with my axe in your skull," said another.

"Shut your putrid mouths," Olavi gnarred. He lowered his shield a fraction and peered at me dubiously. "Surrender?"

"It's what you're burning for, isn't it? Bloody vengeance. Three sons lost, and I am still here. It sticks in your gullet."

At that, he broke formation and strode forward, spear clenched in his meaty fist. He stopped three paces away.

"Here we are again, *Fiskwif,*" he growled. "The same fucking problem. What is the scheme now? You want me to believe you're offering yourself like a steer at the winter *blót?"*

"I'll show you what we have to offer," said Ruarc darkly.

"Don't think I've forgotten *you,* traitor!" The Jarl threw back. "Troll-cursed Irish cur!"

"My loyalty doesn't lie with you, and never did," Ruarc responded. "Gyda, don't play into his hands. Nothing good can come of this."

"I am *tired* of this," I said. "Olavi, listen. I am wounded. I'd like to drown myself in a barrel of ale. So what is it you want from me? My death? To own me as a thrall? To tie a stone to my feet and drop me off a cliff into the sea? Name it and then get on with it. Neither of us will know peace until we settle our scores here and now."

The Jarl dragged his gaze from my head to my feet. His chin jutted and his great beard bristled. "A tempting offer. I expect you want something outrageous in return. You wriggle your way out of your own shit better than an eel through a net."

"Gyda, come back," Eir called, the anguish in her voice raw. "Don't do this."

"Listen to her," Sigtryggr agreed. "You promised me, remember? We fight together."

Sighing deeply, I turned and nodded to Eir, to Sigtryggr, and to the rest. My friends and my allies. Some of them my family. Like Ruarc, standing with me as always.

"I want them safe, Olavi," I said, turning back. "And they won't be if I let them keep fighting my wars. Let this be the end. I am finished."

The Jarl stared at me unblinking. His fingers flexed, and I wondered if he would thrust the spear through my chest and walk away.

But then he drew his beard into his teeth and made a noise in his throat. "Hákon loved you," he said distantly. His shoulders dropped. "He never lost that clear-eyed child's wonder for you."

"What are you saying?"

Olavi turned his head, watching the falling sun. "When his mother died, I know he visited you and Jörund often. He never thought of you as a replacement, but you were close enough. Eventually, I told him to grow up, to stop searching for her shadow in yours. I told him to find his own in mine." He paused, shutting his eyes. When he looked at me again, there were tears. "Is that what killed him? Did I make you the dragon in my saga? Did he throw himself into this fight to seek my shadow?"

Taken aback by his raw grief, I spoke gently. "No, Olavi. Hákon loved you. He respected you. But he was a warrior and a leader in his own right and he protected us all to the end. He died to protect his family. Your family."

"Heimarr and Helgi were also family."

I remained silent until he mastered himself. He turned back to the shoreline and exhaled heavily.

"Killing you does not bring me peace," he said. "It will not bring back my sons. So tell me, *Fiskwif*, what should I do with you? How can I satisfy my honor and my reputation?"

A horn blast cut through the air.

Ruarc's mouth dropped open. "There's a boat approaching!"

We all saw. Not far from shore, ten men rowed a small, broad-hulled craft, its benches surrounding a hold packed full of crates and barrels. Another man had the tiller and, standing tall in the prow with his foot on the strake, was a man with a horn to his lips. He blew a second blast, then waved his arm.

"Some help, please," he called. "Get us up the stones!"

The Jarl looked to Sigtryggr, who stared back, as if each of them expected the other to come to the strangers' aid.

But it was Farajj who answered the request. He barked out an order and five shield-men broke off and loped down the slope to the water.

"What is this? Gyda?" Ruarc's grip tightened as I swayed.

Stunned and breathless, I looked at Olavi and said: "You knew he was coming. You knew and said nothing."

"I knew," Olavi said, expression unreadable. "Turned up in Dyflin with a war-ship and that pack of Córdoban dogs. Man was a bloody nuisance as a *huskarl*, and more now that he's wealthier than Njörd. Followed me all the way here."

I wanted to rail at him then, demand why he'd let the king insult the foreign warriors, why he'd nearly brought all of us to ruin. Instead, I shut my mouth and stared at the boat.

The crew jumped out onto the strand, and with the help of their fellows, whose shining *brynjur* and helmets matched their own, took up the hemp ropes and hauled the boat up the slippery gravel.

Farajj al-Fakhri, smiling at the prow man, offered his hand and helped him down.

This man, tall and with a cloak as blue as the sea behind him, had a limp. But he walked with his head held high. He wore a brilliant, golden neck covering, one that gave him the appearance of a maned lion.

"I think I know him," Ruarc said, puzzled.

"Any man would recognize that one," Olavi muttered. "A strutting peacock, he is."

"Ruarc," I stammered. "Ruarc, take me to him."

We made our halting way back to Sigtryggr, who stared, trying to read me, and Eir, who stood with him.

"Do you see?" I asked her.

"I do," she answered, a grin breaking over her face.

Astrid, Liadan, Guðrun, and Rúna were already striding to meet him, their cheeks red and their hands outstretched for embraces. He welcomed them warmly. He was leaner, sun-browned, and weathered, but his smile was the same.

"Care to let me in on who this is?" Sigtryggr said.

"It's Ragnar," I said. "Ragnar Goldmane."

CHAPTER THIRTY-TWO

As the sun vanished and the moon rose over the bay, Ragnar regaled us with his story.

I listened, half dozing, warmed by a fire on the beach and wrapped in a fur. Rúna, Guðrun, Astrid, Liadan, Sigtryggr, and Ruarc surrounded me. We had our backs against a mountain of crates that, as it turned out, were stuffed full of silver ingots, furs, and amber.

Heimarr's shore-guard had not vanished, after all. Being a handful of ill-favored men with no sword-skill and even less sense, they'd seen how the sea-battle turned and thought it a prime opportunity to try and make off with the hoard.

"I came upon the fools not two miles down the beach," Ragnar said, grinning. "Digging and tossing the crates and barrels into the hold of that boat as fast as their scrawny arms could work. You should have seen how fast they shit themselves when a horde of screaming Córdoban fighters came at them."

Guðrun gave a great belly laugh, and Ragnar tilted his cup to her.

How did you even come upon them? asked Liadan. Rúna interpreted so Ragnar could understand.

He leaned forward with a conspiratorial smirk. "Well, you see, I am a brilliant sailor," he said, which made all Daughters present snort, leaving Ruarc and Sigtryggr mystified.

Ragnar went on, flipping a hand. "I saw a chance to take something back from that troll Heimarr, and so as soon as Farajj al-Fakhri dropped anchor, I took eleven of our men and went off after them. Olavi never even had a chance of catching up."

"Go on, then," said Astrid. "That can't be all of it."

"Of course it isn't," he answered, then turned a bright gaze to me. "Care to explain? I always enjoy your sharp-eyed commentaries."

I rolled my eyes. "Flatterer."

He sat back, looking pleased with himself, and so I picked up a small stone and threw it at his forehead. He flinched when it struck him.

"This turd wanted to make an entrance," I said dryly. "So he waited until we were about to rip each other to pieces. As farcical as the worst skalds, you are."

Ragnar's grin faltered. "Are you annoyed?"

I took a sip of my ale and held his gaze over the rim of it.

He put a hand to the back of his neck and looked away. "I admit, I was rather late in my timing."

Sigtryggr sputtered. "*Late*? That's what you call it?"

The king sat to my left, near enough but not touching. He was very drunk, with his own small cask of ale that he shared with me and with Ruarc on his other side. "Olavi nearly turned this beach into a slaughtering field. He would have but for all the fucking *noise* this one made trying to get herself killed."

Sigtryggr sloshed his cup at me, spilling ale on the corner of my bear fur. I shot him a withering glare, which he returned.

"What about Nashwa and Hadiyya?" Rúna murmured. "They sent for you, didn't they? That's why you came."

Ragnar lifted a shoulder. "Nashwa's brother is a dear friend, and I owed her my life. It is fortunate her message reached Córdoba in time."

And so the tale wove on. He repeated what Nashwa had told me in Jórvík, adding with a scowl that he'd broken his ankle when Astrid punched him through the wooden screen.

"The joint is destroyed," he said ruefully, gesturing at it. "Even the Córdoban healers can't restore me to full strength. I'll never walk straight again, or fight."

"Oh, but a brave, brawny fighter you were before," Guðrun said, eliciting a few muted laughs.

"Serves you right, spying on us like that," Astrid pronounced without a hint of apology.

Ruarc snorted into his ale, and Ragnar sent a flirtatious wink his way. I pretended not to see, for the implications of *that* bothered me more than I liked to admit. Ruarc was my foster son, after all, and Ragnar was—well, he was Ragnar.

"So you let us think you were dead all this time," Rúna said. "Why?"

"Because if I were dead, I was not a target," Ragnar responded. "Heimarr had the ship and the silver. The rest of you were gone, back to Dyflin to face the wrath of the Jarl. I figured sooner or later Olavi would come after me for killing his boy."

"*I* killed Helgi," I pointed out. "You just fought a duel with him."

He shrugged. "What's the difference? I am very wealthy, thanks to loyal service to the Emir and my various charms. For all his faults, Olavi's worst is that he lusts after wealth more than he lusts after his bed slaves. If he wanted the life-price for Helgi, he'd find a reason to take it from my hide. Or so I assumed, anyway. So I hired some fighting men from the Emir's bodyguard and paid them handsomely for their loyalty and their discretion. I bribed a way out of Córdoba and sailed us all to Iceland. I've got an estate set up there now, and people to run it. If the Emir ever goes looking for his missing men, he won't find us any place his trading ships dock."

So you finally made it to Iceland, signed Liadan, delight animating her face. *I had always hoped you would.*

He smiled at her after hearing the translation. "And it is beautiful there, truly. If you ever find yourself in need of a new home, my dear, you are more than welcome. My gates are always open to you."

Liadan flushed with pleasure.

"But Nashwa's message reached you in Córdoba," Ruarc said, frowning. "How is that?"

Ragnar sobered. "I was there with her brother Baqir on business, and by pure chance or the will of the gods, a ship from Jórvík happened to arrive hours before we were meant to depart."

With that, he flipped a hand and brightened. "The rest you all know. Anyone want more ale?"

The stars wheeled overhead. Guðrun stirred the fire. Astrid ladled out more ale. I drank as much as everyone else, listening to Ragnar's recounting of all his achievements under the Emir and all the things he had planned as a wealthy landowner in Iceland.

Drowsily, my mind wandered, thinking of Eir.

She had chosen to remain with Olavi, who had made his camp up the slope and away from the water. She'd wanted to speak to him, to share her memories of Hákon, and who could argue with such a wish?

Hákon's oath-men had gone with her, and that was also good. After all, the Dyflin men were meant to be shield-brothers. Some reconciliation after screaming curses and murderous threats at each other could only be a boon. Helped along by a good dousing of two barrels of fine ale, of course.

Ragnar's fighters made their camp on the far side of the beach, away from the rest of us for their privacy and their need to perform the rites to their god. We looked on discretely, careful to hide our curiosity in favor of respect.

Sigtryggr's men had been tasked with packing up the bulk of the cargo, and would soon haul it to *Hrið-Ormr*. In the morning, all our companies would depart to whichever corner of this wide, strange world we called home.

Sigtryggr, of course, would return to Jórvík with a hold full of his share of the silver, and a renewed thirst to fight Edward, the horse-faced king down in Wessex. A very small, dangerous part of me wanted to go with him.

I watched Ruarc closely, when he could not see me doing so. By the way he studied the king, I knew which direction he would choose once the sun rose. Jórvík had been good to him. It was a great city, bigger than Dyflin, and offered a home with no obligation or expectation. And there was much to learn as a king's oath-man.

The Daughters would return with Eir back to Dyflin in *Sea-Wolf*. There was no question they would join Eir's household and become her companions. She needed them for the birthing and the raising of her child. They were wealthy now, with two chests each between them. Guðrun and Rúna would never return to their families. Liadan would never be a slave again. Astrid was a blooded warrior, and her mother and siblings would thrive with her provision.

And me? Where would I go? Did I wish to go anywhere at all?

Sigtryggr slipped his hand into mine, and I squeezed it tightly. And then I let go, and he gave me a small, secret smile.

One by one, my friends fell asleep, wrapped in their warmth and surrounded by crates of new wealth.

Only Ragnar and I remained awake, staring into the dying flames of the fire and feeling the air cooling as dawn edged closer to the horizon.

"So," he said, rolling his empty cup in his hands and leaning forward. "What an adventure you've had."

I rested my head against the crate and shut my eyes. "Gods, if all this was an adventure, I think I am finally as old as everyone tells me I am. I've got nothing left in me of adventure. Just aching bones, a scorched flank, a hole in my arm, a busted nose, and a new scar across my belly. I'm worse off than a half-gutted fish."

He laughed softly, and after a moment, I smiled too.

"You're just the same as you were, Gyda the Grim," Ragnar said, eyes twinkling from the dying firelight. "Just as much of a hard salt and still stubborn."

"And you're still as immature and absurd as you were the day I found you wrapped in rags hiding in my hold, Ragnar Stowaway," I said. "I wonder sometimes if I should have dropped you over the side when I had the chance."

"I missed you, too," he said, nudging my outstretched leg with his boot.

We fell silent for a while, resting tired eyes and shivering a little as the embers burned out.

"Will you come with me to Iceland?" he said suddenly, and I choked on my breath, having been close to sleep and startled out of it.

"You're asking me to go to Iceland?" I repeated, incredulous.

He nodded solemnly. "I want to repay you, Gyda. For saving my life from Helgi, and for all of it. You'll have land. Power. Influence. More and more people are settling there, all seeking new opportunities and new adventures. Nashwa and Hadiyya are already there. I think you could be happy, if you're willing to give up your life as *Sea-Wolf*'s mother."

I pulled myself up from a slouch, grimacing as the wound in my side twinged. Eir had smoothed a wonderfully fragrant salve on it, which had shoved the pain of the burn and the ache of my ribs far away, but not entirely out of reach.

"Ragnar, it is a noble thing to ask, but Olavi still has a score to settle with me," I said. "In the morning, he will remember that, and when he burns his sons, he might seek to quench their pyre with my blood."

"He won't," Ragnar said.

I scowled at the look on his face. "And why is that?"

"Don't be so suspicious! I'm only quoting the law. Heimarr killed Hákon. You killed Heimarr. The life-price is paid. Legally, if Olavi kills you now, it would be murder. Especially because, in just a moment, I will hold your oath. Olavi wouldn't wish to start a feud with a *very* powerful Jarl from Iceland just for your sake."

I gaped at him. "You bastard! You planned this."

His grin widened. "Give me your oath, let me protect you, and the moment we get home, I'll release you and you can go all the way to Iceland's furthest coast if you want to run away from me that badly. Just let me do this for you. This little pittance of silver is not fair enough payment for saving my life."

As I thought all this over, I watched the women around me. I watched Ruarc's face, quiet and peaceful in the dark. I looked at Sigtryggr, who snored and rubbed his bad eye like he was a child with a lash in it.

"The second we see that coast," I said to Ragnar. "You release me from the oath."

"Done."

"And I get my own estate. Next to yours. But not too close. I like my independence."

"Done."

"I oversee the trade of our stretch of coast. Men answer to *me,* not you."

He furrowed his brow at that. "I take a generous cut of profits," he countered.

"Ten percent," I offered.

"Thirty-five."

I scowled. "Fifteen."

"Twenty!"

"Twenty— *fuck*—twenty. Fine."

"Then," he said, brilliant smile returning. "Gyda the Grim, *Fiskwif* of Dyflin, mother to Rán's Daughters, we have a deal."

"How generous," I said dryly, then turned away from him and shut my eyes.

"Don't sleep yet," he said, barely stifling his laughter. "We sail on the morning tide. I'll need that oath for our scheme to work."

I cracked an eye. "Give me your hand."

"What?"

"Give it to me."

Frowning, he rocked forward on his knees and stretched out his hand.

I grabbed it, kissed his knuckles, then released it like it was a snake. "There. You can tell everyone I had many flowery words and solemn phrases. Tell them I sang you a poem. That's the best you'll be getting from me."

I went to sleep with the sound of his laughter like the rush of surf in my ears.

EPILOGUE

Twenty Years Later

"Are you coming, Mother?" called Háki from the bench on the wagon.

Eir looked up from the grindstone. "In a moment."

"That boy's impatience never stops grating on me," growled Guðrun. She was sitting by the fire, wrapped in a seal-skin cloak, caught and fashioned by the very boy she complained about. She held her hands out, fingers splayed. These days, only warmth could ease the ache of the arthritic joints.

"He's a man. Of course he's impatient," Rúna told her. "Are you not ready yet, my love? Here, put on these mittens, I warmed them on the lava stone."

"Eir, you've put an edge on that sword three times over," Astrid said, hitching the toddler on her hip a little higher. This was her fourth girl, and the only one who'd inherited her lake-blue eyes and golden-hay hair. Her other girls took after Magnus, with his brown hair and eyes like topaz gems. With this one, she'd birthed herself a twin in miniature, and she bragged constantly how Magnus never failed to spoil each one of them.

"The sword needs to be perfect," Eir grunted, pushing the blade one last time over the stone. "I would never forgive myself if it wasn't. She'd scold me."

She scolded all of us for anything she could scold us for, signed Liadan. She stood in the entranceway of the workshop next to her husband Lokur, a giant bear of a man who could speak but never wanted to, because Liadan did all the speaking for them both.

"Mother!"

"We're coming, Háki, shut your flapping gums," yelled Astrid. "I swear, he's pushier than his father ever was."

Eir relished the grin she wore. Any mention of Hákon always

brought forth a smile these days, and that was because she could see him every day in the face of their son, his namesake.

One by one, the women who had been Rán's Daughters filed out of the workshop, each of them bearing something to bring to the shoreline.

Astrid had a seax. Guðrun and Rúna brought a painted shield and an old, but still shining *brynja*. Liadan and Lokur had a huge wooden chair in the back of their wagon, carved by Lokur himself and decorated with intricate, intertwined animal heads.

Eir had the sword.

It once belonged to King Sigtryggr, and still held all its original beauty, though it had been repaired with a new hilt and sharpened until the blade was too thin to be of any use in an actual fight. But it didn't matter; Gyda had no need for blades in the last years of her life.

Once outside, Háki jumped down from the wagon bench and walked around the horse hitched to it.

"Let me help you up," he said, grinning mischievously. Eir stretched out her hand to take his, but frowned as he brushed past her to get to Gunnhild, Astrid's eldest girl who was just two summers younger than himself.

"Hákon Hákonarsson," chided Astrid with a blunt finger in his chest. "Help your mother up first before I skin you alive. You think that's the way to win my approval? Get your hands away from Gunnhild or I'll feed them to the sharks."

Eventually, all of them were seated, including the rowdy younger girls, who would ride in the bed of Lokur's wagon to look after the chair. Liadan and Lokur led the way out of the farmstead, and soon the wagons were bumping down the dirt track to Ragnar's estate on the coast where he awaited their arrival.

"Sigtryggr's sword," Rúna murmured, nodding down at Eir's lap. "It's still beautiful."

Eir shifted, tightening her woolen cloak around her shoulders. Winter was in the air; soon the snows would come and bury this road until the thaw. It was good they were doing this for Gyda today, and not a week from now.

"She was so *angry* when he died," Astrid said, smiling fondly.

The little one sitting in between her legs made a furrowed, scowling face, and Eir laughed.

"Angry?" said Rúna. "She was *furious*. She didn't speak for a month because she was too busy cursing his name in her head. He died a Christian, can you believe that?"

"If Gyda had ever wanted to marry again, I think it would have been him," Astrid replied. "Do you think they're humping on the benches of Valhöll? Now *that* is something I would pay good silver to see. Gyda was a frigid bitch."

Eir's mouth dropped open. "Astrid!"

"What?" She blinked. "You know it's true. She said the same about herself. And I never once saw her with a man. Did you?"

Eir shook her head. "Gyda loved her solitude. She valued it. And she was never lonely with us close."

"Besides, Sigtryggr was married again," Guðrun pointed out. Her hands were tucked under Rúna's, as they often were.

"That didn't stop our Ruarc from running after him to every battle, did it?" Astrid put in. "He worried after that man worse than I do when Magnus goes off hunting."

Rúna snorted. "I doubt he moons like that now. Ragnar keeps him *very* well looked after in that longhouse."

"Ah, but he was never the same after Sigtryggr died," Astrid replied, a touch of sadness in her voice. "And now with Gyda gone, I'm afraid we'll lose even more of him."

"Ruarc is still with us," said Eir, putting a hand over hers. "He grieves, but he's full of the same happiness and light too. He will miss her, but he'll live again. It's what she wanted, and so we all must do the same."

The rest of the journey was spent in silent remembrance.

When they arrived at Ragnar's, the man himself was at the gate, a broad smile creasing his aging face. He walked with a crutch now but still wore the finest of silks and brightest of blades. He was wealthier than ever and controlled a substantial parcel of the coastal lands in the area. This was why Eir had chosen this place to send Gyda off.

"You all look so well," Ragnar declared, hands on his hips and eyes bright. "Please give your horses to Akim there, he'll put them up in the stables. Now, Háki, I hear you've been running after young Gunnhild there. What about Hadiyya's daughter? She's a bit taller than you, but I tell you, she's one of the best loom-weavers you've ever seen. She runs the workshops, you know. You'd do well with her as a wife."

Háki and Ragnar moved away, the younger walking slowly in deference to the older man's limp. Eir watched after them, grateful. Ragnar had been like a father figure the last twenty winters. It had helped to dissipate some of the lingering guilt she carried after leaving Dyflin soon after Olavi died.

All those years ago, Gyda had been stunned to silence to see her arrive with the infant Háki at the farmstead.

The Daughters had all come along, of course. And every one of Hákon's men. With the Jarl dead, they had given their oaths to her, and then again to Háki when he came into his majority. He'd already gone on his first raid this past summer. It was a tad late for a young man; Háki was twenty now, he should have been raiding long since. But the idea had petrified her more than anything, so she'd forbidden it. It was when she'd seen the joy on Háki's face one evening as Ragnar regaled them all with tales of the lands he'd seen and all the rulers he'd met, that Eir realized there was no point forbidding it any longer. And besides, she trusted her oath-men would strive to let no harm fall on the boy. It was time to let go and trust the weave of fate.

"Eir, so good to see you," said a warm voice, still tinged with an Irish accent. She turned and smiled broadly as Ruarc came and grasped her in an embrace.

"Oh, my. You've gone grayer than the last time I saw you," she told him, ruffling his head. He had aged much in the last fifteen years since the king of Jórvík died, but he still had the same crooked smile and the same warmth to him.

"Could say the same for you," he countered. "You look tired; have you been sleeping?"

"Not much," she admitted, and he nodded.

They walked, taking the path they both knew would lead down to the shore, and to what awaited them there.

"The longhouse seems so empty without her in it," she told him.

"We all are sleeping there, of course. It isn't really empty. But *she's* not there. Not even her ghost. You understand, I'm sure."

"I do," Ruarc said. "It's only been a few days, and always the time feels longer. But I promise, you will find ways of comfort in the emptiness, and then you won't feel so empty. She is there, between your ribs next to your heart."

"Easy to say," Eir said, throat closing. "Harder to believe."

Ruarc tilted his face up, letting the dim sun warm it. "I think sometimes I hear her voice," he said. "Since she died, it's in the wind. At night, beside the hearth. But most often, I hear her by the sea."

They stopped then, for they had come to the water's edge.

"The sea was Gyda's great love," she told him after a long moment. "Perhaps her greatest. The luminous blue. Like sapphires. The storm-whipped gray. The lapping breakers against an oak hull. She embraced the ocean like anyone else embraces their lover. She dreamed about it all these years."

"Is that why you wanted her here?" he asked, though Eir was certain he already knew that to be true.

She looked out over the water, to the hulk of *Sea-Wolf* floating close by, waiting for its final cargo.

"To steal the sea from Gyda *Fiskwif* would be a wrong no one could ever make right. And she would curse the fool from the benches of Valhöll for even thinking it."

Ruarc grinned. "That she would," he said.

At sunset, the stretch of shore filled with crowds of people. Many of them knew Gyda. Some of them had only heard about her. She'd had a reputation, that woman. Every year, at the Althing gathering at *Thingvellir,* the assembly field, more of those who had heard of her exploits would approach, seeking tales or conversation. She professed she hated it thoroughly, but Eir saw her secret, pleased smile a moment before she reverted to her permanent scowl.

If Eir didn't know the stories about Gyda were all true, she would have never believed them herself. No one had a right to a life that full, that adventurous. But Gyda *Fiskwif* had lived that life well, and it seemed unfair to Eir that she had died in her bed, her heart giving out, and without getting the chance to face down death and come out the better for it one more time, one more day.

One more day. That's all Eir would have asked for, if it had been up to her. But that was a lie: she would have asked for another day. And another.

The sun had touched the horizon when Gyda's shrouded remains were put into a little boat. Ruarc and Háki rowed her out to *Sea-Wolf,* then lifted her, gently, onto the ship. She would rest on the deck planks over the hold, which was now so decrepit and warped that it was a wonder how they'd managed to keep the old *knarr* watertight for so long. It needed an overhaul from prow-beast to sternpost.

But this would be its final voyage.

After Gyda was laid out, the Daughters' grave-goods came after.

First was Sigtryggr's sword, which Ruarc gripped like a dead man drowning. He placed it down beside her, and did not wipe the tears from his face, for he was unashamed of them.

Next was Gyda's own *brynja* and seax. Then the painted shield. The beautifully carved chair. Strings of beads. Bowls of strong beer. Barrels of sweet mead. Chests of fine clothes.

Gyda had as rich a send-off as any king of old.

"It's almost disgusting, isn't it?" said Astrid, standing at Eir's right elbow. She was smiling through her tears.

"Gyda certainly loved a bit of shine," Eir agreed.

Astrid didn't reply, because her sobbing and smiling had taken her over.

Nashwa, old now and still beautiful, leaned on her daughter Hadiyya. Guðrun and Rúna, still holding hands and still loving each other. Liadan, Astrid, Rúna, and Eir herself. There were no more words, because all they had were tears. Tears and smiles.

With everything in place, Háki let the sail down. Then he and Ruarc rowed back to shore.

Háki joined Eir, taking her hand in his.

"I'll miss her, Mother," he said, under his breath, because he didn't want the oath-men or his friends to see his emotion.

"You aren't alone in that, my boy."

Ragnar took up the bow, lit the tarred end of an arrow on the torch, then let it fly.

Sea-Wolf caught light quickly, having been doused with fish oil and strewn with the driest kindling to be found.

"Sometimes," Ruarc whispered. "A few hardened voyagers return home with tales of adventure, of the letting of blood and of bright, shining silver. And those are the tales that are most dangerous, for we all dream despite the danger. And dreams of that kind do not fade with time."

Eir raised her face, wet with tears. "So shall Gyda's life and deeds echo through the halls of the fallen until the burning of the world at Ragnarök."

Together, they watched *Sea-Wolf* burn, the flames leaping into the sky and shining off the water, like the breath of a dragon in the night.

And Gyda *Fiskwif*, Gyda the Grim, Grim-Bitch, Mother to Rán's Daughters, vanished from the world forever. But not from memory.

The End

AUTHOR'S NOTE

For all the years I can remember, I dreamed of the day I would see my first novel on the shelf. Now that day has arrived, and it is bittersweet. After all, you only get one "first."

Beyond any other emotion, the strongest is gratitude. Fiction has been a home and an escape since I was a child. The adventures within the pages of my books gave me a drive to write my own, and now I am living those adventures in the real world. I can never be grateful enough.

While Rán's Daughters is not my first published work, it is the most difficult piece I've ever written. This book fought me from day one, and given the personalities of these characters, I shouldn't be surprised. Much like Gyda, this book held a grudge. But oh, what an adventure!

I no longer hold the tiller of this story, and so I release it to you, the reader. We authors write for you, after all, as much as for ourselves. I hope you enjoyed this saga. May the wind fill your sail and the tide bear you to a fair shore.

ACKNOWLEDGMENTS

Crafting a book is never a one-person effort. This work wouldn't exist without a multitude of friends and supporters. I shall do my best to name you all, and please forgive me if I miss you.

To my husband Nathan and our incredible son: Thank you both for the unwavering love, patience, and support as I put in twelve-hour days and sometimes forgot how to be human. You were my lighthouse and my anchor through it all.

Special thanks to Prof. Clare Downham, who kindly provided invaluable insight and research on tenth-century Dublin and the women who lived there. Your expertise enriched this tale in countless ways. I hope you'll forgive my inaccuracies.

To Joshua Gillingham, my extraordinary editor and my friend. You made Gyda and her story sharper and stronger. I could not have done any of this without your keen insight and camaraderie. I owe you everything! To the team at Outland Entertainment - thank you so much for believing in my work enough to ask me to write for you again. I am beyond amazed even now. What a privilege it is to work with you.

To Giovanni Barretta, words are not enough. Thank you for the unwavering years of love, support, encouragement, brainstorming, late night crying sessions, and for letting me rant. You've been there every step of the way.

To my bff Kellie Huesler, who celebrated with me from the very first moment and offered constant support and friendship every single day.

To my precious friends Tanya and Hanspeter Erzinger, my deepest gratitude for your endless support, friendship, warmth, advice, and love. The creative life is not for the faint-hearted, and the grace and compassion you manifest in your work and lives inspires me every day.

To Louise Gooding, sister, sounding board, and fabulous fellow author: I miss you! The fearless way you take on the world gave me the confidence to take risks with this book.

To Paul and Kitt Greco, my dear friends and fellow nerds. I love you both.

To Genevieve Gornichec, if we are ever in the same city, I owe you the biggest hug and a giant cup of coffee, friend! Our hours of writing sprints and brainstorming as we wrote our books helped me bring my best self to the page every day.

To Lesley and Ronnie of the Derrybeg B&B in Pitlochry, Scotland. You gave me a home away from home while I muddled through the toughest parts of this book, and I will always remember your incredible kindness. I promise I'll visit you again someday!

To my fellow authors and creators, both online and offline: Kat Orman, Bjørn Larssen, Alex from Spells&Spaceships blog, Cat Rector, Lyra Wolf, Siobhan Clark, Becky Hill, Giles Kristian, Theodore Brun, Steven McKay, Matthew Harffy, Steven T. Dunn, Shauna Lawless, Thilde Kold Holt, Amy Boucher, L. E. Harper, Violet from Wolven Daughter, Morgan Harnly, and the Gwynne Brothers - thank you all from the bottom of my heart. Each of you has been more than generous with encouragement, support, mentoring, reviews, and guidance throughout this journey.

To Carol Brey, my mentor and advocate: thank you for believing in my potential as a writer and encouraging me to pursue this dream. To Francisco Propst, who was my first reader and inspired me to keep going. To Jackie Heinzelmann, who shaped the first ideas for Rán's Daughters with me. To Margaret O'Leary, who never fails to bring me joy.

To the WAC and our book club, for always cheering me on. To the Write Magic community, for being my creative home base. And to my wonderful WIZ group, for the sessions filled with laughter, creativity, and friendship.

And finally: to all those who read, review, and recommend my work–Thank you for giving me a chance. I hope to always bring you new adventures.

AUTHOR BIOGRAPHY

Kaitlin Felix writes Norse historical fiction and fantasy. Raised on the Texas-Mexico border, she now resides in Switzerland with her small family. Her credits include the short story Wave Runners in Althingi: The Crescent and The Northern Star (Outland Entertainment, USA), and the audio drama The Seeing Trees (AltStories podcast, UK.) In her downtime, Kaitlin enjoys crocheting, video games, and collecting too many boxes of tea.